Blanchard Jerrold

Signals of Distress

SALZWASSER
VERLAG

Blanchard Jerrold

Signals of Distress

Reprint of the original, first published in 1863.

1st Edition 2022 | ISBN: 978-3-37500-189-6

Verlag (Publisher): Salzwasser Verlag GmbH, Zeilweg 44, 60439 Frankfurt, Deutschland
Vertretungsberechtigt (Authorized to represent): E. Roepke, Zeilweg 44, 60439 Frankfurt, Deutschland
Druck (Print): Books on Demand GmbH, In de Tarpen 42, 22848 Norderstedt, Deutschland

SIGNALS OF DISTRESS.

SIGNALS OF DISTRESS

IN REFUGES AND HOMES OF CHARITY; IN INDUSTRIAL SCHOOLS AND REFORMATORIES; AT INVALIDS' DINNER-TABLES, AND IN THE HOMES OF THE LITTLE SISTERS OF THE POOR; IN BETHNAL GREEN, AND ST. GEORGE'S, HANOVER SQUARE; IN THE WAKE OF DISTRICT VISITORS; AMONG THE FALLEN, THE VICIOUS, THE CRIMINAL; WHERE MISSIONARIES TRAVEL, WHERE GOOD SAMARITANS HAVE CLOTHED THE NAKED; AMONG THE SHOE-BLACKS AND THE RAG-BRIGADES, ETC.

BY

BLANCHARD JERROLD

"Now the end of the commandment is charity, out of a pure heart, and of a good conscience, and of faith unfeigned."—1 TIM. i. 5.

LONDON:

1863.

TO THE

RIGHT HON. LORD BROUGHAM AND VAUX,

ETC. ETC.

DEAR LORD BROUGHAM,—*I dedicate this book to you, not as of old, the author, on his knees, wrote his dedicatory page to some man of lofty station, who would cast a mite to him. I have been most anxious to seize an opportunity of making public acknowledgment of the gratitude I owe you, for the kind and most earnest manner with which you have met and helped me, when I have submitted to your ripe judgment any suggestions or plans, that bore upon the social progress of our fellow-countrymen. I know that the object with which the inquiries described in this book were undertaken, will command your sympathy. I have endeavoured to reach the truth concerning certain social evils with which our modern civilisation is plagued. During the winter just closed, I have spent many nights and days in the terrible hiding-places of poverty; under the roof of charity, where men and women, worsted in the battle of life, were garnered, to die at least in peace and comfort; among criminal children, learning hard to be honest men; watching the crafty beggar telling his lie to the cunning mendicity officer; in refuges, packed with misery's children in their last rags, sighing or sleeping by the hundred; among the merry shoeblacks in their little tea-room near Temple Bar; or following reverently the footsteps of the Little Sisters of the Poor. I have desired to speak the truth, regardless of theorists,—free from the "bemummying wrappers of sect."*

I am confident then, that this volume, of which I ask your Lordship to accept the dedication, will recommend itself to you, at least by its aim and subject. I assure you that it is in the humblest spirit I ask you, who have circumnavigated the world of knowledge; and have devoted your genius, your eloquence, and your scholarship to the good of your countrymen,—whose name will brighten some of the noblest pages of our history; to permit me the pleasure and the just pride I feel, in expressing how much I am indebted to you; and how highly I value the friendly counsel you have sometimes deigned to give me.

I remain,

Dear Lord Brougham,

Yours always faithfully,

BLANCHARD JERROLD.

REFORM CLUB, PALL MALL.

CONTENTS.

SIGNALS OF DISTRESS.

CHAPTER I.—INTRODUCTORY.

It is high time, when it has become the settled belief of the public that crime has the advantage of poverty in the battle of life, to institute a careful inquiry into the condition of our poor, and to determine whether or not we are too lenient with our criminals, and too harsh towards our pauper population. Penologists who have the most enthusiastic faith in the law of kindness, will not be prepared to maintain that we should make the lot of the burglar and the footpad less repulsive than that of the pauper. When the convict laughs at his sentence, and, rubbing his stomach, tells his judge that now he shall grow fat; while the refractory pauper delights in the decision of the magistrate that relieves him from the penalties of impecuniosity, and subjects him to the milder *régime* of the gaol; a society where pauperism abounds has reason to be alarmed. We are presented with pictures of "gentlemen-workers" who eat two or three courses for dinner, and have surplus food to barter for tobacco, as a punishment for their crimes; while their free and honest competitors sit by, envying them, and purchasing their superfluous food. At Portland the convict has shorter hours, does less work, and is better fed and housed, than his honest neighbour. This is well known in the Cut, the Brill, the Mint of Southwark; in Pye Street, Westminster; and in other festering centres of London crime. The garotter who sallies forth to waylay his victim, knows, almost to an hour and to a grain of meat, what his lot will be if he is caught. He takes a sportsman-like view of his business; at the worst he can only go to Portland—to exchange the food he cannot eat, with free labourers.

Charles Erwood, a convicted thief, was charged with loitering in Fitzroy Square, for a felonious purpose. Two detectives watched him with a companion, examining the houses. Presently there was a crash, and Erwood ran from a doorway; whereupon he was apprehended. Let the reader mark the completeness of Erwood's knowledge. He said to his captor, "Oh, it's all right; you can only make a drag of it, as I have not got the screws." I should explain that "a drag" means three months' imprisonment, and that "the screws" are merely burglar's keys. Erwood had calculated his risks to a nicety; and could realize his position the instant the policeman's hand was upon his shoulder. The screws were not upon him; he had therefore, to his great delight, incurred only "a drag." Thus, criminal risks are calculated by our dangerous classes, with commercial precision; and, with the spread of education, we may soon hope to see the cracksman keep his accounts by double entry.

To discover how our criminals grow; the class that supplies them; the influences under which they are developed, and how they break out into open war with society; and, above all, how the honest poor are compelled to hob-and-nob with the "shoful pitcher" and the "gun," it is necessary to visit the vast nursery-grounds of crime. We must turn from the great London highways into foul and tortuous little cities of sin and sorrow, where the battle of life is fierce always. The distress of Lancashire made the always hard lot of the London poor so desperate, and the help that they had been accustomed to receive was so completely withdrawn in favour of the workless operatives of the north, that the condition and prospects of London alleys were appalling. The mild winter of this year, however, mitigated the calamity. The Registrar-General recorded deaths from starvation. Two great relief societies proclaimed the emptiness of their cash-boxes. The weavers of the north-east of London, their American market destroyed, were silently wasting unto death. Poor lying-in women were left, untended, in the cold. District-visitors went about with empty hands; they hadn't a groat for the hungry, not a blanket for the frost-bitten; and there was comfort and treacle-pudding in gaol!

Comfort! This is Seven Dials. It is Saturday night. The great gin-palaces blaze with gas at every corner. Under their monster lamps are shadows of men, with their hands in their pockets, and oaths on their lips. Men and women are wrangling, joking, and fighting. Shrivelled old women, covered with dark rags, flit in and out, victims of poverty and gin. Children approach, with bare feet, matted hair, and wild eyes; bringing old phials, or broken jugs, for beer or spirits. In years they are the veriest babes; but they are keen over quantities and pennyworths. They have been born and bred in these misty and foul alleys, where their slattern mothers are leaning against the door-posts, wrangling. One cheery young gentleman, who wears his greasy garments airily, passes me singing, with his wiry little costermonger voice—

"Clack! clack! clack! d'ye want any gin?"—

a ditty that passes as wondrously humorous under the glare of these gin-palace lamps! These children who have listened to their father's drunken oaths, and have felt his bestial violence, see all the force of the doggrel. It is a fierce life that is spent hereabouts. The gin-palace on one side of the way, and the empty cupboard and coverless bed opposite, with the pawnshop close round the corner. The black little shops, where Poverty buys its penn'orths, abound. Here are the general dealers, where barefooted children are buying farthing candles; open cellars, with boots ranged upon the pavement before the opening; hideous dangling bunches of old clothes—of clothes so old you wonder where are the creatures so wo-begone, that they must crave these rags; bird shops, with cunning-looking fowlers smoking their pipes within, and thick-necked fellows of sinister appearance, examining the dogs; tripe-shops, where poor creatures are turning over lumps of meat, or cheapening sheep-heads; tawdry finery shops, packed with hideous caricatures of London fashions, at extraordinarily low prices, where Poor Shame buys her scarlet belongings, to catch the eye of the pickpocket or the coiner! Men, their hands deep-planted in their dog's-eared pockets, appear to take delight in elbowing me as I pass quietly on. Some of the loungers are poor labourers who have finished their day's work, mingling with others who have never done a day's honest work in their life; or with the cheats who have flourished by counterfeiting misery. Men and women, honest and dishonest, of fair and foul fame, leaning against the public-house, and children of them, all massed together in the gutter; poverty binding them together within the severe limits of this great slum! Hunger, and crime, and low cunning are cheek-by-jowl, and the world outside is the enemy's country. Let the well-clad pass this way, and they will be jeered at, and hustled. Even the good men and women who approach with help and words of comfort, get, at times, a poor welcome. London is graced with upwards of 750 charitable institutions, the aggregate income of which is nearly two millions and a half of money. We have great orphan societies, infant nurseries imitated from the French *crêches*, metropolitan associations for improving the dwellings of the industrious classes, societies for the rescue of young women and children, institutions meant to teach the poor how to lead an honest life, refuges where the houseless may sleep, reformatories where the young may cleanse themselves of their sins; blanket-clubs, and vast soup-kitchens; cheap, sound literature;—and here are hundreds of children as wild as the inhabitants of a rabbit-warren; mothers, stupified with gin and ignorant as Hottentots, quarrelling with beetle-browed mates, who would not value a human life at the price of a mug of ale, if they had their way. These men and women have their reading, but what reading is it? What is thrust into the hands of the poor, by the hands of the vicious and criminal? I was attracted by a crowd, to a little shop that combined the sale of shag tobacco with that of cheap literature. All eyes were directed, not to cheap periodicals in the window, but to a broad poster. It ran thus:—

"The Fearful and Appalling Dying Confession of Andrew Garrott (a Returned Convict), the King of the Garotters. The horrors of transportation! Life in the bush and at the diggings in Australia, where, in company with other criminals of Newgate notoriety, he murdered 256 unfortunate helpless gold-diggers. In the 'bushes' he cohabited with the paramour of Burke and Hare, who, it will be remembered, was sent, at her wish, to Australia, after she had turned King's evidence against those human butchers. Andrew Garrott narrates this woman's awful end in startling language. She died raving mad! Andrew Garrott studied Thugism, and, having committed a series of fiendish barbarities, he returned to England in the ship 'Mary.' In London he made friends with two ticket-of-leave men, and, having slightly altered Thugism, they at once commenced garotting. The three were termed 'Front Stall,' 'Back Stall,' and 'Ugly Man;' and Andrew Garrott confesses to have murdered six people in London in three months, and to have cut fingers and ears off to obtain jewellery. The back slums of London; the garotters' home and women; depravity and vice; concluding with Andrew Garrott's dying advice to the unprotected populace of London, showing how people may walk the streets in safety."

Boys and men were grinning their delight over this great promise of a feast of crime. It was their sensation novel—their *Woman in White*, or *Lady Audley's Secret*. The rich have their feast of crime daintily served up, their *suprême* of bigamy; and the poor must needs have their fatty cake of burglary and murder. I stepped into the shop, followed by a very ugly customer, and asked for a copy of Mr. Garrott's story. The ugly customer addressed the man behind the counter in a language that was unintelligible to me. I transacted my business with all convenient speed, and took the earliest opportunity of examining my prize.

The writer of the story of crime has seasoned his dish for the market. It is full of the slang of the slum: a rich, unctuous, fatty cake indeed! The writer has the thief's *argot* at his command; nor, in many parts, does he over-colour. He calls "a nettle but a nettle," it is true—not caring to beat about the bush, for refinements of diction. Manifestly, he speaks from experience. This ragged paper before me comes direct from the places it describes. It is a genuine bit of slum literature, that will fall into the hands of many an honest lad, whom poverty has driven to be the next-door neighbour of a cracksman. In the winter nights, with this east wind piercing, like cold steel, to the bones—by the farthing dips that hang from the sooty ceiling of the Seven Dials' general dealer—how many a poor creature, with hunger gnawing like a wolf in his stomach, may read and be tempted! The stories of a neighbour who has dared with success, and who is eating of all the luxuries of the Dials, may serve to complete the resolve. Poverty huddled with crime, and familiar with it, has a hard fight to make, when the tempter speaks, and the cupboard is empty. As Garrott grew, so are thousands of children growing, and wanting—tempted every hour, and with nobody at hand to guard them from harm. I must give the reader an idea, from Garrott, of what the Westminster urchin is made. Mr. Garrott writes in his own proper, or rather improper, person:—

"It is well to be plain. The book of my crimes needs no ornamentation, and my labours of blood need no illustrations. I have 'supped full of horrors,' and I, now dying, desire not the dishes to be garnished, or the cup to be replenished. Would that the terrible history of my life had died with me—but it cannot. Timidity, the timidity of a hereafter, has crept into my soul; my brain begins to reason, and I fear death. Yes, I, who have washed my hands in the blood of 250 human beings, now quail to die. A short time since, death had no terror for me, but lingering on a sick-bed, and dying drunk amidst your companions of depravity and vice, are two very different matters. Now I fear death, and I cannot die till I have confessed my inhuman crimes. . . . I was born in the year 1816, in the parish of Westminster, where my father was well known to a certain class (smashers) as a coiner. But little notice was taken of me, and I was allowed to follow my own inclinations in the 'slums' of Westminster, without any parental interference. My mother, known as 'Flash Poll,' used to take me out with her, dressed decently, to pass money of my father's making. Assuming childish innocence, I had to enter shops, and having purchased some trifling article, do 'a smash,' while my mother waited some distance away. I have 'smashed' as much as 30s. a day. When I was thirteen years old, my father was transported (a 'smasher' having informed on him) for coining, and my mother deserted me to become a 'gay' woman. Thus was I left to obtain my own living in the back dens of Westminster. Continuing to associate with the vilest of society, the reader may as naturally expect a crab-tree to bear forth choice fruit, as for me to bear forth good qualities. Some days I thieved, other days I smashed, but from fifteen I may say that my time was spent in a prison, till ultimately I was transported. . . .

"Doomed at nineteen years of age to transportation! Thoughtless as I was, it made me think. I was to cross the ocean to labour in chains in a land where I should probably die, never having once breathed liberty's sweet embracing air. I thought of the tales I had heard the 'shoful pitchers' (passers of bad coin) tell to each other respecting the horrors of transportation, and I trembled as I thought of the terrible judgment that my misdeeds had brought upon me. The day came when the convict-ship was to bear its living fettered freight of crime to a far-off land, where it would be chained, but not subdued.

"Day after day passed by—it then took eight or nine months for a convict-ship to reach New Zealand from England—and day after day saw us nearer the land where the inheritors of crime stalked about like fiends in chains, and where my father had but a few years gone before me, and where, I had been told, he had died. . . .

"Nineteen years ago, I breathed the breath of life in Westminster; for a few years I squalled and crawled about in deplorable rags and filth, till one day my dissipated mother dressed me decently, and walked me through the paths of vice, as I before said, to pass bad money. A year or two's practice in the delicate profession of a 'gun' (a pickpocket), in gambling and swearing, and exhibitions of atrocious cruelty,[1] in which I thoroughly delighted, and then I was an orphan, as it were, possessing the grossest passions that ever a boy inherited. My father a convict, my mother a prostitute.

"A year or two more, and I was an adept at pulling away 'supors' (watch-stealing), and I pall'd in with a moll (cohabited with a girl). After I had committed almost numberless thefts, I was one day caught, and sentenced by Mr. Beckett to six months' imprisonment with hard labour. From that day I was a marked fellow; my game was up; for no sooner had I done the 'stretch' (term of imprison-

[1] Such as tying the tails of two cats together, and swinging them over the line in a yard, and there letting them fight, their heads, of course, downwards, till they killed each other; making bets as to which would die first. This delight was greatly encouraged by my parents, for my father taught me to skin a live cat when I was but nine years old, and my mother, who afterwards sold the skin for 2s., laughed at the sport.

ment) and commenced my old thieving career than I was again before the 'beak.' Again and again the same thing occurred. I scarcely pulled away a thing but a day after I was doing 'stir' (imprisonment), so sharply did the 'slops' (police) watch me. Then it was my turn to be transported, as it had been my father's a little while before; and here I am on the convict-ship, thinking how strangely and quickly my life, as it were, had been sacrificed to vice. It seemed to me that I had never been a boy, or played a boy's game, or experienced a boy's thought. Why, I had committed ten thousand times more sin before I was nine years old than have men who have lived to be a hundred. My prattle was oaths, my play was brutality, and my thoughts and learning crime. I thought of all this, and I thought of what I was, and I thought of what some men were, and I wept. I had never wiped away a tear from my cheek before, and I never wiped away one since, till to-day—to-day, as I make my confession, with grey hair on my head, and a haggard and wan countenance, too surely speaking of death. The reader will doubtless think it strange that I, for the first time, should think—or repent, if you like the word better—and shed a tear on board a convict-ship. Let me tell you that a man will think of many things on board a convict-ship, for every man must think after his own fashion, and on board a convict-ship thought is part of a man's existence, and it is impossible for the most thoughtless and hardened wretch not to think at times kindly of well conducted society, and regret pursuing the path of ruin, which led him to a convict settlement to be bound in chains."

The writer of this instructive narrative, who has, at least, been the close companion of thieves, or has learned his lesson from felon lips, admits us to one useful view of the criminal's character. The coiner and cracksman have a horror of transportation. I take another extract from Mr. Garrott's ragged page, because it conveys a hint to the public on the art of avoiding the grip of such scoundrels as the author confesses himself to be :—

"Arrived in England, we made our way to London, and 'hung out at a padding ken in the Mint' (lived at a common lodging-house). The police were too numerous, and we were too well known. We scarcely ventured out by daylight. Our money was soon gone, and we became fearfully distressed. We did a little in the 'stoucking hauling' line (pocket-handkerchief stealing) at first, but soon found that 'stoucks' wasn't what they used to be—they don't fetch above threepence or fourpence a piece now! We then commenced doing 'cribs over' (housebreaking), but I found that breaking bolts and bars asunder was too much trouble; at any rate, the reward was not enough for the risk for one who had obtained such gigantic prizes by merely giving a blow on the head. So, while in a state of semi-starvation, me and my mates shook hands together, swore to be true, and commenced my favourite game of garotting, which had obtained for me the name of 'Garrott.'

"We worked our 'garotting business' on principles partly taken from Thugism and Millbank Penitentiary silence system; and I would have undertaken, assisted by my two mates, to have strangled 49 out of 50 persons without once letting them even speak, if I felt so disposed. So those who have been garotted and are living should think themselves fortunate that they were not killed, for it is a question among adepts at garotting, if it is not better to kill their victims than run the risk of being caught.

"My mate, whose business was in front of the man, was called 'Front Stall;' the other mate, whose business it was to be behind the man, was called the 'Back Stall;' and I, who put the 'hug on,' was called 'Ugly man.' We were very successful. But again must I speak of death. In London and round its suburbs we murdered six people in three months. Indeed, it almost seemed that we could commit the same atrocities in police-protected London as we could at the policeless diggings. Amongst other cruelties perpetrated, we have two or three times cut fingers and ears off to obtain jewellery, if we had not time to wrench them off.

"We were drunk—drunk, ay, never sober—and we kept three or four women (I supposed they were women, at least they passed as such), who sometimes accompanied us on our murderous expedition. The swearing, drinking, and depravity, day after day passed by, till the women, while drunk, having made mine and my mates' game known to some other pals of theirs, the game of garotting became a favourite and famous game with all desperate men, and I was called the 'King of Garotters!' . . . .

"But my time has come, as it will come for all men—the good as well as the bad. Drink and depravity has done its work. I am dying lion-hearted; ay, but like the lion, crouching in its den, and afraid to meet his assailant—man; so do I fear to face Eternity. But so, as I have refrained from depicting various scenes of incest, depravity, and vice, knowing that it would only disgust the respectable class of society, so do I feel disposed to die without depicting the agonies of my soul. It shall not be written that the 'King of Garotters!' died a cur. As I have lived in intoxication, so will I die drunk. Brandy! brandy! thou at least wilt make me forget the hour.

"I have but to say to my readers that they would do well to take the following advice:—If you are out late at night, walk in the middle of the road, and, if possible, look both sides of the road at once. If you see three men gradually but certainly nearing you (sometimes only two)—and you must, if not blind, see them, as they cannot seize on you from any court or turning, but must, of a necessity, near you—spring a large rattle (cost 1s. 6d.) and it will directly have the effect of starting them. Or, to be still more safe, have two very sharp spikes attached to your elbows with leather thongs, and one on each heel of your boot. Thus simply equipped, and thus walking in the middle of the road—if you are out late at night—and I guarantee that you are safe from all attacks of garotters.

"Now I have done! my games of death are over. The dark curtain of eternity is about to be drawn between me and you. Angels fled weeping from my side, and the spirits of sin are hovering round my bed in glee. Horror upon horror! Hold! it shall not be said—though I have confessed my crimes—that the King of Garotters 'rounded on his mates or died a cur.'

"Reader, suffice it, may you die happier, and a better man than I. ANDREW GARROTT."

It was very obliging in Mr. Garrott to afford the public the benefit of his experience before leaving for ever the scenes of his unholy labours; but he had done a greater service had he not attracted this laughing crowd about his sensation Dials' poster.

And now, let us see whether it is impossible to separate the poor from the criminal; whether it is wise to keep ill-paid labour huddled in the rents of Drury Lane, or behind Westminster Abbey, and whether we might not aim a deadly blow at the crime of the country, by breaking up its nurseries. I shall endeavour, moreover, to present to the public a full and true picture of the present woful condition of some of the London poor, to this end, viz., that we may not forget the man who is dying of want in the next street, nor the mother who lies, faint and cold, upon our door-step.

CHAPTER II.

DRURY LANE AND HAM YARD.

LIFE is harder, to the mass, in London, than in any other European city; not only among the working classes, but with the respectable, the genteel. It is not long since two ladies were discovered proudly dying of hunger, because they would not stoop to make their distress known. These two proud women, who, in solitude, were battling with hunger to the death, are of a very long list of the respectable who struggle fiercely to keep up appearances; who, in tatters, disdain manual labour; and who rather find themselves by the river's brink on some dark night, than receiving of the bounty of their fellow-countrymen. In estimating the misery that is suffered in London, regard must be had to the poor middle classes, as well as to the poor working classes; to the women tenderly cultured, who suddenly find themselves penniless in the world; to our hosts of half-starved clerks; to the thousands who work their fingers to the bone, in hiding-places away from their friends, that they may still be counted among the genteel. We find that nearly £50,000 are distributed annually among the poor clergy of the Church; while Protestant Dissenting ministers and poor professional men and tradesmen, are yearly helped to the extent of £172,000. Not only our streets proclaim the fact that life is hard in London;—to discover the patient, uncomplaining poor, we must travel beyond the records of our many charitable institutions. The most heart-rending stories of London want are those which are unrelieved. We have hardly a street where there is not a Charity; and yet men, women, and children are known to die, in the midst of wealth and in spite of our poor-laws, of actual privation.

We are told by Mr. Sampson Low, junior, in his admirable book on the Charities of London, that these Charities spend annually, £2,441,967. But it must not be supposed that this enormous sum is disbursed in the relief of positive physical distress,—in feeding the hungry, and clothing the naked; our Home and Foreign Missionary Societies enjoy the distribution of one million out of this sum. London hospitals and dispensaries figure for £183,500. In the relief of the metropolitan poor, then—that is, in relief by public agencies—the sum annually expended is probably half a million sterling. It should be remarked, moreover, that the income devoted to the relief of the London poor has more than kept pace with the increase of population; since within the last ten years our Charities have increased one-fourth in number, and one-third in income. This fact is greatly to the credit of the public; but it does not prove that our London poor are sufficiently cared for. It is active charity—a contribution of time and patience and sympathy—that is wanted. We must go among the suffering poor before we can decide whether all the duties of charity have been fulfilled; and we must go about the streets blindfold if we desire to hug ourselves in the belief that nothing more remains to be done. A severe winter turns thousands of London workmen into the streets. The gardeners sing their annual song in our great thoroughfares; the pawn-shops are besieged; homes are stripped of their furniture; the patient wait, huddled together, for the spring; the bold crowd the workhouses and the soup-kitchens; the cunning know how to turn every charity to their advantage; and the weak and ailing and uncomplaining, die. The newspapers cannot tell the public how many poor each winter starves into the pauper's shell. A long walk through the streets—and the best of them—makes an observer acquainted with a hundred distinct varieties of pauperism. The strange and ghostly figures that flit by: haggard, unshorn men in clothes so grotesque that you wonder where they found them; yellow, lean women, carrying white and flabby babes; children of the gutter, laughing through their sores, turning somersaults for halfpence, to omnibus outside passengers; beggars, artful imitators of all the harrowing forms of distress they have seen; men and children in rags, sweeping every crossing, and fiercely guarding the possession of it; a pauper at hand to hold the head of every gentleman's horse; widows in rusty and scanty mourning selling stay-laces along suburban roads, through rain, and snow, and wind; troops of shoeless orange-girls; along the shore of the Thames, mudlarks fighting over lumps of coal; chickweed vendors in smock-frocks; street quacks and mountebanks at every corner; these are London presences that must astonish every foreigner, and that have made French writers describe England as a country where there are colossal fortunes, and millions of paupers. Without accepting this sweeping reproach (and our neighbours are apt to judge of a country after looking into just one of its back gardens), we may fairly allow that the casual observer sees more destitution in London than he will see in any great continental city. Yet our charities are extraordinary for their extent and variety. We give ten pounds, where our neighbours give ten pence. The truth is, that pauperism is not to be eradicated by charity. Charity, as it is practised in England, has, indeed, rather a tendency to foster it. We are bound to give bread to the hungry. We are bound also to inquire how it is that the man is without bread, and whether there are not steps within our reach, by which we might put him in a way of earning his own living.

In the parish of St. Clement Danes there is a population of about 17,000, the majority being people so poor, so little able to pay for elbow-room, and for the proper number of cubic feet of air, that there are 580 crowded upon an acre of land. There are London poor more crowded than here, about Clare Market; but 580 to the acre suggests a degree of packing exercised upon the human form, very unpleasant to contemplate. The crowded pavements and roadways, noisy with creaking barrows and costermongers' voices, are indeed packed together, to struggle against each other for a living, or rather, for a crust that will keep life together. I have to push my way sturdily through the pack of keen and ragged hucksters, who are in search of bargains. It is Christmas-eve, and every poor creature is striving to cheapen a humble imitation of a Christmas luxury. Here are trucks loaded with holly, ornamented with little flags stuck in turnips; confused heaps of geese near haddocks, red herrings, and mounds of silvery sprats; and a penny appears to be the price paid for everything.

Irish women and children are holding penn'orths of onions in their broad hands; mere babies follow passers-by, and display much ingenuity in provoking customers. "Here you hav'em," cried a gaunt little creature, holding her savoury bulbs aloft. "They'll make your 'air stand on end." Stalls of cheap crockery are besieged; and people are wrangling and shouting over dishes and plates, in every key. Vagrant children, black as the pavement, are staring, with their large and lustrous eyes, at the holly barrows, and dodging about the wheels to filch a sprig—they whose only hope of food to-morrow is in the soup-kitchen, to which I am slowly wending my way. Yonder runs a shoeless girl, carrying a heavy basket of onions upon her head, the hair of the said head being bound in a gaudy net, exactly after the fashion of Belgravia. Indeed, there are fashions in this narrow, noisy street, where the very poor are doing their marketing. A girl is vending turnips—in crinoline! Saucy little children, who are rubbing their noses against the dirty panes of the sweetmeat shop, and are speculating as to the price of Bonaparte's ribs, or a lump of parliament, have hoops upon them, probably filched from a butter-tub. *Le Follet* travels from the boudoir of the countess, to the garret of the water-cress seller. And there is humour in this imitation—as there appears to be humour in all the misery that is around me. A saucy carelessness, a defiant parade of rags, a delight in quaint developments of worn-out costume, may be always remarked among our London poor. They are not chicken-hearted in the streets at any rate; nor shall we find them cowardly in the face of the world that buffets them so hard, in the yard to which we are bound, and where we shall find them receiving the dole of charity —of a charity that is no dishonour to them, I say, this sloppy, hazy winter's night—eve of the day when the coldest of men feels his hand wander instinctively towards his breeches pocket, and when Charity shows her angel face—even in the workhouse!

A navvy lurches out of a public-house, where the "Independent Friends of Labour" meet, carrying, by the neck, the goose he has won in the goose-club; and the eyes of the crowd follow the prize, with most envious looks. Amid the roar of the portable gas upon the barrows, the spitting and hissing of fish lying uneasily in boiling fat—the hallooing, and swearing, and singing—in a narrow, foggy court, stands the Clare Market Colonnade, where the Rev. Mr. Robins is reclaiming a few of these waifs and strays, as we may remark by peeping into the quiet, orderly reading-room, where his *protégés* are spelling over books or papers. The long, low building in which this earnest gentleman works for the benefit of his ragged parishioners, has been by turns a cheap concert-room and casino, then a prize-ring, then a penny gaff. It is now devoted to a noble purpose—a school through the week, and a house of prayer on Sundays. Its aspect is very simple, at the same time presenting a church-like appearance, in some measure attributable to gifts from friends. A hymn-book has been arranged for the especial use of the Clare Market Mission.[1] The mission includes a school, at which every scholar pays a penny per week. There is a monthly examination of the children in the presence of their parents. There are generally about 150 or 200 children present at the Sunday-school. The general number of the congregation at the chapel is about 250. Each Sunday morning there is an offertory, and in the evening a collection. The poor give their pence freely,

[1] We take these facts from Mr. Robins' report.

the pence frequently amounting to 10s. or 12s. In two years their subscriptions amounted to nearly £160.

A very pleasant part of this work is the alliance that has been formed between a small parish in the most lovely part of Kent (where the clergyman in charge of the mission was once incumbent) and Clare Market. The country people, although not rich themselves, have added considerably to the funds of the mission, and have welcomed with great kindness those sick people who needed change of air.

In connexion with the mission a society has been framed, under the title of "The Association of Church Helpers." It consists of the poor people themselves, who take in hand some good work in their neighbourhood; they are humble district visitors. The association has already about seventy members.

A Refuge for homeless boys, taken out of the streets, and instructed, as far as possible, in a manner that would enable them to gain an honest livelihood, was instituted in 1859. Mr. Robins reports that a considerable experience was thus gained of the London outcasts, but it was not encouraging. Very simply but attractively the Refuge was fitted up. A trusty superintendent and his wife were secured, and many kind friends gave their help freely, but still it was no easy task to get these young Arabs to settle to anything like steadiness. They preferred the freedom of the street, with its privations, to the work that was found for them as errand-boys, etc., and to the comforts of a home. What they liked best was shoe-blacking; but after a time they got tired of that, and brought in barely enough to pay for their daily food, though had they tried they might have earned more. A great many of them went back to their former companions and ways of life; at the same time, in many other cases, great and lasting good was done. Mr. Robins appears to believe that the best way of dealing with vagrant boys is to send them to sea, and many of his most wild and reckless scholars are now getting on very well on board ship. Here are two instances:—One boy escaped from his work, and was discovered in Billingsgate three months afterwards in a pitiable state, having roamed about the country in great distress. He, with another boy, who had also run away, and who was found living under an assumed name in a back street on Tower Hill, were admitted into King Edward's school, were sent away as sailors, and have turned out very well. The fact is that boys of this class need watching and restraint nearly as much as actual criminals, and the only successful way of improving them is by removing them altogether from the influence of their old companions; by giving them permanent employment under careful supervision, and thus gradually leading them to habits which they could not otherwise form. The habit of work is the best lesson the schoolmaster can teach a vagrant boy.

I have lingered somewhat about Mr. Robins' Colonnade, tempted by the contrast which it presents, to the noisy, flaring lane that runs parallel with it. But this evening I have a special visit to make to a dark yard in Windmill Street, Haymarket, where crowds of poor people are pressed about the narrow doorway of a low line of buildings, that were once stables, but are now a soup-kitchen and refuge for the hungry and the houseless.

The Leicester Square Soup-Kitchen, founded by the late Mr. Cochrane some sixteen years ago, is an interesting institution to me; because it attracts to its savoury kettles all classes of the London poor.

They flock hither from every part of London, in search of gratuitous soup—from Brompton to Bethnal Green. This soup, made of sound and fortifying materials, is distributed daily to destitute applicants, who apply in numbers ranging from 800 to 1000. Here also is a Refuge, where the homeless (who are provided with a subscriber's ticket) may sleep in a clean and warm bed. The kitchen is, in short, under the following very fair regulations:—

"The soup is ready daily at three o'clock, at which hour the kitchen is arranged for serving it; the holders of single tickets sit down and take their meal of a basin of soup and bread, or if they prefer, take it home in a jug. Those having family tickets bring a vessel, and have two quarts of soup, with a due allowance of bread, to take home to their families; or, in case of a homeless family, partake of it in the kitchen.

"When all applicants having tickets are supplied, the remainder of the soup is served to the most needy and proper persons selected from those who attend the kitchen in want of food; generally one to two hundred are thus daily fed, who know not where to obtain tickets, or, being decent persons out of employ, feel some reluctance to solicit them; yet very frequently a great many have to depart without food, so prevalent is distress at certain seasons. Destitute persons having tickets for supper, bed, and breakfast, apply at nine o'clock P.M., when they have a meal, a comfortable bed, and breakfast before leaving in the morning. Those who come on Saturday evening are allowed to come again on Sunday evening, as on that day they can earn nothing. In some cases, as of servants out of place and in distress, they are allowed to remain till a situation can be obtained; every facility being given them, and occasionally clothes provided, or money lent to redeem things necessary for service. A registry is kept for persons out of place, and may have been provided by that means."

The crowd about the door-way this damp and dark Christmas Eve, is silent and orderly. This is decent, seemly poverty; but it is poverty that bites to the marrow of the bones. The babes are puling in their poor mothers' arms; children are armed with capacious baskets; every one present has either a bottle or a jug. At the door stands an old gentleman, who examines the applicant's ticket. Up-stairs, mounds of excellent tea and sugar are being packed into neat white parcels; and within the kitchen, there is extraordinary activity. It is a low, square, white washed room—a veritable kitchen—with a range of soup-boilers on one side, and, for sole ornament, save the holly, a tablet placed against the wall to commemorate the visit of the late kindly Prince Consort, in 1848. In the centre of the room a lady sits, with two great clothes' baskets, full of packets of tea and sugar. On her left are two bulky barrels of beer and ale, and bottles of port, brandy, and whisky; opposite, upon a long bench, are piles of beef cut in squares; while in a corner, a proud pyramid of plum-pudding rears its aromatic head; and beyond, a stack of half-quartern loaves awaits the coming of the hungry.

I have seen alms doled to the poor often, but I have never seen anything so hearty, so right, and Christian in feeling, as the Ham Yard almsgiving of that evening. All the attendants appeared delighted with their work. As each poor creature came forward, a gentleman stationed at the door, called out the number of children the new-comer had to feed; and in proportion to the number was the joint of beef and the quantity of tea. In the list of this mob of poor (they had want written in their meek features) were milliners, tailors, boot-closers, sick cabmen, street fruit-stall keepers, valets, charwomen, waiters, binders, and mop-makers. Widows, in heavy crape, trooped through the kitchen, by the dozen. For each, the presiding lady had a hearty word. She gave an extra glass of port to the sickly mother who was suckling; an extra packet of tea, to the very old man. She seemed to love the little scared children who came with gaping baskets, and bade them get some of the hundredweight of biscuits Huntley and Palmer had sent for them. A poor woman with nine children was rejoiced with the best part of the shoulder of the magnificent sheep, sent to the poor by Lord Darnley. Many took extra tea instead of beer or wine; but to the mass the barrels of ale and porter sent by the Romford Brewery, and by Messrs. Goding, were welcome gifts. The yellow mugs were brought from under colourless shawls, in such great numbers, that the good presiding lady (who had been up six nights preparing for this holiday evening) rallied the poor women—vowing that she could not be responsible for all these vessels that were so much alike. "They're brothers and sisters every one of them," she said, laughing; and the poor women laughed, and blessed her, by the dozen. I stood by for two hours, while files of the London poor passed through this Ham Yard kitchen. So many children of want (800 in all, and representing at least 3000 hungry creatures) I have never seen arrayed before. One poor blind man tottered to the meat bench, and was helped so tenderly forward, with his meat and pudding, and tea and sugar, that I could not but be touched. How gentle the poor are to the poor! They who come in contact with honest poverty like this, are made better and kinder by the contact, I would fain believe. I cannot conceive a more humanizing scene than this, where comfort was given, for one day at least, to some 800 families.

CHAPTER III.

LONDON MISSIONARIES.

THE recent discussion at a meeting of the Society of Arts, on model cottages for the working classes, was an excellent illustration of the manner in which men, totally ignorant of the wants and feelings of the poor, will dogmatize on their improvement; lay down plans for their dwellings; reform their tailors' bills; change their food, and prescribe their reading. How should my lady know that the society for the diffusion of cheap cambric pocket-handkerchiefs among the poor, is a sorry sham, presided over by a sleek secretary? The Rev. M. A., who designed the rules of a modern lodging-house, was astonished when it was made known to him that the single young men to whom he addressed himself, would not be drilled in their own rooms, for which they paid rent; that they declined to pay for ventilation with slavery. Half the charities of London are encumbered with absurd restrictions and conditions. A man must attend a certain class in order to obtain a crust of bread and a refuge pallet at night; or, the dole belongs only to the hypocrite. Hence the spread of a pauperized class. Poor people learn to conform to the rules of sectarian charities; they whine and mum, and teach their children to whine and mum, after the approved fashion. Then come the gratuitous blankets, the bowls of soup, the yards of flannel, and the well-known packets of tea and sugar. The family, originally in an accidental and passing difficulty, having been helped by one of the good visiting ladies of the neighbourhood, begins to look out for gifts, not help. The tracts are read, because in their wake lie pippins and cheese. It is painful to see the mother first learning to make up her story for her tract and blankets and port-wine purveyor. The mother vows that the winter is the hardest for them she has ever known. She has read the tracts, and would like some more. The lady is delighted with her good work, and gives not only tracts. She does not know that she is pauperizing this family, by teaching them to depend upon her bounty. I shall have much to say on district visitors presently.

All charity should be help—to keep the poor away from the pauper class. It should comfort the man who is out of work, in a way that will stimulate him to seek work. It should teach him all descriptions of social economy; the virtue and the gain of cleanliness; the dignity of independence. It should leave him free, and never debase him by extorting conditions that he must fain pay with hypocrisy. The London City Mission Society has four hundred missionaries doing the work of charity. Here is a little army that might do incalculable good if it would approach the slums of London—the fences and padding-kens, the sloppy alleys and the fever gardens—in a thoroughly sensible spirit. It is the subscribers of the income of £37,000 which this mission enjoys, who are in the wrong. I have reason to know that the city missionaries are zealous, and in a great degree useful men; but they would be more useful, there would be fewer of those barefooted wild children in the streets, if the public who subscribe, would be at the pains of learning how they may best help the poor of London out of the Slough of Despond—out of the inhuman squalor in which they now lie, huddled behind the great and busy arteries of this wealthy metropolis. The city missionary is a good and a brave man, as a rule; but his sphere of activity is foolishly circumscribed. He has only words for the ragged, and tracts for the famished. It is in the following manner he accounts for his large income:—

	1861-2.
Missionaries,	400
Hours spent in domiciliary visitation,	529,030
Visits paid,	1,979,453
Of which to the sick and dying,	251,944
Scriptures distributed,	9,460
Religious tracts given away,	3,069,765
Books lent,	49,208
In-door meetings and Bible-classes held,	43,288
Average attendance at do.,	33
Gross attendance at do.,	1,417,000
Out-door services held,	5,401
Average attendance at do.,	107
Gross attendance at do.,	578,384
Readings of Scripture in visitation,	610,868
Communicants,	1,609
Backsliders restored to Church communion,	262
Families induced to commence family prayer,	709
Drunkards reclaimed,	1,045
Unmarried couples induced to marry,	341
Fallen females admitted to asylums, restored to their homes, or otherwise rescued,	503
Shops closed on the Lord's day,	239
Children sent to schools,	9,716
Adults visited, who died,	6,286
Of whom, visited by the missionary only,	1,747
The proportion visited by the missionary only exceeds	2 in 7

The city missionaries have, then, within the last year, paid nearly 2,000,000 visits, and distributed more than 3,000,000 tracts; they have brought 262 backsliders to the fold, and reclaimed 1000 drunkards. But these operations have been somewhat costly. The half-million hours spent in domiciliary visits have not, I trust, been thrown away; but it is open to grave doubt whether the great and costly machinery of the London City Mission might not be turned to better account, than is shown in the above table.

Let the reader picture to himself, as a field for missionary labour, a famous slum, called Charles Street, Drury Lane. Here, and round about, poverty, vice, and crime are strewn thick as the leaves in Vallombrosa's Vale. The curious stranger may direct his steps to the north-east corner of Drury Lane, which lies against Holborn. He will find women in dirty gowns and shawls, and with matted hair, lounging at the corner, whatever hour of the day or evening it may be. In this north-east block of poverty and crime; men, women, and children are packed so close together that it is wonderful they are still alive to prove the extent of human endurance. The city missionary pays his visits to these 155 houses and 16 common lodging-houses, where the vagrant, the beggar, the prostitute, and the labourer out of work, rest their tired limbs at night —together! There are degrees of misery even here, amid these black and gaunt houses. They who have their own furniture have not reached the bottom of Misery's ladder. Fate has done her worst with a man, when he has come to be the inhabitant of a furnished room in Charles Street, Drury Lane. Here the patterer and the hodman, the thief and the costermonger, the street-singer and the prostitute, the strong boot-maker and the beggar, pay their 7d. or 8d. per night. In King Street are market hands and orange-sellers; in Coal Yard and Smart's Buildings, working folk, who are ready to do any odd work. There are numbers of shoemakers also, hereabouts. The common lodging-houses tempt all who can pay only 3d. or 4d. for a bed, and so the honest, poverty-stricken man finds himself lying beside the felon. Shame festering in rags fills Barley, Fagerty's, and Shaw's Courts. A dense and dangerous mixture of the poor and the wicked! All kinds of cunning and cheating are well represented. About 300 come trooping to these repulsive houses in company—the broken-down labourer, with the beggar, the patterer, and the burglar. In the low, long, whitewashed common room, groups lie and lounge, or huddle over the coke fire; while abandoned women talk the slang of the neighbourhood, and the men curse and swear. It is an evening school for the propagation of vice. If a man is seen to affect reading, he is soundly rated and ridiculed. The sick lie unregarded along greasy benches; and beyond, clothes black as soot, are washed in water dark as ink. For the young who are compelled to pass their nights here, what hope is there? Their daily companions and their bed-fellows, are the vilest of the vile; their nightly supper is seasoned with stories of crime. But they are poor, and the poor cannot choose their companions.

In a district of this description, the city missionary has awkward work to perform. He is the bearer of religious consolation; but the field is not ready for him. All this dirt must be cleared away first. These begrimed patterers and pickpockets cannot jump from this degradation into a state of piety. The missionary is not very hopeful. He says:— "Nearly twenty cases of death have occurred during the last twelve months, some very serious and solemn. I cannot refer to any of them as sleeping in Jesus.

All have left to me, at least, unsatisfactory evidence of their ultimate happiness." This missionary also complains that his prayer-meetings are not so well attended as those where temporal relief is given with the teaching, and where people listen with solid reward before them, to tempt them. This is a complaint we shall have to consider presently. But I protest at once against the style in which the missionaries make reports on their labours. They provoke hostility, and suggest to the mind of the most amiable reader, a certain falsity in the writer. In a word, their tone is canting. I am quite certain that if many of the forlorn creatures of Charles Street and Smart's Buildings, Drury Lane, scoff at the city missionary, it is because he will persist in talking a religious or missionary jargon that is wholly unintelligible to the mass of men and women. The report of an individual case sent in by the Drury Lane missionary is not calculated to impress, but rather to puzzle, and it may be to disgust, the reader. It is choked with hackneyed verbosities. It jars upon the ear, and makes the listener look doubtingly towards the speaker. Is he in earnest, and the right man in the right place, who walks amid ragged savages, uninformed and cold as the ground they tread, and talks of them in this wise?

"Mr. ——, aged 50, of the Model House, Charles Street—the only instance of real apparent good I have seen there—first came under my notice while visiting there, as I have done from time to time. About January 1860, he came to have a more open liking for my visits. Being a man of some education, having been educated in Christ's Hospital, Newgate Street, he was able to express his ignorance of God's plan of salvation, and his own felt need of God's pardoning love, in a straightforward, intelligent manner.

For a very long time he wandered in darkness, seeing men as trees walking. I felt great pleasure in often visiting him. He began to attend Trinity Church (Rev. S. Garratt's) as also a church in the City, and was also an attendant at my Thursday evening meeting. He evidently was seeking salvation. Eventually the Lord led him by a path he knew not. One day, in June 1860, he told me of new light that had broken in upon him, which led to further conversation, during which time, I gathered, he had received great good from one of the Dublin Society's tracts, 'Good News,' and a passage he read there, under God's blessing, was the means of bringing to his soul a sweet assurance of God's pardoning love. This is the passage:—'I say this is the first step to religion, to understand this truth aright, that the Gospel brings glad tidings of salvation to the worst of sinners. Therefore, though I see no good in me at all whereby I might receive good news of the law, and although I do not see that I am a humble sinner, as such a preacher teacheth, or a penitent sinner, or a broken-hearted sinner, yet I know I am a sinner, and, as a sinner, I am the proper object of the Gospel' (p. 5). Since then his walk and conversation have become the Gospel of Christ. I have reason to believe that he is growing in grace and in the knowledge of our Lord Jesus Christ. My local superintendent, the Rev. S. Garratt, expressed satisfaction in visiting him, and brought before him the duty of attending the ordinance of the Lord's Table, which he now does, attending the church next Christ's Hospital, Newgate Street. An instance of his conscientiousness I may here adduce. He gains his living by cutting mural tablets in cardboard, which causes him to go out at night-time into public-houses, etc. Once he minded not the company of such places, now he says that it is hateful to him. He has lost considerably by refusing to join with the general company of such places recently; and although he knows not how to give up such a means of living entirely, for a long time past it has been made a matter of prayer before God that He will guide him how to act. He has recently told me that he thinks he has an opening in the West of England, where he shall be able to go, and thus get his living in an upright manner. I am thankful he is of great help to me among the men in the Model House, as also occasionally at my Thursday evening meeting."

I am glad that the cardboard modeller has listened to the pious exhortations of the missionary; but, at the same time, I am surprised; for I cannot understand how the pious zealot made himself intelligible. I should be sorry to disparage wilfully the doings of the London missionary body. I know that they are a most excellent, earnest, and useful body, as we shall see. I only question the wisdom of some of their modes of proceeding in their noble work. They have presented to the world all the horrors suffered by the London poor. They have valiantly penetrated every dismal haunt of poverty to be found within the bills of mortality. They have set forth the infamies of the Chinese opium-rooms of London; they have lingered by the night cabmen, entered the gipsy's tent, and suffered the dangers and nausea of the padding-ken; they have been most useful moral helps in workhouses. But their knowledge has not been turned to the fullest possible account. They are familiar with families who herd in rooms, as close as sheep in a pen. In Baldwin's Gardens, two families may be seen in one room, and with dogs, cats, rabbits, white mice, etc., to keep them company. "There is an attic in Bell Court," a missionary writes, "occupied by a shoemaker, who breeds dogs, and sometimes has as many as from ten to thirteen at one time. I have for a very long time been fully persuaded that even the manner in which the poor people live together must have a very demoralizing effect, especially on the young. The language of the people, both old and young, male and female, is very degrading and sinful; yet I am sometimes delighted to hear some of the children, scholars at the ragged-schools, sing their little tunes learnt there, instead of profane songs." Such knowledge, the result of experience, might have been turned to most profitable account many years ago. The Society was established in 1835, and has gone on increasing every year from the time of its foundation; but it has never widened its sphere of usefulness; it has never had a care for the physical comfort of its *protégés.* Take the knowledge the cabmen's missionaries have. It is most important, and as unknown as it is important. The East London missionary declares that the difference between six and seven-day cabmen is surprising. Those who rest on Sundays are remarkable for their respectable appearance, as may be easily proved by noticing them on their stands in the week, and by seeing them at their several places of worship on the Sunday; but more especially by visiting them at their homes. The seven-day men have no use for Sunday clothes, since they never have an opportunity of wearing them. Many of them are almost strangers to their own children, and go three or four months without having a day's rest. Such points of information, drawn from the men themselves, would have been useful long since, had the missionaries of our London alleys shown a sense of the importance of temporal, as well as spiritual matters; and had understood the temporal good, as a basis for the spiritual.

CHAPTER IV.

BEGGARS AND THEIR TRAPPERS.

THE officers of the City Mission Society are not the only men with a mission among the London poor. There is another influential London society that has imposed on itself a great and useful task. Established in 1818, the Society for the Suppression of Mendicity was set on foot for the purpose of checking the practice of public mendicity, with all its baneful and demoralizing consequences, by putting the laws in force against impostors, who adopt begging as a trade; and by affording prompt and effectual assistance to those whom sudden calamity and unaffected distress may cast, in want and misery, upon the public attention. The utility of such an institution was at once obvious. While it waged war against the rogue and vagabond, it gave to the deserving poor. It should be observed that this Society holds a place between the Soup Kitchen and Hospice of Ham Yard, and the City Mission. In Ham Yard, only food and shelter are given; from the City Mission House proceeds spiritual exhortation—advice gratis—but not a crumb; while the Mendicity Society gives in cases of unaffected distress, and teaches the poor to work for their bread.

One Baron d'Aguilar, at the end of the last century, set up "Starvation Farm," on the west bank of the New River. He was an old reprobate, and it was the fiendish pleasure of his old age to herd pigs, poultry, and cattle together upon this farm, and starve them to death. The stronger ate the weaker, until a heap of bones was all that remained to tell the dismal story. Now, I make no doubt but that certain wily and reflective dogs in that neighbourhood flourished by counterfeiting the heart-rending howlings and whinings of Starvation Farm, and drew bonés and scraps from housewives' compassionate fingers. The starvation farms of London (and there are many of them), where men, women, and children appear to be huddled by some savage monster, that they may prey upon one another, and presently appear but a heap of dry bones; have unquestionably had the effect of rearing and banding hordes of bowelless imitators of their cries of agony, of their deformities, and sores and sorrows. These sturdy and successful hypocrites became a public nuisance long since.

"It is astonishing the falsehoods they will invent," said a Mendicity officer to whom I addressed myself, speaking of the beggars. "These visiting ladies are not a match for them. They have a story for everybody. It is wonderful how coolly they will invent distresses. As a rule, they overcolour the picture."

It requires the nicest judgment and great experience, to do battle successfully against the craft and good acting of the professional beggar, who has a list of London Charities at his finger-ends. The Mendicity Society have long striven hard to eliminate the professional beggar from the deserving poor. This is their special labour; and they have adapted their premises in Red Lion Square to their worthy object in view. The house is a large, old-fashioned one. On the ground-floor are the offices; behind, a covered yard, in which, on crowded days, applicants wait; and at hand is the constable's room. The constables (seven in number) are very important persons in the transactions the examining-clerks have with their customers. The kitchen department is roomy, and furnished with long deal tables, at which the rations are distributed and consumed. From nine o'clock till twelve, and again from two till four, a constant stream of hungry and workless poor, mixed with lying rascals who are neither very hungry nor very poor, pours through the yard to the examining-clerks' offices, and thence, if deserving, through the kitchen; and so on, to the stone-yard, the mill, or the oakum-room.

In the office, where every applicant for relief is searchingly examined as to his antecedents and his present condition, are two most experienced gentlemen, one of whom has been sifting the falsehoods of vagrants for the last thirty years. Before him is a library of some thousand volumes or more, in which the cases of begging impositions, and of apprehensions by the Society's constables, are kept and indexed—a veritable biographical encyclopædia of beggary and imposture. When the applicant for relief enters the room, he is asked his name and parish. The practised hand is not at all embarrassed. He will, if he believes that the old name may be remembered, give a fresh one. "Why," said one of these intelligent officers to me, "only yesterday a man applied for relief, under the name of Richard Porter, and to-day he was here as Richard Foster. They mostly overdo it. Some time ago a woman applied for relief. She had a pitiful tale quite ready. Her husband had fallen from a scaffold, had fractured his thigh, and was lying in the hospital. She was asked, Which hospital? She answered, 'The Middlesex.' I told her I was very sorry to hear of her misfortune, and that I would send to the hospital to make inquiries about him. She was shown into the constables' room. A man presented himself. I asked him if he was married. Yes, he was married, but he didn't know where his wife was. He was in great distress. I asked him what he would say if I presented his wife to him. He answered that it was impossible. So I sent for the woman from the constables' room, and confronted the pair. They coolly looked at one another, and maintained that they were strangers. The woman persisted in her story that her husband was in the hospital, so I sent her away again, and appealed to the man, telling him I knew that she was his wife, and I had a mind to make an example of him. At last, baffled at all points, he admitted the truth of my suspicion; yet the woman, when he sheepishly confessed in her presence, held for a time, to her impudent falsehood."[1]

The officers, when a man's statement is suspicious, can refer him back from ten to twenty years. Their records include 60,000 cases of begging impositions, irrespective of the great begging-letter department. The Society is very careful not to meddle with cases entitled to metropolitan parish relief. Their object is not to do parish work, but to clear the streets. They test the honesty of every beggar by offering him food—and work.

"Only yesterday," my informant continued, "an able-bodied man applied for relief. He was told to go over to the mill, in Great Ormond Yard, and he would be fed; but the fellow, like many of them, shirked the work." He would, had he not been tested, have had a most excellent and nutritious pint of soup (with plenty of meat in it, as I can testify), and a third of a half quartern of good wheaten bread; and the lazy rascal would have gone off to another

1 "A beggar in Moorfields used daily to have a penny given him by a merchant on his way to the Exchange. The penny was withheld, and the appearance of the merchant manifested his embarrassment and distress. The beggar at length spoke to him, offered him a loan of £500, and another of the same sum if it were required. It re-established his affairs."—*Southey.*

Charity in search of more bread of idleness. As winter comes on, hundreds of country people deliberately crowd to the metropolis with the idea of abusing the Charities of London. The Mendicity officers know how these birds of prey flit from refuge to refuge, and from soup-kitchen to soup-kitchen, and so contrive to live in idleness throughout the winter. This is a system that should be broken up, for it stultifies all the efforts of the charitable, and robs the really deserving. Hence the beneficial operation of such a society as that with which I am dealing. Here the chain of imposture is broken, and the impostor stands a very good chance of finding himself committed to prison, as a rogue and vagabond. The peril is possibly not full of terrors to the old hand, since he knows what prison fare is, and how it stands related to mendicity or other gratuitous soup. But, at any rate, the soup of Red Lion Square is not for the churl who can work and will not. I have tasted the soup, and tested the bread and cheese (double Gloucester) which reward the Mendicity Society's workers at the mill or the stone-yard, and their pickers of oakum; and I unhesitatingly pronounce them a good meal for any able-bodied man. When a man applies for relief with his wife and family, they are all put to work, and have all equal rations; so that they have often more than they can eat. Then money is distributed for the Sunday's dinner—so that no man, woman, nor child, willing to do a day's work in return for relief, need go begging in the streets. The disabled and crippled are sent to the corn-mill, or to the oakum-rooms; while the hale and hearty men are sent to break stones. These, it should be observed, have double rations, having very hard work. The work hours are usually from nine in the morning till six in the afternoon.

There is no end to the subtleties of vagrants. The managers are compelled, when serving out rations to a family of six, to cut the quartern loaf into six parts before yielding it up, because, when they give a whole loaf to a family, the parents would make off and sell it from their children, probably to buy beer or gin.

Tickets, intended for distribution to street beggars only, are given to subscribers. The applicant is then admitted into the Society's office, and examined by the sitting or assistant manager (as I have described), who orders such relief as may be necessary.

To those applicants without lodging, sufficient money is given to procure one for the night. A pauper having any claim on a London parish, is simply referred to the overseers of that parish. Should the applicant be required to return at a future day to the office, a return ticket, entitling him to further relief, is given to him, inquiry as to character being made meanwhile, by the constables. Applicants who have resided for some time in London, although they may have no claim on a London parish, receive an order for six days' work. While at work, the pauper receives two meals a day, and 6d. to provide lodging. A meal a day is also given to each member of the family; on Saturday 1s., and an extra meal to each. A single meal consists, in winter, of a pint of nourishing soup and a sixth of a 4lb. loaf of bread; in summer, of the same quantity of bread, with a quarter of a pound of cheese. On application at the end of the week, the order for work is renewed; but at the termination of a month's employment, the applicant is dismissed, unless the sitting manager considers further relief necessary, when the case is laid before the committee, who renew the order, or give such other relief as is most likely to prevent the necessity of street-begging.

Tramps passing through London, on their way to work in the country, have one ration given to them, and are sent off. Should they return on the morrow, they are set to work before they are relieved. They cannot have a second dip into the 100-gallon caldron of soup that is boiling by steam below, before they have been to the stone-yard or the mill.

The effect of the weather on the London poor is remarkably exemplified on the premises of the Mendicity Society. "We are a regular thermometer," said the cook (who is a constable also). "Directly the cold comes, the distress is upon us." The frost throws thousands of London labourers out of employ. The paviors, hodmen, bricklayers, and navvies, all cease working, and at once they are in distress. At the present moment there is not a man in the Society's stone-yard, nor has it been yet opened during the present winter; and in the oakum-room there are only a few pickers, say from 30 to 40. A sharp day or two would completely change the aspect of affairs. I looked over the constable-cook's soup-book, and it showed that this day (the last of 1862) only 81 had eaten bread and soup; whereas no less than 188 were relieved yesterday. But yesterday's business was very light. On the 16th of last month (it was sharp weather) the partakers of Mendicity Society's soup was 311. On the 24th of December 1861, the number who passed through the kitchen reached 512.

The momentary lightness of the business transacting by the Mendicity Society is due not merely to the mildness of the season, but also to the vast works of demolition that are just now being carried on at Hungerford, and along the line between London Bridge and Charing Cross, to say nothing of the great underground sewerage operations. There is no frost, so that building operations can go forward; but a heavy fall of snow, or weather that would delight the skater, would fill the stone-yard, and people the mill and the oakum-rooms. The Society is always at work, let it be understood, whether there is real distress or not; because sham distress is never over. The vagabonds who have tramped to London, in order to eke out an idle winter on the bounty of the good folk who support refuges and soup-kitchens, will still tax the ingenuity of the Mendicity officers. They will come with the old effrontery to tell their falsehoods. A brazen woman had her tale of horrors complete. Her husband had met with a severe accident.

"Where?" said the acute examiner, sharply.

"Somewhere in this neighbourhood."

"And where did they carry him?"

"To St. Thomas's Hospital," was the prompt response.

This reply set the examiner thinking. It was very strange that a man, horribly mutilated in the neighbourhood of Red Lion Square, should be carried past the Middlesex and other hospitals, to one so far off, and for the moment in complete confusion. In short, the woman was, by her own bungling, proved to be an impostor.

Let me now direct the reader's attention to the present financial state of the Society. The year 1861 showed a great increase of distress among the poorer classes; the diminished supply of cotton consequent upon the American war, and the impaired resources of the consumers of our manufactures, having led to a decrease of employment, and some suffering among those engaged in factories.

During the first five months of the year 1861 there was an increase of 155 per cent. in the number of applicants compared with that of the year 1860; and the first four months of the year presented an increase of more than 300 per cent. compared with that of the corresponding period of the year preceding—distress amongst the working classes being no doubt attributable to the previous bad harvest and the severe winter which followed.

The registered cases, or those which have met with extra attention and consideration, were, during 1861, 446. This was not quite up to the average of the ten preceding years, which was 459, yet it was beyond that of 1860, which was 430. The cases of minor importance, and classed as unregistered, were 7606, showing an increase on the average of the preceding ten years (which was 6159) of nearly 24 per cent., and an increase on the year preceding to the extent of 3382 cases.

The meals given by the Society have also increased from 42,192, in 1860, to 73,077, in 1861; the average of the ten preceding years being 56,802. The increase has been great, yet on reflection it will be perceived that even the relief given in 1861, under this head, did not amount to the half of what used formerly to be given; the average meals of the ten years preceding 1851 having been 152,579.

The sum employed in relieving mendicants was £1470, 19s. 11d. This was much beyond that so spent in any of the preceding nine years, and exceeded the amount spent in 1860 by £564, 10s. 11d. Of this, £153, 19s. was given without work, and £383, 15s. 4d. as the wages of labour; £862, 7s. 7d. was paid for food, £66, 3s. 10d. for clothes, and £4, 14s. 2d. for baths—which appear to be often gratefully received by the applicants.

The list of vagrants convicted during the year 1861 showed a small decrease, being 335 against 350 in the year preceding. Those apprehended were 745; the number in 1860 was 739.

The total amount of expenditure in 1861 was £4242, 3s. 8d. This was an increase of nearly £1100 on that of the preceding year, which was £3169, 16s. 11d. In addition to the extra demand on the resources of the Society, consequent on the greater distress, the expenditure for 1861 comprised the sum of £429, 18s. 6d. for repairs.

It is to be regretted that the income of the Society has for the last twenty years been on the decrease. I find, by reference to the last report, that for the ten years preceding 1851, the average income was £4600, while in 1861 it had dwindled to £2800. I am sorry to hear that during the year 1862 there has been a further falling off in the Society's receipts; that the committee have been consequently compelled to sell out stock to the amount of £801, 15s. 11d.; and that, notwithstanding, the balance in hand on the 23d of last December was not more than £288, 12s. 11d.

A gentleman, in passing over one of the Dublin bridges, was plaintively solicited for charity. He peremptorily refused the mendicant's prayer; whereupon the beggar, whose coat was "a parcel of holes sewed together," muttered to himself, "Well, I know what I will do." The gentleman's mind was disturbed by this threatening remark. He turned upon the supplicant, to see whether he had reached the parapet of the bridge. The man was crawling pitifully behind him. "My man, what did you mean by saying you knew what you'd do?" The beggar answered—despair in his voice—"Why, I meant, yer honor, that if you would not give me anything, I should have to go to work!" This would be the lot of the bands of beggars who now infest the main thoroughfares of London, if alms were persistently refused them. The profession of begging having fallen into decay, the great fraternity of "Whitechapel dodgers" would be positively compelled to earn their bread by the sweat of their brow. They would be actually reduced to the straits which are suffered by the honest poor who shiver at the dock-gates every sunrise, imploring a hard day's work for a shilling. The ingenious dodger who paints a ship upon the flags, flanked by the head and shoulders of a salmon and a couple of mackerel, with a few smelts by way of finishing touches, at a fixed price, and leaves a picturesquely-attired cadger to sit by the performance with doleful face and extended palm, beseeching the charity of beholders for an unregarded Stanfield who has come to this woful complexion—this vagabond artist and cheat, with his lying customer, would be reduced to the dire necessity of doing that which they dread more than prison, viz., earning their daily bread. Children would not be hired to crawl through the mud and snow and rain of quiet streets, at the skirts of hags who beat and starve them, if the public would firmly, and in mercy, set their face against the great impostures which still issue from Whitechapel. Take the case of "two decent-looking elderly men, evidently got up to represent Lancashire cotton-weavers," who were brought before Mr. Combe one morning charged with begging in the public streets. The policeman pounced upon them while they were moaning a lugubrious song about Lancashire distress. They had mastered their new "fakement;" they were *au fait* at the Lancashire dialect, and were robbing the deserving poor of our cotton districts very successfully. At the station-house they "dropped" the Lancashire dialect, being thoroughly identified as "Whitechapel dodgers." Found out, of what avail was the dialect? they would not be at the trouble of acting gratis before the inspector. They had hit upon a happy imposture, and it had been worth the risk of detection. These traders on the tender heart of society watch the shifting phases of our daily life, and appreciate with most sagacious discrimination the direction in which they should seek to invent new traps to catch the pence of unthinking, but compassionate passers-by.

We must confess that the "lay" on which the two rogues and vagabonds whom Mr. Combe sentenced to fourteen days' hard labour were found, was a well-chosen one. These fellows had felt the pulse of society. They had marked how the noble and patient bearing of our starving operatives had touched men, women, and children to the quick; their eyes had gloated over the long lists of subscriptions. And then they had set themselves to work to learn the part of the Lancashire operative. They settled how to dress the character, hired a man of their own kidney to write the "doleful ditty;" and, doubtless, had their dress rehearsals. Whitechapel must be furnished with a professor of the Lancashire dialect, who must enjoy the fruits of an extensive *clientèle* by this time.

Steele, in the *Spectator* (July 14, 1712), writes:— "I looked out of my window the other morning earlier than ordinary, and saw a blind beggar, an hour before the passage he stands in is frequented, with a needle and thread, thriftily mending his stockings. My astonishment was still greater when I beheld a lame fellow, whose legs were too big to walk, within an hour after, bring him a pot of ale. I will not mention the shakings, distortions, and convulsions which many of them practise to gain an alms; but sure I am they ought to be taken care of in this condition, either by the beadle or the magistrate. They, it seems, relieve their posts according to their talents. There is the voice of an old woman, who never begins to beg till nine in the evening, and then she is destitute of lodging, turned out for want of rent, and has the same ill-fortune every night in the year." This picture is exactly one century and a half old—yet it is faithful to Whitechapel life in 1862. The shivering dodge is not extinct. Maimed sailors flourish. The blind are as quick-sighted as ever. The halt have nimble feet when it is necessary to run. Men create sores in their flesh as tradesmen lay in stock. And not only is London worked by these "dodgers"—these actors of distress and disease—whose earnings are so much money filched from the hands of the deserving poor—the country is laid under contribution. The vagabond beggars have their free-masonry, by the signs of which, chalked on doors or palings, each whining rogue may tell how his predecessor has fared. Let any of our readers who dwell in London suburbs or country quarters examine the postern of their gates or their palings; they will discover upon them certain mysterious chalk marks, which are comprehensible to the entire fraternity of beggars. We are told that the passage mark is "a cipher with a twisted tail." There are other marks which indicate whether the house is worth calling at, or whether it is dangerous to apply. The reader will perceive that our beggars have a sense of method. They see that time is money. They spare each other the trouble of acting before the stony-hearted. I have no doubt that "distressed Lancashire operatives"—friends of the vagabonds sent to labour hard in Wandsworth Gaol—have made lucrative progresses round the country. Our army of cadgers could not possibly have a better "lay." They are cunning rogues, and they well know how to make the best of the every generous mood of the British public.

Every penny given to a begging Lancashire operative was a penny given to a rogue and vagabond. I make this emphatic statement without fear of contradiction; since the dignified and patient attitude which our distressed fellow-countrymen of Lancashire have held from the time when work slackened, to the evil hour when the mills were closed, is proof that none of them would beg in the streets. But this is not all. Every distressed Lancashire operative can obtain help enough to keep him from the streets. If he had the will to beg, and sing doggrel along the kennel, he would be without excuse for the proceeding. The great-hearted, open-handed people of England promise him, and give him in his distress, at any rate as much money per week as the Dorsetshire labourer gets in prosperous times. The gift which Englishmen have made to their Lancashire brethren honours both giver and receiver. The London beggar is, it would appear, an irrepressible nuisance. Notwithstanding new and severe laws, and the new police, he still exhibits his manufactured sores, and whines the artful falsehoods he has committed to memory. That he perseveres--that he has held on to his trade from the days when Steele exposed him--is sufficient evidence that his methodical roguery pays; and pays better than labour. And he will ply his shameless trade while the public are thoughtless enough to give without a question.

CHAPTER V.

BEGGING-LETTER WRITERS.

THE begging-letter branch of the Mendicity Society's business is full of melancholy interest. In the vagrants' department, where the idle commit all kinds of falsehoods that they may get a little gratuitous soup and bread, we see a kind of hand-to-mouth immorality that is shocking enough. But the man and wife who forswear each other, and the cunning fellows who give false names, are simple creatures when compared with the knaves whose cases are dealt with up-stairs in the begging-letter office. The common vagrant wanders about with excuses on his lips, and aims only at a basin of soup by day, and a shake-down in a refuge by night. He is a poor, ignorant fellow, upon whom knowledge has never dawned. He was born in a hovel or a court; he has had no "opportunities." But there are knaves of subtler mind than this poor idler; knaves who have been bred at decent seminaries, and have held fair positions in life. To these interesting examples of acquirements misused, the Mendicity Society have devoted great labour.

The begging-letter impostor is as difficult to bring down as the crow. At the sight of a Mendicity officer he wheels about, and gets beyond gunshot. There is William Thomas, surnamed the Black Prince. He has had his laugh for many a year at the expense of the Mendicity Society's visitors, and at London magistrates. He was no bungler. He could define the limits of the law, and keep himself within them. In vain the Mendicity officers sought to convict him as an impostor—they could not prove enough. He collected subscriptions in order to establish a school in the Nilgherry Hills. India was the field of his philanthropic exertions; and who could prove that he had no intention of founding a school for the benefit of the surrounding population? And so the Black Prince prospered, until, in an unguarded moment, he added to his plea in behalf of his school in India a supplication based on the approaching *accouchement* of his wife. He was convicted on the falsity of this statement, and suffered a year's imprisonment, with hard labour.

I presented myself to the gentleman who, since the year 1829, has devoted all his business hours to the detection of begging-letter impostors. The walls of his room are hidden by presses, in which are alphabetically arranged the cases of sham distress which have come under his notice. We had a long and most interesting conversation, which I shall take leave to set before the reader.

The subscribers to the Mendicity Society may send all the begging letters they receive to be examined in this long, severe office, in which I find myself blocked in with the records of roguery. The letters are entered in a book as they are received, and are then handed over to a visitor whose business it is to inquire about, and report on them. In the book before me not less than 54,000 begging-letters are entered. The rate of reception averages between three and four thousand a year, or about ten daily. The visitors, to whom the letters are given, make inquiries in all directions, and take all possible pains to discover whether every statement is true. Their report is submitted to the committee, who decide whether the case is or is not worthy of relief. I may observe in this place, that many men of wealth, who are pestered with applications for money, and who cannot possibly tell which among the supplicants are worthy and which are unworthy, are delighted to hand over the responsibility of distributing alms to this Society, where the false rogue is almost certain to be detected. They are certain, or nearly certain, that the money which they intrust to the keeping of the Society goes into no leering families of black princes. The vigilance and keenness of the Society's officers are displayed in the 54,000 reports on cases which are alphabetically ranged round the walls. I asked the chief of the department how he traced the regular impostors, who so frequently changed their name and abode. "I can tell them in most cases," he answered, "some by their story, but chiefly by their handwriting. We have got all their names in a register."

I was then presented with a mass of letters, arranged neatly and pinned together. These were the papers of a notorious Devonport gang of begging-letter writers. I examined them closely. The story was different in each set. In one series the applicant was a clergyman's widow, with five children, and with a distress for rent in her house. The case was very completely made out. Even the distress warrant was forged. The letter begging help, was signed by a vicar and by a series of subscribers. The ingenuity with which the signatures (all forgeries) were varied, was marvellous. Various shades and colours of ink were used to complete the deception. The second bundle, from the same gang, was the application of a widow for help in order to enable her to place her interesting but demented daughter of seventeen in an asylum for idiots. Forty-five pounds would make the widow for ever grateful. I closely examined both parcels; and, after a little time and trouble, I could see the same rogue's mind and rogue's hand in the two performances. The game in both cases had been found out. The subscribers had proved that their signatures were forgeries.

"They are a low drunken race, these begging-letter impostors," my informant continued, "and they inhabit low lodging-houses, where they associate and plot together against the good nature of the British public. They prefer the country, because they cannot be so rigidly watched as they are in town. They are cunning as foxes. When we try to bring the cheat home to them, by sending them a registered letter, they will not acknowledge that it is for them. It is for a friend in the country, to whom they will forward it." They double nimbly on their pursuers. They are shrewd observers of the world, not to be caught by a schoolboy. They understand the force of every name they forge. They hold that incumbents and churchwardens are impressive. They are careful about their black-bordered paper when they are widows; and they have female confederates at hand when a feminine writing is required. The men engaged in this nefarious war upon the charitable public are often persons who have occupied the position of gentlemen. Indeed, the occupation requires a fair education. "They are mostly clerks who have gone wrong," was the begging-letter examiner's opinion. "They are all drunken fellows. I have seen two of them brought to the police-court with broken heads, having quarrelled over the spoils of their lying tales. Some of them make a great deal of money; they know where to apply, and nothing delights them more than to get hold of one of our subscription lists. By the use of such a list they can ascertain who sends his begging-letters to us, and so avoid the danger of having their letters sent here. There is Lord B—, who was once in the habit of receiving great quantities of begging-letters, many of which he relieved in the dark. This was before he subscribed to the Society. Now the regular traders know that he will send their applications to be sifted here—only the deserving cases, therefore, now reach him." The begging-letter gangs regard the Mendicity Society visitors as their mortal foes, and avoid them always. The manager threw a bundle of letters upon the desk. "This," said he, "is the Dublin case."

The Dublin case, I should explain, is one that has troubled the Mendicity Society for twenty years. In the low lodging-houses of Dublin some very cunning begging-letter writers have had their headquarters. They have devoted their genius to shipwrecks. All their stories have been of poor folk cast on shore on stormy nights, and left friendless in a strange land. They were long accustomed to make capital out of a wrecked colour-sergeant's widow, who never existed save in their vivid imaginations. But this airy lady has been dispersed. She had a hard time of it, and was at last worked to death. The Dublin gang, after a protracted career, are now almost broken up. Some of the more experienced old rascals have done England the honour of taking up their residence in London, and others have gone the way of many begging-letter writers.

When I had sufficiently feasted my eyes on the Dublin case, I was referred to another bulky roll of papers. This was, I was informed, the naval case. The naval case was that of a band of arch-impostors, who pretended to have been sailors. They got up shipboard jargon, mixed with the Greenwich pensioners, and became learned in the names of ships and their commanders. Thus armed with useful knowledge, they addressed themselves to the navy list; and, upon fictitious troubles of poor Jack, they existed a long time. This great bundle before me is substantial proof of the damage the Mendicity Society has done these wicked landlubbers in sailors' clothes. Let me now afford the reader a specimen of the reports the visitors make upon the begging-letters intrusted to them for their inquiry:—

"BEGGING-LETTER DEPARTMENT,
"MENDICITY OFFICE, RED LION SQUARE, *January*.

"No. of case.

"Received (this day), ________ alias ________
(Address.) ________________

"This case is known to the Society, and the following is a copy of the report made upon the last investigation:—

"—— March ——

"The case of this applicant has been known to the committee since 1852, since when no less than thirty similar appeals to the present have been referred to the office. Applicant is the daughter of a clergyman, and a native of ——, about forty years of age. It appears that she married at an early age a Captain ——, of the —— Regiment, and after living with him some years she left her home in a highly culpable manner, and was guilty of adultery, defending her conduct by the assertion that her husband neglected her, and maintained an illicit connexion with other women. She is now endeavouring to raise a sufficient sum to purchase an annuity of £50, and the two gentlemen mentioned in the subscription-list have consented to receive money for that object. One of them, Mr. ——, who is a respectable solicitor, has been seen by the visitor, and it is found that £700 is required, and at present only £240 has been received.

"Applicant is now suffering from a disease of the eyes (which is no doubt caused by mental excitement), and is wholly incapacitated from doing anything towards her support. From the circumstances of the case, it is evident that it would be far better for the applicant to try to obtain admission into some charitable institution, than to be continually appealing to the benevolent for assistance. Her friends, who are in good circumstances, decline affording her any pecuniary aid, in consequence of the disgrace and annoyance sustained by them on account of applicant's immoral conduct."

This case is simply undeserving, according to the Society's estimate. There is no imposture; and, in spite of the Society's advice, the applicant has gained her end; she has obtained an annuity by subscription, and, tempted by her past success, she has originated an appeal for further aid. In this way beggary begins.

There are in Westminster and other low neighbourhoods, not only begging-letter impostors on their own account, but there are journeymen who write for the poor, both deserving and undeserving. These fellows scribble begging-letters at prices varying from fourpence to one shilling, according to the length and importance of the document. They are also good enough to take percentages on the subscriptions received.

By these glimpses behind the scenes of charity the public may learn where and how to give. The poor of London are robbed of nearly one-half of the help that is meant for them, by cozeners in every shape; and every pound robbed from the poor falls into the pocket of a cheat.

It would appear that in 1860 the begging-letters sent to the Mendicity Society's office for investigation were 3601, of which 1080 were received in the first three months of the year. In 1861 the number of such letters sent rose to 4305, of which 1393 were received in the first three months. The sum of £1123 has been disbursed to those applicants on behalf of such subscribers as send money to the Society for distribution, being the largest amount so given since 1849, when the amount given was somewhat greater; besides this, a large measure of relief has, doubtless, been afforded by subscribers who do not constitute the Society their almoners, but who are guided by the reports of the visitors. While the deserving are relieved, as stated, exertions are constantly made to punish unprincipled persons who attempt to practise fraud upon the Society. Thirty begging-letter impostors have been convicted during the year, and sentenced to various terms of imprisonment. Among those apprehended by the officers was a man in robust health named Edward Harper, who obtained from a gentleman the means to buy a trowel to perform a duty at the Exhibition building, and afterwards received a further gift of 10s. from the same source, upon the pretence that he required money to pay the funeral expenses of one of his children. On a subsequent occasion the applicant (who was doubtless a member of the gang of fourpenny letter-writers above alluded to) brought a letter to the same gentleman, purporting to be from the clergyman who had performed the funeral service, recommending the case strongly; but it turned out that the latter knew nothing of the applicant or the letter. It appeared, moreover, that he was a confirmed impostor; and the result was that he was sentenced at the police court, to three months' imprisonment, with hard labour.

Another case is that of a man named James Sullivan, who brought a petition to a lady, stating that a laundress at Paddington having had her horse frightened by the whistle of the railway, the cart which the horse was drawing was dashed to pieces, and her son, who was driving, sustained a compound fracture of the right arm. The petition appeared to be signed by the vestry clerk of a parish, and to be certified by a letter from the clergyman. The lady, suspecting the story, communicated with the Society, and the result was that Sullivan was apprehended, when it was discovered that his story was an entire fabrication, and that he had already been thirteen times convicted of frauds of the like nature. On this last occasion he was condemned at the sessions to twelve months' imprisonment, with hard labour.

Many other instances might be furnished from the records of the Society; and there were also numerous cases in which the persons applying had for a series of years managed to evade criminal proceedings, but who, by their tales of distress and other pretexts, had contrived to support themselves at the expense of the public.

In bringing forward this phase of the Society's operations, the committee may properly express a hope that the pains they take to suppress fraud and professional mendicancy may strengthen the inducements to a judicious administration of charitable relief to deserving objects. That they deserve to see this hope abundantly realized, is proved by the great success with which they continue to combat the difficulties cast in their way by experienced and apparently incurable impostors.

The tender-hearted distributor of alms who is moved at every tale of distress he hears, and who gives money indiscriminately, should pay a visit to the Mendicity Society's offices in Red Lion Square. He will discover how often he has been the dupe of a rogue.

CHAPTER VI.

THE HOMELESS.

THE poor with whom I have been dealing—the casually distressed of Ham Yard; the spiritually-tended poor of the City Mission; the immoral and roguish poor looked after by the Mendicity Society—have all their representatives in the celebrated refuge which I am about to describe. Here, however, there can be no triumphant imposture. The begging-letter writer, the habitual criminal, the artful mendicant, may knock at the door of the Field Lane Refuge, and get shelter for the night. While there is room, a bunk unoccupied, no miserable creature who travels to the little door behind Smithfield is refused admittance. But the man or woman who wishes to remain housed must give assurance that he has

> "A hand to do, a head to plan,
> A heart to feel and dare."

That which the city missionaries preach, the directors and supporters of these noble refuges and schools do, and do earnestly—with that earnestness which Sir Edward Lytton calls "the best majesty of man." The aim is to collect the helpless from the streets, and to teach them how to help themselves. In the stray, homeless boy, tapping at the refuge door, there may be the light of genius, or the high pulse of some moral hero. Many noble heads have been roofless; the stars have twinkled over hedgerow sleepers destined presently to stir the world. "Shall we say," writes Emerson, "that quartz mountains will pulverize into innumerable Werners, Von Buchs, and Beaumonts; and the laboratory of the atmosphere holds in solution I know not what Berzeliuses and Davys?" Ay, Mr. Emerson, or that supplicants at this refuge door—the ragged, homeless creatures—may hold in solution the elements of the highest wisdom, the loftiest purpose, or the martyr's power of endurance! It is with the most earnest faith in the good that is in human nature, these roofless creatures are approached. No lying mendicants are tolerated. The poor who desire to help themselves are helped. Victims of sudden misfortune, Magdalens craving to return to modest ways, pass the doors; and if they be true are fed and housed and clothed, and sent into places where they can honourably live, independent by labour. A mere soup-kitchen is a clumsy charity when compared with that I am now noticing. Soup is given to all who have soup-tickets, and here is an end of the relations between the reliever and the relieved. And we have seen how this soup distribution is often abused. The 154,000 cases of begging-letter impostures on the Mendicity Society's shelves give only a faint idea of the hosts of undeserving vagrants and idlers who prey upon the charity of the public.

The directors of the Field Lane Refuge recognise the right of the starving to a crust, and of the roofless to shelter. The refuges stand in the midst of the poorest of the poor. Where any person may now pass safely day and night, no man who valued his life would have ventured some fifteen years ago. Field Lane was the abode of every variety of the dangerous classes. And now the unpretending buildings on the east side of Victoria Street (in full view of Field Lane) attract the poor, and feed and clothe and teach them. I passed through the crowd waiting at the door of the male refuge, on a gusty and misty night, that by no means recommended it as one to be passed with nothing between a man's head and the thunder-cloud, and made my way into the great sleeping-hall. It had been altered since I last visited it. The galleries had been removed, so that there was a freer circulation of air. The bunks, ranged in rows (very like those on board emigrant ships), are of deal. They are as clean as a Dutch housewife's table, being scrubbed every morning. In each bunk there is a rug rolled up. In the centre of the room is a great stove, over which a boiler full of coffee is sending forth aromatic fumes, that must be grateful to the nostrils of the homeless and foodless. Beyond this well-arranged and airy dormitory, are wash-houses and baths, etc. In the south-west corner of the dormitory is the manager's bed, glazed off from the general sleepers. When I entered, the inmates were up-stairs, in the great school-room, receiving instruction and advice. The man who addressed himself to me was himself a sleeper in one of these bunks, but, being an intelligent and reliable man, had been placed as guard at the door. He told me he had been in every part of London in search of work, and could not get a job. While we were talking we heard a great stir of feet overhead, and then a stream of women and children came pouring down the stairs. I watched them closely. Many of them were respectably dressed, and many were in the faded, scanty garments that betoken poverty's lower stage. The well-dressed were people of the neighbourhood (whom the school has much improved), or servants out of work, who were on their way to the Night Refuge for Homeless Young Females round the corner. After a few minutes' pause, the men came clattering into the dormitory. They first clustered round the stove; then, in the most orderly way, each man seated himself upon a plank placed across the end of his bunk. In this position I could observe them thoroughly. I could see that they were all simply very unfortunate working men. They had not the least relation to the dangerous classes. I have seen strange faces and figures in this dormitory; but there are none here to-night. Poor wretches come, whose rags will hardly bear removal; others enter covered with vermin; but to-night all the inmates are unfortunates whose stories of sorrow have been sifted and found to be true. So that the people who are clustering outside the door, this windy winter night, must go, unrelieved, away, for the bunks are all occupied. I observed one man who was very neatly dressed.

"That man," said the manager, "is going to work at a baker's, at five o'clock to-morrow morning. We have found him a situation; and he has been rigged out in a new suit, to give him a start."

The poor fellow's face was beaming, and he looked very grateful. I could see by his manner and speech he deserved all that had been done for him. The manager questioned him as to his temperance. He answered frankly, "I can't say that I'm a teetotaller, but I am a moderate man; and as for tobacco, I never touch it." The manager said a few kind words on the benefits of total abstinence, and hoped the man would soon be able to provide a comfortable home for his wife. "I'm sure I hope so too, sir," the man answered. It appeared that his wife remained for the moment in the Female Night Refuge.

When the men are ranged round their bunks, their coffee and bread are distributed to them, and then they all go to rest in their rugs, with light and warmth about them. They are up betimes in the morning, washed and dressed. More coffee and bread are distributed to them; and then the master reads from the advertisement columns of the papers all the advertisements which apply for labour. By this most sagacious proceeding, hundreds of men find employment.

"Only the other day," said the manager, "I read out an advertisement for a shoemaker. A man who was here, and who hadn't been in London a fortnight, bolted off on the spot. His character was good, and he got a situation as bootmaker—a mender in a private asylum, at a salary of £20 a year, with a house to live in, and perquisites. And there," the master continued, pointing across the dormitory, "are two men who are going to clean bricks at Hungerford to-morrow." I shall presently set forth the exact number of these and other cases which the directors of this refuge can show for the year 1862.

The varieties of service done to the poor under this roof, and that in West Street, are surprising. Here are Bible schools, special services for parents, day and infant schools, refuge men and boys' class, a penny bank, boys' industrial classes, mothers' classes, girls' industrial classes, girls' night-school, and, to wind up each week of noble work, a ragged Church service—a church where no beadle stands to warn Lazarus from the porch.

During the last twenty years, these useful operations have been going forward. I am assured that the effect in the neighbourhood has been most salutary. The children, who have been rescued from the gutter, have sometimes reclaimed their parents, and led them to school. The depraved and criminal have been cleansed, and placed in honourable positions. Men and women who had strayed from comfortable homes, and fallen into vicious courses, have been led back to their friends. Hundreds of homeless servant-girls have been snatched from the streets, and put out in good situations. It is interesting to see how the managers take the poor from babyhood. There is an infant-school in West Street, Smithfield, where the infants of the poor are taken, kept warm, protected from harm, and presented with the first elements of knowledge in all kinds of amusing forms. It is a scandal to our civilisation that such institutions as this should not exist in every corner of the metropolis, and that the children of the poor should be huddled in pestilent garrets, as they still are in this very neighbourhood. In one small room, not 12 feet by 9 feet, and about 7 feet high, a visitor found the father, mother, six or seven children, a dog, cat, and bird; and here all ate, drank, and slept. The effluvia nearly took the visitor's breath away. No wonder, then, the Field Lane Committee lament that "no enlarged efforts are on foot to improve the dwellings of the London poor." These dwellings are the curse of the poor man's life in London.

From the infant-school the child goes, or may go, to the boys' and girls' school. We are told that the offspring of "the migratory poor of London are here represented in full parliament." The unfortunate children of rat-catchers, prize-fighters, street-singers, professional beggars, hawkers, and others, are brought together, and taught by the power of kindness—not by the fear of the rod. The good done is incalculable. A member of the Council of Education came here, and was so pleased with what he saw, that he said, "I consider it as great a benefit to get a child into the Field Lane Schools, as into a college." The poor girl learns to sew, and goes home to mend the clothes. She is taught to be thrifty. She leaves her farthings with the master; and then, through the Ladies' Clothing Society, she gets various articles of clothing, at one-third less than the cost of material. For the boys, there are the industrial classes, where they may learn a trade. There is the navy also; and at this moment 300 ragged boys, rescued from this neighbourhood, are serving the Queen afloat, and with credit to themselves. The committee are loth to part with their boys and girls before they are completely launched into an honourable career. So there is a secular night-school for the boys who are in situations, at which they can still improve themselves in reading, writing, etc. This school preserves them from the evil tendencies of idle evenings.

Then come the classes for the refuge men and boys. The unfortunate of all descriptions, the fallen gentleman and the gipsy's son, find themselves together. The committee state that "not more than twenty-five per cent. of this migratory section of our destitute poor are originally of the poorest class."

I will now proceed to set forth a series of facts and calculations which I have gleaned about this remarkably various, liberal, and practical institution. The facts I have collected speak for themselves; and the reader will be enabled to judge by them, of the services rendered by these great refuges to the cause of humanity and social order. These figures are brought down to the last day of 1862.

Two hundred and one infants have been admitted into the infant-school in West Street during the year. Average morning attendance, 190; afternoon attendance, 215. Number admitted since the opening of the new school, 591.

Three hundred and thirty boys and girls have been admitted into the boys' and girls' school during the year, making a total of 4370 children who have passed through the new day-schools. Morning attendance, 340; afternoon attendance, 360.

On one occasion, when 359 scholars were present, 95 of them were fatherless, 134 motherless; in 6 cases the fathers were in the poorhouse, in 15 the father had deserted his family, in 6 the mother had abandoned them; 7 were orphans living with relatives, and 8 of them destitute of either parents or home, making 171 children out of the 359 who were deprived of either one or both parents. These 359 scholars represented 256 separate families, comprising a total of 1477 individuals. Forty-six of these families were in the receipt of parochial relief.

Upwards of 80 girls are in the day-school industrial sewing-class, who have made 1125 garments during the year.

During the last year 115 boys and 87 girls have obtained situations from the school; 80 boys have been sent into institutions and refuges; 79 boys have been sent to the royal navy, 17 have been restored to their parents, and 7 girls have been sent to refuges.

In the month of March last, prizes were distributed by the Earl of Shaftesbury to 231 scholars; 105 of this number had received them previously, and 126 for the first time. Of this number, 88 boys and 38 girls received 7s. 6d. in money, a certificate of good conduct, and a Bible; 5s. of this sum is a gift of the Ragged School Union, and 2s. 6d. from the school funds. Sixty-five boys and forty girls received a prize card from the Union, and 2s. 6d. from the committee. Of the 126 who received the prize for the first time, 97 kept their places from 12 to 18 months, and 29 from 18 to 24 months.

Of the 105 who had previously received prizes, 45 had kept their places from 12 to 24 months, 42 from 24 to 36 months, and 18 from 36 to 54 months. Of their ages, 52 are in their 12th, 67 in their 13th, 43 in their 14th, 44 in their 15th, and 25 in their 16th year. Of the entire number, 91 are orphans.

There are 300 boys now in the royal navy, who have been connected with the day or night schools as scholars.

No instance is known of a lad sent from the school having run away from the service, but two or three have been discharged through accident or ill health.

The boot bill alone during the year has amounted to £46, 16s. 9d., while the children's entire contributions have only amounted to £44, 12s. 3½d., leaving the difference to be defrayed by the members and friends of the institution. Upwards of 900 garments have been purchased by the children.

The average number in attendance for the past year in the secular night-school for boys in situations has been 180, the highest number 251; when on one occasion 193 were present, 187 had passed through the day-school, and received from it their situations.

The average attendance in the refuge secular evening-schools for men and boys has been 76.

The average attendance in the elder girls' industrial class has been 120.

There have been 810 lads admitted to the shoemaking class, in the boys' industrial classes, the average nightly attendance being 18; and 915 to the tailoring class, the average nightly attendance being 22.

In the elder girls' night-school for teaching reading, writing, and arithmetic, the attendance, out of more than 200 entered upon the books, has been, during the summer months, about 40, and 80 during the winter, the general average being 55.

In the penny bank established by the committee there are now about 500 depositors, who have paid in during the year £231, 16s. 5d.; amount repaid during the year £158, 16s. 2d., leaving in the hands of the treasurer £73, 10s. 3d.

In the mothers' class the average attendance has been 50 to 80.

In the maternal department 59 mothers have received help during the past year.

In the male refuge 233 have been sent into situations, 181 have obtained work, 54 have been sent to reformatories and refuges, 41 have been restored to friends, 25 have enlisted into the army, and 106 have entered the royal navy and the merchant service. During the past year this department has admitted 6537 persons, who received 25,550 lodgings and 64,450 loaves of bread.

In the Female Refuge for the Homeless (as in the male) all applicants are admitted till the 87 beds are full, and they are generally full throughout the year.

Into the servants' room 278 girls have been admitted, and 2300 into the large dormitory. Of these, 350 have been provided with outfits and sent to domestic service, 99 into situations and homes, 86 into constant needlework, 16 to unions, 15 to their own parish in the country, 23 to hospitals, 78 restored to their friends, 14 boarded and lodged away from the institution till provided for, 2 provided with stock for sale, and 156 with different kinds of employment. Besides the servants' outfit, many poor women received boots, or some kind of clothing when they left. The above numbers do not include those who have obtained work and left. These inmates received 28,392 lodgings and 56,784 loaves of bread.

In the Bible-schools the average attendance on Friday evening has been 200; on Sunday morning, 175; afternoon, 200 to 300, and evening 300 to 500.

The average attendance at the Lord's-day evening service for parents has varied from 80 to 100.

Between 300 and 400 families have been visited and relieved out of the Special Relief Fund, while the following articles have been given away: 1500 articles of clothing, 57 beds and pillows, 40 rugs and blankets, 395 half cwts. of coal, 510 loaves of bread, and, in pound cases, meat, grocery, etc.

In the Ragged Church the average attendance during the winter was 225, and out of 250 present on one occasion, 130 were inmates of the Male and Female Refuges.

The school missionary has access to upwards of 900 families, and there is scarcely a child throughout the entire route who does not attend a school of some description.

The committee commenced the year's operations with a balance of £945, 17s. 3d., but the contributions have so fallen off during the year that this balance has been more than absorbed to meet the current expenditure. The expenditure of the past year amounts to £2634, 4s. 1d., and the income to £1938, 14s. 7d., showing that the former has exceeded the latter by £695, 9s. 6d. A balance of £750, 7s. 8d., in the hands of the bankers, arises from money withdrawn from deposit.

The reader will perceive from these facts and figures how wide are the operations of this institution, how well they are planned, and how sensibly carried out. Yet the subscriptions have fallen off—indeed have almost ceased.

A gentleman connected with the Field Lane Refuge told me it was his belief, after an experience of fifteen years, that there was a certain amount of floating benevolent capital. Any extraordinary claim or excitement diverts it from its ordinary channels, and leaves old and useful institutions high and dry. I remember a point recently made by the accomplished vicar of Dartford, when he was arranging a subscription for Lancashire distress in his parish. He urged his parishioners to bear in mind that they would do no good if they deducted what they gave to Lancashire, out of the sum of their usual donations to public Charities. Had all the active gentlemen who worked through last winter in behalf of the distressed Lancashire operatives been as thoughtful as Mr. Bloomfield showed himself, we should not now have to deplore the state of impecuniosity to which many of the finest of our London Charities are reduced. The recent experience of the Field Lane Refuge managers is woful. In June, July, August, September, and October last their subscription did not average £3 per month, whereas their outgoings were £240! But this is not all. Last December (and December generally produces enough to carry the institution through the summer) there was a great falling off. They usually received about 100 parcels of clothing weekly, and last December not a dozen parcels reached. The honorary secretary said that the reason of this was clear to his mind. Only a certain amount of money was given away, and nearly all went to Lancashire. In the beginning of 1862 the sufferers by the Hartley Colliery explosion drew the benevolent towards them, at the cost of this and other kindred institutions.

It would be a sin and a shame to London, if this West Street Female Refuge for the Destitute, in which I find myself, were allowed to fall into decay. It is a clean, well-ordered, quiet sanctuary, to which the hunted and hungered innocent may fly from the coarse temptations and the hard-heartedness of the world. Its doors are open to the fallen also, who would fly from their shame, and in quiet and comfort pass back to the home they have left, or to a humble independence that will keep them from the streets. Country girls, who have been lured by deliberate seduction to the wilderness of London, wake up from their dream under this roof, and are thankful for its protection. There is a breadth of sympathy floating about these corridors of unpainted deal, that must touch the heart of every visitor.

I was led into the great dormitory. The bunks are built on the plan of those in the Men's Refuge; but the women have a mattress, while the men lie on the bare boards. The dormitory is a lofty, well-ventilated room. All the arrangements are neat and sensible. Everything in its place, is the guiding motto. The bonnets are ranged upon even rows of pegs; and the inmates are comfortably sitting at long tables. Perforated tubes along the roof insure an equable temperature. The women appear to be of all classes—domestic servants, needle-women, street-sellers, etc. One bunk is already occupied.

"That is a sad case," said my companion. "She went out to spend Boxing-night, and has returned to us in a bad condition; very ill. Boxing-night is a very trying time to us."

There is every comfort here. Warm baths, washing-tanks, with warm and cold water laid on, books to read, and work to do. Pursuing their wise plan, the managers proceed to sift the good from the bad, in this general hall. The deserving, who desire to go into service, are removed to a separate apartment, called "the servants' room." Here they are employed, by day, making clothes. They look snug enough sitting at their long table, with the decorations of Christmas twined over their heads, and a comfortable bedroom at hand. On the opposite side of the corridor is the spacious kitchen. This is kept by some of the inmates. Beyond it is a compartment in which there are three bunks, and a bed for a watcher. In these beds, apart from the rest, lie the utterly unknown, who have been picked up in the streets. They are often foolish servant-girls who have been locked out, and who, but for this refuge, would have found their way to some place of infamy. Waifs and strays picked up by the police in the streets, here they lie, to be judged of presently. Sometimes they are sent back to their mothers or mistresses, and sometimes new situations are found for them.

"We are very particular about them when we send them to service," said my informant still at my elbow. "We have our duty to perform towards their masters and mistresses, as well as towards them. Our aim is to do some permanent good to all who appear desirous of helping themselves. We encourage the girls by prizes, etc., to keep their places a long time. My experience proves to me that the practice of giving servant-girls a day's holiday out every month, has created a vast amount of ruin. They are off to Greenwich or Gravesend with anybody. The result is often the streets. They should be allowed a week with their friends and relatives once a year. We treat them with the greatest kindness. The law of kindness is our rule. We want them to consider us as their parents. If a girl goes out, she goes with the sub-matron."

The observations I have made on the treatment of servants by their mistresses, and on the temptations to which they are exposed, may be supported by a case that has been brought before a London magistrate. A poor girl, brought up in an industrial school, is compelled to seek the protection of the law against the brutality of her mistress. The assertions made by the poor white slave are denied by the mistress; but the magistrate thought the matter grave enough to be submitted to the judgment of a jury. On the same day another London servant figured in a police court. This unfortunate creature was charged with the crime of concealing the birth of her illegitimate child. The reader who would take the trouble to watch the number of these cases would find that the female servants of London are exposed to temptations, and fall victims to them, in vast numbers. There is little or no sympathy between the parlour and the kitchen. The old family servant, who was treated with affectionate regard, and who considered himself almost a relative of the people he had faithfully served throughout his life, has disappeared, as the nurses of two generations have disappeared. In their place we have Jeameses, and flaring illustrations of servant-galism. The employer and employed stand on their dignity, so that the servant-girl is a solitary creature in a houseful, and she is apt to fall a victim to the first comer. And so these poor women lose character and self-respect. Some accept all the horrors of the streets as the price of existence; others, as we have seen, beg a mattress and a crust of bread at a refuge door; and others are found on the parapet of one of the bridges, or stealing by night to the banks of a canal. The sudden transition from the comfort of a good house to the rigour of a refuge, is too much for many; the streets and a luxurious home of shame, are preferred. From this fate a few kind words spoken occasionally by master and mistress, would have saved thousands.

The Female Refuge, it will be perceived, is on a plan almost identical with that of the Male Refuge. I regret to find that both are threatened with destruction by two great London improvements; and that up to this time no appropriate new site has been found in the midst of the poor, where such a great and healthy Charity must be.

I have conducted the reader to refuges where the beggar, the pickpocket, and the prostitute may be found. Let us now turn to a "House of Charity" where the homeless deserving man or woman may enter and be comforted. This house is situated in Greek Street, Soho, at the corner of Soho Square. It is a fine house of the old school, with highly ornamented ceilings, fine carved mantelpieces, and a lofty hall. The rooms are square, roomy, and lofty. The apartment that is the temporary chapel, was the court-room in days gone by, when the great held revels and high ceremony here. It is a strange, weird place now; with its irregular ground-plan and its many staircases. There is a silence in it that strikes the visitor when he enters. He is shown into the somewhat sombre and severe room of the lady superintendent. The voices are subdued, and the contrast with the hum in the street is striking. The world appears to be completely shut out, and it is difficult to believe that only a few minutes since we were in the midst of merry children, tripping from dainty broughams, to buy toys in the Soho Bazaar. The ladies who, with the warders, govern this quiet realm dedicated to charity, are sisters, and are severely habited in black and white, with crosses pendant upon their bosoms.

With the most courteous *empressement* they offer to show me over their House of Charity. Sister —— will do the honours. Clanking a goodly bunch of keys, she starts on her journey, and we gossip about the institution by the way. We enter the room where the women are sitting at work or reading; if at work, on their own clothes. The House of Charity makes no calls upon its inmates. In return for its roof, its warmth, and shelter, it asks only the gratitude of honest hearts. The women are in a fine room, with a pleasant fire, chatting and working. They are poor governesses, seamstresses, or invalids. It matters not, so that they have kept in the right path through their distress: they may be Mormons or Papists; from the icy north, or from the sunny south. Let them be recommended by reliable people as of good character, and the lady superior throws the door of the House of Charity open to them. This is a resting-place to them, where they may recover from illness, or seek in security a new way in the world.

From the women's sitting-room we pass to the refectory—a spacious and lofty room, hung with Christmas green. Here Christmas has been better kept—that is, in a truer spirit than in many a gorgeous hall. The good sister explains that one long table is devoted to the men, one to families, and one to the unmarried women. The diet is generous—good roast and boiled; for the partakers are all reputable folk—victims of misfortune only—who are to be comforted and helped, and not punished. Here have dined poor governesses, matrons, nurses, housekeepers, merchants, farmers, clergymen, clerks, tutors and schoolmasters, servant-maids, artisans and labourers, men-servants, porters and shopmen, and ex-soldiers and policemen. All these, be it remembered, have been well recommended as deserving objects. The sister is anxious to impress me with this fact. He who recommends an inmate to this House of Charity must be a man of position: neither publican, nor coffee-house keeper, nor landlord of a lodging-house. He must fill up a form, and prove his complete knowledge of the case he recommends. He need not be a subscriber. All that is required from him is that he shall be able to vouch for the worthiness of his *protégé*. The governors lament that many who recommend to the House of Charity do not help to support it; but the deserving man or woman is never turned away on this account.

The sister related a touching story to me, as we stood before the long dining-tables. A poor Pole, who, in his time, had occupied the position of a gentleman, had fallen into terrible distress. He had six children and a servant. This servant had been at the wife's death-bed, and the dying woman had implored her to be a mother to her children. The servant had promised, and she was true to her trust. She was found with the starving family, and was brought to this House of Charity. Not one of these eight unfortunates could speak English. They sat week after week at this table spread by charity, and the servant remained faithful to her late mistress's children. They occupied a family room up stairs, in which the devoted creature performed, without reward, all the duties of a nurse. The sister appeared to be greatly touched by the story of their misfortunes, and told me how they all remained in the house during six months, and were at last sent at the Society's expense (amounting to £50) to Queensland, where the father might earn money in the vineyards. Had this house been closed upon this hapless family of refugees, they must have perished in the streets. We passed through a clean and light corridor to the sitting-room devoted to the men and boys. It was as snug and well-arranged as that of the women. There were only three or four persons in it, the rest being out in search of employment. One lad, who was subject to epileptic fits, was too delicate to do work. The dormitories for the men, which we next visited, were scrupulously clean. Each inmate had a compartment parted off to himself, in which were his bed, jug and basin, etc.; all in the best order. Everything was plain, but solid and healthy. As we approached one of the male dormitories the sister turned to me and said, "Here there is a poor man dying of consumption." We glided quietly along between the beds. The poor fellow was lying in bed, not far, I could see at a glance, from his last rest. He was patient and quiet, and answered the sister's question in a weak, calm voice. She talked to him as one who had sat long hours at his side. She looked about to see that his orange was by his bed, and that he was comfortable. She exclaimed that she had been very busy throughout the morning, but that she would be with him presently, to read to him. And then we turned to a youth who was seated at a table near the fire, writing. The sick watching the dying! A young, earnest, pale face was turned upon us. "And how are you to-day?" said the sister. "I feel very weak," he answered, and he looked so. The sister suggested a re-arrangement of the table, that the fire might reach more freely the face of the patient in bed, and we made this change. "He has studied too hard," said the good sister. I asked the pale student what he had studied. He had tried to master several languages, and had overstrained a very weak frame. He was now in a state of feverish excitement over a manuscript that lay open before him. "I am writing an essay," he said, "on self-improvement;" and he hoped he should have an opportunity of reading it in public. He spoke so earnestly and confidently, and withal so modestly, that I could not but be touched to see the strong will and high purpose burning in the frail vessel.

A most melancholy picture were these two invalids, stricken in the morning of life, by disease and poverty. They were housed, however, in this home of charity; with gentle hearts about them, and a shield of love between them and the pitiless rigour of London streets.

The House of Charity is adapted both to the single and to the married. Its foundation is of the most liberal character. The warden and council call to the mind of the public that "scarcely in any other unendowed asylum are deserving cases received solely upon the recommendation of any trustworthy person, without regard to their being contributors to the fund." The House of Charity is open to all the deserving unfortunate. It is not filled by the nominees of subscribers. Distress is not in need of a moneyed patron that it may find a refuge in this home. The poor sick who travel from afar to have recourse to the skill of London physicians find a welcome here. We have only to mount the stairs to the family rooms to find an instance.

The sister conducted me from the dormitories appropriated to women (which are like those arranged for the men, with the addition of a few necessary feminine comforts) to the "family rooms." I saw that which the Polish family had lately inhabited (a comfortable nursery), and was then led by the sound of infant voices to a second family room. There were two beds in it, together with the furniture of a plain sitting-room. A bouncing child cried lustily from one bed on our appearance, and was immediately hugged in the sister's arms. On the other bed lay a little quiet baby, purring and playing with its little hands. The mother was at hand, arranging and mending clothes. "The baby," the sister said, "goes to the Orthopœdic Hospital; its feet are deformed."

So the young patient was here, in good quarters, to be within reach of the highest skill of the country. Indeed, the wise and tender forethought that presided over the foundation of this Charity, is shown in every detail of its administration. In the women's dormitories, for instance, there are regulation deal boxes—one to each bed. Herein the inmate puts the clothes, etc., she requires at bed-time, or on rising. The dormitories are kept under lock and key throughout the day, that they may not be disordered. The various luggage of the inmates would create confusion if brought into these prim rooms. It would, moreover, introduce certain lively but inadmissible visitors, against whom the sisters have a strong antipathy. The inmates' luggage is therefore kept below, in a place to which they have constant access. This regulation is made for the convenience and advantage of all. On the basement of the building there is a lavatory, where the inmates may wash their linen; a hot room, where they may dry it; and there are appliances for mangling and ironing. There are hot baths, also, into which the suspicious are dipped when they enter the house. Without the most rigid cleanliness this house, like the refuge in West Street, Smithfield, would be unendurable. In the latter place, where every precaution is taken, it is impossible to secure the entire absence of certain minute but obnoxious specimens of the animal kingdom. The visiting ladies find that these minute monsters have a knack of colonizing in their ample skirts, so that all kinds of offensive and defensive operations are necessary in order to defeat the enemy.

An ample kitchen, a school by day for the children, and religious service three times daily, are the remaining features of the House of Charity to which the sister directed my attention. Under the wardenship of the Rev. E. C. Chambers, M.A., who lives on the premises, every possible attention is paid to the development of the religious principle in the inmates. These, let me repeat, are all deserving poor, as—out-door patients of hospitals, emigrants waiting to embark, unfortunate widows, or orphan or friendless girls. Every form of destitution that is not the result of crime or profligacy, may find shelter in the House of Charity. The object of the friends of this retreat is to shield the poor, who have not fallen, from temptation. The cost of this good work is estimated at something less than 11s. per week per inmate—this sum including all expenses of management, etc. Some 600 unfortunates pass through the House of Charity every year. The list on the Society's books illustrates every accidental form of misery. We find young girls who have come to London in search of situations, and have found none; the fatherless girl, whose mother has been committed to prison for ill-treating her; the unfortunate commercial traveller; the lunatic, discharged as cured, but still requiring careful treatment, etc. These are among the unhappy accidents which have been solaced in this sanctuary. By the agency of this house, vice and crime are prevented. Help is given to the sorely tempted before they fall, and thus the council invites the offerings of the calculating economist, as well as the Christian philanthropist.

I find, by reference to the last report of the council, that, as in the West Street Refuge, the great majority of inmates are servant-maids. In an analysis of inmates for 1861, out of 526 admitted to the house, 323 were servants, while there were only 51 artisans and labourers, and 22 dressmakers, needlewomen, shopwomen, etc. The large number of domestic servants to be found in this and kindred institutions is, it must be confessed, a reproach to all people who employ servants. Poor girls are sent forth suddenly, possibly for some venial fault, alone and friendless, upon the great world of London. They are surrounded with dazzling temptations. We have learned from West Street that even "the day out" is fraught with danger to them. As a rule, the mistress does not trouble herself to learn whether her maid-servant has relatives within reach. The girl may go out for a day, with the sole provision that she shall return early. She may spend her day as she lists, or as the first comer suggests that she should spend it. She may become associated with dissolute companions. Let her do her work in her place, and no questions will be asked. Her mistress does not take her into her friendship. It was this lack of sympathy which Judge Talfourd deplored in the last speech he made from the bench. It is beyond a doubt, that careless and unsympathizing mistresses help to people the refuges and establishments like this House of Charity in Soho Square. In *The Greatest Plague of Life*, the brothers Mayhew set forth, with a humour that had something grim in it, the differences which often exist between mistress and maid. There was truth in the broad caricature; and it was nowhere truer than in the parts where the female tyrant was dealing with the drudge. If the parlour would deal with the kitchen in humble imitation of the Christian spirit that pervades the House of Charity, we should find fewer outcast servant-maids in Soho and Smithfield. There is not a more helpless and miserable creature within sound of Bow-bells, than the poor servant-girl suddenly turned out of her situation. If she be young and pretty, she is to be pitied indeed!

CHAPTER VII.

THE HOMELESS.

THE best test of the gravity of London distress is to be found in the night refuges, two of which I have already described. It is here that the poor who are always on the verge of starvation, and the men and women out of work, who have travelled hopefully to London in search of employment, find themselves directly the frost sets in, or there is the least dearth of work. The Field Lane, Playhouse Yard, and Dudley Stuart Refuges are thermometers by which we may always test the condition of the London poor. These refuges are of vast importance, since they help to clear the streets of the unfortunates who, but for their agency, would spend winter nights on door-steps or under archways. There are 46 refuges, reformatories, and industrial schools in London alone, capable of accommodating 2931 inmates. The return for the United Kingdom shows 248 of such institutions, capable of accommodating 17,955 persons. The refuge in Playhouse Yard, Whitecross Street, is undoubtedly the most important of all the night refuges in the United Kingdom. It is absolutely free to all who are destitute, without regard to colour, race, or character. It is open to the miserable of all ages and nations, and it accommodates 700 persons.

I should recommend any charitably-disposed person, who may desire to see for himself where the worst misery of this great city is to be found, that he may help to lighten it, to take a walk some cold night, about ten o'clock, towards Whitecross Street, through the dismal slums beyond Smithfield—itself as dismal a wild as can be conceived to exist in the centre of a great capital—past the wretched general shops, lighted by a solitary dip; past dirty and untidy women, squatting in dark doorways, and through sombre lanes, lighted up only by the flaring, noisy, gaudy gin-palaces,—for no locality is too poor to support a splendid gin-palace. They are gilded and pretentious hard by Charles Street, Drury Lane; gorgeous at the corners of the New Cut, and brilliant in Whitechapel. The human creatures at the bright zinc bars are in tatters. Shoeless children enter with physic phials they can hardly place upon the bar, to buy that universal curse of the London poor—gin. It is probably the last twopence in the garret the little one holds in her hand, and while the parent takes the dram, the child will go supperless to the heap of rags that is called its bed. The industrial schools and suburban reformatories are filled with the children of gin-drinking parents. "What became of your mother?" "Please, sir, she took to drinking." This is question and answer heard daily by all who are in constant contact with the London poor.

In the streets round about Barbican I find misery shivering under the public-house gas-lamps. I see labourers in their flannel jackets, spending the money for which their children are crying far away up the narrow courts it would be perilous to enter; but which we must enter, nevertheless. Women pleading for the hungry children, plead in vain. Made desperate, they themselves take to the gin; and, savage and unsexed, they shuffle about the streets—bonnetless and with matted hair—cursing the fruit of their own womb! Playhouse Yard is not an inviting place to enter. It is difficult, indeed, to find the refuge. I had to ask my way, and was directed to some green gates, barred at the top. It was eleven o'clock at night. The doors were closed, but we could see the lights through the bars. The bell soon brought a man to the door. I entered a rough kind of ante-room, on one side of which was an opening or wicket, at which the superintendent, Mr. Billing, stood, ready to receive new-comers. I was conducted up wooden steps to the first great dormitory. It was like a gigantic hayloft, trimly kept. By the dim light of the lowered gas-jets, and of the great fire, by which a helper had fallen asleep (contrary to rules), we could indistinctly see long series of boxes, like orange-boxes, that appeared to be filled with sacks. On nearer inspection, I made out the faces of some hundred sleepers—lying in every extravagant form of rest, and closely enveloped in the covering (four skins sewed together) allowed by the institution. There were young, fair, handsome faces, dreaming, and sighing or coughing in their dreams, with their ragged clothes folded up for pillows. Some were evidently of gentle birth—poor fallen men from fair estate. Here were three negroes huddled in their skins, snoring with a will. Beyond lay a bearded, handsome German, with a greasy, broken hat carefully deposited at the head of his humble couch.

"I have no doubt that man has been in a very good position," said the superintendent. "He tells me that he expects 400 francs from Germany in a few days. They are of all classes. You would be astonished to see the people who are glad to come here."

In this, the last place to which poverty betakes itself, when the crowded and bare garret is a luxury no longer to be afforded—this last step in the social ladder, as I shall presently show, is not taken only by the humbly born: labourers, charwomen, domestic servants, and hawkers are foremost in the list; but it includes schoolmasters, surgeons, artists, and clerks! A more affecting scene than this long, dim room, filled with sleepers packed like mummies, wheezing, coughing, and sighing in their feverish sleep, it is impossible to conceive; for every sleeper is absolutely penniless and roofless—a wanderer on the face of the earth. Hardly one knows his neighbour to the right and left. Every sacrifice has been made, every shift has been borne, before it has come to this. There are not many bunks empty. This winter refuge has been open, at this writing, for the season of Lazarus, only two weeks; yet, said the superintendent, "we had 530 of them here last night." Huddled with the rest, was a ticket-of-leave man.

"He had permission," said the superintendent, "to stay out a little later to-night, that he might attend a meeting of ticket-of-leave men. These meetings are held three times a week in Wellclose Square, St. George's-in-the-East, under the management of Mr. Jackson, a city missionary." The object of these meetings is to promote the reformation of the men; and the superintendent declared that the man in question appeared most anxious to lead a good life for the future.

We passed from the rooms devoted to the men and boys, down the passage between the bunks, marking the varieties of men by the way, some with their bare and muddy feet protruding beyond the sheepskin covering, to the rear of the premises, devoted to the female department. The long room we first entered was arranged like that in which the men were sleeping. There was the great fire, as in the men's room—arranged so that the poor creatures might cook any bit of food they were able to bring in. The bunks were on the same plan, and the sleepers looked as much like swathed mummies. The bonnets and shawls, hung against the walls over the sleepers, were the first points that reminded me I was in the women's ward. The coughing was gentler; and the sighs were deeper, welling from sad hearts, oppressed with all the ills that flesh is heir to. There were, I doubt not, Magdalens by the dozen—chained by iron necessity to their life of shame and want. None could look more miserable than some of them. One, in shreds of old satin—a shadow of a woman—was still sitting upon the edge of her bunk, her nimble fingers plying the needle in the half light; her face, meek as that of Charity herself. She never raised her eyes, nor appeared conscious of our presence when we passed close to her. "Stitch, stitch, stitch," she went; and, if she were not making her shroud, it was not because she could think of Death as so very far off; for death, "like an untimely frost," seemed upon her.

"They work often when they come in," said the superintendent. "Some of them knit nightcaps and other things to sell in the street next day."

Not far off from the patient ghost of the worker, a woman was lying asleep. The face was fair and gentle, and the hair was braided over the white brow as only very delicate fingers could braid it. Her sleep was deep and silent under the rough sheepskin. Had the coverlid been an eider-down quilt, the canopy silk damask, that face would have been accepted as a fine type of the beauty of blue blood! Nobody there knew her story.

"As a rule," the superintendent remarked, "we don't know who or what they are. All are admitted without let or hindrance. We exact no compliance with irksome forms from them. It suffices that they are utterly destitute. They have half a pound of bread when they come at night, and half a pound when they leave in the morning."

In answer to my questions, the superintendent continued:—"It depends on the weather when we open the refuge, but we open it directly there is anything like frost. When destitute persons apply, we question them as to their parish, calling, etc. We pass them on the first night, and look a little closer into their case on the following morning. Then we give them a ticket for seven days, and they come every night for that time. As a rule, we expect a person who has been an inmate for seven nights to remain away a fortnight, in order that other houseless applicants may have their turn of relief; but we make exceptions in special cases. We have Church service twice a day in the upper room, and it is generally crowded. We don't allow smoking or talking in the wards; this is for the comfort of all. There is an overseer and two helpers up in each ward throughout the night. We allow them to go out at three or four o'clock in the morning, if they have work to do betimes, but the time for turning out is between eight and nine o'clock in the morning. We make every one of them have a good wash before he goes to bed, and an assistant-surgeon examines them if they come in early. If late, the storekeeper, who is a good chemist, and has great experience of these class of cases, looks at them. Any who are taken ill are conveyed at once to St. Luke's Hospital, under the care of one of the helpers. Our committee have made special arrangements with the hospital authorities for this purpose."

A heart-rending scene remained for the last. We were led from the single women's room, to a side dormitory, called the Nursery Ward. It was reserved for women who had children with them. It was a sight that every mother's eye should know. I have seen poverty in a hundred different forms, but in none so pitiful as this. The poor mothers lay in their bunks, withered and ghastly pale, some with three babes upon their arms. The squalor and the care that were heaped within this narrow space would have wrung pity from the most cold-blooded witness. In the stillness of the night (it was now nearly twelve o'clock), the only sounds being the deep sleep-heavings of the exhausted mothers, and the puling of the sickly babes, struggling amid the rags; the tragic picture appeared to me to be of another world, or of a far-off time. It was hard to believe that all this woe and want of mother and child, were within half an hour's walk of the ranks of brilliant equipages that were taking up the bejewelled mothers of Belgravia, and their laughing children, to carry them to their palaces hard by. I could not help thinking that it would do their hearts good if some of our softly-curtained ladies of the West, would drive through Smithfield to Playhouse Yard, on some winter's night, and see what befalls some mothers and some babes in this modern Babylon. *Res est sacra miser*, is the refuge motto. To give heedlessly and from afar, the trifle that will provide these shells for houseless mothers to nestle in with their children, is only to make up this picture, in proof of how much yet remains to be done.

I now pass to a statement of facts that will further elucidate the aim and scope of this, the greatest refuge in the United Kingdom. These figures and dates will help to fix any impression I may have made in the reader's mind.

In 1860 and 1861 the subscriptions and donations amounted to £1151, 5s. 1d., and in 1861 and 1862 to £519, 7s. 10d.—difference to the prejudice of the asylum of £631, 17s. 3d.

From the classification as to the occupations of the persons admitted, it would appear that out of a total of 6785—there were 4 artists, 170 boot and shoe makers, 87 carpenters and joiners, 671 charwomen, 17 clerks, 57 errand-boys, 44 persons employed in factories, 25 French polishers, 19 gardeners, 99 garden-women, 201 hawkers, 2211 labourers, 663 needlewomen, 120 painters and glaziers, 31 porters, 31 printers and type-founders, 199 seamen, 262 servants, 89 smiths, 84 stablemen, 95 tailors, 19 waiters, 57 weavers, 586 women and children without occupation, etc. Comparing these numbers with those referring to other pursuits, we find, for example, there were 4 bill-posters, 4 boot and shoe cleaners, 4 butchers, 4 button makers, 3 chemists, 2 chimney sweeps, 1 coachmaker, 1 coach trimmer, 3 colliers, 5 compositors, 5 cutlers, 4 discharged soldiers, 3 engineers, 3 engravers, 3 farriers, 3 fishermen, 2 gas fitters, 3 hatters, 2 lucifer-match makers, 6 milk carriers, 2 musicians, 1 optician, 1 pianoforte maker, 1 portmanteau maker, 3 schoolmasters, 2 school mistresses, 12 shopmen, 4 staymakers, 16 stokers, 1 surgeon, 1 tanner, 3 tobacconists, 4 travellers, 7 umbrella makers, 3 upholsterers, 3 writers and grainers, etc.

Looking to the countries (irrespective of the United Kingdom) from which the different inmates came, it appears that, exclusive of 95 who were classified as "unknown," the largest numbers were as follow:—59 from the United States of America, 13 from the British Provinces of America, 12 from France, 34 from Germany, and 14 from the West Indies; whilst the smallest numbers were—1 from the Cape of Good Hope, 2 from Belgium, 1 from Gibraltar, 1 from New Zealand, 1 from Peru, 2 from Portugal, 1 from Rio Janeiro, 1 from Russia, and 2 from St. Helena.

The total number of individuals admitted from the 13th January 1820, to the 24th March 1862, was 261,040, while the number of nights' lodgings afforded was 1,682,809, and the rations of bread given was 4,041,691.

The receipts and expenditure from April 30, 1861, to April 30, 1862, showed that the former amounted to £1414, 3s. 3d., and the latter to £1303, 4s. 4d., leaving a balance in the treasurers' hands of £110, 18s. 11d.

So small a balance and so much to be done! A peep into that nursery ward would open a thousand purses could a thousand children of luxury be brought to gaze upon these wasted forms of mothers and sucklings.

The founders of the Dudley Stuart Nightly Refuge knew how to fitly perpetuate the name of an amiable and philanthropic English gentleman. They established an institution "for the temporary relief of extreme want during the severity of the winter season." This institution is now a handsome building in Market Street, Edgeware Road. It is something more than a refuge that affords shelter and bread; it seeks to separate young women of good character from the bad, and to get them situations. The fallen are sent to friends or reformatories. There is a home, in fact, within the refuge; and poor girls of good character have entered it in rags to come forth to comfortable situations. In other respects this refuge is sagaciously managed. For instance, trifling sums of money are given in certain cases; and an officer is attached to the house whose business it is to give his advice to the inmates, and to detect the tramps and professional beggars who make a home of the refuges and workhouses during the winter. He also looks after work for the unemployed, and has a parental care for destitute children. In short, the operations of the institution are adapted as far as possible to the various exigencies of the average 170 men, women, and children who are in nightly attendance. Tools are supplied to poor men who could not accept a job without them. Even furniture has been contributed to put a broken home together once more.

The committee have sad cases to cite; indeed, the case-books of London refuges are chronicles of vice, and want, and suffering, that will give some future historian a comprehensive idea of the variety and extent of the suffering endured by the humbler clsses during the Victorian era.

The committee's last report gives the following summary of the number of persons received into the refuge during the year, distinguishing ordinary cases from special cases:—Number of ordinary refuge cases of men, women, and children admitted from the 17th of December 1860, to the 23d of March 1861, 10,196; from the 8th April to the 22d June 1861, 3847. Number of ordinary cases of women and children from the 22d June to the 2d November, 3078, making a total of 17,121. Number of girls and women admitted into the girls' home, and provided with situations and employment, from February to November 1861, 124. The number of special cases entered in the books (which include those of girls and boys sent to training-schools, to their parents, to institutions and employment, to hospitals, etc.) was 196. The number of persons assisted with small sums to redeem their clothes, and to wash ditto at the public baths, to set up a trade, to help them on the road, to buy tools, and to buy small articles of furniture, etc., was 586. The number of men, women, and children allowed to remain in the refuge for that period till provided for, was 2013; making a total of special cases amounting to 2919, and a grand total of all cases amounting to 20,040.

The balance-sheet shows that this large amount of help and relief was afforded at the comparatively small cost of £1017, 9s. 7d., exclusively of a sum of £67 owing for outstanding claims, and independently of several valuable presents of clothing.

The report of Mr. Reece, the medical superintendent, states that out of the 19,000 poor persons who were admitted, sheltered, and fed at the Refuge during the past twelve months, no less than 2294 received advice or medicine; sixteen cases were of a nature requiring admission into the public hospitals; fourteen were admitted into St. Mary's Hospital, two into Middlesex Hospital, and two into Queen Charlotte's Hospital.

The victims of cruel parents and of seduction abound in the committee's list of cases. Let us take an example. A girl, from Hounslow, aged eighteen, was admitted. Her mother was dead. She was left unprotected; her father being a gardener. She went to the parochial school, and there, at the age of fourteen, she was seduced by a boy in the school. She managed, however, to enter service, but was enticed from her situation by a soldier. He, of course, deserted her. Her rapid descent now began. She was homeless and degraded. She wandered from union to union; she took to the streets, she was laid up in hospitals, and at last she reached the Refuge. From the Refuge she was conducted to the Magdalen. Another girl, only thirteen years of age, had lost her mother, and had been deserted by her father. The poor child got a situation, but she was too weak to perform the duties. With the scanty wages she had earned she paid for lodging at night, until every farthing had disappeared. She was found wandering hopeless about the streets, and was directed by some kind passer-by to good Dudley Stuart's Nightly Refuge. Another poor soul, who had travelled all the way from Montgomeryshire, was found by a lady in the park in a most shocking condition. She had been sleeping in the open air—in the park, or in the streets—several nights. She was another victim of seduction. She had been decoyed from her home, and cast ruthlessly away, in London. Happily this poor girl was rescued from the streets, and received back into her home.

The Dudley Stuart Refuge, then, comprehends a place of permanent help and reform. In this respect it is more valuable than a mere bread-and-shelter refuge. In Playhouse Yard, I should observe, the superintendent helps some of the inmates to find work. He told me he thought he should get one of the negroes we saw asleep, taken home by a West India captain; and he had received, for instance, an application for a man to carry show-boards. I think that the Field Lane plan of reading all advertisements for labour in the daily papers to the inmates, is one that should be copied in other refuges. For, after all is said and done, the best help man can give his brother is to enable him to help himself.

The obvious danger of these refuges is one which I pointed out in my chapter on the Mendicity Society. The committee may be made the dupes of artful rogues, to whom the half-pound of bread at night is sweet—as the bread of idleness; who avoid work or do very little, keeping an attentive eye on the soup-kettles of Ham Yard, the cocoa-fibre mattresses of Playhouse Yard, and the bread and coffee of Field Lane. It is quite clear then, in order to keep down the ranks of professional tramps who come up to town for a begging and cadging season, so that nearly all that is distributed by charitable people shall reach the really deserving; the relief should be scanty and rough, until the applicant has proved that his misfortunes merit the commiseration of his fellow-creatures.

CHAPTER VIII.

THE CHILDREN OF THE STREETS.

EVERY earnest inquirer who will resolutely study the gradations by which the simply poor man glides into the dangerous classes, and how vagrancy and immorality in one generation create criminals in the next, must come to the conclusion that to sweep destitute and vicious children from the streets, is at once the wisest and most economical method of dealing with crime. To rear a race of spendthrift convicts is extravagant, when we might rescue all Blueskins in the bud, from crime, make honest and useful citizens of them, and at the same time put money into our pockets by the transaction.

There is a humble little Home in the Euston Road that will teach us what ought to be done in every

London parish. It is called "The Boys' Home" for unconvicted, destitute boys. Like the House of Charity, the Home is a refuge and protection for the outcast who are liable to fall. That which the House of Charity accomplishes for the needlewoman, the servant, the poor clergyman, and the houseless clerk, the Home offers to the neglected or abandoned children of the London gutters. It snatches ragged babes from their sleeping-places under dark arches, even from drain-pipes and market-baskets. A savage woman has left a little boy upon the kerb-stone, telling him she will be back to him presently. We stand appalled at the depth of human wickedness as we contemplate this wretch, turning her back for ever, with a lie in her mouth, upon this innocent child, who has faith in her still, and love for her, although she has beaten him in his cradle. He will cry his little heart out when, after hours of watching, hungry and cold, the idea bursts in all its horror upon him, that his mother will not come back. He is alone in the world; and he creeps into corners, eats the garbage of the markets: it will be strange indeed if he escape the temptation to steal. Haply his misery, when it has reached its worst—when he is covered with dirt and vermin, and the pitiless rain is coursing down his black cheeks—haply he will attract the attention of a policeman, and be carried before a magistrate. From the police court he will be conducted to the Boys' Home for the unconvicted and destitute.

The boy whose case I have set forth is now actually in the Home; and is a cheerful, active, and bright little fellow at his work in the firewood yard—young Tom Allalone, snatched from the gaol and the hulks, to be, in full time, a gallant soldier or sailor. To this Home the managers of refuges send destitute boys.

The very first boy who entered the Home was a deserted costermonger's child, from Grotto Passage Refuge, and now he is a sailor of good character; and has been back, happy and healthy, to tell his old school-fellows of the wonders he has seen on the Pacific station. Other little Arabs wandered rapidly in—each boy with a tragedy to his bare back. No. 10 lost both his parents by the cholera, and was sent from the Field Lane Refuge. Here is an account of No. 7, in a few words, by the manager. He was "fearfully destitute and helpless, yet honest. He came to Euston Road—covered with a few rags, and many vermin—on a snowy night, shivering as much from hunger as from cold. He had been on board a merchant ship, of which his father was one of the crew. The father had been lost at sea, having fallen from the masthead. The boy had then been turned off by the captain, who found him useless without his father; for he was very slow both of speech and understanding. He was, therefore, put ashore at a strange port, hundreds of miles from his mother and home. He made his way to London, and came to the Home, literally starving." In the end, by the agency of the Home, he was restored to his relations. Had there been no night refuge, and no Home, No. 7 would now be an Arab of the streets, or a pickpocket. The committee have cases as touching as this, by the dozen. Some are the children of soldiers; others are refractory boys who had the vagrant tendency strong in them, and made bad associates in their neighbourhood; others, again, are the children of very poor parents, to whom this Home is the best school and industrial training they are able to give their boys. Mr. G. W. Bell, the tried and enthusiastic friend of the Boys' Home, puts an instance of wide application, where institutions like this may do great good. "Take the case," he said at one of the Home meetings, "which must be common to many here, of a domestic servant who has married a man in her own rank of life. It may have been right that she should do so. She and her husband may have been in health and strength; but at the end of a few years the man dies, and the woman is left unprovided for. If she has been a prudent woman, she has perhaps a few pounds to fall back upon; but she has a couple of children—say two boys. She can do nothing whatever except earn her bread by domestic service; and her two children, instead of being a help, are a clog to her. Perhaps you say she might earn her living, and put her boys to school. But we all know that the wages of a domestic servant in this country range from £8 to £20 a year; and she could not put her two boys to school and provide for herself even out of the larger sum. I believe I may confidently say that there is no such thing in this country as a school into which a person in that rank of life can put a boy or a girl and maintain them there. But by a little help she may do it; and, therefore, a portion of our boys is received from that class. We take part of their maintenance-money from father or mother, as the case may be, and we depend upon your contributions to assist us to the rest of their cost." This hint about schools for the poor recalls to my mind a suggestion I made about the year 1847, for the establishment of ragged colleges, to which the poor might send their children. Mr. Hughes (author of *Tom Brown's School Days*), another valiant and active supporter of the Home, states that the cost of the boys is about £12 per annum for clothing, lodging, and maintenance. Now, thousands of labourers could afford, say half of this sum, or about 2s. 6d. per week, for the clothing, food, and education of a child;

and with help from the public and the State, with endowments and subscriptions, people's boarding colleges might be established on a grand scale in every great centre of population. By the agency of such institutions, thousands of children now playing about courts and alleys of our cities and villages, would be educated, and taught industries that would make them robust and industrious men. Such institutions would lessen the criminal army that now preys upon society, and thin the ranks of those most expensive luxuries, full-blown criminals.

The managers of the Home to which I am about to introduce the reader, have insisted on making the boys feel that they all belong to one happy and united family. They are taught to be gentle and forgiving towards each other. The rules upon the walls are for the regulation of "the family." The master and mistress of the Home, with their children, live with their interesting little charges. All are together day after day, learning and toiling and eating in a common Home. In the master's wife these reclaimed outcasts find a mother. She knows all their names, and keeps childish indulgences for the good boys. A pat on the head for one—a tit-bit at dinner for a second. These are humanizing agencies when administered by a kind-hearted woman. The wild and idle are reclaimed, and lured to industry; the stubborn are softened. The boys, when first taken to the Home, are often sullen and dissatisfied, and have an aversion to work. The vagrant habit is not easily shaken off. It is this habit which induces a love of positive idleness; and is the most important vice with which masters of reformatories have to deal, since the young vagrant is the criminal in the bud.

The Home consists of two moderately-sized houses

in the Euston Road, thrown into one. The door is opened by one of the boys, an intelligent lad, coarsely but warmly clothed. In the hall there is a printed list of rules for the regulation of the family, all conceived in the kindest spirit; also, a syllabus of lectures to be delivered in the Home. The lectures are of an instructive character, as on "The World we Live in," "Bread and Water," "A Pictorial History of Robinson Crusoe, with Illustrations," "Sugar," "Coals," "Salt," etc. Amusement is promised in the shape of mechanical views, dissolving views of day and night, summer and winter, protean figures, and Chinese fireworks. Each lecture is varied with vocal music.

The matron conducted me over the establishment. We first passed into the carpenter's shop, where the boys were sawing and planing; and seemed to be proud of their work. I noticed in this first room a spirit that pervades the establishment, viz., one of thorough cheerfulness. The boys did not appear to be doing distasteful task-work. Beyond the carpenter's shop was the brush-room, where there were brushes of all descriptions—from the scrubbing-brush to the lady's hair-brush—the handiwork of "the family." "We're not working here now," said the matron, "because we have no orders. We depend entirely on private orders. The boys spoil so much hair while learning, that we cannot supply the shops at wholesale prices. It's the same in other departments; they destroy much material while learning." I peered through the back window, attracted by an enormous stack of timber. "That," said the matron, "is to be cut up in fire-wood, or used in the carpenter's shop." I could see the family, busy as bees, under the sheds at the end of the yard, cutting and packing wood.

The dormitories were a series of folding iron beds, with the bedding rolled up upon each. The front room I examined was spacious, and free from smell, and over the beds were the rules for the conduct of the family, with wholesome moral maxims. The Home provides in this way for the accommodation of 50 children, and there are 50 in it at the present time. From the dormitory I descended to the back kitchen, which was the shoemaker's shop—a shop that might be in many respects improved. Three or four very diminutive workmen were busy over "boys'" strong boots and mendings. They all bowed as we entered. The master shoemaker said that the boy near him (who looked baby enough to wear hat and feathers) could almost make a pair of boots. I guessed that he was eight years old, but he was thirteen. A busy lad, with a fresh, open face, walked briskly in.

"That is the best hand I have," said the master. That mite of a boy, with a bag over his shoulder! "They are all very small," the matron said, compassionately. "They come here in a deplorable condition, having been neglected all their lives, poor fellows."

I remarked that nearly all these baby lazzaroni were spare, dwarfed creatures. It was only by looking in their old faces that their age could be correctly judged. The "best hand," who had just entered with the bag, had been to the Soldiers' Daughters' Asylum at Hampstead, with repaired shoes. He had had a good trudge, and still appeared fresh.

The kitchen and refectory is just a plain ordinary London kitchen, with long tables in it. We found two boys at work, cleaning. The kitchen usually employs three of the family. It is a privilege to be in this department, because it is warm, and the matron sends the young cooks a tit-bit from her own table sometimes. Beyond, in the second kitchen, a tailor and a seamstress are at work, and under their superintendence half a dozen boys (generally new arrivals or weak boys) are sewing and tailoring. "The first thing I teach the very young ones when they come," said the matron, "is to practise sewing on a piece of rag. They become very expert at last."

Ranged against the wall were the boys' haversacks and comb-and-brush bag; the former being for the reception of their humble private properties—toys, etc. Upon the floor are heaps of boys' clothing waiting to be mended. So we see that the Home requires no hired servants. These miniature workers are turned to all domestic, as well as industrial accounts.

"Some of them mend socks beautifully," said the matron; "we teach them to be useful in every possible way, and we look after them as far as we can, after they leave us. A boy we sent out to a situation as page a short time since, has just been discharged because he is too little for the place. We will not leave him to the temptations of the streets: we haven't room for him here; so he goes to-night to our farm-school at East Barnet."

The school-room is in the rear of the house, and by the side of the wood-yard. It has been tastefully decorated with holly, and with portraits of the great friends of the Charity, encompassed with evergreens by the boys' grateful fingers, and emblazoned with good inscriptions, as—"Blessed is the man that considereth the poor and needy."

The hissing of a circular saw, and the babble of young voices, draw me to the wood-yard. It is a lively scene. The staid and business-like air of the workers is wonderful. On one side the stronger boys are giving power to a circular saw; and at our feet is a busy group sorting the sticks from the chips. I can hardly believe that these mere babes in appearance are doing serious work. One child looks as though he could only just run alone.

"He's much older than he looks. Here, Tommy!" The bright fellow jumped up, and came confidently to the matron's side. This ingenious, fresh face was that on which the heartless stepmother looked when she abandoned an infant to the mercy of London streets—as I have already described. Another boy was carrying wood in a basket. "That boy," said the matron, "is the son of a soldier. His father, wounded in India, died on landing at Gravesend. The boy was left on the wide world, and he was brought here. These are our cases. Absolute destitution is the best claim on us."

A gate was opened, and some of the boys wheeled a truck into the yard. "They have been out delivering wood. We trust them after a time all over London; and they receive the money, and account honestly for it. There are boys in the Home we would trust with any sum. Remark those two elder boys, who are tying bundles. They wear 'good conduct stripes' upon their arms. One of them can tie up 800 bundles of wood per day. He has been here five years and a half. We like to keep some of the good boys, because they act as monitors and examples to the new-comers, who are sometimes very refractory and difficult to manage. They are all, however, as a rule, happy together, and very fond of each other. They squabble occasionally, but never fight. The chief vices they exhibit when they first come, are laziness and dirtiness. We have one boy of thirteen who has been here only four weeks; he will complain of work that the rest would take as a light task." I asked about the system of rewards and punishments. The matron described them:—"The boys who behave well get a mark a day; and at the end of the year they are entitled to a certain sum of money for every seven marks they have received. Bad conduct entails the forfeiture of marks. Stealing is punished with confinement, and bread and water; and grave disobedience with one or two stripes across the hand with the cane." These punishments are not severe; while the rewards are those that will stimulate their labour. To stimulate industry in these young Allalones is more important than to make them expert at pothooks. There is something of the Mettray spirit in the Home; more of it than is to be found in the pretentious school at Feltham. The boys are watchful of each other. They are warm friends, and have an *esprit de corps*. They have their pleasures and indulgences, as well as their school and work. If, as Richter says, "play is the first poetry of the human being," the poetry of these little hewers of wood is not neglected. The younger ones have a penny a week pocket-money, and are permitted to go out to buy apples or cakes. They are treated, in short, with a generous trust, and taught to love the Home as a place where there is some affection for them. No wonder, then, that the Home boys prosper when they grow up. They are surprisingly healthy, when the state in which they usually reach the Home is taken into consideration. Only one child has died, and this child, the offspring of an abandoned mother, was "too far gone," when it reached the Home, to be saved. The following facts will describe the progress of this, the first school certified in London under the Industrial Schools Act:—

Since February 1858 to last March, 139 boys had

been admitted, of whom 52 are now in the Euston Road Home, and 12 in the Barnet Home.

Of the total number admitted during these four years, 1 has emigrated to Canada; 3 have been received into other institutions; 8 have enlisted in the army; 7 have entered the royal navy; 1 has entered on board a merchant ship; 16 have been placed in tradesmen's employment or domestic service; 18 have been restored to their friends, and most of these are known to be now doing well, either in trade or service; 1 has died of pulmonary disease; 7 have been dismissed for misconduct; 13 have absconded from the Home, 4 of these had been only a few days in the Home; 64 are still inmates of the Home.

Of the 64 boys in the Home last year, 8 are total orphans; 36 have lost one parent; 20 are believed to have both parents living. The fathers of many of the latter are disabled from earning their livelihood —one is blind, one a lunatic, two are cripples, and two are invalids from chronic rheumatism.

The oldest boy in the Home is 17 years of age, the youngest 7; the average age of the whole school is 12 years and 4 months.

The results of the industrial work becomes yearly more encouraging. The past year's account contrasts favourably with that of the previous year, and shows a clear profit on the carpentering and the firewood, while the tailoring and shoemaking have also been carried on at a small profit.

The average cost per head has been £17, 2s., exclusive of rent, during the past year; and £25, 4s., including rent, printing, and all contingent expenses.

The dietary rules allow to each boy—On Sunday —½ lb. bread, ½ oz. butter, and ½ pint cocoa, for breakfast; ¼ lb. beef, ¼ lb. bread, potatoes, and pudding, for dinner; 6 oz. bread, ½ oz. treacle, and ½ pint coffee, for supper. On Monday, Wednesday, and Friday—¼ lb. bread, ½ pint porridge, ¼ pint milk, for breakfast; ¼ lb. bread, ¼ lb. meat, and vegetables, for dinner; 6 oz. bread, 1 oz. cheese, ½ pint tea, for supper. On Tuesday and Saturday—½ lb. bread and ½ pint cocoa, for breakfast; ½ lb. bread and 1 pint soup, for dinner; 6 oz. bread, ½ oz. butter or dripping, and ½ pint tea, for supper. On Thursday—½ lb. bread, ½ pint cocoa, for breakfast; ½ lb. bread, ½ lb. pudding, for dinner; 6 oz. bread, ½ oz. butter or dripping, and ½ pint tea, for supper—so that no complaint can be made on this score.

The statement of income and expenditure for the last financial year showed that the former amounted to £3121, 8s. 5d., and the latter to £2930, 6s., leaving a balance in hand of £191, 2s. 5d.

At a quarter to six, this hive is up and doing. The rooms are cleaned and dusted; then breakfast, prayers, and play till nine. From nine till a quarter to one, work. At one o'clock, dinner; clear away, and play till two. From two till a quarter past four, work again; then wash, and school to six. From six till seven, supper and play. From seven till eight, school again. At half-past eight, prayers, and to bed —to rest, after, it must be owned, an industrious and well-spent day. I warrant the young bees sleep.

CHAPTER IX.

THE CHILDREN OF THE STREETS.

THE goodly band of charitable folk who support and govern the London refuges for the homeless have a just and reasonable cause of complaint. Let any man who doubts the utility or questions the social importance of these homes be at the trouble of spending an afternoon in one of them. Let him question the little workers one by one. He will listen to extraordinary chapters of woful accidents. One child has been abandoned in the streets by a heartless stepmother. A second has worked his lonely way from the Indies in search of relatives of his dead parents. A third cannot tell who was his father or who was his mother. A fourth has run away from a cruel home, and tramped and begged from Yorkshire to London. The father of a fifth is transported. The observer must be struck with the fine courage there is in most of these infant wrestlers with an adverse faith. They show that they are of the British race, as, shoeless, and moneyless, and friendless, they set out on a walk of two hundred and fifty miles, to London—to London, the golden. In London they will find food and clothing with little difficulty, or they will discover places where charity will cover their nakedness, and set a plate before them. They find dark arches and hordes of juvenile criminals, for associates. Without work, and forbidden to beg, they sink day by day; until their poverty has taken a sufficiently picturesque exterior to attract the attention of some charitable passers-by; or they become members of a thieves' school. If begging is their first offence, they are committed to prison for fourteen days as rogues and vagabonds, and their hair is cropped after the penal pattern. All the law does for them is to punish them. While they remain good boys, the Government will have nothing whatever to do with them. They may serenely starve in any quiet corner they may choose for the operation; not in the highway, because the wasted limbs and glazed eye would attract a crowd and hinder traffic. To a good, vagrant boy, who has tramped to London, misled by the golden promises, probably of people who wished to get rid of him, the Government offers no help. He becomes interesting and fit for protection only after an appearance before a London magistrate.

The Privy-Council grant has been withdrawn from one of the most important refuges in London, on the ground that the destitute children whom it collects from the streets, are not criminals. The grant was at the rate of five shillings weekly for each child—a great help to an institution raised and supported by donations and annual subscriptions. This grant withdrawn, and the funds reduced by the drain of the Lancashire Relief Fund, the managers of the refuges situated near Seven Dials and Drury Lane found themselves suddenly crippled, at a time when London distress was abundant, and houseless children were in every byway. The operation of these refuges is to prevent destitute children from becoming criminals. They are whipped out of the streets, and taught to earn an honest livelihood. They are sent into the army and navy; prepared, if they be girls, for domestic service, or shipped for Queensland, or Natal, or Port Elizabeth. The cost to the community for this conversion of our London Arabs into useful and honourable men and women, is very small. It appears to be hardly £12 per annum for each rescue from the streets. When we compare, then, the cost of clothing, feeding, and teaching a destitute child, with the price which the public pays for rearing colonies of criminals, the extravagance of the latter proceeding will be evident "to the meanest intellect." It may be safely asserted that every professional criminal costs the country over £200 before he is disposed of. The accomplished thief is a plant of slow and expensive growth. A clever young thief appeared before a London police magistrate. He was an infant prodigy. Still in his teens, he had been already convicted some dozen times. Another promising criminal, who bids fair to reach the honours of his profession, was known by the policeman in attendance to be the tutor of thieves. Under his auspices, destitute children whom he can find in the streets—sleeping under arches or in common lodging-houses—are initiated into the noble art of dipping felonious fingers into strangers' pockets. Should the refuges, which endeavour to save the honest destitute from the wiles and lessons of such precocious young rascals as this felon tutor of the young idea, now find themselves without money, we may expect a large addition to the juvenile crime of the metropolis. The number of eligible, well-conducted boys ready to serve in the army and navy, will be diminished; Queensland and Natal will have some skilful immigrants the less; the ranks of efficient domestics will be thinned, while the passers of base coin, shofulmen, "wires," and "covers" will be sensibly strengthened. We shall show that we prefer raising ornate varieties of the criminal class, to the tameness of conducting humble schools of industry, and converting ragged urchins into mere carpenters and shoemakers. There is something picturesque—there is a dash of romance about the beetle-browed burglar, with his watchful eye and stealthy step; and we must pay for the picturesque. The ragged-school is a bit of vulgar cheapness when compared with the padding-ken in which Blueskin assembles his pupils, and exercises them in the light-fingered art, on a dummy with a bell. So we enjoy our £200 criminals. They are part and parcel of our greatness. We must show that we can still afford our full-blown convict show. Carpenters, and shoemakers, and servants are only so many ordinary figures, common to every civilized community. So the Privy-Council grant is withdrawn, and will be restored only when the refuges confine their humane attentions to criminals, who have proved their prowess in a house of correction. Prevention is less expensive, but, according to the Privy-Council, not better than cure. There is no great merit in putting a shield about an honest orphan who has been basely left alone in the wide world, but there is a triumph in curing the very sick. Let us, then, leave the ragged and hungry in the frost, and see to the warm water of Jack Sheppard.

The more I dip into the sad histories of the children of want, the more I am impressed, not with the evil there is in the young, but rather with the good. Some of these gathered waifs from the wilds of London have shown the most heroic courage and the most extraordinary self-denial. They have seen themselves suddenly cast upon the world, moneyless. The devil has appeared to them, as in Ingoldsby's "Legend of Cornelius Agrippa"—

> "He drew the mystic circle's bound,
> With skull and cross-bones fenced around;
> He traced full many a sigil there:
> He muttered many a backward prayer,
> That sounded like a curse.
> 'He comes!' he cried, with wild grimace,
> 'The fellest of Apollyon's race!'
> Then in his startled pupil's face
> He dash'd—an Empty Purse!"

Into the face of a bright-eyed boy, lying sick in bed before me, the empty purse was dashed. His mother and father were dead, and he was alone in Jamaica. He shipped as a cabin-boy for England, having been told that his father had relatives at Bristol. He walked all the way from Liverpool to his destination. After some trouble he found those relatives, in search of whom, alone and unfriended, he had travelled thousands of miles. But they would have nothing to do with him, he was in such a plight. "I don't much wonder at it," he said, "I was a dreadful figure to look at."

And so, with a courage wonderful in one so young, he turned his steps back towards Liverpool. In this bustling city he found a humble place, in which he remained eighteen months. Then he was turned upon the wide world once more, and kept body and soul together by begging. At last he was told that food and lodging were easy to get in London. So he started.

"How much money had you in your pocket when you set out?" I asked him.

"Money, sir? Not a farthing."

In reply to my questions as to how he lived, he answered (and in a voice and language that showed he had received some education), "I got on pretty well. I begged, and slept in the workhouses at night. They're obliged to give a night's lodging; some of them give a bit of food. I managed till I got into the cotton districts, between Huddersfield and Manchester. Here I couldn't get anything, for people hadn't got it. I lived on swedes I got from the fields as often as not. I was three weeks on the road. When I arrived in London I went to a baker's shop, and they gave me some bread; they'll generally give a bit of bread at a baker's. I had been in London four days when Mr. Williams (the Refuge secretary) met me by Blackfriars Bridge. I was thinking of getting into a Reformatory."

Mr. Williams concluded the boy's story. He met him on Christmas-eve last with another boy; and heard them speculating as to what kind of a Christmas dinner they would have. The boy who had walked from Liverpool was in a most deplorable condition; he had no jacket, and but a very ragged shirt. He asked them whether they had a place to sleep in, and they replied in the negative. Whereupon he gave them a paper, copies of which he always kept in his pocket. Upon it was printed, "If you want a home, take this to Mr. Wood, No. 8, Great Queen Street, Lincoln's-Inn-Fields."

It was here that the boy was lying when I saw him, suffering from an affection of the chest caught by exposure. A few beds off was his friend, breathing stertorously. The secretary told me that many of the boys suffered in this way when they were first brought into the Refuge. They are pretty well while the street life lasts, but they break down at first when they are brought into a house, and have a regular diet. The change is too sudden and complete.

The refuges for homeless and destitute children of St. Giles's and St. George, Bloomsbury, are more important, or rather more extensive, institutions for the rescue of houseless children, than that in the Euston Road. The Society that manages the Girls' Refuge in Broad Street, Bloomsbury, and the Boys' Refuge in Great Queen Street, Holborn, have ragged schools and other classes in Little Coram Street. They now command an income approaching £5000 per annum. This is the result of a small beginning, made with determination and zeal. A few working men held a meeting at one of their lodgings, in 1843, with the object of raising money to have a missionary placed at their disposal by the London Mission. They succeeded, and planted a missionary in the Rookery, St. Giles's. In this year a school, held over a cow-shed in Streatham Street, was opened. In the first year the income was only £180, and in the following year it was less; but in 1845 it advanced to £315, 19s. 9d., and thenceforth it has increased year by year, until we find a powerful committee doing good on a large scale in two great refuges, and in several ragged schools.

The Boys' Refuge is an old coachbuilder's place of business, the front of which is nearly opposite the Freemasons' Tavern. Where my lord and lady's new chariot stood, boys are now learning "the gentle craft" of shoemaking, and beyond is a vast carpenter's shop, where once wild children of the streets are carpentering, or picking hairs from hides for a neighbouring currier. The lads looked up curiously at us as we passed them. We halted before the group, who were as busy as monkeys, over a hide. The secretary singled out a red-headed boy, upon whose head the prison shears had made their mark.

"This is a sad case," he said. I asked the boy to tell me his story. The substance of it—given with emotion—was this:—He was an orphan. His father was killed in a colliery accident; and he, being alone and penniless, tramped to London in search of work in one of the match factories. No work, however, was to be had. Homeless and moneyless, the poor boy begged. A policeman seized him, and took him before a magistrate, and he was sentenced to fourteen days' imprisonment, and—this prison crop! On his release, one shilling was given to him—and the streets. Nobody was at any pains to discover whether the boy's history was true. The Government had only a gaol and a prison crop for this houseless orphan, who, hungering after a long tramp to London, had begged! The last hope of obtaining employment had been taken from him by the prison shears; and had not Mr. Williams met him as he was in search of a night's lodging in St. Giles's workhouse, it is not unreasonable to presume that he would very shortly (and thanks to these prison shears) have made his first steps in crime. Thank God, here is one brand snatched from the fire! Yet the Government have withdrawn from this establishment the 5s. poll-money per annum granted to reformatories, on the ground that these children are not all unconvicted criminals! It would almost appear that "the powers that be" are displeased to see philanthropy busy in the old nurseries of crime. The governors of the Bloomsbury and St. Giles's Refuges, however, are not to be daunted. They take boys who have been in trouble, in spite of Government unfriendliness; holding that there is small blame to be laid at the door of such a lad as this one, with a prison crop, who is now busy over a hide.

In the shoe shop, among the boys at work, I noticed three negroes. They had come over in ships, and had been ruthlessly turned adrift. One was the son of a runaway slave from the States. I remarked two bright deal boxes, one marked "W. Gibbs, emigrant to Queensland." "Those two boys," pointing to two young carpenters, "are off to Queensland on Saturday. Our colonists have been very successful. One we sent out, who is nearly out of his apprenticeship, has just written to us to say that he shall want us to send him out an assistant shortly, and he begs for one with a high forehead." Boys from this Refuge are doing well in both services, as well as in the colonies. There are other features of the Refuge worthy of remark. Beyond the firewood-chopping department (practice in which makes a boy's hand firm and true) there is a covered playground, with a swimming-bath in it. The school-room (a very large one) is on the first floor. I found it covered with holly garlands, and decorated with devices. The master was giving about 20 boys a lesson in dictation. They would have charmed Webster's pencil, as they screwed their lips and knit their brows over the hard words. Behind were a few refractory scholars who were learning their lessons on their knees, by way of punishment. One crafty little fellow (he was a tailor in the bud) had crossed his legs, and was suffering punishment at his ease. The secretary pointed out another boy to me who had been abandoned by his mother, and who had been found almost naked, looking wistfully into a Long Acre cookshop. There was a little boy, nine years of age, in the dictation class. He was too young to be admitted without payment; so a kind lady pays £13 a year for him.

The boys do all the work of the Refuge—the cooking, sweeping, and cleansing. These duties will make them useful to themselves in after life. While they make shoes for the Girls' Refuge, the girls make the boys' shirts and mend their clothes; and the linen of both refuges is washed in the industrial branch, at Acton. These economies are of great importance. They lighten the cost of every child, and so make places for new-comers. As I survey these hundred boys, results of so many unhappy chapters of accidents, and hear their various experiences, I am struck with the infinite variety of circumstances which life in the streets presents. Here are two boys, sons of a widow who walks daily from Southwark to Hoxton to earn 10d. for a day's needlework; there is a boy who has been the pet of a regiment at Chobham, an orphan, to whom the men took a fancy.

The Girls' Refuge, in Broad Street, was built for a great gin-palace; its rooms are, therefore, comely and spacious. That part which would have been the bar, had the architect's original plan been carried out, is the infant ragged-school, where, upon benches raised like a theatre gallery, crowds of Seven Dials children sit all day, secure from harm, under the eye of a teachèr who was once in the Refuge overhead. To hear the shrill little voices sing in time and tune, or count in concert, is a most amusing sight. Some wriggle and shrug their shoulders, others play with their tiny shoes, but most of them sit at attention with their arms crossed. The teacher keeps them all under control, with an energy that never savours of unkindness. On the same floor is a school for the ragged of a larger growth, where sewing, etc., is taught. But the most interesting part of this home for poverty is the Refuge, where girls picked from the street are housed, clothed, fed, taught, and put into situations. Their dormitories are pictures of cleanliness and plain comfort; the kitchens are admirably ordered; the school-room is without a fault, and the girls themselves are as neat as Dutch dolls, in their clean grey pinafores. There was a great Christmas-tree in the school-room when I paid the institution a visit, with 300 presents upon it—six for each girl. These presents were little toys and utilities suited to various ages. Up-stairs—in the mistress's room—were two sweet-looking girls, furtively preparing two presents for their teacher, and they appeared delighted with their task. In the board-room I found a touching evidence of the good feeling which exists among these poor girls. A girl was in disgrace, for having lit a candle in the housemaid's closet, where the clothes are packed. The head-teacher had sentenced the culprit to early bed and absence from the Christmas-tree distribution. This sentence had pained the entire community, and a petition had been drawn up, on a slate, and left upon the mistress's desk. It was couched in these words :—“ OUR DEAREST TEACHER,—We feel it is our duty to write these few lines to you. We all feel very unhappy to think that one of our school-fellows cannot enjoy the pleasure which we are about to enjoy. We want to ask you, as a favour, if you will please to forgive her, for she seems very sorry about it. Please, our dearest teacher, do not be offended with us for taking the liberty we have in asking you to forgive her. Because we know that it is painful to you when any of us are in disgrace, and especially at such a time as this. We all thank you for the treat which you have in kindness given to us; and now we think we must conclude, beseeching you to forgive us in the request we have asked you. From all your affectionate scholars. Will you please to answer this letter?" This letter—brimming over with feeling that would do honour to the best academy in England—was written by the daughter of the well-known blind beggar who walks the Bayswater Road! The lady (Miss Dickson) to whom it was addressed (who has spent seven years in Jerusalem managing an industrial school for Jewish children) smiled at the petition, and told me that she should forgive the poor child at the last moment, but that she must make an example when so dangerous an infraction of the rules had been committed, as that of carrying a candle into the clothes closet.

More cheerful, well-spoken, frank, and comely children I never saw than these pickings from London streets. They are taught to be useful, to earn their own living honourably. Every branch of domestic service is gone through. They sew, and wash, and cook, and scour. They clothe dolls, instead of wasting time over crochet: this fits them for places as nursemaids. Whether offspring of a Seven Dials costermonger, a Chelsea pensioner, a blind beggar, or found (as one was found only a few days since) weeping in the rain, hungry and in rags, the Refuge welcomes the destitute and abandoned, and makes them, what we see these happy children at their tea this January afternoon—good, brave, industrious girls, and grateful women.

I will add to this brief description of these Bloomsbury charities, a few suggestive facts and figures that will correctly indicate the extent and cost of their operations.

During the year described in the last report, 75 boys were received into the Refuge. Of this number, 15 were admitted on the application of friends interested in their welfare, 10 applied of their own accord, 8 were brought by missionaries and Scripture-readers, 8 were brought by the secretary and members of the committee, 5 brought in by the superintendent, 19 sent direct from the other ragged schools, 8 sent by various friends, 2 sent by magistrates.

At the close of the year 1860, there were 104 boys in the Refuge, which, with 75 admitted in 1861, makes 179 lads who derived benefit during the year from the Refuge.

Of the 104 in the Refuge on the 31st December 1860, and the 75 admitted in 1861—1 entered the royal navy, 10 emigrated to South Africa, 9 emigrated to Canada, 2 emigrated to New Zealand, 6 entered the merchant service, 26 were sent to situations in London and the country, 12 were restored to parents and friends who had lost them, 1 sent to another institution, 8 left of their own accord, 1 died, 1 sent to infirmary—leaving 102 in the Refuge at the end of the year 1861.

The industrial work sold and done for customers has produced the sum of £502, 16s. 5d., and the work done for the institution amounts to £362, 17s. 9d.—making a total of £865, 14s. 2d.

During the year, 1289 pairs of new boots and shoes were made, and 1369 repaired; 366 new articles of clothing were made in the tailors' class, and 1776 repaired; 31,600 bundles of firewood were made up and sold, and 3270 for the use of the institution. The errand boys' work produced £71, 12s. 6d.

During the past year, 52 girls were admitted into these refuges. Three applied of their own accord, 16 were sent direct from other ragged schools, 27 admitted on application of friends, 3 found in the streets by secretary, committee, etc., and 3 brought by missionaries.

Of the 66 in the Refuge on the 31st December 1860, and the 52 admitted in 1861, 21 were sent to service, 23 restored to friends and left of their own accord, 1 emigrated to Tasmania, and 2 died—leaving 70 in the Refuge on the 31st December 1861.

The total number of children admitted into the Refuges up to the end of 1861 was 1047—viz., 618 boys, and 429 girls. Of these, 225 applied for admission of their own accord, 187 sent from other ragged schools, 321 admitted on application of friends, 132 brought by missionaries and Scripture-readers, 105 found in the streets in a state of destitution, 20 sent by magistrates, 29 sent by chaplains of prisons on their discharge, 8 sent by clergymen, 5 sent by policemen, 1 sent from another institution, and 14 re-admitted.

The total number of children who have left the refuges for service, etc., from their opening till December 31, 1861, is 736—400 boys, and 336 girls.

The ragged-school operations show that during the thirteen months the night-school for elder girls in Great Queen Street had been established (up to the date of the last report), 122 were admitted, some of whom went to service, and many removed from the neighbourhood, so that at the end of the year there were only 26 in attendance.

In addition to this night-school for girls, there is a Sunday night-school for boys and girls, and men and women, carried on in the same building. The attendance is often over 200.

In Broad Street there are a girls' day-school (the number on the book being 136); a girls' night-school (50); an infant day-school (120); Sunday night-schools for boys, girls, and infants (200); a mothers' meeting (80); lectures to working men (100); working men's benefit club; provident and clothing club; a penny bank.

The average attendance in the girls' school was 80. The mothers' class was attended by 80 poor women. They had their annual excursion to Hampton Court, and 76 availed themselves of the pleasure.

The infant-school has a large attendance of little ones.

At the close of the year the number of members in the working men's benefit club was 128. During the year, £27, 12s. 6d. was paid out to sick members, £7 to one widow on the death of her husband, and £3 to a member on the death of his wife.

In Little Denmark Street there are a boys' day-school (the attendance being 80); boys' night-school (40); a Band of Hope class (40); Sunday-school, morning (60); Sunday-school, afternoon (101); provident fund—number of depositors, 162; sum deposited during the year, £29, 6s. 5d.

In Little Coram Street there are a day-school for boys and girls (the attendance being 100); an infant day-school (90); a night-school for boys (25); a night-school for girls (30); a Sunday-school for boys and girls (160); religious service for the poor on Sunday and Wednesday evenings; a penny bank, in which there were 258 depositors last year; a lending library. All these operations are working well.

The teachers, paid and voluntary, connected with the various refuges and schools number more than 60.

The finance statement showed a balance in hand at the last audit of £133, 4s. 1d., and £500 on deposit at the bankers'. The receipts during the year amounted to £4786, 8s., including £300 drawn from the deposit account (but exclusive of a legacy of £900 hereafter mentioned), which, with the above balance, made £4919, 12s. 1d. The payments in respect of the Refuge and Ragged School operations were £4832, 19s. 1d., leaving a balance in hand of £86, 13s.

During the year 1862, two legacies were received —£20, free of duty, from Miss Mary Ann Pippin, for the ragged-schools, and £1000 (less £100 duty) from the late Countess of Haddington, for the Boys' Refuge. This institution, like all I have visited, felt the effects of the Lancashire Distress Fund.

The Boys' Refuge in Commercial Street, Whitechapel, is an industrial school, to which destitute and vicious boys are sent by parents or guardians, or kind strangers. The committee charge £13 for each boy admitted, if he has parent or patron able to pay this sum. The utterly destitute are not, however, turned from the gates. Sad-faced, stunted children they looked, as they stood in line undergoing military drill. In most of their faces I could read their story. They were no more like the children of well-to-do people, lively as "troutlets in a pool," than our battered Greenwich pensioners are like the hearty boys of the Naval School. This little regiment in corduroys is composed of men in miniature, who have spent their babyhood in the school of adversity. Many of them have been in prison. They have a careworn, doleful, and at the same time "knowing" look. Left to themselves, they would undoubtedly have graduated in crime. It is pleasant, therefore, to see them manœuvring in their playground, or working in their shops, or turning into their comfortable dormitories. They are training to be useful members of society. They will be coopers, tailors, shoemakers, wheelwrights, hairdressers, turners, or printers, and not vagrants, vagabonds, and thieves. The rules by which this reformation is worked are strict, but they are kind. The boys applying for admission must be between eleven and fourteen years of age. Once admitted, they are cut off from the influence of parents or guardians. Only one visit per month is allowed. The committee have taken the right course in appealing to the heart and honour of the boys. The restraint it is necessary to impose in order to govern more than a hundred vagrant and idle boys, whose previous life has usually been totally idle, galls these errant natures; it is too much for some of them. Many have absconded from all the comforts and promises of this clean and kindly home to return to pocket-picking in the streets. They will refuse to work, and refuse to be apprenticed, and persuasion will be powerless against their dogged determination to live a life of idleness. They are treated in all respects as though they were perfectly honest; they are trusted with money and errands; they take their holiday out alone. This treatment has been eminently successful, as it always will be. The boys are flourishing in various parts of the world. One bounced one day into the playground dressed as a drummer and fifer. He was splendid in scarlet, and was surrounded by his wondering and jealous old school-fellows, who wondered when they would be big enough to be soldiers.

A day at the Home is anything but an idle one. The boys are aroused at six, and are expected to be washed and dressed at half-past six. Then they hear prayers till seven. From seven o'clock till eight they are put through various military exercises; from eight to nine breakfast and play. Then the serious business begins. From nine to eleven, half the boys are learning their trades in the industrial department, while the rest are in school. From eleven to five minutes to one, all the boys are at industrial work; and then there are dinner and play to pass the time till two o'clock. From two to four, half of the boys go to the industrial department and half to school, as in the morning; and then from four to six everybody is at industrial work. A quarter of an hour for supper precedes an hour for washing and play; an hour and a quarter for school; and, finally, half an hour for prayers. Bed at nine o'clock. This represents a good day's work, and I can understand its severity when imposed on a boy who has been accustomed to the idleness of the streets. Nor is the fare these workers enjoy luxurious. Breakfast and supper mean bread and cocoa with milk, butter being added to the bread on Sunday evenings. Sunday's dinner consists of bread, meat, and pudding; but Monday is only bread and cheese; Tuesday, soup and bread; Wednesday, meat and potatoes; Thursday, dumplings; Friday, Irish stew; and Saturday, soup and bread. Yet this modest fare acts upon the boys when they are first brought in as it was acting on the brave boy I talked to in the infirmary of the Bloomsbury Refuge.

There is nothing peculiar to remark in the workshops. They closely resemble those I have already described. But the out-door system is worth special notice. The boys are put to work out, remaining still under the supervision of the governor. There are sixteen of these boys now earning wages outside the walls of the Home. They contribute to the Home in proportion to their earnings. The boys who earn 8s. a week, pay 5s. for their board and lodging, and 1s. 6d. for clothes. Then they deposit 1s. in the bank, and retain the remaining 6d. as pocket money. By this means the boys are guarded through their first steps in life; they are taught to be provident, and their example acts as a good impulse to their younger companions, who are still in the school workshops.

I give a few statistics from the report of that year:—

During the year there were 120 applicants, 69 of whom were admitted; of those admitted 60 were partially paid cases, and 9 were entirely free. Although the number of paid cases appears large, yet the money received for them does not equal one-third of their expense.

The number of boys disposed of during the year was as follows:—22 apprenticed, 7 sent to sea, 10 provided with situations, 8 restored to parents, 4 (for whom further payment was declined) sent home, 10 absconded, 3 died, 1 joined her Majesty's service, 1 sent to another institution, and 1 expelled, making a total of 67, leaving in the Refuge 103: 12 of this number were orphans, 40 had both parents living, 36 were without fathers, 14 without mothers (of these 8 had stepfathers, 7 stepmothers).

Of the seven sent to sea two were engaged as ship's fifers, for which they received 15s. per month extra; the others are doing well. Of the three that died, one died at the Small-pox Hospital, Holloway, and two at the Refuge; one of consumption and the other of "black scurvy." The boy that joined her

Majesty's service entered as drummer and fifer. The boy that was expelled had been sent to the Refuge from a country prison, and after a residence in the institution of a year and six months, was placed out on trial as an apprentice to shoemaking, the committee engaging to bind him; but he refused to be bound or to work. Of the 103 remaining in the Refuge, 29 were engaged in carpentering, 35 in shoemaking, 30 in tailoring, 4 in wood-chopping, and 5 in sundry employments.

In the school 25 read well, 40 read fairly, and 38 imperfectly; 72 wrote in copy-books, and 31 on slates; 1 worked algebra, 10 the higher rules, 50 compound rules, and 42 simple rules. The balance-sheet shows that the receipts amounted to £2198, 7s. 1d., the expenditure to £2129, 6s. 9d.; leaving a balance in hand of £69, 0s. 4d. The industrial department (comprising tailoring, shoemaking, and carpentering) exhibits a loss of £22, 19s. 4d.

In a narrow street, by Dorset Square, a row of three or four shops, closed, and painted bright green, attracts the attention of the passer-by to the Cripples' Home. A more affecting sight than this refuge for deformed children it is not possible to conceive. A lame child opened the door to me. In the workroom some 30 or 40 cripples—showing every variety of deformity—were plaiting, and making up articles in straw. What wan, pale faces were there! what poor, palsied limbs! A row of baby-cripples, just painfully trying to master the rudiments of straw-plaiting—so many motherless Tiny Tims—stared wistfully at me as I passed along, and still went silently on with their work. The more advanced were making ornamental baskets, or bonnets. There are not many industries open to these afflicted children; so that nearly all of them are here, busy over straw, while two of their sisters keep a counter in the Soho Bazaar for the sale of the Home handiwork. The Home had a very modest beginning. A few charitable ladies set up a small place, and their first inmate was a wretched beggar-girl, who used to wander about the neighbourhood of Bryanston Square.

This Cripples' Home is ingeniously contrived, every part of it being turned to good account. Thus on the ground floor there is a public nursery—a clean warm room—where workwomen can leave their babes in safety while they go out for a day's work. There are all manner of appliances and toys. In the centre of the room is a "fold," railed off and padded with a mattress, wherein sucklings may lie, and kick, and crow, without harm. Against one wall there is a row of cots; and against another are rocking-horses. To the gentle duties of the nursery some of the cripples are equal. But the ingenuity of the contrivers of this home has not ended here. Beyond is a laundry, where women are employed washing. These are destitute refuge girls, and they are learning the duties of domestic servants. They are very useful —"the cripples being so helpless, need a great deal of waiting on." These refuge girls wheel out the cripples to the Regent's Park in perambulators.

The Home is under the management of a committee of zealous ladies, and is under the care of a matron and four sub-matrons. It is not, however, a home to which the moneyless can resort. Each cripple must have parent or patron willing to spend £8 per annum. Even this payment covers only one-half of the maintenance of a cripple; since the diet of these invalids must be adapted to their weak constitution. Two doctors do what science can to straighten and strengthen the crooked limb; and when what the Home can do has been fully done, the unfortunate cripple goes forth into the world, armed with a trade by which she can earn her living. It is to be hoped that this good work will prosper. Let any man or woman who doubts the truth of the picture I have drawn, glance into the work-room where that row of deformed babes is to be seen; and, I answer for it, he will be a friend to the Cripples' Home.

The whole amount invested as a building fund is now £2000 Consols, and £910, 2s. cash in deposit at interest in the London and Westminster Bank.

The entire income this year is less than in the preceding year, being £2845, 9s. 6d., against £2856, 9s. 8d., while the balance carried over is also smaller, being £148, 10s. 7d., against £248, 11s. 10d.

The diminution in the receipts appears to have arisen from a decrease in the subscriptions, donations, payments for girls, interest on Exchequer-bills, and the seaside fund. Moreover, there has been no Government grant, which amounted last year to £133, 2s. 6d. On the other hand, there has been an increase of £390, 16s. 11d. under the following items of receipts—Laundry, nursery, straw-work, and collections after sermons.

The entire diminution in receipts on deducting the decrease from the increase is £41, 15s. 1d.

Looking at the expenditure during the year, there is an increase of £413, 2s. 6d. under the heads of food, nursery, raw materials and tools, general expenses, salaries, taxes, gas, seaside expenses. To the above amount the bazaar expenses (£86, 13s. 8d.) should be added, making a total increased expenditure under the heads mentioned £499, 16s. 2d.

On the other hand, there has been a diminished expenditure amounting to £221, 13s. 10d. under the heads of clothing, laundry, house, advertisements, etc., rent, sick expenses, building expenses.

The entire calculation of receipts and expenditure shows a total diminution in the income amounting to £769, 18s. 8d.

The most prominent feature in the balance-sheet is the large amount of work done by the girls, which this year is £1062, 1s. against £708, 3s. 11d. last year, being an increase of £353, 17s. 1d.; and although, when put in connexion with the greater number of girls employed (70 to 72 instead of 60), and the increased amount expended in food, raw material, and bazaar department, which is in all £379, 13s. 6d., there is an apparent diminution of some £25 as compared with last year. This is more than corrected in regard to the amount of stock in hand, which is valued at £450. This amount has been obtained, under fortunate circumstances, to meet the increasing demands upon the charity.

CHAPTER X.

THE SCHOOL OF DISCIPLINE.

THE atrocities committed by ticket-of-leave men were put forth as the direct results of our mild penal *régime*. We beheld the innocent poor maltreated in the workhouses, babes and sucklings left to die miserably, and convicts bartering their superfluous food for tobacco. In approaching the questions involved in these strange and jarring social scenes, I deemed it prudent to deal, in the first place, with the institutions the object of which is to rescue the poor from temptations to crime. I have inspected the nightly refuges, the cheap or gratuitous homes, the industrial schools, and now I come to glance at the reformatories.

The homes with which I have dealt have been industrial homes, into which the children of dissolute or destitute parents, intractable children, abandoned children, and also children committed by magistrates for theft, have been received, and so brought up that they should lead honest lives. I have described also the house of charity, where the good conduct of the destitute finds its reward, and where the poor cripple is tended and taught remunerative employment. It is because I believe that the industrial home system is capable of great extension in the direction I have already indicated, that I add some little more experience I have bought on this head.

The matron of the School of Discipline, held in an old commodious Chelsea house, near the Chelsea Hospital, and which was instituted so far back as 1825, said to me: "These homes have become old-fashioned. People turn to new fashions in charities as in other things; and so some of them are not so well supported as they used to be." Yet the house was a clean, quiet, well-ordered establishment. From without it had even a handsome appearance. All that suggested "discipline" were the green horizontal blinds that were fastened outside, nearly two-thirds up the windows, to baffle the designs of would-be truants. Within, were forty girls, with fresh faces and in clean clothes, playing noisily in their schoolroom. At the side was their refectory, with two long white deal tables—in the room that had been the dining-room of some well-to-do cit. Overhead were their trim dormitories, a bed for each sleeper; and below was a kitchen in which many a maid-of-all-work would be glad to find herself. Peering through the back windows I could see the long strip of playground. The pantry was garnished with piles of substantial loaves. These children have, surely, to behave only moderately well here to be happy, learning the little useful arts of good domestic service. "I find that kindness will do everything; that is, kindness and firmness. They were in a state of insubordination when I came here. A few hours of firm treatment were enough to bring them to order. We have very few cases of theft, and very seldom resort to punishment."

My inquiry into the kind of punishment that was used to compel obedience led us to a cell (adjoining one of the dormitories) so dark that when the door was open I could hardly distinguish the bed in it.

"When they have committed any grave error, we put them in here two or three days and nights. It is just light enough to allow them to knit stockings. But I seldom have occasion to make use of this last resource; during the last four months only twice. They are very good and tractable."

The dormitories were placarded with scriptural quotations and with rules. "Thou shalt not steal" was painted over the head of one of the beds. This commandment suggested an anecdote to the matron. A child was taken ill there; and in her illness read this again and again. It fastened itself upon her mind, and she said that it had done her good. At last she begged that the board might be placed close to her; and it comforted the poor little penitent in her dying moments. The child had stolen probably, and was sent here, possibly by a London magistrate, for correction. This home takes Government cases of children brought up for robbery, at the Government rate of 5s. per week per child. Under the old system of punishment, many of these children would have become the companions of thieves, and the mistresses of convicts. Under this system there are good results to show. There are now eleven Government cases in the School of Discipline; and since they are behaving well, it is just to anticipate that they will turn out as good servants as nearly all their predecessors have been. Among these good examples are girls who have gone into domestic service, behaved well, and married well.

There are now forty girls in the school, many of whom come from comfortable homes, and many of them from homes where drunkenness and vice are the rule. All are paid for, but the money paid in no case suffices for the cost of maintenance, clothes, and instruction. Voluntary contributions make up the difference, or should make it up, if noisier charities did not step in to mar the usefulness of this quiet labour. I remarked that some of the girls wore ribbons and medals. The matron explained that the medals represented good conduct, and the ribbons monitorship. The girls, as in all the industrial schools, do the entire work of the house; the sewing, the scouring, the washing, and the baking. They go out for walks, in neat uniforms, twice every week. They are well fed, having meat six times a week. Good ladies of the neighbourhood visit them continually, and hold Bible classes with them. They are constantly under the doctor's eye. These charitable aids given to unfortunate children are so much good done, not only to the girls themselves, but also to the generation in which their adult life will be spent. We have so many honest workers gained, and so many criminals destroyed.

Close at hand, in Sloane Street, there is an Industrial Home for girls, that differs from the School of Discipline in this, that the former does not take Government cases. It is simply a boarding-school for the very poor and intractable, conducted with less severity than the School of Discipline—with its old-fashioned and foolish lock-up. The mistress of the Industrial Home for Girls told me she had very little trouble with the children. She punished them by sending them to their bed-rooms, or separating them from their companions. They were playing lustily in the open ground behind the house while I was talking with the matron; and when I presently saw them tumbling into their meal-room before a blazing fire, I thought of the advances society has made in the treatment of the young since "Do-the-boys Hall" was the picture of a Yorkshire seminary. There are thousands of men and women born of the middle class who can remember their schooling given in dens, compared with which many of these industrial homes and reformatories are homes of luxury. I can remember a certain provincial French academy I passed some time in, the *salle-à-manger* of which was a kennel compared with the meal-room of the Industrial Home in Sloane Street. We had no brilliant fire, no law-of-kindness government. We went cold and half-fed to bed, and rose and went to the icy school-room miserable and unkempt. We learned very little that was useful or morally elevating, yet the school was founded for the sons of gentlemen!

I might describe other homes and schools for girls to which the destitute and the criminal are committed, as the Lisson Grove School, but the discipline varies so slightly that the task would be almost useless. I may note, as I pass to a more general view of the reformatory and industrial systems, that the establishment at Lisson Grove has a feature that might be imitated with advantage in others of its class. The inmates are taught cooking, not mere roast and boiled, steaming potatoes, and concocting refuge soup. The charitable ladies of the neighbourhood send orders for all kinds of delicacies to be cooked for the sick poor; and by this means they enable the girls to try their 'prentice hands at jellies, custards, etc. This apprenticeship makes them more valuable as domestic servants. They can boast that they are able "to dish up a dinner." A revolution has taken place in these most useful establishments. The Government grant has been withdrawn this year, and the schools and reformatories are handed over to the care of the Home Secretary. The Committee of Council on Education has got rid of a great expense; and now the only assistance granted by Government to the schools which are registered under the Industrial School Act consists in a weekly payment of 5s. for any child that may be sent to such school by order of a magistrate. The fallacy of the reasoning by which the Government has arrived at its present position will be shown by some facts and statements which I have been at some trouble to collect and arrange.

The Industrial Schools Act was intended to clear the streets and highways of destitute and criminal children. It was a confession of the wrong that had been long left without a remedy. The intention of the promoters of the Act was to enable Government to sap at the foundation the criminal nurseries of our great towns. The children of bad or neglectful parents were to be taken from the pernicious parental control, and handed over to kind and experienced teachers and matrons, who would bring them up carefully, and guard them from the companionship of the vicious. The Government would no longer give grants in aid to private industrial schools, even when they were supported mainly by voluntary contributions. The Committee of Council on Education would no longer recognise these institutions as popular educational establishments; they must be handed over to the Home Secretary; their grants must be withdrawn; and the care of rescuing children from London streets must be confided to London magistrates. Scattered over the United Kingdom there are about 248 reformatories, refuges, and industrial schools. Some of these private charities flourished many years before reformatories, Magdalens, and homes became fashionable hobbies. The Magdalen in Blackfriars Road, for instance, was founded more than a century before there were midnight meetings. The Dublin Magdalen was established in 1767, and that of Edinburgh in 1797. There was a Lancashire female refuge at Liverpool in 1823. The Philanthropic Society's Farm School dates from 1788. The refuge for the destitute of Dalston was in existence in 1805. So that the refuge and rescue systems, homes, and industrial schools, are not of yesterday. There were industrial schools in London, Bristol, Sutcliffe, Birmingham, Derby, Hull, Manchester, Newcastle, Sunderland, etc., in 1849. The Perth Boys' School of Industry was in existence in 1843; and the Aberdeen Female School of Industry was founded in 1842. The good done by these humble charities that have risen in every part of the kingdom is more, I venture to assert, than Government is ever likely to do by any patent Parliamentary system. A rate-in-aid was exactly the help the benevolent required to stimulate them. It never sufficed for the outlay; it was a drop in the ocean of charity that blesses this country. It enabled certain tremulous committees to undertake humble contracts for the welfare of their institutions, that must now be left undone. It was a fair levy made on the uncharitable section of the public. It forced the thoughtless to give their mite *quand même.* The withdrawal of the grant has embarrassed hundreds of these homes and schools. Every report expresses the embarrassment into which it has thrown committees. The ninth report of the Industrial Home for Girls in Sloane Street—to take one at random—reminds all persons interested in the school that "the income of the year has not been sufficient for the expense," and that the expedient of selling out a portion of the reserve fund cannot be repeated with justice to those gentlemen who have undertaken the responsibilities of the lease. "The only resource, unless further assistance be given, consists in refusing all candidates for admission, except those for whom a payment of 5s. per week, either from friends or subscribers, can be secured; a step which the committee grieve to be compelled to take, believing, as they do, that the most urgent cases of rescue which come before them are just those for which no payment can be obtained." Let the reader mark that these cases are, moreover, precisely those which are not likely to be brought before a London magistrate. They must be left unregarded then, while the homes are crippled by the withdrawal of the Committee of Council of Education grants, unless they offend the law.

How many of our London or provincial Arabs reach reformatories or homes, or have reached them since the Amended Industrial Schools Act was passed in 1861? Their way to them, unless they are patronized by some good Samaritan, or are admitted when the voluntary contributions support free cases, as at the Bloomsbury refuges and elsewhere—their way to reformation is through the police court. "And observe," said a gentleman to me, who knows the system and working of it *à fond*, "the London police magistrates have great reluctance in committing children to reformatories. They never send them if they can help it."

I had made the same remark. I had watched the police reports, and found children sent to prison just tainted with some petty larceny, to come forth ready to complete their education in knavery. The country has saved 5s. a week, and made a rogue for whom £1 per week will have to be paid in a few years. The magistrates have not the excuse that the facilities for finding places for budding criminals and infant vagrants are not kept before them, since there is a Reformatory and Refuge Union at 118 Pall Mall, that has every reformatory and industrial school in the United Kingdom under its thumb. This Union, moreover, takes care to provide every magistrate with printed application papers to reformatories or certified industrial schools. Every magistrate wishing to commit a child to a reformatory is requested to cause this form to be filled up as accurately as the case will admit, and to send it at least a fortnight before the expiration of the imprisonment, to the Secretary of the Reformatory and Refuge Union. In the case of a child not committed to prison, the form should be sent at once. In this the name or "known alias" of the child is requested; his or her age, height, state of health; name and address of parents or step-parents (an important query); statement as to legitimacy or illegitimacy; occupation and earnings; number and ages of brothers and sisters; whether now going to a reformatory or refuge for the first time; whether the applicant has been in a workhouse, and if so, how long; at school, and how long; if previously convicted; offence now committed; where and by whom convicted; date of conviction and sentence; name of gaol; whether in separate confinement or not; and lastly, will the county the offender belongs to make an allowance for his reformation—and how much? These questions are all necessary to the governors of reformatories. They require to know as much as possible of the antecedents and disposition of the child who is to be sent to them. Yet these forms are very reluctantly filled up. Let me call to the mind of the reader the case of the boy who travelled to London after the death of his father in a colliery accident. It was a brave thing on the part of this child to tramp to London—having been told that he would be able to get employment in some match-works. He reached London, but he could get no work. The empty stomach is a potent logician: he overrides many social refinements and drawing-room moralities. The boy begged for bread. Alone in the world—ignorant as the stones his bare feet pressed—he implored bread. The law that would have let him hunger in the streets while he could stand, was down upon him directly he spoke. He was dragged in his rags before a magistrate, and committed to prison as a rogue and vagabond. His hair was cut prisonwise, and at the expiration of his sentence he was turned once more into the streets, with a shilling between him and starvation. Mr. Williams, of the Bloomsbury Refuge, found him looking wistfully into a cook's shop in Long Acre, on his way to ask a night's shelter in a work-house. That which the law would not do (although the magistrate had the power to secure this homeless child from harm, and had the form at hand ready to be filled up that would have sent him to honest employment), private charity cheerfully did for him, and he is in a fair way of earning his own livelihood. He would have cost the Government 5s. a week, and now he will not touch one halfpenny of the estimates. Had he been committed once or twice for theft, a London magistrate might have deemed him ripe for Government interference.

It is true that reformatories and industrial schools are doing much good. Juvenile crime is on the decrease. About 17,000 individuals are in these private asylums for the destitute and fallen; but Government has done little of the work, and has now resolved to make that little less. Magistrates, as a rule, are indisposed to convict a child under the Industrial Schools Act, although some county magistrates have shown a good example. In one instance an admirable lesson was read to the Home Office. The grant was withdrawn from a certain school; whereupon a county magistrate, whose school it was, turned his sixty *protégés* adrift. Found in the streets, they were brought before him; he, in his magisterial capacity, sentenced them under the Industrial Schools Act; whereupon they were conducted back to school, and the Home-Office was compelled to pay £13 a head for them. The injustice committed by the Government towards the refuges, reformatories, and industrial schools is made more apparent when it is borne in mind that some of these institutions—and among them the most useful—have one Government case in the course of the year, and some have none. It would be difficult to pick out a more useful refuge than that in Long Acre, yet it secures no Government cases; and, consequently, has no Government help. It is not certified under the Industrial Schools Act; and will not be so, in all probability, because there appears to be little or no good to come from such a certificate.

There is one way, and one way only, in which the Home-Office can be made to do its duty by the houseless and criminal children of the country. These should not depend for their rescue on the fitful impulses of private charity. No babe should be left to crawl from the gutter into prison because vast sums of money are wanted in Lancashire or elsewhere. At this moment many unsupported refuges see before them the near prospect of a disastrous early-closing movement. Let them close, and the result will speedily be seen in London streets. They desire Government cases. They ask, and with justice, that the national purse should come to complete the noble work of private charity. Let their friends take a leaf out of the books of the Roman Catholic asylums. Let them see how the Roman Catholic priests have been at work—how they have been busy in the purlieus of Westminster, seeking the ragged, homeless boys of their religion, bringing them before magistrates, and insisting upon their being brought within the scope of the Industrial Schools Act.

But a few facts and figures will set the operation of the amended Act before the reader.

A return relating to industrial schools, dated March 31, 1862, shows that the total number of children committed by justices or magistrates up to that time was 84. Of these, 39 belonged to the county of Middlesex; 47 of the entire number were Roman Catholics, and 27 were Protestants. In the county of Middlesex alone the whole number were Roman Catholics; the other counties mentioned being Essex (St. Nicholas Industrial School), Glamorgan (school-ship Havannah), and Lancaster (Liverpool Industrial Schools). The statistics of the various offences show that 6 were charged with vagrancy, 1 with stealing from parents, 10 with theft, 2 were not under proper control, 36 were charged with begging, 1 on suspicion of stealing, 6 were homeless, and were companions of thieves; 4 were found sleeping out; 1 was discovered "in a shop;" 1 was charged with petty thefts; 7 were destitute; 1 was charged with larceny; and 1 was beyond parental control.

In addition to the schools included in this return, as certified under the Act, 19 industrial schools are in operation in England certified under a former Act, and 18 in Scotland, also under a previous Act.

The whole number of children under a magistrate's order in certified industrial schools, at the date of this return, is 339 in England, and 283 in Scotland, making a total of 622.

These figures are proof of the successful activity of the Roman Catholic clergy. More than half the convictions under the Industrial Schools Act, according to the return moved for by Mr. Newdegate, were the handiwork of Roman Catholic priests, or, at least, the offenders were Roman Catholics. This energy on the part of the Roman Catholic Church should tempt all earnest Protestants to exert themselves in the cause of houseless and criminal children, and force upon the magistrates the duty of acting, in every case within the law, on the Industrial Schools Act.

CHAPTER XI.

CHILDREN OF THE STREET.

THE Boys' Home at Wandsworth is by far the largest and the most vigorously managed London private reformatory school for boys I have yet visited. When you halt before the handsome iron gates, at the side of the canal bridge, you might imagine you were at the entrance to some sleek alderman's suburban retreat. A zinc plate brings the imagination to a halt. Behind the evergreens at the end of the long broad walk, in the solid square brick building, are 180 boys—about 140 of whom know what a gaol is like. My ring at the bell is answered by a brisk boy, dressed in grey, corded with red—the uniform of the institution; and I am conducted to the hall-door, where I am met by the head of the establishment. It is difficult, as we walk into a well-furnished drawing-room, to understand that there is not some mistake. Through the window there is a broad lawn—and beyond—ay, just a faint suggestion that busy hands are there. The long, low buildings; the waggon passing down a lane on the left, conducted by boys, in the grey and red of the diminutive gate-keeper; the stacking of bundles of wood to the right (with which I am by this time so familiar, and know its meaning so thoroughly, that I shall never see a bundle of firewood again without remembering the unhappy little fellows whose fingers chop and tie it) set my mind at rest. This is an industrial home, a reformatory, and a refuge, certified under the 17th and 18th Vict. cap. 86. It is an industrial home for convicted or unconvicted criminals, and destitute boys, from the counties of Surrey and Middlesex. The boys are taken between the ages of ten and sixteen, and .put to the usual industrial work. These Wandsworth boys appear to attain a higher degree of excellence, even in the higher branches of industry, than is usual with reformatory or industrial school lads. In the master's room there was a ship beautifully built by one of the boys, who showed a strong aptitude for engineering. The master, being himself an engineer, encouraged the lad's proclivity; and now he is a man, well placed at his favourite employment. He was found by a city missionary, begging in the streets. He had been turned out of home. A religious quarrel had divided his family, and he was left to cleave his way alone through the wide world. In this Home, being an apt scholar, he was promoted to drive a little engine in the sawmill. He was only fourteen years of age when he left. The ship he built and left behind him, as a memorial of his skill, stands upon a highly-finished marquetrie table. "That," said the master, "was begun and finished here by three of my boys. It has been exhibited, and was much admired by the late Prince-Consort." I inspected other samples of the boys' skill—a working model of a screw propeller, a massive tool-chest of complicated design, etc.

"Here," the master said, "we really work." What I subsequently saw proved the truth of his words, else this institution were an impossibility. Who ever hears of it? It never figures in the advertising columns of the newspapers; it has no committee, no president, no honorary secretary; it cannot boast even a printed report; it has never aired a long list of fashionable subscribers. And wherefore?

There are people, as I discover daily on my way through the charitable institutions of the metropolis, who pass their lives doing daily good by stealth. This important institution is, however, a monument of private charity, so nobly and perseveringly exercised, that it is difficult to celebrate it. Rich words, "to hang trophies on," proclaim that which has been done unostentatiously from year to year, with earnest heart and open purse, by a single lady. In the "Fable for Critics," the poet sings of Emerson :—

> "To the men he thinks worthy he frankly accords
> The design of a white marble statue in words."

I leave it to him who hath the gift to record that holy, unregarded work which Miss Portal has been doing these many years. The power of Fortune falls at times into strange hands, but it falls occasionally into the lap of human creatures who are nobly touched. It has cost the guardian gentlewoman who has held this refuge for children together, "generally £3000 a year, according to the master. Last year the lady's outlay was over £1000. These free gifts, most heartily bestowed, are repaid to the lady by the affection with which the reformed boys write to her from all parts of the world. I looked through many of their letters in the master's office. Some of them were remarkable for sound sense and strong determination to do good; and all for a generous spirit of gratitude that pervaded them. The letters addressed to the master were signed, as a rule, "your foster son." Two letters from boys who had gone out to Canada together, were interesting. Both boys were doing well. One was earning ten dollars a month on a farm. They had both joined the Volunteers, and had sent home their photographs (taken together) in uniform.

"Most of them," said the master, "write every month, and send me papers. They are pretty well all over the world. One who has just written to me is a clerk on a railway. He was sent here from a prison."

Another letter was from a boy in Canada, who was training for a schoolmaster. He was a bright, quick lad. He had made up his mind, at an early age, to devote his life to teaching. When he reached Canada he worked only to save, and go to college. When his money was spent he was going to work again to obtain means for the completion of his training, when a kind neighbour, who had noticed his self-devotion to the object of his life, stepped forward and offered to lend him the money he required to qualify himself as a teacher. The offer was accepted. The loan has been repaid long ago; and the brave fellow is now at the head of a school, with a first-class certificate. His gratitude to the Home, and to the beneficent lady who supports it, he has lately expressed in a long, affecting letter. It is addressed, "Unto thee who hast been the chief of all my friends." Here is a lad rescued from crime. He was not on the brink of crime when the doors of the home were opened to him. He had been committed to prison for robbery five times; and had been described, in all probability, by some police-court reporter, as "an incorrigible young vagabond." I opened another boy's letter, from Canada West. He was doing well.

"He," said the master, "was one of the gang of young roughs who pitched into the master at Pye Street, Westminster. They were sad young savages. I was asked if I would take the risk of them. I accepted them at once, and never had any trouble with them. This boy, now in Canada West, had a sweet disposition."

The master pointed to a group of flowers, in water-colours, framed and glazed, and hanging over the mantelpiece. "That picture was painted by one of the stupidest boys I ever had in my life. I couldn't make anything of him at first. I used to see him always scribbling on his slate. I looked over once or twice, and saw that he had some idea; his rough sketches were better than any I could have managed. So I gave him some bits of colours, and he did that."

"That" was a cluster of flowers skilfully grouped and delicately manipulated. Near it were some smaller works, by the boy's pupils.

"He's all right now," the master continued; "he's a chemist's assistant, and he is about to be married."

In this way we discussed the careers of many of the boys, and found by their letters, and other evidence, that nearly all of them were doing well. About 50 are in Canada, and not four of this number have done badly. There are also 47 boys from this Home, serving in the navy. These facts will show the public the good that may be done with "incorrigible rascals" who have been committed to prison five times, or more. Of the 185 lads now under the care of the master, not more than 40 have been admitted without payment; and for these 40 the beneficent patroness of the Home provides, as she provided for all until the Home was certified: as she still pays apprenticeships, guarantees rent—in short, everything that it is necessary for her to pay, in order to secure the continued prosperity of the Home. Many of the boys are from Lancashire; some are sent by the Surrey Society (a benevolent society of Surrey magistrates who make a fund together), who pay 5s. a week for every boy they send; some are brought by the city missionaries; and some are sent by benevolent people round about—who often recommend when they decline to pay. The boys brought by private individuals are free to go when they choose; but the rest are strictly prisoners under the Reformatory Act. For the convicted boys, Mr. Leyland receives 6s. weekly per head; the allowance was 7s. The lesser sum is enough, if not more than enough, as I shall endeavour to show.

It is most important, since the number of children confined, convicted under the Reformatory and Industrial Schools Acts, is yearly on the increase, to discover the just price due to the masters of reformatory homes like this admirably administered one in which I find myself. In 1854, there were only eight reformatories in England and Scotland; in 1861, there were 64. In the year 1854, just 29 boys and girls were sent to these eight reformatories; in 1861, no less than 1743 children were rescued from the streets and prisons—the total number of inmates of English and Scotch reformatories being 4337. While the reformatories have increased, the commitments of juvenile offenders have decreased 48 per cent. The decrease was, according to Mr. Sidney Turner, greater in 1860. The late increase of juvenile crime is fairly attributable to the prevailing distress, which has promoted tramping in search of work, and has so produced begging and crime. Mr. Turner believes that the increase is also due to the temptations the reformatories offer to parents, to get their children committed to them, and to the difficulty of making parents contribute to their maintenance when the State has once got hold of them. It is with infinite regret that every man who has thought this question over will learn that very little money is got out of the parents of children in reformatories. Take this Wandsworth Home for Boys as an example. Of 83 boys admitted in 1861, 57 were received on first conviction. There were 119 boys in the home; their cost was £17, 12s. 5d. per head; and the parents' payments were £69, 18s. 11d.! If Miss Portal were not at hand—and if the Government refused here the grant of 6s. a week for each boy—these boys would, with one or two exceptions, starve or steal. They are here in comfort; and many a working man who has his children huddled in a garret, would be glad to see one or two of them enjoying the comforts and the education these juvenile criminals are enjoying. The temptation is strong; and it is dangerous to society, since it would make the cost of juvenile reformatories and industrial schools an intolerable burden. I believe that the present most excellent and experienced Inspector of Reformatories and Industrial Schools has looked sharply after the parents of children in the institutions under his control; yet he collected only £2439 in 1861. He recommends that children shall not be sent to a reformatory after a first commitment; holding that this rule would decrease the parents' temptation to get rid of their children. I believe such a rule would have no good effect; since children once committed to prison, and sent forth at the expiration of their sentence into the streets, start at once on the round of wrong. If their parents desire their removal to a reformatory, they will carefully incite them to the commission of the second felony. The twice convicted are more expensive, it must be remembered, than the once convicted. Again, if by this rule Mr. Turner suggests within reformatory wards, we shall crowd our houses of correction; and the reformatory costs less than the gaol. I would venture to ask Mr. Turner whether the law might not be made more stringent against parents?

When a father abandons his child; when, by his neglect or evil teaching, he brings it to the felons' dock before it can see over the bar; and when he commits it to the care of the State in its tender years, he shows himself a bad member of society, or, at the least, an incapable one. The child he calls incorrigible, is found to have a sweet disposition in a reformatory; the boy he thrust out of his door is now a school professor in Canada! He owes the public the cost of this duty done for him, and he should be made to pay it. If every defaulting parent were severely punished, registered, forced to keep the reformatory in which his child was living informed of his whereabouts; and, if they who could not pay in coin were compelled to work out the debt, Mr. Turner would soon find a difference in "parents' payments." This payment to the reformatory is a sacred debt. It is only a poor atonement to the outraged State at the best. Put the defaulting parent in the stoneyard, or at oakum-picking, or, if possible, at more remunerative employment, and he would not hang back a second time. The sick, and lame, and crazy should be excused; but every man and woman who can pay in work or money should be compelled to pay.

The admirable organization of the Wandsworth Home for Boys, where "they really do work," will most forcibly fix in the mind of any visitor this pregnant question,--Should these boys cost six shillings a week each? Their labour is great and various. All the work in the house is done by themselves. They wash their own linen, make and repair their own clothes, and cook their own victuals. In addition, they raise their own vegetables, or enough for a part of the year, and actually build their own workshops and dormitories. They tear rags for the paper-maker; and a party of them—builders—are building some little villas for the master hard by. Yet I find in Mr. Turner's last report that the industrial profits derived from the industry of 119 boys throughout the year 1861 were only £66, 19s. 11d.—say 10s. per boy per annum! Now, many of these boys are verging on manhood. They cannot be committed to a reformatory when more than sixteen years of age. Many, however, who are nearly eighteen, declare to the magistrate they are not sixteen. Surely such boys can earn more than 10s. per annum. In the Warwickshire Reformatory for Boys, at Weston, near Leamington, 29 boys earned £118, 1s. 4d.

The lads at this institution are older than the average of boys in reformatories; but I would undertake to pick out 29 from among Mr. Leyland's colony as old as the eldest of the Warwickshire boys. The Redhill boys are credited with about £4 per annum each against their cost. When I said that six shillings per week was enough for the Government to pay for every boy sent to a refuge, I did not go far enough; since I am confident that these boys could be maintained with profit to reformatory keepers or managers for a much less sum. A manager pointed out to me the absurdity of limiting a criminal boy's labour, more than the labour of a free boy's labour is limited. What is a fair day's work for a boy outside a reformatory is a fair day's work for one in a reformatory. Now, six hours of every day must be set apart for instruction; whereas three hours would be ample time. We are not seeking to rear Admirable Crichtons, but skilled working men, who shall have the best of all education for a child of the working class, viz., that which will enable him to earn his daily bread. If the cost of the reformatory and industrial school systems could be lessened, they might be extended. The less the cost of each boy, the more boys the State will be able to maintain. But this is not all. Why should boys be set free directly their labour becomes valuable? Why should the elder ones not help to keep the younger? They owe this to the State, which has been a father to them. By the adoption of this principle, reformatories might be made almost, if not quite, self-supporting, and reformatory lads would not be sent out into the world until they were fully able to earn their living, and were thoroughly habituated to a regular, industrious, and moral life. The present reformatory system includes that which has become so odious in the sight of the public—viz., the ticket-of-leave. Boys are sent to a reformatory for not less than two nor more than five years. If a boy's conduct is good, he is let out with a license at the expiration of one-half of his term. The aim of the Government is to get rid of the cost of his keep as soon as possible. He is kept while his labour is of little or no value comparatively, and is parted with directly he is able to support himself. That he is not thoroughly reformed, then, is proved by the license which is given to him: he must still be guarded; he must report himself personally at his reformatory once a month; or, if at a distance, he must send a certificate from his clergyman and his employer. Agents from the reformatory visit him at his work. In short, he is not deemed strong enough to run alone. I believe that if the evidence of all masters of reformatories were taken, it would point to the expediency of keeping boys until they had returned to the State, by the proceeds of their industry, the money the State had spent on their reformation and tuition.

I made a minute inspection of the Boys' Home, at Bridge House, Wandsworth. The apartment or hall (for it was as spacious and ornamental as many an assembly-room in a second-rate provincial town), which is school-room, chapel, and dining-room, is filled with transverse rows of desks and forms. Tin mugs were placed at numbered intervals upon the desks, and under the desks were recesses for books, etc. Leading from this comfortable apartment, where one or two boys are engaged drying linen at a roaring fire, was a long, broad workshop. On each side the boys were ranged at workstands behind great upright knives, tearing rags for Messrs. M'Murray, whose paper-mills are at hand. They were all hard at their work: some were sharpening the knives, others were carrying the torn rags to be weighed, and others, again, were sorting the rags. They are allowed 1d. or 1½d. per diem for their work, according to the skill and energy displayed. Every boy has a sack marked with his number, so that the overlookers know who has been adroit and who has been negligent or lazy. Two boys were literally employed jumping in sacks, to press the rags into them. This is the probationary room, where the new-comers begin their industrial education, and remain six or nine months. Behind is a large garden and orchard. Twelve boys, under two head boys or directors, are digging or clearing parsnips, and sifting ashes for the garden walks. In this garden is a covered bath, where the young fellows disport themselves once a week, having tepid water from the engine-boiler in the winter. These garden boys are being thoroughly educated as gardeners. While I was walking in the grounds, watching the workers, the master told me some anecdotes about them.

"I had one boy here," he said, "who was about nineteen years of age when he came. Of course he had sworn that he was not sixteen; and how are the magistrates to tell? One day he lifted the poker at one of the masters, and swore he would strike the first person, on the head, who approached him. I heard of this, and went into the room with a stick. I desired him to put down the poker at once. He still threatened; but a sharp rap over the knuckles knocked it from his hand; and now there cannot be a better fellow. He was a desperate customer from Coldbath-fields, but now he is as tractable as a child, and can be trusted away alone, a mile off, to dig in the gravel-pits. I have always eight boys outside taking the vans about with firewood, or fetching rags from the paper-mills. They go as far as Richmond. Sometimes they bring £5 or £6 a day in. In five years only two boys have kept back part of the money. One made off, but I caught him in the pit of the Victoria Theatre. I punished him with three days of bread and water. He is all right now; in a good situation; doing well. The other young defaulter is now trustworthy, and is overseer, with about fourteen men under him, in a bedstead manufactory."

"Some of them are the most cunning rogues on the face of the earth. One, a bit of a boy, wanted to have a little time out, and he proceeded in this way. He fell down in one of the dormitories, clasped his elbow, and set up a howl that soon attracted me to the spot. He had, he said, hurt his arm. Every touch gave him excruciating pain. I took him next morning to the doctor, who examined the elbow, which was very red. He said no bone was broken, but the arm was injured. It was suggested that he had better go to St. Thomas's Hospital. He returned with his arm neatly bound in splints (which it was afterwards discovered the artful scamp had cut out of two lesson boards), and an order, duly drawn up, that he was to go on the morrow. This continued for a day or two; and at last he brought an order in which the arm was described as in a state of mortification. This aroused my suspicions; but there was the order on the printed hospital form. I went to the hospital, and had a sharp interview with the young dressers. They knew nothing of the case. I returned to the boy, and told him to take his jacket off. He pretended that it was impossible to move his arm; however, I stood over him with a rope, and he took it off as well as I could. There was nothing the matter with his arm. He had contrived this plot in order to spend a day or two with some friends of his—publicans. He obtained the order by going to the hospital, getting his blank ticket, and leaving with it before he reached the surgeon's room. He had been in prison many times, although he was only fourteen years of age. He is now in America, preparing to be a schoolmaster.

"Then we had a boy who shammed fits. In his feigned delirium he called out, 'I'm to be hanged to-morrow morning!' I sent for the doctor, who laughed, and said, 'You can cure him better than I can.' He suggested a shower-bath. We carried him to it; and he kept up the deceit all the time. He was stripped and put in the bath. The instant the water fell upon him he leapt up. I was at hand with a rod, and gave him one cut, and he was off, running as fast as his legs could carry him, to his bed. I asked him his reason for the sham, and he said the boys told him I had released a boy who had fits, so he thought he would try. He is now in the army, and as good a boy as ever broke the world's bread."

Gossiping in this way, we passed back through the cotton-tearing department, to the playground. It was a cheerful place enough. There were pigeons flying about; there was a swing for the boys, and two vans were being loaded or unloaded. I watched a group of boys counting and stacking firewood. There was one distinguishable at a glance from the rest. He was a merchant's son, sent here for having committed some crime in his family. The master said he had a boy who could speak three languages.

We visited the tailors' and shoemakers' shops, which led the master to observe that the boys had made everything he stood upright in, except his hat and overcoat. It was as we were mounting the steps that lead to the firewood department, that the master called to my mind Squire Baker's Reformatory in

Gloucestershire, where the boys' industry pays all their expenses. The firewood department is carried on in an airy and lofty gallery. The wood is cut with circular saws, into blocks. Along the gallery are compartments or berths; three boys work in each. One chops the wood, one sorts it, and one presses and ties it into bundles. Each party must do at least 600 bundles per diem. This done they may off to play, having earned one penny each. In a corner berth were two boys, one was chopping and one was tying bundles. A window behind him was broken. The master inquired how it was done. A boy had pitched a block of wood at it. "He was not at work, of course," said the master. The boy replied in the negative, and we passed on. The master told us a tragic story.

"That boy," said he, "who was tying up the bundles, had a narrow escape of his life a little time ago. He had offended another boy in the course of the day, a boy who had been with us about three months. This boy secreted a chopper when he went to bed at night; and about three or four in the morning, when everybody was asleep, the little fellow—for he was a very small boy—crept out of his bed, and went from sleeper to sleeper until he had found his victim. He then pulled back the clothes, and before he could be reached had given four frightful chops on the sleeper's head. The boy you saw has a bit cut out of his skull now. It was found in the blood on the bed-clothes afterwards. The teacher rushed into the room. I was called up, and found the boy lying, I thought dead, in the school-room. All his ferocious assailant said was—'I've done the deed.' He was tried, and coolly pleaded guilty, but was prevailed upon to withdraw the plea. He was in the end condemned to fifteen years' penal servitude."

This revengeful young monster came from Nottingham, where he had already committed violence on a companion, a fact that was not sent with him.

There are three dormitories in the Home; one for unconvicted boys, one for boys who have been convicted once, and one—a fine gallery with top-lights, like a South Kensington picture-gallery—for boys who have been convicted more than once. I will conclude by a reference to Mr. Sidney Turner's last report on this Home. He complained that it was too crowded—considering the little out-of-door work it offers and its position—when there were 119 boys in it: now the numbers are 185; but I confess I saw ample accommodation and employment for the present number. I protest, with him, however, against boys being sent hither from Lancashire because they are admitted without immediate payment.

CHAPTER XII.

HARD DRILL.

WHEN I stepped out of the train at the Feltham station I found no difficulty in tracing my steps to the great Middlesex Industrial School which has been so frequently and so severely criticised. A policeman was at hand, with a boy about whom there could be no mistake. He was most unquestionably bound, under a magistrate's warrant, for the reformatory school. There was that in his appearance, shambling gait, dog's-eared pockets, and sharp, troubled face, I have never been able to reduce to words. The anxious, assured, querulous look of these men-boys who offend the law and take their punishment, is familiar to all who have had to deal with large numbers of juvenile criminals. I followed in the wake of the policeman, through the quiet village of Feltham, and along a pleasant English road—speculating how it had come to this pass with the urchin before me, who was now and then talking to the policeman, and who, as we approached the school—a vast pile of red brick buildings—took an apple from his pocket, and munched it rapidly. He had some misgivings as to the rules of the establishment, the handsome lodge and iron gates of which he was approaching; and was making sure of his apple. I rang the lodge bell, and, as I waited the arrival of the gate-keeper, my eye wandered over the broad acres about the school, where the boys, in grey gangs, overlooked by masters in the county uniform, were digging in lines. The boys wore blue-grey blouses, and close round caps, variously bound. Some caps were bound with white, others with yellow: the colours marking the section to which the wearer belonged. I signed my name in the visitor's book, showed my magistrate's order to inspect the establishment, and then passed along a smooth-gravelled road, past the gangs of boys at work, who stared at me as I went by; and then turned, not too energetically, to their work again. The policeman, with his charge, was close behind me. In the clerk's office I found the officials ready to give me every possible assistance, and I should have been at once despatched on my rounds had I not expressed a wish to see the new-comer installed. The policeman entered, followed, meekly, by the boy.

"What have you been about?" said the clerk.

"Taking my master's money," the boy answered.

I questioned the policeman, who had been very

kind to the lad on the road. It appeared that the boy was in the employ of a milkman, and that he had robbed his employer more than once, whereupon a magistrate had made out a warrant for his removal hither, to be schooled and reformed for three years. His parents were to pay 1s. 6d. weekly towards his support; little enough, since the cost of each boy in the establishment is about 10s. a head per week. The doctor entered briskly, and told the boy to take his jacket and shirt off. The boy slowly and clumsily obeyed. He was then examined on the head, between the fingers, etc., and passed. Hence he would be conducted to the infirmary, where he would have a hot bath, be divested of his rags (which would be fumigated), and habited in a suit of school clothes, bound in the colour of his class. The plan of this, the largest industrial school in England, is well thought out and well carried out. It is spaced off into sections, each section being a complete and distinct establishment in itself. A description of one section or school, which is made to accommodate fifty boys, will suffice. Long, light, clean corridors stretch throughout the building. Having passed through the handsome entrance-hall (which is like that of a nobleman's mansion), with the justices' rooms on one side, and the superintendent's and chaplain's dwellings and offices on the other, we entered the first corridor. The doors on our left led to the various domestic offices of the vast establishment. The boys, as in other industrial schools, do all the work. They scour, wash, mangle, and fold; just like so many girls. Here are some dozen boys, in their comfortable loose uniform, counting linen for their companions, who are labouring in the fields yonder. Others are managing the patent drying apparatus; others, again, are cleaning the coppers, and making all neat about the washing troughs. The kitchen, where an old soldier presides as cook (and where the policeman whom I followed from the station is waiting to have that "bit of something" to eat that was ordered him in the clerk's office), is a wonder of cleanliness. The deal tables are as white as sheets of paper; the metal utensils sparkle in the light. Against the wall the framed diet-table of the boys is suspended—whence I gather the fact that the youngsters have six ounces of meat three times a week, and one pound and a quarter of bread daily. There are all kinds of amusing economies hereabouts. The steam-engine close at hand, has its work cut out for it. It supplies the establishment with water, and the cooking is done by steam. All is on a large scale, for the establishment was built to accommodate 800 boys, and there are nearly 600 within its walls at the present time, to say nothing of some 50 officers of various grades. "We have three cardinal points to which all our exertions tend," said the superintendent, "cleanliness, order, and industry."

I had already seen samples of all the points. Every operation appeared to be going forward with the regularity and quiet of clockwork. As we passed along the corridors, we met boys at intervals, who saluted us in military style. Each had his duty in hand; not one was idle, and not one was where he should not be. I remarked that there were doors across the corridors at regular intervals.

"These doors," said the superintendent, "completely shut out one school, a section, from the other, making each an establishment complete in itself."

The tailor's room was a lofty, well-ventilated apartment, where some five-and-twenty boys were sitting cross-legged, busily plying the needle, under the vigilant eye of a master. By the fire stood a most miserable-looking lad, whose hair had been cut close to his head, so that it looked like the back of a mouse. I inquired what his offence was. The superintendent ordered him to stand forward. He was asked why his hair had been cropped. He answered—"For taking money from my friends." The answer was given in a meek, subdued voice. The boy was dispirited, and thoroughly ashamed—a picture of dejection. He had not, it should be understood, stolen one farthing, but he had accepted money from one of his comrades, and the school rules forbade this. While the master-tailor showed us the stout pilot suits making for the boys who were going into the navy, this cropped boy stood at hand, and I could not help thinking that the punishment he was suffering was disproportioned to his offence. I marked a second cropped boy among the budding tailors, and was told that he had been cropped by mistake.

We returned to the endless corridor, passing doors on each side, until we halted by a narrow transverse passage. This led us to the bath. Some five-and-twenty boys, under the superintendence of a master, were bathing, or drying, or dressing themselves. They looked blue with cold; their teeth were chattering. Over the bath were the solitary confinement cells. They were dark and bare enough—four walls, and a rug to lie folded in, at night. The superintendent opened one of the doors, with a loud noise; but the prisoner was fast asleep, and had not been disturbed. He woke as by instinct, at the superintendent's summons. He was a runaway, who had been brought back that morning. He looked dejected and wo-begone, while the superintendent described his case and fate.

"He will remain here," said the superintendent,

"till the magistrates meet eight days hence. They will deal with him. He will be flogged."

The next cell contained a second runaway. I remarked that the boys had neither socks nor braces.

"We remove them always; it's military rule. They are wonderfully cunning. There's one here (in another cell) who was found altering his blouse, to make it like a coat. This was his preparation for absconding. He will be flogged to-night by the drill-master."

As we descended to the corridor, the boys were issuing from the bath-room in double file, and to military word of command. Along the corridors we constantly caught the master's sharp words, "Right wheel. Halt. Left wheel." Along the central line of the corridor lay bundles of the boys' clothes, and they marched until they faced those bundles, when they were halted, and they clothed themselves with military precision.

Let us now turn from the corridor at a broad opening, and wheeling to the right, enter the first schoolroom. No plan could be better devised. This room is the refectory and school-room of fifty boys. In the centre is a large open stove, well protected by a high screen. Behind it, raised, are the masters' desks; facing the masters are a series of desks, raised like the gallery of a theatre, to the wall, and railed off from the centre of the room. On the central floor are four deal tables, with forms, etc. These are for the boys' meals; the raised desks for their lessons. Everything is as clean and trim as the cabin of a man-of-war. A door by the side of the master's desk leads to the distinct and separate playground belonging to the school; a door in the playground wall leads to the general grounds and workshops. By this arrangement these fifty boys are kept distinct from the rest while they are taught, while they sleep, and while they play; the sections mingle only to work in the fields or in the shops. When I was walking in the grounds in the evening, I was amused to see the companies of boys marching with military precision, and one to the lively airs of a penny whistle, skilfully played by a little fellow in the ranks. They were going from the various workshops to their respective sections—the boys belonging to each section being dropped at the door of their school playground. This arrangement worked admirably. I inquired as to the school hours, and found to my great satisfaction that the chaplain has arranged that every boy shall have eighteen hours schooling per week. He is at liberty to do this, since the school is under its own special Act—an Act, by the way, which has its serious defects, as I shall presently show. The superintendent wisely insisted on the primary necessity of teaching the boys to work, and to work hard. Idleness and uncleanliness, those two foul fruits of life in the gutter, are their main vices. Industry and cleanliness will bring moral susceptibility and a desire for knowledge. In an industrial school, therefore, the workshop is the first and best school. The strict attention which is paid to order struck me. The boys are compelled when they enter the school-room to take their boots off, and put on slippers. The boots are neatly arranged in rows along the corridors, and the draught of air dries them. The slippers are unpacked and put on —the boys standing in lines like soldiers, as they stand when they begin or leave off work, and when they are summoned to meals. The master always speaks to them with the voice of a drill-sergeant. The seventy or eighty tailors, and the fifty or sixty shoemakers fall in, and wheel and face about. I saw them sit to their supper. They were marshalled by word of command, and marched to their bread and cocoa with the precision of Guards. They even raised their hands, and clasped them, and sang grace to the sharp orders of the master. This constant attention to time and regularity gives a military precision to their conduct and movements.

The superintendent repeated the complaint I have already had occasion to make two or three times. "It is constant teaching," he said. "Directly they begin to be thoroughly useful they leave. Most of them remain three years—that is, are committed for this time; but then they leave and others come."

I observed that the boys on leaving are more rationally treated here than they are at Redhill. A Redhill boy has sometimes as much as £20 to take away with him when he leaves the school. Such a sum is a temptation to parents. The few pounds a Feltham boy has carried off with him on his dismissal, have been known to be spent, or half spent, by him and his parents in the village hard by, and they have left for London in a state of intoxication. The three years would be thrown away, and the school gratuities won by good-conduct badges would be spent in the public-house. There are many of these boys whose parents would imitate this execrable example if the opportunity were still afforded them. In order to take from the bad parents of reformed boys the opportunity of robbing their children, the good-conduct money due to a boy when his term is completed, is given to him in two or three instalments, according to the character he can send from his employer, after he has left the school. By this means the chaplain keeps some hold on the boys after they have left school. They are compelled by self-interest, to report their whereabouts and conduct, in order to obtain the money that is due to them.

The police of the school is ingeniously provided for. "We want no police," said the superintendent to me as we walked through the hedgeless grounds, past the carpenter's and smith's shops, to the infirmary, a large square building apart from the rest of the institution. "Every man and boy round about is a guard; for we give any of our neighbours who bring back a runaway, 5s." While the superintendent was talking, I watched the drill-sergeant walking stealthily round the outer walls. "He is looking after skulkers," said the superintendent. The infirmary was a quiet, comfortable place. Nearly all the windows were darkened. They had remained so since the ophthalmia had broken out among the boys. Now chilblains were the prevalent ill. Every comfort was at hand that could minister to a body diseased; as in the institution itself every human want appeared to have been the snbject of attentive study. There were no luxuries, save that of cleanliness. The work was hard; the hours were long—from six in the morning in the summer: and the punishments were not of the mildest. Boys were reduced to No. 10 or No. 16, letter A or B. They had neither affection nor even regard about them. A line of conduct was traced out for them, and they must keep to it, or suffer the penalties prescribed for the government of the school. They could see their parents, or receive letters from them, once in three months only. The chaplain would speak some comforting words to them; they might get a pat on the head from the superintendent; but they must remain apart, wrapped up in their own thoughts, cut off from the world, and without the gentle tones of one womanly voice to expand and soften their nature. It is said to be the best that can be done for them, their natural parents having failed them; but it is a cold, and harsh, and desolate place, to abide in, for the young, who should still be under the maternal wing. As I watch the little fellows marching in columns from the fields, to the hoarse word of command, and see how completely the will is curbed and the heart is disregarded, in order that these large numbers may be dealt with; I look back to one or two little artificial homes I have seen supported by voluntary contributions, and am inclined to favour the less pretentious place of reformation, where the boy is not A 42, but still Jack Collins, with his own story about him—Jack whose idiosyncrasies are known to his master and mistress, and who is made to feel himself part of a new family. At Feltham he is one of a regiment. He is being kneaded in a vast, beautifully polished, complex machine; and he is expected to turn out a perfect specimen of humanity. The machinery is costly—some £14,000 last year for these 561 boys. Redhill, however, is a much more expensive machine, since it holds about 260 boys, and costs about £9000 annually.

It is instructive to see these intelligent lads, in the turner's shop, turning red-cedar candlesticks, or building shapely chests of drawers, or delving lustily in the gravel-pit, with their good-conduct stripes upon their arms, and health in their cheeks. But I doubt whether this constant strain on the spirits, and this incessant wheeling to the right and left are good. The boys are apt to become dogged. A very wise head has told us, that "the bow should be sometimes loose." I was struck with a remark from one of the authorities, that the boys would not play. When they had a half-holiday lately, and foot-balls were given them, one school was incited to challenge another; but no match could be got up. The boys held sullenly back, and broke into groups, and chattered. I saw them at play; one or two appeared to be endeavouring to be cheerful, and the rest were leaning so silently in line against the school-room wall, that I thought they were under punishment. A tame, meek boy, who was idly kicking a stone about, seemed utterly unable to rouse himself. He was going into the navy in a few days.

"We give them what will be useful to them when they leave," said the superintendent. "If a boy wants to emigrate, we help with £5. We give shoemakers one pound's worth of tools, when they leave; and carpenters two pounds' worth."

We were entering the farm-yard as we talked. It is a vast model yard; large enough for a farm of 350 acres, instead of 94 acres—the extent of the school farm. A long row of neat pig-styes (built by the boys), inhabited by prime Berkshire porkers, and mounds of potatoes laid up for the winter, were evidences that the farming of this great Middlesex industrial experiment had been begun in earnest. The pigs are consumed by the officers of the school, the boys not being allowed to taste pork. The consequence is, as the superintendent's punishment-book shows, they frequently steal it. In this book I found this entry—"Stealing piece of pork, six strokes on each hand with cane." There are regular farm-boys, who will be brought up to agricultural pursuits exclusively.

Corporal punishment, it will be seen, is known in this Middlesex model school. It may be necessary here, but it is not in smaller schools. Here no boy is ever trusted beyond the grounds on any pretext whatever. No faith, therefore, can be placed in him. There is no strong appeal to his honour possible.

When he enters the school he is a prisoner; and when he leaves it he is absolutely free. The special Act of Parliament under which this school exists—faulty in many respects—is especially faulty in this: that it does not permit the authorities to put a child out under a letter of license, that license being revocable. None of these boys go out with waggons and wood, and receive money and return honestly home. They remain close prisoners, well housed, well fed, well washed and clothed, and sufficiently educated. But they are automata, wound up by the visiting justices. They have no more volition than pith figures upon a piano. Sapient magistrates play, and they dance; an oracular nose pronounces over their meat and cocoa; a mentor in blue and buff frowns over the chaplain's regulations. If the great machine moves smoothly, it is because the superintendent is one of those men with will at once firm and gentle, with a manner made to command, and with a free, fresh nature, and a head wise and orderly; a man made for the place, if ever there was one. His voice is never angry, and he will not allow the boys to think for one moment that he has a personal interest in punishing them. When they steal from his private rooms, he takes no notice of it. Captain Brooks is fortunate in his chaplain, the Rev. N. G. Pilkington, who has drawn up the most sensible rules and regulations for his schools I have yet seen; and who carries out all the details of his interesting mission with the most exemplary zeal. He follows his scholars to their places of employment after they have left the school; and encourages them to keep up a correspondence with him as their best friend. This is the best side of the system. On the other hand, there is an elaborate detective machinery kept up, by which officers of the school, some of whom are sworn in as constables, can swoop upon runaways, and carry them back to their section and the birch. The birch, the cane, bread-and-water, solitary confinement, and incessant drill—these are the terrors ever present to the Feltham boy's mind. It was painful to see them march from the school form to the supper form; 1, 2, 3, lift their hands in prayer; again, 1, 2, 3, lower their hands, and take their seats before their iron mugs of cocoa, and set to in solemn silence. Not a word must be spoken during meal-time. And why? The day has been spent in the workshop, in the fields, and in school. It is dark. The boys are weary. Why should they be doomed to sit elbow to elbow munching their dry bread? It is enough to freeze the heart out of them, and it is through the heart they must be reformed.

One of the happier features of this gigantic institution was the singing. Some of the masters are very proud, as well they may be, of their scholars' musical accomplishments. I heard two or three of the sections sing choruses, sacred music, "The last rose of summer," etc., with excellent effect, and with delicacy of execution. They have a band also, and many of the boys play a musical instrument well—as witness the little penny piper I heard a while in the grounds. Boys are rewarded with grants of little plots of ground, that are marked off outside the playground walls.

I have now a few words to say on the instrument of terror that overshadows the school, and may well make the stoutest boy tremble. The corporal punishments are administered by a tall, muscular drill-master, who has, I believe, been in the army. The punishment-book shows that his muscle is not seldom brought into requisition. Strokes on the hand, and a dozen with the birch, meet many offences, as "very gross insubordination," and altering blouses with a view to absconding. I witnessed three canings and two floggings with the birch. I may be chicken-hearted, but I confess that when I saw a boy stretched upon a table—when I saw him stripped, and held by two or three stout men, while a fourth —a stalwart, deliberate disciplinarian—with a long birch, struck the naked flesh with his full might, pausing between each blow, while the urchin shrieked with agony, and implored forgiveness, I confess I thought it was a brutal sight for any eyes to look upon, and I pitied the forty-nine boys who were bound to witness it. Again, when this same stalwart drill-master took a heavy cane, and struck a boy's hand with such force that the cane whistled through the air, and the boy in his agony writhed like a cut worm, I looked on with a strong feeling that this was bad and brutal. I am told that it is necessary, but I should like all who advocate the birch to see it in operation. It is said it flogs the vice out of a boy, but I am inclined to think it is apt to flog the heart out of him.[1]

[1] REFORMATORY DRILL AND DISCIPLINE.

One of a series of papers appearing in the *Post* on "The London Poor," in an account of the Middlesex Industrial School at Feltham, contains the following statements, amongst others, respecting the discipline to which the boys at that establishment are subjected:—

"I saw them sit to their supper. They were marshalled by word of command, and marched to their bread and cocoa with the precision of Guards. They even raised their hands and clasped them, and sang grace to the sharp orders of the master."

This devotional drill, then, at the above-named Reformatory, forms part of what is meant by the "religious instruction," which it is so necessary, as we are told, to combine with secular teaching.

Again, we read that—

"It was painful to see them march from the school form to the supper form; 1, 2, 3, lift their hands in prayer; again 1, 2, 3, lower their hands, and take their seats before their iron mugs of cocoa, and set to in solemn silence."

When the consecrated wafer is carried about the streets of some

I will now afford the reader the few facts and figures Captain Brookes was obliging enough to let me glean from the MS. of his forthcoming report of what has been done at Feltham during the year 1862.

The annual report of the superintendent up to the 1st January 1863 gives the following details:—

During the past year, 193 boys have been admitted, being an increase of 4 as compared with last year, the annual admissions since the opening of the school being as follow:—In 1859, 103 boys were admitted; in 1860, 210; in 1861, 189; in 1862, 193—showing an average annual admission of 173¾ boys.

During the past year, 89 boys have been dis-

foreign town in which British troops are quartered, our soldiers, if it happens to be borne past them in procession, are sometimes commanded to present arms to it, for the purpose of conciliating the priests and humouring the natives. The result of this compulsory manual exercise of idolatry, on the part of those who are obliged to perform it, is perhaps considerably more beneficial than the devotional manœuvres above described as executed by the scholars of the Feltham Reformatory at the word of command. Both the soldiers and the boys are likely to be impressed with a contempt for the mechanical observance imposed upon them; only in the case of the soldiers that contempt is contempt for the worship of a cake; in the boys' case it is something more.

The Middlesex Model School at Feltham is an institution for the reformation of young thieves, but its arrangements for developing the religious sentiment in the youthful mind appear to be such as may be conceived to have been devised for mutual edification by the inmates of an asylum for idiots.

For the encouragement of aspirations to endless bliss, the plan of accustoming children to obey the command "1, 2, 3, lift your hands in prayer," and making them sing grace "to the sharp orders of a master," does not promise to be successful to a certainty. Of another place than Heaven, however, from what the writer above quoted says further on, it seems likely that these lads are sufficiently well impressed with some idea:—

"The corporal punishments are administered by a tall, muscular drill-master, who has, I believe, been in the army. The punishment book shows that his muscle is not seldom brought into requisition. Strokes on the hand, and a dozen with the birch, meet many offences, as 'very gross insubordination,' and altering blouses with a view to absconding. I witnessed three canings, and two floggings with the birch. I may be chicken-hearted, but I confess that when I saw a boy stretched upon a table—when I saw him stripped, and held by charged, 5 have absconded (of whom 4 are still at large, and 1 in Coldbath Fields Prison), 2 have died, 2 have been sentenced to 3 years' penal servitude, and 1 has been granted a free pardon.

The number now in the school is 561, independent of 4 at large, and 2 in Coldbath Fields Prison.

The gross expenditure for the year amounts to £13,207, 14s. 9d., which, when compared with that of similar institutions, shows (says the superintendent) that care and economy have been exercised in the management. For instance, the Redhill Reformatory during the year 1861 contained an average of 261 boys, and cost £9337; whereas, during the same

two or three stout men, while a fourth—a stalwart, deliberate disciplinarian—with a long birch, struck the naked flesh with his full might, pausing between each blow, while the urchin shrieked with agony, and implored forgiveness, I confess I thought it was a brutal sight for any eyes to look upon, and I pitied the forty-nine boys who were bound to witness it. Again, when this same stalwart drill-master took a heavy cane, and struck a boy's hand with such force that the cane whistled through the air, and the boy in question writhed like a cut worm, I looked on with a strong feeling that this was bad and brutal."

If such tortures as those above detailed are possible in this world for naughty children, what limits can be imagined to the penal possibilities of the next? If a drill-master exists, capable of using all his might to scourge a naked little boy who shrieks with agony, and vainly implores forgiveness, or of slashing a lad on the hand with a heavy cane while he writhes like a cut worm, the sufferer who realizes these horrible truths will find little difficulty in accepting all that literal orthodoxy teaches about an ulterior executioner with horns and tail.

It may be impossible for a reformatory to go on without some corporal punishment; and flogging, merciless as that which is inflicted at the Feltham establishment, may be necessary in the case of a boy who has no feeling sufficient to restrain his evil passions but fear. Only, it would be as well to keep such a boy in confinement for life, and never turn him loose on society with all humanity whipped out of him, and his hatred, malice, and lust of vengeance lashed into madness. Flogging is a fine thing; but how strange that its application is limited to boys and soldiers and sailors: to children of tender age, and members of an honourable profession! Wouldn't it be at least as suitable to garroters, and even to cruel swindlers, whose exemplary torture, in comparison with the misery caused by their crimes, would be the lesser evil of the two?—*Punch*, Feb. 14, 1863.

year, this school at Feltham contained an average of 385 boys, and cost £9350; that is to say, that this school maintained an average of 124 more boys than Redhill, at the same expense.

Captain Brookes, however, trusts that the cost of this establishment (now the first heavy outlay is over) will show a material reduction at the end of next year. Up to this date, provision has had to be made for the requirements of a constantly-increasing establishment. The establishment, it is believed, has now reached its full growth.

A table showing the ages and number of previous commitments of 193 boys admitted during the year 1862, states that 36 had been in prison once, 10 twice, 4 three times, and 3 above three times.

The total number in the school on the 1st January 1862, was 464; 3 were re-admitted, and 193 were admitted during the year—making a total of 660. These were disposed of as follows:—89 were discharged on completion of the term of detention, 5 absconded, and were not retaken, 2 were sentenced to three years' penal servitude, 2 died, 1 received a free pardon.

A table showing the various offences of the 193 boys admitted during the year 1862, states that 143 were charged with larceny and petty theft, 5 with larceny by servants, 3 with larceny from person, 2 larceny in dwelling-house, 7 with attempting to steal, 2 with unlawful possession, 2 fraudulent offences, 1 housebreaking with theft, 4 wilful damage, 19 vagrancy, 1 obtaining money under false pretences, 3 uttering counterfeit coin, 1 forgery.

Speaking of the ages of boys at the time of admission, the report shows that 29 (out of the 193) were under 10 years of age, 29 were 10 and under 11, 39 were 11 and under 12, 64 were 12 and under 13, 32 were 13 and under 14. Of these, 71 have lost one parent, 16 have lost both parents, 8 have been deserted by one parent, and 2 by both, 12 have a step-father, and 12 a step-mother, 3 have one parent in prison, 9 were uncontrolled by one parent only, and 4 by both, 81 were under the control of one parent only, and 85 of both.

The chaplain has submitted to me the results of his extensive experience, which I shall present to the reader in a separate chapter. They are too important to be dismissed in a few words.

CHAPTER XIII.

RESCUED FROM THE STREETS.

A CLOSE examination of the Feltham Industrial School has led me to the conclusion that it is a very costly experiment. It is built regardless of expense, its rooms are well finished and lofty, and architectural. The scent of the justices' dinner preparing while the sitting is going on suggests some good port not far off. It is evident that there is no voluntary contribution element in this "monumental" machinery for the reformation of the young Arabs of Middlesex. The Home-Office allows 5s. a head per week for every boy sent to a private reformatory under the Industrial Schools Act; and 6s. for reformatory boys who have been convicted; yet the Feltham boys, who are supported out of the county rates, cost more than 10s. a head per week. I am not prepared to dispute the assertion of the friends of this county school that it is most economically administered, and most efficiently conducted; but I present the facts of the case. I have given a truthful account of what is done at Wandsworth and what is done at Feltham. I confess that the latter institution, with its noble iron gates and its elegant hall, has advantages over the humble premises where Mr. Leyland rules, and where the munificence of Miss Portal is displayed. At Feltham all is done in the light of day. The floggings are severe, but they are regulated and recorded. Not a stroke of the cane is given without the sanction of authority. Here is no sly rope-end used to make a boy remove his jacket; no master who is monarch of all he surveys. Mr. Leyland is absolute master of a certain number of criminal and vagrant boys. The Government pay him 6s. a week for the criminals they send him, and Miss Portal pays him for the houseless whom he takes in free. He acts, and bargains, and chaffers on his own responsibility. He scorns the idea of a committee of control over him; he laughs at the idea of an annual report. I am not prepared to say that he is not a model reformatory master; a being specially fashioned and set apart to teach "the young idea" the way out of the crooked paths of life; so far as my observations extended, he appeared to have a rough but kindly view of his duties. The boys appeared to like and fear him. He walked about his premises —smiling, and full of encouraging words—*en souverain.* I only point to what might happen in an establishment like this, the sole control over which is an occasional visit from the Rev. Sidney Turner. Mr. Leyland finds that an Industrial Home pays at Wandsworth, with a Government allowance of 6s. a head for the criminal boys; and the question naturally suggests itself, why, if 6s. per week per boy suffices at Wandsworth, it should be insufficient at Feltham?

I have received a communication from Mr. Leyland, in which he assures me that my statement as to the money spent by the benefactress to his institution "needs considerable qualification." He remarks that "this sum would cover the whole expenses at the present time; and as the great majority of the inmates are received under magistrates' orders, of course the payment comes from the Home-Office." My reply is, that I took down Mr. Leyland's statement as he gave it to me, on the spot, in the presence of a gentleman who confirms my report of it. Mr. Leyland further observes that "it is only as regards the forty voluntary cases that we are dependent on private sources; and here again there is an error, as the £1000 which you state as having been the lady's outlay for last year would include payments for cases sent by other individuals, as well as those sent by the Surrey Society. Before the school was certified in 1858 the expenses were in a great measure borne by our benevolent foundress." If Mr. Leyland will be at the trouble of reading my description of his school a second time, he will see that my statement is almost identical with his own. I could not have made a mistake as to the figures, inasmuch as I wrote them down as they fell from his lips, in the presence of a third party.

I am free to confess that I prefer an establishment on Mr. Leyland's plan, to that which is paid for out of the county rates at Feltham, because I think the Middlesex school is an unwieldy one, in which no special influence can be brought to bear on any individuality. The boys are so many pegs on a cribbage-board; this is a vice or a weakness inseparable from a great school.

I will now glance at the Feltham chaplain's report, which I am happy to discover bears out, in many particulars, the remarks I have made on the industrial schools and reformatory systems. In the first place, Mr. Pilkington pronounces against Mr. Turner's idea that boys should not be put under reformatory discipline until they have been committed to prison more than once. He says:—" Waiting till a boy is convicted two or three times only renders him less susceptible to reforming influence when it is eventually brought to bear upon him, while it considerably increases the difficulty, upon his discharge, in providing for him some trade or occupation to enable him to earn his bread by honest industry; and if this is not done we suffer him to return to the same evil associations and neighbourhood reeking with crime, to sever him from which, three years' more or less expense and labour have been spent. When this is not prevented there is danger lest we should educate the thief." Nothing could be clearer. The boy who has once become a gaol-bird is much less likely to show a permanent reform than the boy who, after a first offence, has been at once severed from his bad associates. This, the most successful, is also the most economical course. Should we determine to permit boys to be committed to prison several times before they are eligible candidates for a reformatory school, we should be at the risk of educating astute thieves. They will only profit by the teachings of the schoolmaster, in order to carry on their future depredations on a more scientific basis. Mr. Pilkington justly remarks that his observations " apply more especially to London boys, as it is with them we have mainly to deal, and their real reformation is, in the majority of instances, only half completed unless combined with total separation from all former connexions upon their discharge, and anything tending to increase the difficulty in effecting this cannot fail to be an evil." Mr. Pilkington goes on to observe that boys easily learn to take a pride in their reputation as thieves when once they have graduated—a truth to which Mr. Henry Mayhew, and other gentlemen who have closely studied the criminal character, bear witness. Such boys undoubtedly exercise a harmful influence over all with whom they associate; and it is therefore for the sake of the better class of reformatory and industrial schoolboys, as well as on the grounds already stated, that it is expedient to whip the criminal urchin from the streets of London at the earliest possible opportunity. It is easy to discover whether a child who has been guilty of some trifling theft is in a fair way of becoming a habitual thief, or whether the parental control is sufficient to restrain him. We must always keep this point in view when we are dealing with juvenile crime—viz., that the rearing of a thief is much more expensive to the State than the rearing of an honest man. We go with the financial reformers when we advocate the speedy removal of criminal and vagrant children from London streets.

I agree with Mr. Pilkington that drunken and profligate homes are the chief nurseries of London juvenile criminals. Teaching by example is the most powerful teaching. When this teaching is bad, it is rational to remove the child from its influence, with all possible speed. It is a wrong done to the child, and a waste of money to the State, to send it again and again to prison, and still again and again to send it to its pernicious home. There is a wise distinction, however, which the chaplain draws between town and country children. He says, "On the other hand, a county may justly complain of having to support and teach for two or three years a young country urchin who may have been convicted for robbing an orchard, breaking down a mill-dam, stealing a fagot, or any similar petty theft, unless previous convictions can be proved against him. If it is a first offence, a month or two's separate confinement in prison would have, in most cases perhaps, the desired effect. But a country and a young London thief regard the same punishment in a totally different light; the former will, in very many instances, remember it with shame (and the chaplain, after four years' experience in a county house of correction, has had some opportunity of judging); the latter will look on it as a natural event in his life—certain to come sooner or later, as it had happened more or less to all about him." This distinction is astutely drawn. It puts the finger on the sore. The town boy, if very poor, lives in a criminal atmosphere, whereas the country boy has about him only the salutary anger of his neighbours, when he does wrong. The chaplain has been at much pains to trace the antecedents and surroundings of the boys who were sent last year to the school, and he has come to the conclusion that 140 out of 193 were entered in the annual returns as never previously committed; their *entourage* was such that their criminal career was cut out for them.

Another anxious task which lies before the chaplain of an industrial school is to provide for the reformed boys on their discharge. The leper has been cleansed. He is clean and whole. How shall he be put in the straight path so that he may have resolution enough to keep in it? Experience of the boys who have been set free unconditionally, shows that the return to bad associates and the old neighbourhood generally ends in a return to evil ways and to a speedy appearance in prison. The object, then, is to turn their thoughts and energies in a new direction—to "pastures new" in our colonies, or to the deck of a man-of-war. Employment in London has been found by the school authorities for many boys, but that which they obtain easily they value lightly. The chaplain's experience is that places obtained by him for discharged boys are not kept so long as situations obtained by their parents or themselves; so that he recommends the authorities to refrain from interference when parents have obtained situations for discharged boys, and merely to give pecuniary encouragement to the boys when they have held their situations a certain time. These are the fortunate cases. There remain the destitute, friendless boys, or the boys of depraved parents. For these there are the two services, the merchant service, emigration, and I should specially and honourably mention the Barking fishing-smack service of Messrs. Hewitt Brothers. The musicians of the school are easily placed in regimental bands. The navy is open only to boys who are under 15 years of age. And the chaplain points to a difficulty that affects the other outlets during the winter. These are closed, and yet boys are discharged in the winter as well as in the summer. Months of idleness lie between the discharged boy and the work for which he is destined. He must reach Canada in the summer, when there is a great demand for labour. The chaplain tells us that "in the fishing-smack service they positively refuse to take the boys between the months of November and March." This difficulty operates seriously against the success of the Middlesex Industrial School. The superintendent holds every boy in custody under a warrant, and he cannot discharge him one hour before the expiration of the time for which he has been committed. The boy must leave in December, when the school has no work to send him to, if his time expires in December; whereas, if the Act under which this school is conducted allowed letters of license, the superintendent would be able to part with boys when favourable opportunities offered for placing them well in life. The chaplain is right in urging upon the visiting justices the expediency of at once applying for power to do that which is done in every other reformatory, and with the most satisfactory results.

I am pleased to be able to record that the boys who have left Feltham have, with very few exceptions, turned out well. The chaplain speaks from experience which he has obtained with great labour, during the last three months of 1862. If 81 out of 128 are known to be doing well, and earning an honest living; if twelve only are "in very doubtful circumstances, living in bad neighbourhoods, without any stated employment;" and if fourteen have relapsed into crime, we may safely assert that the result of the system pursued in this great institution is satisfactory, especially when we bear in mind that the machinery is new and hardly yet in full working order.

I have had much experience of report-writing of late. Before me lie masses of secretarial eloquence, garnished with Biblical quotations, generally so suddenly and clumsily introduced, that they jar upon the reader's ear, and suggest cant rather than devotion. The process of filtering facts out of such verbiage as one generally sees presented as a rational account of a charitable society's doings, is a tedious and depressing one. The relief is delightful when one comes in contact with a chaplain of an institution who sets about his task earnestly and sensibly; and draws up his views of the work done and to be done in plain English, leaving the sermon for the pulpit, and the Bible for the closet. We know that we shall learn something from the experience he has to describe, and from the opinions he has based on his experience. Such an observer is this earnest, practical thinker, whose ideas on the duties he has done, and on those which remain to be accomplished, I have dwelt upon. I now offer the reader a few figures from his most interesting and instructive report.

The respective number of boys sent to the school in the years 1860-1-2, were 210, 189, and 193. Of these, 31 were deprived of mothers, 45 of fathers, and 20 were more or less nearly destitute; 34 did not know the alphabet, and 71 may be said to have known the alphabet only; 176 did not know the multiplication table, 107 could not write a line, 48 did not know the Lord's Prayer, and 76 did not know anything whatever of Jesus Christ, who he was, or how he died; only 25 out of 193 had apparently ever been taught a prayer, exclusive of the Lord's Prayer.

After this statement with reference to the general ignorance of the boys sent to this school, a table is given showing the educational state of 94 boys discharged during the year. Of this number, 48 could read well, and 25 very fairly; 62 could write fairly, 53 could do the compound and higher rules of arithmetic, 75 were able to pass a good examination in Holy Scriptures, 86 could repeat the Lord's Prayer, Creed, and Ten Commandments perfectly, and 87 knew as perfectly their morning and evening private prayers.

On referring to the educational system pursued throughout the school, we find that for three months during the last year the schools were more or less broken up on account of ophthalmia, which prevailed to such an extent as to necessitate three of the schools being turned into eye-wards.

The minimum weekly hours allowed for schooling are eighteen, and in no case has this time been exceeded. Each section is divided into two divisions, the latter containing two classes. The first division is in school on Monday, Wednesday, and Friday, from 9 to 12 A.M.; the second division on Tuesday, Thursday, and Saturday, from 6.30 to 7.45 P.M. daily. In October last a senior section was formed, into which 38 boys were drafted on account of their advanced state of education. All boys in this school are exempt from morning school, while their evening school is increased by three-quarters of an hour.

There is a prospect of having, in a few months, at least 100 boys in advanced sections, thus enabling them to devote the whole of the day to their respective trades and occupations.

The general conduct of the boys is good, the majority giving little or no trouble, and a few only being constantly reported and punished.

The journeys I have described among the refuges, reformatories, industrial schools, in and about London, will have given the reader a fair idea of the kind and extent of help which is extended to the poor, helpless, and fallen of the metropolis. Two or three more visits will complete this part of the task with which I set out on my travels among the London poor. This part is not one-third of the whole. Having examined the machinery already in existence for the mitigation of the sufferings of the poor, and for the reformation of the fallen, it remains to be seen how far this machinery may be beneficially extended.

There is a ship off Purfleet which is arranged as a reformatory for criminal boys. The first boy was admitted to it in June 1859. From that time the number of boys on board has steadily increased; and the discipline which prepares youths for life at sea, appears to have been attended with encouraging results. The adventurous nature of a sea-life, with its changes and dangers, accords with the roving disposition of the vagrant boy; who is, as a rule, the criminal boy. Let me tell the reader what the managers of the good ship "Cornwall" have to show by way of result after two years and a half of experience.

The "Cornwall" frigate was certified as a reformatory school on the 2d of May 1859, and, as I have said, the first boy was admitted on the 6th of June in the same year. On the 31st of the following December there were 46 boys on board, and during 1860, 81 were received. In 1861, 103 boys were admitted, and on the 31st December in that year the entries amounted to 230. Of these, six have been discharged to friends, five have absconded and been since reconvicted, three have died, six have been transferred to other reformatories, twenty-one have been provided for at sea, three have emigrated—leaving on board, December 31, 1861, 186. The Reformatory and Refuge Union contributed £15 towards the cost of the emigration.

The average number of boys on board in 1861 was 168. Of those discharged to friends two have gone to sea, one to Australia (doing well), one to a ship-building yard, one has left on the expiration of his time, one has been pardoned. Since the above date the entries have been 22. Of these, one has been discharged to friends (sentence expired), and 17 have gone to sea on license, making from the commencement 252 entries and 62 discharges, and leaving on board, on the 29th February last, 190 boys.

Of the 230 admitted to the 31st December 1861; 111 had not been previously convicted, 42 had been once, 36 twice, 20 three times, 6 four times, 4 five times, 11 above five times. Of these, 3 came from the county of Bedford, 3 from Devon, 1 Essex, 1 Herts, 5 Kent, 180 Middlesex, 35 Surrey, and 2 Yorkshire.

Their educational state was as follows:—11 could read well on admission, 53 could do so at the date of the report; 68 could read fairly on admission, 124 could read well at the date of the report, 55 indifferently; 30 well at the date of report, 96 not at all, and 23 well at the date of report.

Thirty-six could write well on admission, 84 afterwards; 70 indifferently, 124 well afterwards; 124 not at all, 22 well afterwards.

Eleven could cipher fairly on admission, 63 afterwards; 42 indifferently, 89 fairly afterwards; 177 not at all, 78 fairly afterwards.

The average age of the boys is between fifteen and sixteen years. The staff consists of ten persons, viz., captain, superintendent, schoolmaster, assistant-schoolmaster, chief officer or boatswain, boatswain's mate, carpenter, three seamen instructors, a cook, and steward.

One death occurred during the year, and that from disease of the brain; but the health of the boys has been remarkably good.

The good-conduct list contains 33 names. These are divided into three classes, the first receiving 3d. per week; the second, 2d. per week; the third, 1d. per week.

The treasurer's account, from the 31st December 1860, to 31st December 1861 (the last published), shows that the receipts (including a balance of £1193, 8s. 4d. in hand at the previous audit) amounted to £4326, 5s. 1d., and the expenditure to £3845, 19s. 11d., leaving a balance of £480, 5s. 2d.

The majority of the boys sent out from the good ship appeared to have fared well. Some are in the Indian navy; some are in merchant ships, earning 30s. a month; and many have reported themselves with pride and gratitude to their old masters. The "absconded" appear to relapse. I find that No. 37, F. S., who made off successfully from the ship, has, marked against his initials, "Since re-convicted, and sentenced to fifteen months' hard labour;" another truant (No. 52, J. A.) has been since sentenced to three years' penal servitude; a third has been sentenced to fifteen months' hard labour; the fourth and fifth, to penal servitude. These reckless boys, once more in the streets uncontrolled, have gone directly back to the old vile haunts,—and thence to the inevitable prison. The truth is that no boy should be free. Parental control is the natural and the best control; but, this failing, other control should be substituted. I was lately in a very small industrial school, situated in Constitution Row, Gray's Inn Road. It is a small, insignificant industrial school, with a few pairs of boots in the shop-window, and a *laissez-aller* air about the premises. A shambling boy, in soiled shirt-sleeves, opened the door, and led me into a back parlour, where some children were playing, at the end of a long deal table. The superintendent advanced from the back-yard, and willingly offered to show me over the establishment. It was on a small scale, and kept cleanly. In the back-yard, under a shed, some eight or nine boys were chopping and stacking wood—on the universal industrial plan. They were talkative, laughing boys, who could hardly be kept quiet while the superintendent spoke. The eight of them had managed to chop and bind between 500 and 600 bundles for their day's work. The superintendent informed me that the school was not certified.

"We have no control—save moral control—over them," he said. "One made off last week; and we don't go after them. By the rules of the committee every boy is bound to give a week's notice of his intention to leave; and then he is permitted to go. We can't help it. The school is for poor and destitute boys in the parish, and for attendants at the local ragged-schools. We endeavour to find situations for them."

The vagrant boys, then, in this uncertified school are free as birds. They can fly when they will, back to the thieves' haunts that are close round about, and that present attractions to them not to be found here, where the hours are regulated, where the labour is systematic, and where they are constantly under the eye of a master. It is clear that every industrial school, whether supported by voluntary contributions entirely, or mainly relying on convictions under the Industrial Schools' Act, should be certified. The boy once recovered from the haunts of thieves, or rescued from starvation in the streets, should be compelled to work his way into an honest path, and be held until he is firmly fixed in it.

The regulations of the St. Pancras Industrial School closely resemble those of most industrial schools. The diet is good, the work-hours are not excessive, and the boys receive part of their earnings. Some of them work out of doors. These receive one-third of their earnings, the remaining two-thirds being spent by the committee for their support. They do all the house-work, except the washing; as in other schools. This work, I must observe, cannot possibly be of great use to them in after life. It may make them handy, but it will not give them the means of earning their own living—the most important gift industrial schools have to bestow. Wood-chopping—which in most industrial schools is given to a boy as a probationary industry—is here the sole industry at present. It is hardly skilled labour, and certainly not profitable. It is barely possible to earn a crust and a pitcher of spring-water added.

The inmates are twenty-five, including a lodger, who pays his own expenses. They are all fed and clothed in the establishment; and fourteen of them are in situations, some partially, some regularly employed, their earnings varying from 1s. to 5s. per week. The time occupied in the house is from half-past six in the morning till nine at night, the employments being of an industrial or scholastic character. The present industrial occupation, as I have said, consists of wood-chopping, and it is intended to add to this the manufacture of hall-door mats of cocoa fibre, in place of the shoemaking, which is now abandoned as unprofitable. But of what avail will mat-making be? Better gather up these boys, and make ploughmen, or soldiers or sailors of them! I was much pleased, however, with the manner and tone of mind of the superintendent, Mr. Stocks. He had been a city missionary. Some years ago he set sail for America, and was wrecked on the Irish coast. He found himself at Cork, and, being without employment, started a reformatory there.

"I was at the head of that reformatory, sir," he said, "for eleven years, and I had only ten cases of flogging all the time. I am strongly against corporal punishment. I never flog here. I consider it brutalizing, and these boys have nearly all been brutalized when they come. When I came here a few months ago, there was a kind of conspiracy against me, but I have managed to destroy it. I punish with bread and water, solitude, and fines."

Where one master finds it necessary to rule by the rod, another dispenses with it, and still maintains strict discipline. And surely he who spares the rod and improves the child, is the better teacher.

Anxious to learn how it has fared with the children of the poor of Whitechapel and Spitalfields of late, and how a well-known institution of the locality was progressing, I pushed through the crowded thoroughfares that lie between the busy thoroughfare of Bishopsgate and the dreary homes of the weavers. At the corner of Brick Lane there was a monument of local distress—the deserted houses of the weavers; the broad windows cracked and broken; the doors nailed up, the rusty shutters closed! The poor were in the streets—loitering on all sides, and smoking and chattering, with a careless air: tired of the misery, and content to take what might come. On one side is the vast brewing establishment of Truman, Hanbury, and Co.—a monument of wealth, about which the square-built draymen are rolling hogsheads; and opposite are the silent looms in the denuded garrets! Much has been done to alleviate the misery that clouds this unhappy district. The story of the Spitalfields weaver is a plaintive one, familiar to all classes of readers. The pots of flowers that were at their windows have disappeared; and the looms may go for firewood. The ruined men will, by degrees, betake themselves to more profitable work than Spitalfields silk-weaving; and these hundreds of children who are now chattering, laughing, or intoning their lessons in the two great, free school-rooms of the King Edward Ragged and Industrial Schools, in Albert Street, Spitalfields, will,

I trust, be far away—gaining a fair livelihood as honourable and industrious men and women.

Spitalfields has now long been a disorderly and criminal district. Its dense population has suffered all the demoralizing influences of a failing industry. There was a time when the quaint weavers of Spitalfields were a most happy and reputable race. But poverty befell the little streets where the weavers threw the shuttle. There were protracted pauses of silence when the welcome whirr of industry was stayed, and the weavers were at the street corners. The distresses of the Spitalfields weaver obtained universal commiseration; poverty and Spitalfields became synonymous. I have no doubt that the friends of the King Edward Ragged and Industrial Schools are correct and moderate in their description of the locality as it was when, in 1846, they began the work of moral improvement. The vice, we are told, was appalling. This was a vast nest where criminals were reared. It is not the chosen residence of the virtues and the graces now. The schools have done much good, but they have not yet vanquished the natural growth of poverty.

The superintendent said to me, as I watched the little children tumbling into the great schoolroom, "Many of them wouldn't have clothes to come in, if they did not get them from us. They come hungry and ragged; very hungry if the father has not been able to bring home a few pence for dinner, as often happens. We give them clothes from the bundles of left-off apparel charitable people send us. The children that come dirty are sent home to wash."

They seemed happy, romping and chatting together. I never saw a more various and grotesque collection of children's clothing. The girls (we were in the girls' school) were of all ages, down to stumpy and unsteady little babies, bearing up with difficulty under capes and frocks and caps intended for children twice their years. They were ranged in groups about their teachers, learning from a board, or being drilled to answer questions with one voice. The boys were in a room on the basement of the building, and were scarcely to be heard amid the clatter of the girls. To my remark that the girls made infinitely more noise than the boys, the superintendent or matron pleasantly answered, "It's generally said that women talk more than men, and I suppose we must allow that it is so. They 're very merry."

King Edward Ragged Schools and Refuge for Destitute Girls is a handsome building, in Albert Street, Spitalfields; the first stone of which was laid in 1861. It is conspicuous in this poor neighbourhood. A passer-by would decide off-hand that it was an hospital; but it is neither too spacious nor too solidly built. It is a well-arranged, well-ventilated home, where the children of weavers and costermongers can find recreation and education, ay, and clothes to cover their feeble limbs. There is a gymnasium where they may exercise, a dry playground, which is a good exchange for the gutter; more, there is a refuge where utterly destitute children may find instruction in homely duties. This is not a certified institution. The forty or fifty girls who are here at work, in their striped grey loose gowns, leave at any moment. They are only too free agents; for some of them have not a relation in the wide world. They have been culled from the streets by some gracious hand, and put under this protecting roof. Here I find them, washing in a model laundry, or working in the sewing-class, or learning lessons in the school. They are bright, cheerful, well-spoken girls; growing, to be the fit and true helpmates of honest working men, or prosperous settlers in New Zealand, or some other British colony. While the poor little *externes* come often hungry to school, these refuge girls have their assured meals of wholesome food, and their meat three times a week. Their work is not hard, and every hour of it advances them in the right direction. There is a library where they may read good, instructive books.

Under this roof there are not only day-schools and a refuge; there is also a Sunday ragged-school, which between 200 and 300 children attend. There were bread and coal tickets, for the mothers of the ragged *externes*, kept under this noble roof; and the poor women of the neighbourhood were very glad of this help, in their struggle to warm and feed their little ones.

"But," said the superintendent, "none have been sent to us this year for distribution, although the distress has been as severe as usual. The poor have not suffered much from the cold; but they have had their full share of want. I am afraid we have no tickets, in consequence of the drain on the charitable made by the Lancashire distress. We have suffered; I know our funds are very low."

We find, then, as one certain result of the aid given to Lancashire, that the poor woman of Spitalfields have missed their usual bread and coal tickets. The Registrar-General records deaths from starvation in our midst. How many have died of positive want lately the coroner can tell. The shadows of men, women, and children, I passed on my way to this school, looked like dried mummies endowed with motion—human atoms, so bent and wasted, and beaten by hard fate, that I passed them wondering how much more the human form could endure, and still hold the soul within it. To think of the tens of thousands of London folk who live idle and luxurious at the West End; to think of snug Clapham and haughty Eaton Square; nay, to think of little Daffles, of the Post-Office, going home to his tea and muffins, or of Mrs. Grundy's very humblest relation, and then to look upon these pictures of skeleton want, framed in London fog, and beaten upon by a north-east wind! Men and women are thoughtless in the happy west, dancing, eating, and dreaming behind the splendours of Mr. Cubitt's stucco town, or many a dainty foot would press Brick Lane, and many of the sighs with which the atmosphere of Spitalfields is weighted, would give way to laughter.

In no former year have the applications for admission to this refuge been so numerous, but the want of sufficient means has obliged the committee reluctantly to refuse many. Thirty-five, however, were admitted, and the number in the refuge at the date of the last published report was 42. Of these, 6 were orphans, 12 have both parents living (2 deserted by father), 13 were without father, 11 were without mother; 24 could read well, 13 could read fairly, 5 could read imperfectly; 36 wrote in copy-books, 6 wrote on slates; 4 were in the highest rules of arithmetic, 20 in compound rules, 18 in simple rules; 14 were returned to their friends; 12 were provided with situations, 4 left without leave, 2 were transferred to other Homes, 1 was expelled. Two of the girls formerly in the refuge, who had received good characters from their employers, were assisted with passages and outfits to Tasmania.

Considerable progress was made by the children in the day and evening schools. The number of children who attended the day-schools during the year was 504, of whom 307 were still in the school. There were about 60 girls able to learn needlework, and they were almost constantly employed in making every description of clothing for themselves and others. Since Christmas, 40 frocks and 146 pinafores were distributed, besides trousers, jackets, etc., for the boys, and a large amount of under-clothing for the girls.

The boys' day-school was equally satisfactory. The average attendance was 109.

One great difficulty with which the teachers have to contend is the irregular attendance, arising from the casual employment to which the children are put, for the general support of the families of which they form a part.

In the evening school, there were nearly 80 of both sexes in attendance, varying from 11 to 18 years of age, who from various reasons were prevented from attending during the day.

The Sunday-schools are open in the morning and afternoon of the Sabbath. In the morning a special service, suited to the capacities of children, is held in the large schoolroom, at which from 250 to 300 children are generally present, while the average attendance in the afternoon was 246 children, presided over by 20 voluntary teachers.

The library was augmented during the year by 250 volumes, making a total number of 320 books for the perusal of the children.

The Sunday-evening ragged-school is also another important branch of the operations conducted in this building. The number in attendance was 255 children, and 19 teachers; 26 boys and girls received prizes of 5s. and 10s. each, awarded by the committee of the Ragged School Union, for having kept their situations with credit to themselves and satisfaction to their employers.

No less than 3261 periodicals, together with 129

Bibles and 154 hymn-books, were purchased by the children during the past year.

The penny-bank was continued during the year; £52, 9s. 6d. had been deposited by 160 depositors.

The schoolmaster, then, is doing good service in this sombre locality; come in what guise he may—whether offering clothes, and bread and coals with the horn-book, or merely with his books and pens. The late Earl of Portsmouth presented a schoolmaster to a village in Devonshire in a peculiar way. The village was in the darkness of complete ignorance, and consequently prone to use the comforts of the ale-house. "They shall not escape my schoolmaster," said the Earl. So he built a village inn, and he made the schoolmaster the landlord thereof. The sign of the inn was, and is, "The Schoolmaster," a strange name for a public-house, it must be owned; but it served to familiarize the country bumpkins with the teacher and his vocation; and so, I trust, led many to seek him for the reading and writing he could teach, as well as for his ale.

Being not far off the Fenchurch Street Railway Station, I took the opportunity for a visit to the Home in the East for Criminal Boys. This is a regularly certified Home, where only boys who have been convicted of crime are received at the Government reduced rate of 6s. a week. It is a small edition of the reformatory at Feltham, conducted by private enterprise in a corner of London, called Old Ford, Bow. The journey thither, over the houses of Stepney, through Shadwell, is a run through some of the more notable quarters of London poverty. The Home itself is reached after a most tortuous and puzzling walk. Any place more adapted to a quiet, unobserved business I never saw. An illicit still, or any illegal trade, might be carried on in such a happily chosen retreat, with particular confidence. The approach to, and appearance of, the house vividly reminded me of the Wandsworth Reformatory, conducted by Mr. Leyland. A reformatory boy was gate-keeper. He was a smart, bright lad, and informed me, with a self-possessed air, that "the governor was not at home." However, I would see the establishment; and the master tailor, aided by the matron, did duty as guides.

There was nothing very remarkable in the house. It was neither better nor worse than Mr. Leyland's. The boys were in a comfortable school-room—some 68 in number. A large group of them was collected about the stove, talking freely. There was a happy, unconstrained look about them; they were very unlike the sad automata I had seen in the Feltham school-rooms. There was heart in them. In the playground some were singing, and others lounging about the gymnastic apparatus. Their workshops were roomy and well arranged. The master tailor was evidently a little proud of them. He showed me some of their handiwork.

"These blue guernseys and trousers," he said, "we are making for the Union Jack Blacking Brigade"—a new blacking force which is the good work, I am told, of a single private individual. Behind the house are some acres of land which the boys cultivate. There is no wood-chopping on the establishment. The gardening is probably the most remunerative employment.

I accepted the master-tailor's explanation of the little disorder I saw, for the boys had been playing a cricket-match that afternoon. Indeed there was not the least disorder worth an excuse. I could see the spirit in which the establishment was conducted. The boys are taught to make shoes and clothes, and to garden; they are moderately fed, having meat twice a week, and meat soup twice; they are warmly clothed in blue, with red collars to their jackets; they are drilled by the master tailor. They play together in a band; and when their term of restraint has expired, they are helped to situations. Some go to sea, and some have been sent to Canada, but the emigration has been discontinued of late, for reasons which the matron could not explain to me. So far, good. The Government does not provide employment for the criminal boys it reforms. The conductor of a reformatory like this is bound to keep and instruct his pupils, while the State pay him six shillings a week for the task; but when the money is withdrawn, the master's duties cease. He has reared a shoemaker, but he cannot force him to stick to his last; therefore the master of a certified reformatory (who deals in reformation as a shoemaker deals in shoes) is bound merely to fulfil his bargain; he is not responsible for the future of his boys.

The reformation of juvenile offenders having become a trade, and not an unprofitable one, it should be most strictly overlooked. In this Home in the East there are the comforts, and I think only the wholesome restraints, of a well-regulated establishment. But much is left to the temper of the master, governor, or speculator. He must live out of the labour of the boys, and the grant of the State. The temptation of the position must be to put the boys to the labour that is profitable to him, and not to that which will be most advantageous to them in after life. The shoemaker's and tailor's apprentice spoil quantities of material in the process of acquiring skill. This waste is complained of in every reformatory. The boys are very young, as a rule, when they enter. They are committed for three, four, or at most five years. The average age of the boys in the Home in the East is between thirteen and fourteen years. As skilled workers they are not likely to progress rapidly. They have been accustomed to vagabondage in the streets. It is the universal complaint of their masters that idleness is their peculiar vice. Their rough labour is most likely to be profitable. They can dig, and weed, and carry as well, according to their strength, as men. Hence broad acres cultivated by them. Now gardeners are not in very great demand, nor are unskilled agricultural labourers, in this country. To bring town boys up to gardening, is not a rational way of rearing them, except when they are destined for the colonies. At this Home in the East there is much gardening, and no emigration. This is a mistake, as far as the welfare of the boys is concerned, but is a good business arrangement for the governor. Reformatories should be classed; the boys in each should have a prearranged destination. The discipline and teaching should be adapted to fit them for the life that has been marked out for them. A hodge-podge of industrial teaching makes a jack-of-all-trades. Jack is an unsteady, thriftless, capricious fellow. Before bidding good-bye to the Home in the East, let me notice the punishments. There are cells, and there is the cane. Boys who abscond are reformed with both. "Are they caned on the hand?" I asked the matron. She answered, "Sometimes on the hand." My inquiry could go no further; but her answer was suggestive enough. The cane in the hands of a hot-tempered man, who has nobody to restrain his anger, is a dangerous instrument. It is severer than the birch, for it raises wheals of flesh. We have seen what the birch can do at Feltham under the strict supervision of magistrates; what might not be done in this obscure corner of London with a cane applied —not always—to the hand?

CHAPTER XIV.

INDUSTRIAL BRIGADES.

THE ragged-school movement has had a marked effect on the poor of London. In some of the neighbourhoods where ragged-schools exist, lanes that, ten years ago, were impassable dens of infamy have become safe and reputable localities, as I have already led the reader to notice. These schools have succeeded and extended, because they have been enlarged in plan, and have added industrial tuition to the teaching of reading and writing. The 52,000 attendants at ragged-schools are evidence that the work directed from the central committee in Exeter Hall, is useful. It may be remembered by a few readers that, some ten years ago, these schools were assailed and condemned as only so many centres where thieves and beggars might congregate, and, over a gratuitous fire, concoct elaborate robberies. Indeed, there appeared to be cause for alarm, since the children who were tempted to school were the offspring of poverty and vice, and were likely to have a bad rather than a good influence on each other. In the beginning I have no doubt some harm was done; and some sorry young rascals only learnt how to steal to better advantage. But years have passed over these Lazarus schools. They have been watched by zealous friends, led by the Earl of Shaftesbury; they have been modified and remodelled according to circumstances; and that which, to my mind, is their most important feature, they have been made to include that which is the first, best lesson you can teach the vagrant child—to bear the labour by which the honest man lives. It is this industrial feature of the schools to which I shall direct my attention. It is important, since great numbers of the ragged scholars are, through the school agency, put into situations; while many a helpless, homeless boy is set in a way of earning enough to keep him, with a little to spare for the savings'-bank. The friends of ragged-schools have been ingenious creators of work.

The idea of establishing shoeblacks in the streets of London occurred to Mr. J. Macgregor, of the Temple, in the spring of 1851. The idea was merely an importation from that nation which is said to manage so many things better than John Bull. But it was an excellent idea for giving employment to a number of destitute lads. It enabled the supporters of ragged-schools to offer a premium to their scholars, and, at the same time, to show the public the good the schools were doing. The first International Exhibition of Industry was about to be opened; there would be thousands of foreigners in England who would be familiar with the street shoeblack system. The promoters of this importation from Paris had little hope, however, beyond the year. They thought it would last through the summer, and be an advertisement for their schools; but they never dreamt it would be adopted heartily by the London public, and become a great and flourishing employment to destitute boys. It will interest the reader to learn how the germ of 1851 has grown and taken root, and become a goodly tree, under which hundreds of poor boys find comfort and shelter. Such a result has not been obtained without much thought and trouble. The promoters of shoeblack brigades had to guard their boys against the dangers of the streets. We shall see how they have accomplished their task.

We will first glance, however, at the operations of the entire Ragged School Union, and mark the progress and present state of its operations.

The number of schools in connexion with the Union is as follows:—In 175 school-buildings there are 202 Sunday-schools, with 25,000 scholars; 172 day-schools with 18,000 scholars; 211 evening-schools, with above 9000 scholars.

The above is the average number in attendance, the number on the books being larger.

The following figures show the progress of the Union during the eighteen years it has existed. Taking each six years from its formation, it appears that in 1850 there were 95 school-buildings, 53 Sunday-schools, and 10,439 in attendance; 45 day-schools, and 5558 in attendance; 74 evening-schools, and 5332 in attendance. In 1856, there were 150 school-buildings, 128 Sunday-schools, and 16,937 in attendance; 98 day-schools, and 13,057 in attendance; 117 evening-schools, and 8085 in attendance. In 1862, there were 175 school-buildings, 202 Sunday-schools, and 24,256 in attendance; 172 day-schools, and 17,658 in attendance; 211 evening-schools, and 9032 in attendance.

The industrial schools are this year 3600. The voluntary teachers, 2800. The paid monitors, 420. The paid teachers, 317.

The number who regularly attend the parents' meeting is 2850, while those who attend other religious services held in ragged-schools by the teachers, city missionaries, and others, is above 5000.

All these are the average numbers and attendances throughout the year.

The number reported as sent to situations from the various ragged-schools during the year is 1130. The number rewarded at the last prize meeting was 960; viz., 540 boys, and 517 girls. All these had certificates of good conduct from their employers, for twelve months at least.

Among the scholars there are now 170 who have become communicants at various Christian churches, and among the voluntary teachers, 150 who were formerly scholars in the ragged-school.

The shoeblacks are, on the whole, getting a fair living—some of them being really well off. Their united earnings were last year £4665, the total number of boys being 362.

The number of refuges on the list has this year been reduced in consequence of several not now receiving the scholars from ragged-schools, but rather convicted children sent by magistrates, or those who are paid for by friends.

The Union continues to give help to those that remain on the list by a capitation grant, to provide every child admitted from a ragged-school with food and lodging.

Above 18,000 were rewarded during the year, from 120 schools, with summer treats and country trips; and in addition to these a special fund was raised, whereby 2000 children, from twenty-seven schools, were treated on one day to an excursion to Richmond.

The penny-banks, clothing-clubs, and provident funds continue to prosper. Eighty penny-banks collected during the year £9175, and fifty-five clothing-clubs collected nearly £950.

Two magazines—a large one and a small one—

are issued by the Society. Of the large, 3500 are circulated; of the small, about 7500.

The receipts and disbursements of the Union from April 1, 1861, to March 31, 1862, showed that the former amounted to £8695, 16s. 10d., and the latter to £7456, 8s. 9d., leaving a balance in the bankers' hands of £1239, 8s. 1d.

The earnings of the shoeblacks have been as much as £4665 in one year, a large sum to be collected by blacking boots in the street. The dangers of the shoeblack's calling are obvious. He is sent into the streets with his brushes and blacking; he is uncontrolled; he is a loiterer at street corners; his work is light and fitful; he is his own master. A boy so placed is likely to fall among bad associates, unless strong incentives to good conduct are given to him. The Ragged Shoeblack Society has undertaken to do this work, and is doing it most successfully. It has parted the boys into brigades; it has put them under strong and salutary laws; and it has compelled them to lay by a share of their daily earnings. A brigade boy is watched; he must attend school; he must account for his earnings every evening; and he must be active at his duties. He is liable to observation from head-quarters at any moment of the day. He is easily detected, if he gives in a false account of his earnings. Let us follow him to his quarters, whither he repairs at dusk; his day's work done. I select the Central Ragged School Shoeblack Society because it is the original one, and its boys (the Red Brigade) have a deserved reputation for their behaviour. The head-quarters of this brigade are in an old house in Ship Yard, Temple Bar. As we turn out of the Strand we find ourselves in a dark, densely-inhabited court, that suggests anything save order or improvement. The house is on the left hand.

On opening the door I found myself in a large square room, filled with forms and benches, at which numbers of boys were seated, chattering happily. There was a blazing fire. The air was charged with the aroma of coffee. Two women were near piles of tea-cups, ready to receive the boys' orders. Most of them had just arrived. These were wiping their faces—having washed in a convenient lavatory on the kitchen floor—or combing their hair with combs tied to the wall.

"Do they give you hot and cold water?" I asked a boy who was sluicing himself vigorously in the lavatory.

"Oh! no, sir; cold water. Never use hot water, sir; makes you feel so cold afterwards."

The little fellow answered so briskly and cheerily, and seemed so full of health and spirits, with such evident contempt for the effeminacy of hot water, that he convinced me at once he was one of the boys who would earn briskly and save perseveringly, and be a hard-working citizen presently in some part of the world.

The boys now gathered in these warm and pleasant head-quarters are not, it should be understood, Arabs taken without discrimination or trial from the streets. No boy is admitted who has not been recommended by the superintendent of some school in connexion with the Ragged School Union. They come from Huntsworth Mews, New Pye Street, One Tun, Westminster, Fox Court, Agar Town, and other localities of this not very promising description. I looked through the book in which their names and the occupations of their parents, are entered. The boys are the offspring of hawkers, char-women, cab-drivers, dock-labourers, bricklayers, etc. Some have lost both parents. One is described as "a great beggar, but not known to be dishonest." It will be seen that the recommendation of a ragged-school superintendent being necessary to the admission of a boy as a shoeblack, the superintendent has an inducement to offer to his scholars to behave well; for a boy who is once brigaded with the "Reds" has a good chance of making his way in the world. This prospect, opened by the Ragged School, is, to my mind, the most important feature of it. The urchin is first dragged from the gutter; he gets a little learning; and, as a reward for good conduct, the prospect of living to be a prosperous working man.

I will now follow the superintendent through the establishment, in which he has already given me a most courteous reception. The great room on the first floor is furnished with forms, upon which the boys are sitting in their red jerseys, while the superintendent from his desk (which is railed off with an open wicket, through which the boy called upon, settles his account) summons them one by one to give an account of their day's earnings. Before him are tall columns of halfpence. The boy summoned advances to the wicket.

"How much?" says the superintendent.

"One and ninepence," the boy answers, depositing the money.

The superintendent explained that the wind and dry weather were against them. "But," he continued, "the boys vary very much: some boys will make shillings where another will earn a penny. They stray from their posts, or gossip; but we give every boy 6d. for his day's work, whether he has earned it or not. The money is divided in this way: Suppose a boy brings 9d., 6d. of it is his—he is entitled to this absolutely; then the 3d. would be divided in this way—he would have 1d. of it, the

Society would have 1d., and 1d. would be put into the bank for him."

This distribution of the boy's earnings is well calculated. The boy is certain to receive 6d. for his day's work. When he earns more, he is compelled to save one-third of the excess. The third that goes to support the Society is little enough, and he has it back, as I shall show, in various forms. 4s. or 5s. are considered a good day's work. The Society, I should add, takes nothing until the boy has earned 9d. The best station is by the Duke of Wellington's statue, opposite the Royal Exchange. Here four boys will earn 30s. in a day. A boy who has been stationed under London Bridge brings 9d. as the fruit of his day's work; he is one of those boys who never show a brilliant return. I remarked that the boys paid borrowed money, and left something with the superintendent.

"That boy," the superintendent explained, "has earned enough to leave some with me for him. He will probably draw it in a lump at the end of the week. It is in addition to his bank deposit. The other boy paid me 2d. he borrowed this morning for breakfast."

Another boy advanced to the wicket and put 3d. upon the desk. "He's always bad," said the superintendent; "he doesn't do his best." This was a bad bargain for the Society, since the idle boy's 6d. had to be made up out of the Society's fund. I could read success or failure on the boys' faces. Some were open, full of courage, bright and clean: these were the boys who had done their fair day's work, and were content with themselves. The skulkers and dullards were morose and whining; these are the boys who sell their brushes or mats. The dishonesty of this will be apparent when I inform the reader that brushes, mats, and jerseys are furnished to the boys at half their cost price. A brush that cost 1s. 1½d. is delivered to the shoeblack for 6d. When he sells it, therefore, it is a grave offence.

Some of the boys have earned as much as 11s. in the course of a day. It is difficult to convict them of a false statement when their receipts are large, because so much of the money is what is called "over-money," or money given to the boys in excess of the penny they have a right to demand.

When a boy has appeared at the superintendent's wicket, he delivers up his jersey to the inspector, and it is placed in a separate room, where the blocks, brushes, and blacking are kept. This side-room is pungent with the smell of the blacking, a great cask of which is in the centre of it. "We consume here," said the superintendent, "from £70 to £80 worth of blacking every year; and our brushes come to £40. Twelve gallons of blacking last us about a fortnight. We fill the boys' blacking-pots on Saturdays and Wednesdays."

From the brush and blacking room I was conducted to the school-room on the second floor. Against the walls are photographs of shoeblacks and their friends, and upon the mantlepiece a china figure of the familiar red jersey. Here, too, is a stuffed gull, sent by an old brigade boy from abroad to his companions. I had some conversation with the superintendent on the histories of some of the boys who had distinguished themselves. We examined a framed list of the boys' earnings, which is drawn up every month or five weeks, the earnings being counted in pence. The boys are, of course, anxious to be at the head of the list. They have equal chances, since their stations are changed every three days. At the head of the list was a boy named M'Carthy.

M'Carthy is one of those determined, strong-willed, quiet boys who travel slowly and surely to their goal. He is not to be put aside by the noisy. He has certain work to do, and he does it with a will, or why should he be at the head of this list of bread-winners, having earned 1091 pence in five weeks? To begin with, he is lame; he was born lame. He was in a deplorable condition, and so weak he couldn't carry the box the brigade boys carry. But the superintendent was loth to part with him. His case was a pitiful one: and he was quiet and gentle under his misfortunes. A light box was specially made for him, and he took up his load once more. He, the weak cripple, showed that he deserved all the kindness he had experienced. He returned to head-quarters day after day, having done his work thoroughly. And now he is the best bread-winner in the brigade. "He's as quiet as when he first came," the superintendent said.

I saw him in the general room on the ground-floor, sitting among his companions. They were talking and laughing over their game of dominoes, or fox and geese, sipping their halfpenny cups of tea or coffee, or munching thick slices of bread and butter, and he still seemed to be the quietest of the party. I was glad to perceive that this honourable little society of shoeblacks were free to laugh, play, and talk—their day's work done. There was just sufficient control over them. They were not drilled till the heart was out of them. I could not help, as I stood in their cheerful kitchen, contrasting their supper and games with the supper of those mute Feltham boys, who say prayers to the word of command, and clasp their hands at the call of the drill-sergeant. Between the Feltham boys and these there lies the prison. It is, I know, by the merest accident that these happy lads, who have just doffed their red jerseys, are not in the duller clothes of the Middlesex Industrial boys, and this thought must lead us to applaud the good work done by Mr. Macgregor. He has given easy work to these vagrant lads, by which they will be led to depend on their own honest exertions for their own living. He has brought them out of low neighbourhoods to this comfortable fireside, and made them feel the blessings of industry, cleanliness, knowledge, and forethought. Presently they will pass up stairs to the school-room, that their industry may be fortified by education. They have many good examples before them. Their superintendent, who has been here twelve years, can tell them stories of boys who have gone hence into comfortable situations, or who have emigrated and are doing well.

It was with just pride that the superintendent drew my attention to the subscriptions which these shoeblacks had made to the Lancashire Relief Fund. Out of their earnings and savings they had subscribed £8 in one week. No. 49, I see, gave 15s., and others gave 10s. and 10s. 6d. This 49—our young friend M'Carthy—is progressing wondrously indeed. I see that he has already saved more than £15.

The boys of the Red Brigade assemble here every morning at seven o'clock, and open the day with prayers, after which they go off to their respective stations to work. A boy once accustomed to these regular hours, and this regular employment, who has money enough to keep him, and some in a post-office savings'-bank, feels that he has a stake in society. He is no longer an outcast. He has a positive gain in sober conduct, and vigilant attention to his duties. He will find that many situations are open to him:—of 177 boys in the Red Brigade, 38 obtained situations, and 69 left of their own accord to seek other employment, or have been discharged. He will see how his Society has progressed from year to year; how his comrades earned £1824 last year, and will earn £2000 this year. A spirit of emulation will be awakened in him. He will enjoy the winter and summer treats. He will be jealous at last of the reputation of his brigade; and so, like many of his predecessors, he will find his way to honourable employment. The Society gives him three commandments—"Bring in all your money; keep to your station; spend Sunday properly." Obedient to these he may flourish, and leave Fox Court and One Tun, Westminster, far behind him.

The Government, however, decline to protect these brigades of poor boys, who are seeking, with all their might, to make their way out of the pestilent neighbourhoods in which they were born. The brigade boys require protection against the assaults and competition of impostors. Boys of bad character and loose lives, who decline to submit to any moral control whatever, who never put a groat in a savings'-bank, elbow the brigade boys, and endeavour to oust them from their stations. The Ragged School Union have sought redress, and in vain. The redress of this wrong must remain, then, with the public. The brigade boys, and these boys only, should be patronized. These boys are known to be living honest and reputable lives. They are regular attendants at school; they are depositors in savings'-banks. They are children of the poorest of the poor who are striving to become honest working men. Their ragged and riotous competitors are lawless young scamps, who give no guarantee for their good conduct, who spurn control, and who even jeer at the seemly bearing of the brigade boy. Every brigade boy wears a uniform; and his uniform is an honour to him, that should give him the favour of every passer-by who needs a shoeblack's services. This shoeblack industry is a creation of the ragged-school promoters, and if these gentlemen had done only this work, they would have deserved well of their countrymen. But they have done much more, as the figures I have already given testify. They seek scholars where no other teachers penetrate, although it has been said by Government Commissioners that ragged-schools are useless, because there are other schools open to the poorest. The evidence given before a select committee of the House of Commons conclusively proved that these schools attack, and are helping to break up the nurseries of crime. They have regard to the physical as well as moral well-being of their scholars; they seek out the felon's babe, and endeavour to rescue him from the evil of parental example; they gather classes together from the ragged sleepers in refuges; and they are content to depend upon the charity of the British public, which, up to this time, has not failed them. If the existence of ragged-schools is unnecessary, how is it that they have gone on steadily increasing during eighteen years? How is it that some 50,000 children are taught in them in and around London? These are children on the verge of starvation—crossing-sweepers, vendors of penny trifles in the streets, etc. The starving child is not only taught that it is wrong to steal, but is also helped to find food in return for labour. The schools where this work is done are in the most crowded and poverty-stricken parts of London. They are connected with mothers' meetings, ragged churches, bands of hope, penny-banks, and clothing clubs. They pay for the admission of destitute boys to refuges. If all this were so much useless work, as stated by her Majesty's Commissioners, would the charitable British public give—and heartily give—some £8000 every year to the Ragged School Union, and would her Majesty head the list of donors?

The two International Exhibitions of Industry which have been held in this country, have marked the introduction of two new industries by the governors of London Ragged Schools. The first, that of street shoe-blacking, I have already noticed; the second, that of rag-collecting, remains to be touched upon. This collecting, which gives employment to a number of poor lads, does good, not only to the boys whom it supports, but also to the housewives, whom it tempts to be more provident than they have been of late. Time was when the rag-bag was a domestic institution, and when every frugal housewife would have been ashamed to own that she cast aught away that might be turned to profitable account. Some treasured broken articles and victuals for the poor; others for their own profit. The good done by this frugal system was twofold. The housewife helped a poor pensioner, or added to her purse; and much material adaptable to human purposes was saved. It was in the days when women were content in "homespun kirtle," that every scrap of cotton or linen found its way into the "tidy;" before work-boxes were made of buhl or marqueterie. It was not in an age of veneer that the British matron saved every bit and scrap, and when the careful broom collected every atom of linen or paper.

In the beginning of 1862, the friends of the ragged scholars of London, stimulated by the dearness of the rags which go to make paper, bethought themselves that vast quantities of this precious material must, in these wasteful times, be cast to the dust-bin to rot. The rag-pickers of Paris have long driven a trade that cannot be said, indeed, to be a greatly profitable one, but which has kept them clothed and fed, and would produce a frugal, decent livelihood for them if they were not as a class addicted to the drinking of *camphre,* better known in Paris as chiffonnier's brandy. I had occasion, in the year 1854, to inquire closely into the habits and earnings of the Paris rag-pickers. I found that they were the refuse of the Paris population, and that they were, as a rule, reckless and dissolute. I estimated their average earnings, and found that a fair specimen of the class could earn about twenty pence per diem. To earn this sum the rag-picker had to sort what he collected in the streets; but many of them would not take this trouble; and those who shot their basketful into the dealer's shop could not earn more than fifteen pence. The idea of starting a rag-brigade in London, was no doubt suggested by the trade of the drunken population about the Montagne Ste. Geneviève. There was no machinery in operation here for collecting rags and useful refuse. The earnings of the Paris rag-pickers amounted to a very important sum per annum. Why should not the unemployed boys of London create such a trade in London, and appeal to London housewives to be thrifty once more?

The success of the shoeblacks encouraged ragged-school promoters to answer this question with an experiment. They appealed to all classes. They desired to collect rags and refuse, and, by this collection, to give fresh employment to their poor scholars. The young poor were to be benefited and reclaimed, by carrying off the sweepings of the rich. The Ragged School Union appealed to the public, saying—" You will benefit the deserving poor, your houses will be cleared of waste refuse, and you will be in pocket by the transaction; and the demand is increasing for the waste our boys will carry away. There shall be a regular tariff of prices; the brigade of refuse collectors shall be under strict regulations, and shall be honest, hard-working, school-attending boys; you and they and society shall be the gainers."

With this appeal, made under the auspices of Lord Shaftesbury, the Rag-Collecting Brigade of the London Ragged Schools was formed, at the beginning of 1862. It offered employment during the day-time to the elder ragged-school boys.

This brigade is now in active operation, and collects rags of all kinds, waste paper, and worn and broken metal, in all parts of the metropolis. They call at houses to purchase these articles at fixed, fair, market prices. The boys call with a covered truck, furnished with weights and scales. They buy according to weight, and give and take a receipt for all moneys they receive. They are clothed in a distinguishing uniform. Every boy has given a guarantee for his good conduct. He has some claim on the kind consideration of the householders, as he goes his rounds. This daily work is a good education to him, that will enable him to take employment in a shop or warehouse. He offers fair terms for that which would be wasted, if not sold to him. "To show the need of more systematic arrangements for gathering the rags of this country," according to the Ragged School Union Report, "we need only refer to the evidence given before a select committee of the House of Commons, which sat during the last session of Parliament (1861). It was stated before that committee, that not more than four-tenths of the rags of this country are preserved. If the remaining six-tenths of the rags were carefully preserved, and returned to be re-manufactured, there would be no necessity to go to foreign markets for meeting the deficiency of some 25 per cent. in the amount of rags now required for the paper manufacture of this country." Enough to establish the utility of the Rag-Collecting Brigade.

The inhabitants of London should know all the precautions that have been taken to make this Rag-Collecting Brigade a trustworthy body. They are furnished with trucks marked "The Rag-Collecting Brigade of the London Ragged Schools." Every member of the brigade wears a dark-green cord jacket and waistcoat, and a badge marked R. C. B., and bearing the wearer's number, on his arm and on his cap. Each truck is attended by three persons, viz., a collector, and two assistants. Every member of the brigade must be at the warehouse in the City at seven in the morning. He must breakfast there in the morning, and take his tea there on his return in the evening, his meals being charged to him at cost price. The boys are separated into three classes, viz., collectors, assistants, and sorters. Of these classes the sorters are the lowest, being employed from eight to four daily, in the warehouse, to sort the contents of the trucks, and receiving 1½d. per hour for their labour. The sorters become assistants, and may, finally, collectors, according to their deserts. No sorter can become an assistant until he has 5s. in the brigade bank. Again, no assistant can become a collector until he has £1 in the brigade bank. The assistants draw the truck, and are under the command of the collector, who makes all the purchases, and is responsible for all the cash. To be a collector a boy must be a fair reader, writer, and arithmetician. The payment which the collector receives is 2s. per day, the assistants receiving 1s. each. With strict regulations for attendance at school, and for order and cleanliness, this wise and humane code is calculated to rear a set of orderly, honourable, and industrious men. The effect of it is already becoming apparent, as the institution grows.

The court or mews by London Wall, in which the young rag and refuse pickers sort the contents of their trucks, is indeed a busy place. I reached it about one o'clock in the day. The premises appeared well adapted to the business in hand. Indeed, they cost the promoters £75 per annum, and were a drag on them when the brigade was in its infancy. When in March last there was only one truck, the outgoings greatly exceeded the incomings. One poor detachment could not show profits sufficient to cover the expenses of machinery intended for a brigade. The public would not, at first, understand the experiment. Fine ladies would not condescend to know what became of the rags, paper, bones, and bottles of their establishments. The boys distributed circulars at every house of the locality in which they wished to make a footing; and called the next day. They suffered repulses at first; but their mission became known by degrees, and they obtained a footing. Their orderly behaviour, their just measures and fair prices, and the good cause which they represented, have, at last, made them welcome wherever they are known. They are now known at Highbury, Hampstead, Brompton, Finchley, on the Surrey side of the water, etc. They wander so far off from head-quarters that the establishment of local depots is in serious consideration. From Hampstead to London Wall is a long journey with a full truck of rags, bones, paper, and bottles. Every day the collecting-house of the boys is increasing. They appear to be thorough little men of business. At the entrance to the warehouse two or three of them are weighing basketsful of bones, and casting them into a cart at hand. Within, countless wine bottles are stacked round the room, and in the centre are great pans, full of beef dripping. An inner room is devoted to the boys' prayers, breakfast, and tea. Round this room their own clothes are hung, under numbers, while they are out at work in the uniforms belonging to the brigade. There are now 24 boys in the collecting and sorting force, in addition to adults.

I should explain that when this brigade was formed it was found necessary to intrust the collectorships to adults only. No boys who could be trusted with the bargaining, handling of money, etc., were to be had. But presently the superintendent was able to select three boys who could be trusted alone with a truck. They have thoroughly learned their business, and are able to show a result equal to that accomplished by a party officered by an adult collector. I glanced over their account for one day. They had bought goods to the value of 16s. 11½d. These consisted of bones, broken glass, dripping, doctors' bottles, rope and bagging, mixed rags, etc. A very good and profitable day's journey had they made, and their example had created a ferment among their companions. Their promotion afforded the superintendent an opportunity for addressing words of advice and encouragement to the entire brigade. The boy selected to be the first juvenile collector in the brigade was a little fellow, but he was shrewd; and above all, he could read, write, and calculate well. All his shrewdness would not have given him this proud position, had he been idle at school. Therefore his companions should emulate his example. They should strive to learn their business and their books. The effect created by this appeal, and by the picture of the promoted boy's successful campaign, has made a stir throughout the brigade, and all the boys will strive their utmost to be worthy of being trusted out without an adult collector. The promotion is valuable. The young collector gets 7s. 6d. per week, his senior assistant 7s., and his junior assistant 6s. 6d.

The rag-room, on the first floor, is crowded with heavy sacks of rags, some for the paper-mill, and others ready to be sent to Yorkshire, and to become shoddy-cloth for cheap tailors. The sorters are ranged at a long, perforated bench, upon which the many-coloured rags they are sorting are tumbled. Every separate bit of rag is felt and torn, to see whether the wool contains cotton. To detect the cotton in the woollen fabrics requires an experienced touch. Round each sorter is a row of baskets, into one of which he throws each bit of rag, according to its quality. The white clean rags have a compartment of honour to themselves—being very precious. The brilliant colours of the scraps that lie in masses about the room make it cheerful. Behind the sorters a man is engaged tumbling the sorted rags out of sacks, to examine them on the part of his master, who is the purchaser thereof. The dyes of these bits are bright—for the scraps are new—from the workrooms of Messrs. Silver and Co., the great emigrant outfitters.

"We get great quantities in the City," the superintendent said. "I can venture to say that one-half of what we collect would be cast away, burnt, or lost, if it were not for our brigade. The people who allow us to call upon them would not permit any one else to call. We get about one ton of these cuttings from woollen shirts from Messrs. Silver every three months."

The men were busy filling the sacks that were suspended from the ceiling; here with piles of old, dark, greasy cloth, not worth much—there, with more delicate fabrics. Beyond the rag-room was a store, where the sacks of valuable refuse were heaped almost to the ceiling.

"We take everything," the superintendent said, as he showed me his miscellaneous treasures: "old books, lamps—even to hearse trappings"—the truth being that in these days it is difficult to find an article, let it be the oldest and most battered of its kind, that is useless. On the opposite side of the court to that in which the rags are sorted, and the kitchen stuff is preserved, is the paper department. This department is a rough, stable-looking place. Round it are stacks of ginger-beer bottles, ink-bottles, jam-pots, and flower-pots. Upon the ground lie masses of soiled paper. At a board a man is neatly arranging the cardboard and whole newspapers that have been brought in with the scraps. All these bits and odds and ends are the sweepings of City warehouses. The long bits of cardboard are carefully tied together, and will serve as shapes for cheap caps. The superintendent explained—"We carefully take out of the sweepings all written documents and destroy them, as we do all accounts. We don't reduce them to pulp ourselves, but we guarantee that they shall be reduced. We have had as much as five or six tons of account-books from the Underground Railway contractors. I give an undertaking to destroy them. We have great quantities of ink-bottles and jam-pots. It is not the season for jam-pots now; but when it is we sell them to the confectioners. I rose, myself, from a ragged school. I first went when I was about six or seven years old; and I am now 26. I married, like most young men, and did the best I could. I was a barman, and then in a pork-butcher's. At last when the gentlemen agreed to start this place, they remembered my character, I suppose, and put me in here." This account of himself was so modestly and truthfully told by the superintendent, that I saw at once how fully justified the ragged-school authorities were in choosing him from among their old scholars.

For each truck a special book is kept in the office. In this book the earnings and disbursements of the truck are recorded daily. Then the doings of all the brigade are summed up in a weekly account. Some of the items of a week's account are startling. The boys brought home 97 dozen bottles; 31 cwt. of various kinds of waste paper; more than 8 cwt. of bones; 7 cwt. of rags; and nearly 8 cwt. of fat. They purchased these goods for £20, 13s., and the expenses of the brigade in wages were £14. The average purchases made by each truck per diem range between 15s. and 30s. The purchase money is given to the collector every morning. He is solely responsible for it. It is almost impossible for him to cheat. He must be able to read and write, and be a good arithmetician; so that he shall have no excuse on the score of ignorance. His accounts are balanced every evening. The superintendent can see whether he has brought back money's worth. Any discrepancies are at once deducted from his money. And, to crown the precautions taken by the authorities, every collector carries a tariff of prices, to which he is bound to adhere. The tariff, it should be understood, is a guarantee of good faith to the sellers of refuse, as well as to the governors of the brigade. The collector's card tells them what they have a right to expect, and what the collector is justified in asking. This tariff varies a little, as the market price varies. Even the refuse which thousands cast away to perish, rises and falls in value in the public market. The cast-off clothes of the most forlorn of beggars have their value when brought into the market-place.

The following are the prices at which the boys are allowed to make purchases just now.

In the article of rags: new white cuttings, 2½d. per lb.; white rags, 1½d. per lb.; dirty white, 1d.; coloured or mixed, ½d.; new cloth cuttings, 4d.; old do., 1d. Paper: clean white shreds, 1½d. per lb.; inked do., ¼d.; clean cardboard cuttings, ½d.; dirty do., ¼d.; newspapers or old account-books, 1d.; office and warehouse sweepings (paper only), 1s. per cwt. Broken glass (white), ½d. per lb.; old rope (hemp), ¾d.; horsehair (clean), 5d.; do. mixed, 1d.; old brass, 4d.; pewter, 6d.; copper, 7d.; lead, 1½d.; old zinc, 1d.; old iron, 6 lb. 1d.; good beef dripping, 4½d.; kitchen stuff, 2d.; bones, 5 lb. 2d. Bottles: wine, 5d. per dozen; champagne, 2d.; French do., 4d.; beer, 4d.; doctors', 2d.; do. small, 1½d.; ginger-beer (glass), 5d.; do. stone, 3d. Why should there be a sudden fall in the price of champagne bottles from 3d. to 2d. per dozen is an industrial mystery. Stone jars, 2 gallons, 3d. each; do. 1 gallon, 2d.; ½ gallon, 2d.; hare-skins, 1s. per dozen; rabbit do., 6d. per dozen; old carpets, ¼d. per lb.; Kidderminster, ½d.; india-rubber galoshes, ½d. This tariff varies only slightly; but it is necessary to adjust it continually, keeping an eye on the markets, and noticing when "good beef dripping" is worth 5d., and when it will not fetch more than 4½d.

The labours of the brigade are relieved by six days' holiday in the course of the year, viz., three treat days, when they are provided with amusement, and three days when they are left to themselves, receiving their wages as though they were at work. With eight trucks, and another building, and the machinery in good order, our London rag-pickers are confident of a great success. Their indefatigable honorary secretary has been good enough to let me glean a few facts in anticipation of his report. I find that during the short time the brigade have been in existence they have bought from 40 to 50 tons of waste paper, between 3000 and 4000 dozen bottles, between 5 and 6 tons of metal, between 18 and 20 tons of bones, and about 20 tons of rags.

In conclusion, I will put an anecdote on record. Some boys with their rag-collecting truck were stopped in the streets by a gentleman, who appeared most anxious to know how they were getting on. He very cordially wished them succcss on one condition—that they would manage to put down all the marine-store dealers in London. When the gentleman passed on, the boys noticed that the policemen at hand touched their hats to him. This stimulated their curiosity, and they asked who their questioner was? "Sir Richard Mayne, our governor," was the answer.

I cannot help thinking that more industrial brigades might be started. Why not news-boy brigades; messenger brigades; and why not a great central agency for the employment of boys?

CHAPTER XV.

THE LITTLE SISTERS OF THE POOR.

WHEN at St. Servan, a little town on the coast of Brittany, opposite St. Malo, two or three humble townsfolk schooled themselves to be "Little Sisters of the Poor," and took an old woman to their humble home to begin with, they little dreamt that they were founding a charitable institution that would spread over France first, and then travel abroad. Only twenty-three years have passed since a few earnest women, under the direction of the Abbé le Pailleur, took vows of hospitality, and gave up their lives to the care of the aged poor; yet 1500 women have already followed their example, and now the little experiment first made in the humble dwelling of Fauchon Aubert is being successfully carried on in seventy-five houses in France and elsewhere. By the tender hands of the Little Sisters of the Poor, between 8000 and 10,000 aged poor are now fed and nursed. The Abbé le Pailleur, the founder of this wide-spread family of charitable little sisters, is now its superior-general. I need hardly add that the Little Sisters of the Poor are a Roman Catholic family; but to their great honour be it recorded that they gather the aged poor to their homes without regard to the sufferer's religion. The Jew is as welcome as the Papist.

Many Londoners must have remarked a little dark cart, driven by a woman in conventual dress, driving about the streets. Strange stories floated in metropolitan society about some devoted sisters who were tramping about the streets of London, begging food, left-off clothing, and money for their *protégés*, and that these servants of the poor were content to live on the refuse their inmates left. To exclude a charity so peculiar and so admirable from a review of the institutions which endeavour to mitigate the suffering of the London poor was impossible. I therefore determined to obtain accurate information about the Little Sisters, and to see them at work with my own eyes. The Little Sisters of the Poor have two establishments in London, viz., one at

6, Sutherland Gardens, Maida Hill, and one at 11, Paragon, New Kent Road. I visited that situated at Maida Hill. I expected to find a by-street, and to see some of the outward aspects of poverty. I was prepared for mews, or rents, or dark and muddy lanes, and I found myself between two rows of handsome modern houses, that appeared to contain about the luxury that £1500 a year will bring. These great stucco houses, in any of which a rich alderman might dwell, the abode of the Little Sisters of the Poor, and their aged men and women! I was speculating and doubting, when a hooded face appeared behind the blinds. The face was that of a Little Sister of the Poor, and I rang the bell.

A sister opened the door, and I was admitted to the hall. I begged to be allowed to see the good mother. The sister went to speak to the superior, and I remained examining the fine proportions and high finish, and expensive fixtures of the house. Presently the Little Sister returned, and showed me into the receiving-room. Had the house been put to its destined purpose, this would have been the dining-room; and here thirty guests might have comfortably ranged their knees under the mahogany. Over the massive marble mantelpiece, built to support Sèvres china and some of the glories of French ormolu, a large crucifix was nailed against the wall. The pictures were portraits of the Pope and Cardinal Wiseman. The room was not carpeted, and, for all furniture, contained a deal-topped table, a few cane chairs, and a case full of drugs and bottles. From the window of this bare and fireless apartment, I could see the rich hangings at the windows of the houses opposite.

The good mother entered, followed by a Little Sister—the begging sister. I was motioned to a seat; and explained the object of my visit. The good mother was a Frenchwoman, and understood very little English, so that we conversed in her native tongue. The begging sister (who was French also) spoke English remarkably well. Indeed, in this establishment, there is only one English Little Sister. In reply to my inquiries, most kindly and courteously received, the good mother said:—

"The object of our work is to take aged people for the remainder of their lives. The only payment we require—this we do not always insist upon—is £2, 14s. on the entrance of each old person, to pay for a bedstead, etc. Friends may help, but they are not compelled. Our inmates—and we have 94 with us at this moment—are provided with everything, and we ask nothing. We are supported by the broken food, clothes, and money the Little Sisters are able to collect. They go to the great hotels and to rich people's houses. Some are very kind to them; but they get many rebuffs. The Great Western Hotel, the hotel by Hyde Park Corner, and others are very good to us. We are very poor, and depend on our begging sisters. The rent of the house is paid for us—we couldn't afford it. The house is not large enough for our numbers; we haven't room for even one more sufferer. We want to build new houses on plans suited to our object, but we must wait for help. We are almost unknown in London, but our sisterhood is all over France. We want to be better known. If you wish to see over the establishment, the Little Sister will show you over it with pleasure."

The Little Sister entered upon her duties as guide with alacrity. She was a bright and cheerful body, and seemed to think all matters connected with the establishment the merest holiday work. The old men we met on the stairs or in the passages were greeted with a kind word or friendly recognition. They looked like Greenwich pensioners out of uniform. There was the same mild and contented expression which bespeaks a mind at ease. It is for these, the scarred and maimed, vanquished in the battle of life, that the sisters toil by day and watch by night, and beg along the highways of London.

The premises inhabited by the Little Sisters of the Poor in Sutherland Gardens are three fine houses thrown into one, or rather, communicating by the garden in the rear. The centre house is inhabited by the Little Sisters, and the other two by the old men and women. It was in the sisters' house that I first presented myself. It is by far the least comfortable of the three. On the first floor is the chapel. When I entered it, some half-dozen old folk were silently praying before the altar. On the second floor, reached by broad stone staircases, was the sisters' bed-room, trim and sweet, but without a feminine comfort save that of cleanliness. The Little Sisters sleep on straw; but sleep soundly, I have no doubt. Behind the bed-room is the linen-room, where the aged people's linen is kept distinct in numbered boxes. Two Little Sisters were busy sorting it for the Sunday's wear. The handsomely-finished bannisters were covered with old clothes, spread out after having been cleaned. We now descended to the kitchen-floor. A great, well-furnished, savoury kitchen. Some tempting morsels were hissing and spluttering in the frying-pan; and Little Sisters, dressed for culinary duty, were busy preparing food. At the dresser the Little Sister who was my guide opened a deep drawer.

"This is the bread we collect," she said. The drawer was half-full of broken bits of bread from sumptuous tables. I pointed to stacks of fresh slices upon the dresser. "Yes," said the Little Sister, "that is for the old men and women. They never eat the broken bread we pick up except in their soup; and we never touch the fresh bread while there are any scraps. We live on what is left—on anything. The best of everything we give to our old people; and if any meat, etc., is left, we have it. They have four meals every day. For breakfast, they have bread and butter; for dinner, soup, meat, vegetables, and beer; and then they have tea, and something for supper."

This is bountiful fare, collected by the little begging sisters of the poor. Their *protégés*, however, are so old that they require plenty of nourishment.

The back kitchen is the sisters' dining-room. A long deal table was laid for their afternoon meal. I have never seen a more touching sight. Two piles of broken odds and ends of stale crusts, and two heaps of cheese-parings—all leavings from good tables; with some brown jugs of water, and mugs set to each plate—were all these self-devoted women had laid for themselves. That which gave a refining touch to the whole was the arrangement of coarse *serviettes*, tied with black strings, against each plate. The Little Sister smiled, as I lingered over this feast of scraps that any London beggar would scorn. The fare the Mendicity Society give to passing tramps is a meal for a club *gourmet* when compared with this severely frugal spread. Yet, eaten with a hearty will, and by contented lips, it becomes dainty food, whereon the Little Sisters flourish. It is sweetened day by day with the knowledge that comfort has been given to ninety of God's creatures. I could not forbear from contrasting charity as it is here administered, unregarded by the world, with London Tavern feasts, where hearts are opened by guinea dinners, to the strains of hired singers, and where applause is modulated to harmonize with the amount given—a slight rattling of glasses, accompanying the gift of two guineas, and "great applause" proclaiming the fifty guinea donation. Unseen and unknown, the Little Sister of the Poor, her hard day's work done, munches her stale crust and rind of cheese, content to carry out her vow of hospitality, and to sleep upon straw!

I followed the Little Sister from the house into the garden. An old man was wandering about it, dabbling with the beds. The old men cultivate plots of ground here in the summer. We entered the old men's wing. The plan of the house was exactly like that of the Little Sisters'.

The front-kitchen was a smoking-room, in which a few old men were enjoying their pipes. "This," said the Little Sister, "is where they smoke, as you see. And shoe-mending goes on here, but nothing is doing this afternoon; they are all resting, and making ready for Sunday." They were all more than sixty years of age, come to the asylum for age, to wear away in rest the few remaining years of their unfortunate lives. To age this is in truth

"A chapel of ease
For all men's wearied miseries."

"We are now going to see the younger men," said the Little Sister, as we mounted to the ground-floor. Some five-and-twenty veterans were seated round a fire, or at tables, in the handsome room, that had been built for a luxurious dinner. They rose as we entered. The Little Sister went up to some of them cheerily, and talked with, and rallied them. "They play all their money away," she said, laughing—"all of it." They turned from their dominoes and laughed. One advanced, and spoke to me—in praise of the good sisters—hinting, a little coarsely and strongly, at a lack of money. I didn't pause to inquire whether he was touting for the charity or for himself, for his manner and speech were jarring. I followed the sister to the back-room, where two old men were tailoring. "These men, you see," she observed, "are earning money. Get up; a gentleman has come to pay you a visit." This request was addressed in raillery to the senior of the tailors—a very old man—who could not easily rise from his seat. He endeavoured, but I stopped him. He looked happy at his work, with his spectacles perched upon the tip of his nose; but his fingers were unsteady; they had lost their former strength and cunning. Yet he had a mind to work on while he could use the needle, and he was earning a little money by his feeble labour. All the men in this room were over sixty.

"A curious collection of old men," I said to the Little Sister, when we reached the landing. She laughed, and answered—"Those are not our old men. You will see some now, up-stairs, in the infirmary."

They were very old. A knot of them bent, and dozing, and mumbling over the fire; in all kinds of old men's loose clothes, and quaint head coverings. They rose with difficulty; and turned their wrinkled faces towards us. They were quiet and gentle with the sisters, who treated them like so many ailing children who should be coaxed and petted. "They have been all shaved to-day. Haven't you?" said my guide. "Yes, all of them." I turned to the back part of the room, where two invalids were lying. One was propped up in his bed: an old man whose face was wasted almost to a skull, and in whose sunken eyes there was an expression of anguish that thrilled through me. Poor, worn-out traveller, longing to be at rest; borne down with unhappy years, and, in the end, racked with rheumatic pains! Beside him was another invalided veteran, whom a Little Sister was tending. In a corner was a bed, upon which a younger man was stretched. "He has been paralysed fifteen years," the Little Sister whispered to me. "We take him out of bed once a week—to make it—that's all." Fifteen years spent upon his back! This is a living death. The world has been wagging apace since he was laid upon his back to wait for the great change. Palsied, and upon a bed of poverty. Fate could not hit poor human flesh a harder blow. He is here, however, under a noble roof, protected by the vows of hospitality of the Little Sisters, and has all the comforts it is possible to give to one so deeply afflicted.

As I stood in the midst of these old, old men—all solemnly gathered here in the ante-chamber of death, waiting meekly and cheerfully the summons that could not tarry long—I remembered what their fate must have been had they been left where the brave Little Sisters of the Poor found them. The man, now cold with agony, about whose bed the screen will come soon, would have been lying in some garret, with want added to his sorrow. And I thank God, who directed the gentle steps of the Little Sisters to him.

The Little Sister stopped as we were leaving the room to talk to an old, laughing man. "Are you very good?"

"No," he answered, shaking his head; "I'm not good; none of us are good."

Above the infirmary were the sleeping-rooms, in what housewives would call "apple-pie" order, and with the Sunday clothes and clean linen of each old man upon his bed. The Little Sister told me that two Sisters remained in the men's house, and two in the women's, all night, to be at hand if any inmate should require assistance. The wonder is that with such inmates the Sisters can ever have a good night's rest.

We returned to the garden, and entered the house devoted to aged women. The arrangements of this house resembled that of the men, save that the women had no smoking-room allotted to them. The ground-floor room was the work and sitting room. About thirty old women were assembled in it, chattering together. The work was at an end, and they were taking rest for the morrow. They were all comfortably clothed, and were sitting about the room—a cosy party, probably waiting for that which old ladies love so much—their tea. They looked so unlike the miserable crones I had seen in London alleys, that I asked the Little Sister whether they had been in a state of absolute destitution.

"They are all the poorest of the poor," she answered. "If you had seen some of them when they came to us, you would not believe that they were the same women. Cleanliness and good living soon alter them. But these are the younger women; you will see some much older in the infirmary."

The infirmary was disposed like that of the men. The women were crowded about the fire, with the exception of one or two, who were in bed, and one who was sitting apart between two of the beds.

"Here is a gentleman come to see you, Mrs. Nugent; come along; come and speak to him." The old lady, with a slight help, came towards us. The Little Sister took hold of her affectionately. 'Why, this is the beautiful cap that was given to you the other day." The old lady smiled at the Sister. "How are you to-day?" She replied that she was pretty well. She was ninety-seven years of age, and was consequently a woman—possibly married—when the first French Revolution happened, and past her prime when the battle of Waterloo was fought. She was not less than fifty-four when the First Gentleman in Europe died. Yet she had many of her teeth still, and could walk and talk cheerfully. When it was suggested to her that she would more than complete a century of life, she shook her head and said, "I hope not; I'm sure I hope not." This was truthfully and emphatically spoken. Her face looked wondrously old; not touched in the least by illness, but withered and blanched by time. She shook hands, and said "good-bye" more brightly, however, than many women of eighty could take leave.

Up stairs, in one of the dormitories, we found a solitary old woman in bed. The Little Sister had a few kind words to say to her. The poor creature tried to rise from her couch and bow to us, but the effort was too much for her strength. When we had left the dormitory the Sister said, "She has been here only a few days. We hadn't room or bedding for her, so one of the Sisters gave up her bed. I found her in a cellar, and she was almost black. We had the greatest trouble in making her clean. She is very grateful for being here;" as well she might be, in that spacious room, upon a clean couch, and nursed by the Little Sisters of the Poor. On our way out —I had now seen all that was to be seen—the Little Sister showed me the inconveniences of their premises. They were built for rich folk, bent upon enjoying all the good things of this life on a large scale; not for the waifs and strays of Whitechapel and Westminster. To begin with, they are too high. Old people cannot mount three or four flights of stairs without being much distressed. The neighbourhood is too genteel. Around are the children of prosperity, who are sometimes proud with their prosperity, and are therefore not always well pleased to see an asylum for aged paupers next door to them. The begging Little Sister, and the cart on its way to fetch broken victuals, may offend the eye of pride, who has paid a heavy rent to be with, if not the *crême de la crême*, at least the *crême*.

The Little Sister conducted me to the street-door. She opened it, and an old man with a wooden leg was on the door-step. He was an inmate who had been out for a holiday. "They are allowed to go out once a fortnight," said the Little Sister, as she welcomed the wooden-legged holiday-maker home, and bowed to us.

I would have the reader observe that I did not see the houses of the Little Sisters of the Poor prepared, as many charitable institutions may be, for a visit. I merely called on the first convenient day, and the good mother frankly and freely threw the premises open to my inspection. I saw the "servants of servants" at their daily work, doing the most menial offices for the aged and widowed poor, and taking the stalest of the crusts for their own daily food. I was not asked whether I was Roman Catholic or Protestant. I saw that which is going on every day, and that which any reader who rings at the Little Sisters' bell may see for himself. I saw "widows indeed, and desolate" cared for, and dutifully and humbly nurtured. It is a happy place of rest for indigent old age, and he who casts his mite into the slenderly-stocked treasury that supports it will help to smooth a pillow for a helpless grey head.

CHAPTER XVI.

POOR INVALIDS' DINNER-TABLES.

THE poor of London are an improvident and a stubborn class. They learn very slowly. As an old-fashioned, ignorant cook will not deign to be taught the mysteries of a new dish by the most skilful mistress, so the poor woman who almost works her fingers off to give bread to her children will not listen when she is told she might save much that she throws away, and purchase with better advantage. She dismisses the advice as new-fangled, and goes on her own wasteful way—as Soyer showed—throwing aside, if she be in a well-to-do establishment, what would keep a poor family in France. The woful ignorance of cookery shown by the poor, who should at least know how to economize food, is not assailed in any charitable institution I have yet visited. There is a school of cookery in Berners Street, Oxford Street, where women are taught to make *omelettes, soufflées,* and Palestine soup. It is prospering mightily, and people flock to the school's *table-d'hôte* to partake of the results of the pupils' lessons. All this will be of no service to the poor. It will only tend to make good cooks cheap, and so add to the luxuries of the middle class. The best lesson the charitable can teach the poor is how to help themselves. At ragged and industrial schools poor children are taught how to hem and sew, or ply a trade; but in none is the important lesson taught how to turn to profitable account every atom that is purchased out of labour's modest wages. If a sensible, scientific cook would mount a platform, arrange his culinary utensils, and show the million how to make a good dinner out of mere odds and ends, and if the wives of working men would attend and listen to him, he would do more real good to his fellow-creatures than the hack purveyors of moral platitudes, who command the audiences of mechanics' institutes now-a-days, can show as the fruit of their lips. The cook would teach the humble housewife how to make home happier, and so he would smooth the way for the schoolmaster and the clergyman. When the workmen of France were in great distress, the Empress of the French gave her patronage to public kitchens, adapted to their purposes. Food being scarce, it should not be wasted. Many a poor man's family would be rid of half the privations they now endure if *mater* had the knowledge that a cook could give her. Soyer could make excellent soup out of refuse, left by very poor people for the dust-cart. I propose to submit to the reader, in this chapter, what has been done in London, to give invalided workmen and workwomen a good dinner at a cheap rate, that they may recover the strength which is money to them.

There are very few persons in London who have heard of the Invalids' Dinner Table. Who wants a good dinner more than the invalid, who has been impoverished by illness, and who cannot regain his strength without nutritious food? A lady lying ill thought of the poor on a bed of sickness, and resolved that, if she recovered, she would establish a charitable dinner-table for the sick. In time her health mended—hence the first Invalids' Dinner Table. The original table was laid in Duke Street, and was removed last spring to Earl Street, Lisson Grove, at the end of 1859. The plan is simple. The tickets for dinner are valued at 6d. each; and all benevolent persons are at liberty to buy as many as they please. These tickets are distributed among the sick poor, each ticket entitling the holder to a dinner. If well enough he must present his ticket at the house where the dinner is held, at nine o'clock in the morning, that the matron may know for how many she has to provide. The dinner, which consists of the best beef and mutton, bread, vegetables, and beer, takes place at half-past twelve o'clock. The diners who eat in the little Earl Street *salle-à-manger* pay nought for this substantial and wholesome fare. A workman reads to them while they eat; grace is said before and after meat; and the establishment closes for the day. The invalids who are not able to reach the dinner-table may send for their dinner; but for this privilege they must pay a fine of one penny. At the St. Pancras Dinner Table (held at No. 4, Woburn Buildings, behind St. Pancras Church), all diners pay twopence with their ticket. Care is taken that no person afflicted with an infectious disease is admitted. Extra comforts can be had by special tickets issued to subscribers. Thus, green tickets are issued by medical gentlemen for medical diet. Red tickets are for extra medical comforts, as ordered by the physician, surgeon, or the dispensary.

This invalids' gratuitous dining-room, in which I find myself, is only a little shop, with a long deal table in it, the little back parlour being the kitchen. There are now four of these dinner-tables in London, viz., this, the parent one; the parish of St. Pancras Dinner Table; one at 65, Upper Ebury Street, Pimlico; and one at 5, Poplar Place, Moscow Road, Bayswater. These four establishments distribute about 14,000 good dinners annually among the invalid poor of the metropolis. It is stated on the dinner tickets of the St. Pancras Dinner Table that "the object sought by this charity is to help the honest, industrious working man and his family, after they have been (by no fault of their own) thrown upon a bed of sickness, and are slowly recovering from its effect, and to enable them to resume their occupation as soon as possible." It is such as these who deserve assistance; the more so, because they are the last to urge their claims before the public. When a working man leaves the hospital, he may be cured, but he is by no means in a condition to resume his work immediately. His strength wants recruiting. The hospital has done its part, and others are waiting for the bed just vacated. The patient, therefore, is dismissed at the earliest possible period. It is at this stage that the action of this charity comes in, and offers to such as are ascertained to be deserving of it, a little wholesome, nourishing food for a few days or a week, as the physician or surgeon may recommend. This timely help must be most welcome to workmen and workwomen who never received a groat in the shape of charity. One of the noblest charities that have been built and set in motion, since the establishment of the second French empire, is the hospital for convalescent workmen in the Bois de Vincennes, near Paris. We have no such institution near London, and these invalids' dinner-tables are therefore doubly welcome.

The original Invalids' Dinner Table appears to be the best ordered of the four, perhaps because the lady superintendent has more experience than her imitators. Her regulations meet all kinds of cases. She desires that the diners should come to her board, that while they eat they may get a little religious instruction. She therefore places a fine on the dinner that is carried away; the fine is 1d., and "those who are not prepared to meet this payment will forfeit the bread and the beer." The dinner is served under medical inspection, and doctors attend occasionally to test the wholesomeness of the food.

The usefulness of the parent institution does not end with the distribution of food to poor invalids, since the matron undertakes to teach respectable young girls "the rudiments of cooking" for 2s. a week. This cheap instruction may open a career to many a poor girl, and teach many a poor maiden to become a useful working man's wife.

The table is laid only three times a week in the summer; not, it would appear, because there is an absence of poor invalids at this period, but because the subscribers who distribute the dinner-tickets are nearly all out of town. This thoughtlessness merits the reproof it has received in last year's report. The people who forget the poor directly they cease to be in contact with them are feeble sympathizers—their charity is of the poorest. I find that some contributions of port wine have been made to the Invalids' Dinner Table, "by adopting the suggestion made in the last report, of saving for the sick that small portion of every bottle of port which is unfit for the decanter!" This is charity made easy. The lees of wine from the healthy rich man's table are sent to the ailing poor man! The lees may be welcome, but the donor had better have spared a full bottle. To give away that which is not good enough for our own use is hardly charity. The matron receives presents of wine, home-made jam, cod-liver oil, linen rags, flannel, etc. The patrons of this institution can already lay claim to many cures. The invalided poor require a good dinner rather than medicine. They want strength. A boy came to this little place in Earl Street severely afflicted with St. Vitus' dance. The poor child wanted good nourishment. He received it, and was cured. A single dinner-ticket given away does little or no good. The invalid requires good living for a week or two to make a permanent effect upon him. The poor man often complains that his physic makes him hungry. It is intended to stimulate his appetite; but he has no dinner.

The cook, a matron at the Earl Street dinner, was most anxious to give me every kind of information. Most unlike, in this respect, the lady who presides behind St. Pancras Church.

"We buy the very best beef, mutton, and vegetables," said the Earl Street lady. "Yesterday, I cooked dinner for twenty-six, and to-day for twenty. Every diner has half a pint of beer and a roll with his meat and vegetables. I give a quarter of a pint to very young children." I remarked on the smallness of the kitchen. "Yes, but I have cooked dinners for a hundred people in it."

I inquired how often the same people returned to dine.

"Some come every day for a week or two. I had one woman and a little boy who dined here every day for a year and a half. She was very ill when she first came, and her little boy had been run over. Just now, two or three young men, who have been in the hospital, dine here, to recover their strength."

It is gratifying to learn that the Invalids' Dinner Table is becoming known in provincial towns. The matron of the Earl Street table told me that a lady had recently called upon her for the rules of the institution, in order that she might be prepared to spread an Invalids' Dinner Table in the Isle of Man, where, she said, such an institution was much wanted.

It should be observed of these charitable dinner tables that they are not likely to be abused. They are instituted to help needy men and women at a time when they are least able to help themselves. Employers might take advantage of them to do a gracious action to workmen who have fallen ill. A bricklayer falls from a scaffolding, and is laid up for weeks in an hospital. He is a member of a benefit society, and he is entitled to perhaps 10s. or 12s. a week from the fund to which he has subscribed. This sum will help to keep his *ménage* together while he recovers; but it will not afford him the nutritious food he requires when he leaves the hospital, that he may regain the strength necessary to his vocation. He is in a sore dilemma. To him strength is money, and solid food is strength; and he cannot afford to eat of roast and boiled daily. Help extended to him in this moment of trouble will not demoralize him. It will not lure him into the fraternity of beggars. His health and strength regained, there is no longer a knife and fork for him at the Invalids' Dinner Table. He will rather return to work with the new courage that belongs to a heart made grateful. The timely charity of which he has been the object will have refreshed his moral nature. He will see that he is cared for, in his hour of misfortune, by people placed by accident above him. We may dwell, then, with unmixed pleasure on these humble tables spread for the suffering poor.

A few more facts, which I glean from the last report of the Earl Street table, may be added, in order that the reader may have a complete idea of the operation.

As far as the work of the past year can be stated in numbers, it is as follows:—Meat dinners, 3045, of which 1913 have been eaten at table, and 1132 taken home. Four diet tables, each representing ten or twelve light nourishing meals, have been given, besides other occasional supplies of invalids' food. These are always taken home, as those who require them are generally seriously ill.

The number of tracts distributed has been about the same as that of the dinners given, and the Scriptures have been read and prayer offered about 260 times in the hearing of companies varying in number from two or three to between twenty and thirty. Up to the present time no special provision has been made for incidental expenses: they have been defrayed out of the contributions of those who did not require tickets, added to the small sum obtained by the pence charged to the invalids for dinners carried home; but three years' experience has shown that these resources are both too small and too uncertain to be relied on.

Every effort is made to reduce the working expenses to the lowest point, but they cannot be stated at less than between £50 and £60 under ordinary circumstances. During the past year, owing to special circumstances not likely to occur, they have been unusually heavy, and consequently the disbursements have been some pounds in advance of the receipts. It has, therefore, been resolved to form an expense fund, to which special contributions are invited.

It should be borne in mind that the expenses of rent, cleaning, matron's stipend, and master and matron's dinner do not vary according to the number of invalids fed, so that the larger the number of dinners provided, the less in proportion is the cost of working the charity. Notwithstanding the smallness of the *locale*, it is quite capable of dispensing five or six thousand dinners annually.

The rent of the premises is 9s. a week; but arrangements are being made to lessen the amount by letting the room for the sale of pure literature on certain evenings in the week.

A kind of sick-club has been formed, from which the members who contribute as much as 4s. receive a depositor's ticket, which entitles them in time of sickness to eight dinners, without further payment. Any sum, from ½d. upwards, is received until the required amount is reached.

The balance shows that the receipts amounted to £158, 15s. 8d., and the disbursements (including a sum of £97, 12s. 0½. for 3045 people's dinners, together with 259 matron's dinners and 250 master's dinners) to £158, 3s. 10d., leaving a balance of 11s. 10d. due to the treasurer.

These dinners have been so successful, that it is in contemplation to extend the benefits of cheap dining to healthy work-folk. From time to time endeavours have been made to draw working-men from the public-house by providing them with airy, well-lit reading and coffee rooms. In the manufacturing districts millowners have built fine news-rooms for their men adjoining the mills. The success of these endeavours to wean the operatives from the beer-shop has been only moderate. I remember that when I was travelling through the manufacturing districts, about two years ago, I was shown, within the handsome walls of a factory at Church, a spacious, even elegant, suite of rooms. "These," said the owner, "were built for the use of our hands. You will see that all the periodicals and newspapers are here. The rooms are well warmed and lighted. I have studied every comfort. But very few of my people use them. No, sir, they prefer the dark and comfortless tap-room in the ale-house opposite." It did appear unaccountable on the face of it that the men should prefer the tap-room to all this comfort.

But, on closer examination of the matter, the reason for the preference became as clear as noon-day. A glance at the regulations justified the men. When an operative has completed a hard day's work he desires relaxation. He has been under the watchful eye of a foreman all day. He has been the slave of regulations all day long. To him, then, complete liberty is the keenest enjoyment he can have. He wants to chat with his friends over his pipe and his mug of ale. In this model suite of rooms he must drink tea or coffee, and he may *not* smoke! Teetotallers and anti-tobacco advocates will applaud this prohibition of the pipe and of malt liquors; but I venture to assert that it is a most irrational one. I gave my reasons to the millowner who was showing me his model reading-rooms. I told him that his men would not be put under regulations in their holiday hours, since liberty was what they enjoyed most in these hours. The absurdity of the smoke prohibition was illustrated by our own party; we were all smoking while we were discussing the question. Smoking-rooms are in our London clubs; men of all classes are addicted to tobacco. Then why should we endeavour to force the workman, who finds enjoyment in a pipe after his day's labour, to forego this humble luxury, and be content to have a cup of tea in a model reading-room? The promoters of working men's clubs and reading-rooms may depend upon this, that the class to whom they appeal will not be won from the tap-room until there is all reasonable liberty in the club.

At No. 6, Mount Row, Davies Street, Grosvenor Square, there are working-men's coffee and reading-rooms. These rooms appear to be in a flourishing condition, the average weekly attendance being 500. As the situation suggests, "the class of persons making use of these rooms are stable-men, servants out of place, coachmakers, labourers," etc. There are prayer-meetings, a lending library, a benefit society, and a penny bank connected with the club. This club was set on foot in 1858, in "very dilapidated premises in Adam's Mews." Its success has justified removal to commodious premises which include a hall capable of holding 200 persons. I am happy in being able to record the complete success of this experiment, carried on among gentlemen's stable-men and grooms, under missionary influence; but I am certain that large clubs carried on as this is carried on could not be made self-supporting. Mr. G. M. Hicks, who established the St. Pancras Invalids' Dinner Table, has in contemplation, I am informed, a working-men's club, at which dinners shall be served at club prices.

The cooking depots of Glasgow have, it appears, already stimulated a number of gentlemen to form themselves into a committee for the purpose of affording the London working classes good dinners. These depots are to be paying speculations. There is to be no charity in the matter. Working men are to feel as independent in them as his lordship feels at the Traveller's. Twenty depots are to be simultaneously formed in various districts of London, at a cost of about £5000. There is every reason to believe that the speculation will be a remunerative one. These depots will tend to draw working men from the public-house. When the workman's dinner-hour has come he will not be compelled to seek the nearest tap-room to eat his dinner. He will find a well-ordered and strictly economical dining-place in the neighbourhood, where there will be no landlord to tempt him to drink. But these depots do not dispose of the question of cheap food for the London working classes and poor. Everybody who has studied the progress of the co-operative movement in Lancashire and in London must have been struck with its rapidity. Working men are becoming alive to the fact that they pay dearer for their food than their rich neighbours. Buying in small quantities, they pay more tradesmen's profits than the consumer who is able to purchase in larger quantities. So they have banded themselves together into little societies, and gone to the wholesale vendor, and put the petty retailer's profits into their own pockets. They have thus secured to themselves cheap and unadulterated food. A workman who has once found his way to a co-operative store never deserts it. He becomes a partner in it. It teaches him prudence, while it gives him his full money's worth. The workmen who are members of co-operative stores are thrifty, saving men. The principle of these stores is exactly that which governs our large West-end clubs, where luxurious living is afforded to members at cost price. There is no reason why these working men's stores should not become clubs, all massed together under one management, so that a member might get his dinner at cost price at the club nearest to his place of work. These clubs would be well-regulated establishments, where there could be no drunkenness; where the working man would find only worthy associates. He would be subject to rules of his own making. If he spent his evenings at his club, they would be better spent than in the tap-room of a public-house. He would learn to take a pride in the good conduct of his club. Every member would be a wholesome check upon his neighbour.

Cooking depots might flourish in spite of the organization I have suggested. The clubs would include only the regularly employed. The masses of workmen who are continually moving to and from London would not belong to them. They would be beyond the reach of the very poor. Women and children would be excluded from them. They would not be available for tramps, dock-labourers, the majority of costermongers and hawkers, nor for the many varieties of vagrant poor who pick up a living in the streets. The poorest man feels the greatest necessity for economy. The dock-labourer feels the evil of the present system of buying and selling provisions more than the mechanic. If food can be given to the former at cost price, it is of the first importance that it should be done. As trade is carried on in Whitechapel, Drury Lane, and behind Westminster Abbey, the poor are robbed of one-third of their earnings. They eat bad food at a higher price than they would pay, under a good system, for wholesome food. They are plundered in the pawnbroker's, the tally-shop, and the pot-house. They pay, for dog-holes, rents that should afford them decent lodgings. In short, one pennyworth is not one-twelfth part of a shilling's worth. The acute operatives of Lancashire were the first to see the ludicrous error in which they were living. They ended by buying their own corn and grinding it in their own mills. They would have twelvepence-worth of flour for their shilling. To help the poor of London to get full value for the little money they earn would be to do more for them than almsgiving. These invalids' dinner-tables are timely aids to the poor sick, and they deserve the cordial support of the public. I trust that they will soon be spread in every town of the United Kingdom. These are charities, however. To teach the poor how to go to market is merely to give them a lesson in domestic economy that will affect both the sick and the healthy. It will have a salutary effect upon every member of the working classes, since it will increase the value of his wages, and make his household happier and healthier.

CHAPTER XVII.

UNFORTUNATES.

THERE can be no longer any doubt that the distress in the poor districts of London is at least fully up to the average. The first sharp frost ripens this our great sore—as it ripens the medlar. The refuges and workhouses, the soup-kitchens and the hospitals, will be crammed; while the resources of these institutions will be less able than ever to cope with the difficulty. I find on all sides the same exclamation—"Lancashire has crippled us, and we may have a hard winter yet." The experience of the Mendicity Society, and the Bloomsbury and Field Lane Refuges, is that of nearly all our London Charities; of those that attend to the moral elevation of the poor as well as of those that give food, shelter, and clothing.

There is, perhaps, not a charity in London which more deserves the attention of the public, at the present time, than that which seeks to rescue young women and children from "the great vice of cities." The extent of this evil, and the horrible distress that accompanies it, are among the blots on our generation. A walk by day or night along our London streets will prove to any who may need proof that there is work enough to be done by the

Rescue Society that seeks to snatch fallen women and fallen children from their loathsome trade, and make good and industrious women of them. These brazen creatures, who openly flaunt their finery of shame, and elbow our wives and daughters, are vixens and brutes—not to be mentioned to ears polite, nor to be thought of as human creatures. It is in this spirit that society has been wont to regard them; they are lost—lost beyond redemption; their touch is pollution, their breath is poison. Gentility frowns them down so vehemently that it is difficult to make a plea heard in their behalf. Yet they are sisters! But then they are fallen, and can never be erect again. Society will give them no quarter. Let them out into the wet or frosty night; let them shiver with the cold, or soak in the rain, or bend before the wind. The charity of society was scant indeed towards these fallen creatures. Ugly names were hurled at them, and they were left to their miserable lot, until they were brought into operas and were prettily christened. Traviata and Anonyma may be talked about; theirs is splendid sin; shame accompanied with all conceivable pomp and circumstance. Hence midnight meetings, and the discovery that there may be some good left in the woman whom a man has betrayed to her ruin, and whom loss of character and poverty have driven into the streets. The Rescue Society show that out of 400 outcasts received into their homes, 324 were domestic servants; these were victims of unscrupulous men, driven from honest employment to the streets. Fallen they were, into mire; but why should they be irreclaimable? Why should the sentence of society upon them be irrevocable? The ranks of poverty in London need no recruiting; then why so belabour these victims, as to make them desperately wicked and keep them so? Let the "ferociously" virtuous be at the pains of watching these, their fallen sisters. Many of them are fair and blooming still; and many have kind words on their lips. They have not lost their charity; they will be seen to help the halt and blind. They are not demons. Then why should society say to them: "There is no way back into the presence of the virtuous; no hope, save in death. The scarlet letter must be worn to the end of the chapter, and the eyes of the pious remain averted." Society keeps the seducer an honoured member of its ranks; but, with refined cruelty, strikes the seduced to the earth. It is perhaps too early to ask that society shall fully and amply acknowledge its injustice, and henceforth be kind and gentle and forgiving to the humble Traviata; but we may demand that society shall be just.

The poor creatures who find their way to the homes of the Rescue Society have fallen, as young boy outcasts fall, into crime. Unkindness or death at home, or a cruel mistress, drive servants forth into the world, where there are tempters at every street corner. The soldier, the policeman, the schoolmaster, the theatre, the fair, and the public-house are at hand. The Rescue Society show the case of a schoolmaster who ruined his pupil, aged thirteen. They have also cases of ruin accomplished at the ages of seven, nine, and ten. They show us, in fact, that these "sad wanderers" of our streets are only poor women who have been sorely and shamefully tempted. The majority of them have been betrayed by their employers; they are martyrs of the very humblest origin, and they deserve our pity more than our scorn.

The incredulous, the hard of heart, should visit one of the Rescue Society's homes—say the Hampstead Home, the most interesting and important of the eleven homes which this admirable Society has opened to the fallen women of England. It is one of the old houses in Church Row, solidly built, and on very high ground, commanding a fine view of London. Behind it is a drying-ground, and next door to it is the Home for children who have been in peril. Mrs. Golding, who presides over the Home "for thirty young women," received me most graciously, and showed me into her sitting-room, which was ornamented by some handsome curtains that had been worked by one of her pupils. In this room were some portraits of fallen women whom the Society has rescued, and who are now leading honest and industrious lives in domestic service. The house was decorated throughout with holly and flowers, and banners. "Welcome to the Home" was embroidered upon a banner across the passage. The ceilings were all tastefully decorated, and in Mrs. Golding's room were vases of exquisitely cut flowers, the work of the women in the Home. "You see, sir," said Mrs. Golding, "we have been having our annual treat. We had the house so full: quite full. We gave them a good dinner and supper; and they sang. Eighteen who have been in the Home, and whom we have placed out at service, came to pay us a visit. They were as bright and happy as could be. When they come to us we teach them to be good servants. They work in the laundry. We are obliged to humour them and lead them by kindness. This is the only hold we have upon them, for they can walk off at any moment. We live like a family. They may quarrel a little among themselves occasionally, but a word from me stops them. I have never, however, heard one of them make use of an oath. Their conduct is wonderful. They stop from six to eighteen months, according to conduct; and if, after we have got situations for them, they lose them, we receive them back. If they go wrong again we still receive them, if we see a chance of ultimate amendment. We have had some back three times. When a girl has been in a situation for six months she gets a character, then she goes to the Servants' Home. From the Servants' Home she can get a better place than she generally has at first, because on the second occasion she can leave her old story behind her."

We proceeded to view the Home. It is simply a very large, well-ordered, scrupulously clean house. On the ground-floor is a long laundry. The women, neatly clad, were busy ironing and folding. Below is a wash-house, where the women are at the tub from nine o'clock in the morning till five in the afternoon. Above are the dormitories, where the little white beds are ranged. There is also a long common room.

When we entered it the women, about thirty in number, were ranged in two rows. They were all neatly dressed—as a very tidy nursemaid would be dressed—with snow-white aprons. The room was decorated from ceiling to floor with evergreens and flowers, and these, and rows of cheerful faces ranged round it, made a very pretty picture. In a corner was one girl who would not be diverted from her work. It was she who had knitted the curtains in the parlour. She had begged that she might be up at sunrise to work, so completely was her heart in her employment. I remarked that all the women called Mrs. Golding "mother." "Yes," she said, "I am always called 'mother' by them. We really want to make this their home, and to let them feel, wherever they may be, that there is a place where they are cared for."

At the mother's desire the girls sang three or four songs, all conveying wholesome moral or religious precept. They sang charmingly, in harmony and time, songs, some of which had been composed by themselves. When we left the room, I heard them break into conversation cheerfully and without restraint. An interesting, earnest-looking girl followed us out, and put a paper into the mother's hand. It was a very well-written manuscript of the songs they sang.

"They are all there, mother," the girl said, and slipped slowly back into the room. The first was a hymn on the New Year. It appeared that "mother" had suggested the first line, and the girls among themselves had added the rest. The song, or hymn, is one of gratitude for the Home in which the singers find themselves, neither hungry nor thirsty, nor cold, nor ill-clad.

The mother pointed out a fine, fresh-complexioned girl. "That girl," she said, "was brought here in a most deplorable condition only a few weeks ago." She is now on the high road to respectability. She has been snatched from the streets, and she will become a decent domestic servant. Surely to accomplish this reformation is a deed that is good in the sight of God and man. To do this is better than to throw stones at the fallen, and to bring them under the weight of our wrath. It is done on the most sensible principle by the Rescue Society. Their Homes are conducted on the family principle, by carefully chosen married women or widows. There is nothing in the houses to distinguish the Society's Homes from ordinary private residences. The inmates are neither put in uniform, nor subjected to the scissors of the hair-dresser. The Homes are situated in widely separated parts of London, in order to separate the women from their old, bad associates. The inmates learn washing, sewing, knitting, baking. They are religiously instructed. There are no harsh punishments; separation from their companions in the Home being the severest. All friendless girls in London, whether of good or bad character, may seek the help of the Rescue Society. Poor servants without suitable clothes for a situation; girls discharged from hospitals; and wanderers from the country,—are to be found in the eleven family Homes of the Society. All these have been saved from the sum of misery that is in London. Left to themselves they must have perished miserably after lives spent in vice and want.

It is nine years since the committee commenced their labours, and during that period 3041 outcasts have been relieved, sheltered, clothed, fed, instructed, and sent forth into the world again.

During the past year the committee have received into the Homes, or otherwise taken under their care, 591 young persons, including 203 who remained in the Homes at the end of the previous year.

The total admissions of the previous year were 756, showing a falling off in the number received to the extent of 165 persons, and this was attributable solely to the want of funds; but the vacancies being filled up towards the close of the financial year, when the necessary contributions came in, the Society had a larger number under its care on the 31st March last than at any single period in any previous year.

The 591 young persons (400 fallen and 191 unfallen) received into the Homes during the year were thus disposed of—200 were placed in situations; 25 were placed in other institutions; 1 was sent out as an emigrant; 11 were placed in hospitals; 67 were restored to their friends; 67 left of their own accord;

7 were dismissed; 211 remain in the Homes; and 2 died.

In viewing the occupations of fallen ones, it appeared that 324 had been domestic servants, 37 of the servant class had been living at home assisting their parents, 6 had been needlewomen, 4 had been dressmakers or milliners, 3 had been shopwomen, 2 embroiderers, 1 a factory girl, 1 an envelope-maker, 1 a teacher, 1 a schoolmistress, 1 a bar-maid, 1 a book-sewer, 3 charwomen and laundresses, 2 companions to ladies, 1 theatrical, 1 a shoebinder, 1 a trimming-weaver, 1 a waitress, 1 a straw-plait maker, and 8 followed no occupation, their parents being in respectable positions.

125 fallen and 42 unfallen had lost both parents, 68 fallen and 42 unfallen were fatherless, 90 fallen and 43 unfallen were motherless. Of two fallen and one unfallen the parentage was unknown; 115 fallen and 64 unfallen had both parents living.

Five fallen and six unfallen were well educated; 58 fallen and 82 unfallen could read and write tolerably; 227 fallen and 40 unfallen could read and write a little only; 70 fallen and 26 unfallen could read only; 40 fallen and 36 unfallen could neither read nor write.

343 fallen and 149 unfallen had attended Sunday-schools; 55 fallen and 39 unfallen had not.

Sixteen fallen and 105 unfallen were under 15 years of age; 209 fallen and 60 unfallen, from 15 to 20; 139 fallen and 19 unfallen, from 20 to 25; 36 fallen and 7 unfallen, above 25 years of age.

In the preventive cases, girls who have not strayed from virtue, 47 were homeless or outcasts; 58 were rescued from evil associations or bad examples at home; 86 were otherwise destitute or refractory.

Of the entire number of cases—591—394 were from

the country, and 197 from London and its vicinity, showing a large proportion of young persons from the country.

The ages at which the young women were received into the Society's Homes showed that the majority entered the path of sin when under or not more than 17 years of age. One was led from the right path at seven years of age—2 at 9 years, 2 at 10, 1 at 11, 15 at 12, 18 at 13, 31 at 14, 65 at 15, 54 at 16, 65 at 17, 49 at 18, 33 at 19, 28 at 20, 10 at 21, 2 at 22, 3 at 23, 1 at 24, 4 at 25, 2 at 26, 1 at 27, 1 at 28, and 1 at 31 years.

The statement of the funds showed that they had so far increased that in the year ending March 1862, the amount received was £6478, 12s. 8d., as against £250, 5s. 1d. in the year ending March 1854.

During the year, no less than 707 applicants applied personally at the Society's offices and Homes, but could not be admitted, while a large number of Christian persons applied on behalf of poor girls with the same result.

In the Dover Home (to which the Society contributes an annual sum of £30), 59 young women were received during the past year. Of these, 14 had been placed in situations, 5 had been sent to other situations, 10 restored to their friends, 4 had left of their own accord, 1 was dismissed, and 25 remain in the house.

In addition to the grant of money, the parent Society received into its Homes 13 young women, with a view to providing situations for them.

The receipts of this Home for the past year were £447, 16s. 1d., and the expenditure £435, 7s. 8d.

I find, from my experiences in the Refuges, as well as in these Homes, that London domestic servants are a most unhappy and unfortunate class; and that much of their unhappiness is due to the harshness of mistresses and to the immorality of their male employers.

The Home of Hope is in Regent Square, Gray's Inn Road, a square of pretensions not transcending those of College Place, Camden Town; a luckless place upon which *Mr. Punch* once turned his humorous eye. Number 6 of this humble square is a house which an auctioneer would describe as "a comfortable and genteel residence for a small family." There is no mark by which it can be distinguished from the houses around. Yet it is at this door that fallen and friendless young women are invited to knock, and obtain shelter, advice, and comfort. It is hither that the foot sore wanderers of our London streets, by midnight, are led, while words of hope and of kindness are ringing in their ears; to this quiet, ordered, seemly house, where there are little white-curtained beds that are as clean and as fresh as those which hear the dreamy words of happy school-girls.

Let us see what has been done under this modest roof by the voluntary charity of good folk, and the earnest gratuitous work of friends.

During the year, 73 young women (including the 11 remaining at the close of the previous year) were admitted into the Home; the whole cost being only £462. Had the funds at the disposal of the committee been larger, many more would gladly have availed themselves of this door of escape.

The committee give the following statement respecting the young women admitted into the Home:—40 had lost both parents, 6 were motherless, 11 were fatherless, 16 had both parents living.

Fifty had been domestic servants, 12 had been milliners, dressmakers, and needlewomen, 1 had been a nursery governess, 1 had worked at a silk mill,

1 had been a shopwoman, 1 had been a bookfolder, 6 had not been brought up to any regular employment, but lived with their parents.

Ten were 16 years of age and under, forty-three from 16 to 21, eighteen from 21 to 26, two above 26.

Twenty-nine had attended Sunday-schools, 44 had not, or were not known to have done so.

Twenty-six were placed in situations, 11 were restored to their friends, 1 was sent out as an emigrant, 11 left of their own accord, 7 were placed in hospitals and other institutions, 3 were dismissed, 1 was placed in business, and was since dead, 13 remain in the Home.

The funds raised on behalf of the Home during the year amount only to £462, showing a diminution on the previous year of £146.

As the matron was the only paid person connected with the Home, every sum contributed was expended upon the objects intended to be benefited.

If the whole cost of the Home (£462) be divided between the number reached and benefited (73) it would be seen that the average cost of each admitted case was £7.

An analysis of the coroners' inquests in London for a few years, on children under two years of age, shows that the crime of infanticide is greatly on the increase. In 1857 there were 177 cases; in 1858, 190; in 1859, 242; in 1860, 272.

The return of the verdicts of coroners' juries during the year 1861, on infants under two years of age, show that in the eastern division of the metropolis alone, 421 inquests were held. In seventeen of these cases the jury returned a verdict of murder. In the western division there were 316, the verdicts being generally "found dead," or "found dead in a box." In the city and liberty of Westminster, there were

91 inquests, and in the city of London and borough of Southwark, 84. In the metropolitan part of the county of Kent, there were 43 investigations by the coroner. In the parishes under the coroner for the Duchy of Lancaster, there were six in Middlesex, and in Surrey no less than 142. In all, the number of inquests holden on infants under two years of age amounted to 1103 in the course of one year.

In few instances is the mother able to recover from the putative father the small weekly payment called legal compensation. A return entitled "Bastardy," presented to Parliament in 1861, states that 157,485 summonses were issued from the year 1845 to 1859, both inclusive, against putative fathers; of these, only 124,218 came on for hearing, and of that number orders were made in only 107,776 cases, 15,981 being rejected. The committee find from experience that the great majority of mothers are unwilling, either from shame or misplaced affection, and often from not knowing the real name and residence of their seducer, to appear against the father, while in many instances he has been lost sight of before the child is born. Moreover, it frequently happens that, though there is no doubt where the guilt lies, it is difficult to produce sufficient corroborative evidence.

Should the mother obtain the sum called legal compensation, as the highest amount recoverable is only 2s. 6d. per week, and the charge generally for a nurse child is 5s. a week, she would still have to pay £6, 10s. yearly, besides clothing herself and child out of the scanty wages she must naturally expect to receive on entering service without a character. The committee have, therefore, opened a separate fund, out of which to pay for the child at nurse while the mother is under their care at the Home, and for a short time when she is in service or otherwise honestly and respectably employed; but in no case do they take charge of the child.

This system is very well considered. It would be highly dangerous to permit young women whose children are out at nurse to feel that their responsibility with regard to the "little strangers" had ceased. A benevolent gentleman who took an unfortunate mother and child into a Home of Hope he started, found after a short experience that he had a houseful of children. The mothers, relieved from their maternal responsibilities, had flown. They had flown, and they would come to no good; whereas, had they been held to their maternal responsibilities; had they been taught to work for their offspring, they would have been stimulated to take situations, and to have worked for the sake of the dear little one. This plan is found to answer in the Home of Hope. The women bring their wages in aid of the keep of the child that is out at nurse in a respectable family.

The Home is conducted on the most rational principles. It is most comfortably furnished. The table is a good *bourgeois* table of roast and boiled. The women have their time to themselves after five o'clock. They are not suddenly taken from the free living to which most of them have been accustomed, and put on gruel diet. The change would be too severe to them. They find in the Home of Hope a home of comfort such as they may some day keep over their own heads, if they will be industrious and well conducted. The success of the Home proves that it is conducted on sound principles, and that it deserves the support of the charitable public. It is a Home of charity, and rest, and good-will; where a Christian spirit may grow and fructify, and whence a new and honourable start in life may be made.

CHAPTER XVIII.

DISTRICT VISITING.

An important association has lately sprung into existence, viz., the Working Men's Club and Institute Union, for promoting the social, mental, and moral improvement and recreation of the working classes. This association is under the presidency of Lord Brougham, and is supported by some very active social reformers. The object of its honorary officers is to promote the formation of working men's clubs throughout the United Kingdom. They confess that mechanics' institutes have not been made amusing enough to counteract the allurements of the public-house. They declare that "recreation must go hand-in-hand with education and temperance." They seek to kindle a brotherly love among the working classes. They say, "The aim of the Union in all cases would be to help working men to help themselves, rather than to establish or manage institutions for them." Yet the council, "in justice to the true interests of these institutions, deem it right to stipulate in regard to every association, club, or institute, received into membership with the Union, that no intoxicating drinks, betting, or gambling be allowed on the premises or in the recreation-ground; while they would recommend that at least one-half of the managing body should be *bonâ fide* working men." Of course the council of the Union, who will not allow a tired working man to drink a glass of ale in his club, will not allow him to smoke a pipe. He must be resigned to his three-halfpenny cup of tea and his twopenny round of toast—and diagrams lent to him by the generous Union!

The Society's printed law, that no club in which intoxicating drinks were sold should be admitted into the Union, was felt by some members of the council to be a little too strong, and a meeting was called to reconsider it. After a warm debate it was agreed that the Union would exercise a wider influ ence by strongly recommending the exclusion of in toxicating drinks than by making that exclusion a condition of membership and assistance. It will appear strange to any unprejudiced mind that there should have been a moment's doubt on the question. Mechanics' institutes have passed into the hands of the middle classes because they have been too strait-laced. They have been less free clubs than educational penitentiaries. The working man, who has only his evenings to himself, insists upon his freedom. He will not be drilled into total abstinence, nor be frowned at because he blows his evening cloud. Preached at in model reading-rooms, over tea-cups, he takes himself off to a freer atmosphere. The blame is with the misguided social doctors who wish to prescribe for him. He hates to find a hobby-rider always at his elbow, preaching at him, and droning in his ears the praises of water. He is not a drunkard; and he would be glad to be in a club of his own, if he could have the freedom in it which gentlemen of high degree have in theirs. But he will not be put through his facings, nor abdicate his idiosyncrasy, and sing the "Song of the Pump" in chorus. Let him govern his own club; have his mug of ale and his pipe there without rebuke from certain temperance preachers, who are more intemperate on tea than many drunkards are over grog, and he will remove his benefit club to it, and transact there the business of his life. Some twenty clubs for working men are already in existence; but the clubs that will effectually clear the public-houses remain to be created. Such clubs will be a great saving to the working classes, and a blessing to their families. More money will be carried home from the club than reaches it from the public-house. Tavern landlords will cease to hold the boxes of benefit clubs—always provided the clubs are based on rational principles, and not upon hobbies. The Union will do infinitely more harm than good if it operates through the agency of temperance apostles. You cannot drag a man up in the social scale by the hair of his head. Give him a club-room instead of a tap-room; set him to regulate it himself, for his own comfort and that of his fellow-members. The dignity he hereby acquires will lead him to frame decent rules, and, by the potent example of the mass, to become a sober and a thrifty man. Working men hate busy, meddlesome councils, which deal with them as so many black sheep, and talk about elevating them, as though they were little better than Ojibbeways.

It was under the auspices of the late Bishop Blomfield that a most influential and comprehensive association was organized, "for the relief of destitution in the metropolis," just twenty years ago. The attention of the public had been forcibly drawn to the severe sufferings of the houseless and foodless. Various charitable societies were at work alleviating the metropolitan distress; but a wide-spread reliable system of relief was wanted, and the metropolitan clergy hit upon a distribution of help by means of parochial and district visiting, under their superintendence. The Association which was founded, and which is now in a flourishing condition, set its face against indiscriminate alms giving. The funds at its disposal were handed to the metropolitan clergy, to be applied to the relief of the deserving poor of their parishes, and to the promotion of their permanent welfare. The district visiting societies which are dotted over the metropolis are intrusted with the duty of inquiring into the causes of distress, and, where it is possible, of applying a remedy. The pecuniary gift is generally but a momentary palliation of misery. The cause of the empty cupboard is often ignorance and often vice. The visitor who comes with help comes, then, with conditions that are laid down for the good of the sufferer. It is not enough to raise the morally blind from the slough of despond; they must be so guided as to keep them from it for the future. With this just aim this great Association was formed in 1843.

The promoters found that there were seventy metropolitan visiting societies in existence. In the districts where the poor were massed the visitors were crippled for want of funds, and were disheartened, seeing so much destitution which they could not relieve. To these crippled almoners the new Association made grants of money. The committee of the Association next discovered that there were sixty metropolitan parishes in which there were no district visitors; and in these very parishes the sufferings of the poor were most acute. Here district visitors were appointed and provided with funds, so that the protecting arms of the central Association were extended all over London. More: a district association to promote district visiting, and to give it pecuniary support, was established in the parishes south of the Thames. These institutions, the creation of the Association located in St. Martin's Place, Trafalgar Square, have become permanent; and the wealthy of the West are enabled to give to the really deserving poor, through an agency which is beyond suspicion. When the cholera raged in London, preventive measures promptly reached the poor through the machinery of this Association.

Having helped the needy in their distress, the Association, true to their origin, turned their attention to the means within their reach of inculcating economic habits among the poor. They afforded all persons with whom they came in contact, the opportunity of putting aside profitably the smallest savings: this at a time when there were few poor men's provident societies in existence. It is curious and gratifying to notice the rapidity with which these societies have grown, and how the poor have been taught to husband their pence in them. When these societies were originated, in 1845, they were twelve in number. There were 3744 depositors, and their united deposits amounted to £1451. In 1846, after one year's experience of the use of these savings' banks, their number was twenty-six; they were supported by 6574 depositors, and the amount deposited reached £2797. Still these provident banks grew, and many of them were able to stand alone. In 1853, the central association assisted thirty-five banks, which mustered 30,451 depositors, the amount deposited being £14,665. In ten years 100,000 depositors availed themselves of the advantages offered by the Association's savings'-banks; and in pence deposited more than £100,000. In a little statement of the origin and operations of the Association, the committee refer to this striking fact, saying: "Here you have thousands of poor families making themselves each successive year independent of charity. You have, amongst the class in which you desire above all others to implant it, not only the seeds of prudence sown, but absolutely the plant itself in vigorous and healthy growth. You are giving to a people who have hitherto depended too much on others, that self-esteem which leads them above all other feelings to self-reliance and self-exertion." This saving habit is a moral as well as an economic education. The tipsy-footed man grows steady. He interdicts himself the luxuries of vice that he may add to his store. He subdues his rising gusts of anger, and moderates to the cheerful, constant worker, who is at ease with his conscience. This saving habit taught is worth more to him than

"A very unedifying stuffage of mind,"

picked up in a lecture theatre. The moral improvement of the parents is reflected in their children. The mother trusts her little one to carry the garnered pence to the local provident fund. This confidence put in children is good teaching for them. "Many a child," says the rector of a large parish, "now in my schools have I first met as a depositor for its parents in my provident society. If I bring parents to church through the instrumentality of the society, I no less attract their children to my schools through the opportunities the same machinery affords me." The plan on which this great metropolitan association is conducted is at once simple and effective. The funds at its disposal are distributed at the weekly meetings of the committee amongst the district visiting societies of the metropolis, in sums ranging between £10 and £150. The sums are entirely devoted to temporal relief, and are gratuitously distributed, chiefly in kind, in the homes of the poor "without distinction of religious persuasion." Not one shilling may be given to the district visitors, nor employed in payment of rents. The grants are made to the clergy, who are the natural heads of the district visiting societies, and who are expected to call personally for the grants made to them by the Association. If any clergyman makes an appeal to the public, on his own account, for the poor of his district, the Association will make no grant to his district "for a period of six months from the appearance of such appeal, except in special cases to be considered by the committee." These are sensible rules, by which the committee guard the Association against giving too much in one locality, and too little in another. Every precaution is necessary that the utmost amount of good may be accomplished with the means the Association have at their disposal, for every district visitor is disposed to overstate the cases she has in hand. Her very earnestness and tender heart lead her to colour her pictures of her poor. The cut finger we see has more effect upon us than the broken thigh that is described to us.

At Midsummer 1861, 83 societies, each having a separate staff of voluntary district visitors, were working by the aid of this Association amongst an aggregate population of nearly a million souls. The number of visitors thus employed was reported to be 1178, and in the year terminating at that date, £5845 had been granted by the central Association, and £4223 raised by local exertions; thus constituting a fund of upwards of £10,000, available for the relief of destitution in the poorest quarters of London. In the last year, £4075 was granted to 84 societies claiming aid from this Association. These calculations do not include the operations carried on in Southwark under a separate committee, to which the sum of £500 was granted during the last winter, or in those portions of London which are visited by societies maintained entirely by their own resources. Besides the assistance granted to visiting societies, the committee still continue to promote the forethought and self-reliance of the poor by making grants to provident institutions, in which they can store their little savings throughout the year, to meet the wants of the coming winter season. At the close of 1861, applications were received from 41 of these institutions, in which the aggregate sum of £15,659 had been accumulated by 31,983 depositors. This large amount of resources, available at a time when the earnings of the poor are unusually small, and their expenses enhanced, was raised at a cost to the association of less than £400.

During the last year, the sum of £1991, 2s.·10d. Consolidated 3 per Cent. Annuities was received by the trustees on account of a legacy left by Miss Mapletoft. During the year, the contributions received were about £2500, whilst the committee felt themselves compelled to expend nearly double that amount in relieving the pressing wants continually presented to their view.

The balance from June 30, 1861, to June 30, 1862, shows that the receipts amounted to £6682, 12s. 8d., and the expenditure to £6219, 12s. 8d., leaving a balance of £463. The Association will not hear of paid district visitors. All must do the work—which is harassing, and at times repulsive—and find sufficient reward in the knowledge that they have done a little good to a few of their fellow-creatures. The visiting is chiefly needed at the East end of London, where want is the rule of life, and whence prosperity flies with hasty wing. It is to these, the realms of Lazarus, the rich of the West are invited, to improve themselves, as well as the ragged and famished, " by bringing into direct and more friendly intercourse classes too widely separated by worldly circumstances. If those who occupy the higher positions of the social estate are made familiar with the cares and necessities of the poor, the natural consequence is sympathy and kindly feeling on the one side, whilst respect, gratitude, and confidence are engendered on the other." Many refrain from undertaking districts through positive fear. They are terrified at the idea of entering the cellars and garrets of East London, lest they should be repulsed with oaths and threats. These are visionary fears—at which the initiated cannot but laugh. Do we ever hear that harm has come to the City missionaries, who almost live in the dens of thieves? I have been in the vilest of London's vile haunts, and no harm has reached me. Only a few nights since I made my way through Whitechapel, down Leman Street, past groups innumerable of men and lads, about whose profession there could not be two opinions, to the further corner of Wellclose Square. It was Saturday night, and the pavements were packed with somewhat unsavoury crowds, who were shouting, or bargaining, or loitering under the flaring gas-lamps. The Jews were selling coarse food and shoddy-cloth suits to the thieves. Faces flitted past that were terrible to see, there was so little humanity in their expression. The thieves were sharp as terriers, and the gaberdined Jews chattered incessantly, seeking a profit, it mattered not whence. The boisterous, keen-witted, rapacious crowds, all in search of "lumping penn'orths," gloating over the tripe-shops, or pressed against the cook-shop windows, were a saddening sight. They made a long, broad torrent of poverty, and crime, and ignorance, and misery. Women, with their matted hair, screaming over the babes that lay, swathed in foulness, in their lean arms; the frequent quarrels; the language unutterably low; children at play, with obscene words tripping in very sport from their tongue; and all around, the hideously deformed, the aged, and the scarred. In this sea of abomination where is the safe life? I reply, the stranger is safe. In the corner of the square dwelt a missionary, who had passed a long life in the midst of this savage wilderness of London. His house had been and is a refuge whither the most abandoned may fly for advice and comfort, and help to a better life. He has had ticket-of-leave men by the score within his gates, and no harm has come to him, while good has come to them. He can trace his penitents, who are thriving in various walks of life; his pickpockets, who are steady seamen; his couples who, after years of illicit life together, have married. The postman brings him letters from all parts, filled with the gratitude of those who have had the fortitude to follow his teaching. He has spent his lusty days in humble striving to do good where the gay and prosperous would not trust themselves an hour. He learned the thieves' *argot*, that he might make his mission understood among them. And now, after years in Goodman's Fields, he yearns to have some closing days away from the depressing scenes of his labours. I looked over the well-kept records of his doings. The outcast and criminal have paid him 116,509 visits. He has restored 174 to their homes, sent 221 to asylums, procured employment for 447, and enabled 85 to emigrate, induced 361 couples, who were living together in an unlawful state, to marry; and to these ends he has devoted not only himself, but his family also. While we were talking, swearing and quarrelling of the most savage description could be heard outside. The untried district visitor may tremble indeed in such quarters; but here is a family that has dwelt unmolested in the midst of this broad acreage of guilt, and dwells here still.

The district visitors who have reported their experience to the Association for Promoting the Relief of Destitution in the Metropolis, have not a single instance of an ill reception by the poor or fallen on whom they have called with advice or help. Guilt and misery are not enjoyed by the criminal and the miserable. They would gladly be helped to tread the bright ways of the world; and, therefore, he who comes to them to lift them from their squalor, and cleanse them of their shame, has an assured welcome. Dr. Chalmers, who tried district visiting on a large scale, bears witness to the gratitude and cordiality with which he was received in the lowest dwellings.

The committee of the Association advise their district visitors on many important points. The poor are to be approached sympathetically, and with delicacy of feeling. The cause of their distress must be probed from house to house. They should be advised how to help themselves out of their trouble, and not to depend on gifts. The visitor must have his wits about him, and guard himself against deception. He must beware of the very importunate, and inquire about them in their neighbourhood, as to their character, and the relief they are obtaining from various sources. The active charity necessary to do these things is the charity of which the poor of London are most in need. There are hundreds who will write cheques for Londoners over the border, but the ranks of the visitors are thin.

Between June 1861 and June 1862, the committee of the Association sent £795 to the clergy of Bethnal Green, £260 to the clergy of Clerkenwell, £255 to the clergy of St. George's-in-the-East, £145 to the clergy of Limehouse, £280 to the clergy of Newington, £410 to the clergy of St. Pancras, £290 to the clergy of Shoreditch, £210 to the clergy of Stepney, and £305 to the clergy of Whitechapel; and they gave away £392, 13s. in grants for premiums on deposits, in order to encourage the poor to save their pence.

The vast field which the Association occupies, extending from one end of London to the other, leaving the poor south of the Thames to a separate body of charitable workers, makes it most important to inquire how the field is occupied, and whether all the good that might be done by this extensive and well-contrived agency is accomplished.

In the first place, the means of the Association are extremely limited. Some £6000 to £10,000 per annum, spread over all the pauper districts of London, can do very little to alleviate the horrible effects of that system of driving the poor into overcrowded dwellings, which is the result of the manner in which our poor-rates are levied. The good clergy, who strive to their utmost to make headway against the tide of pauperism that rolls into the parishes, where there are courts and alleys which will receive an entire family in a garret or cellar, are disheartened. London improvements mean new streets of fine houses, where only the well-to-do can abide. The poor workman must shift his quarters to the already overburdened parishes, where there are low lodging-houses to receive him. We break up St. Giles's, and the pauper crowd flocks where the slums are intact. The St. Giles's rate-payers rejoice, as well they may. Their poor-rate is lightened, but other already severely taxed parishes pay the difference. The parishes where the rich dwell are quit of their poor. Model lodgings for working men are not built in the vicinity of palatial dwellings, and they rise in neighbourhoods already over-populated. Belgravia may well send a few cheques to mitigate the miseries of Bethnal Green, Whitechapel, and Shoreditch, since no rich man's contribution, in the shape of a subscription, equals the just proportion he should pay towards the maintenance of the poor. Now the Association, which has centres of activity throughout London for the relief of metropolitan destitution, might (since one of its objects is to put the poor in the way of helping themselves) take the causes of London pauperism and crime broadly under their consideration. The clergy of the poor districts might appeal to the clergy of the rich districts, to awaken their wealthy parishioners to a proper sense of their duty in regard to the poor population they have driven from their neighbourhood. The handsome suburbs which have been added to London of late years, have arisen at the expense of the comforts of the poor, who are now compelled to travel many miles daily to their work from the poor quarters. I am certain that the band of district visitors who work under the protection and by the money aid of the Association for the Relief of London Distress, are brave and conscientious workers. Their aim is to better the condition of the poor. Will they ever accomplish this their work of Christian chivalry while whole regions of the metropolis are given up to pauperism, and the West is not responsible for the East and South? A few pounds given and a few families visited will close a few sores, but the ulcer remains eating into the body social. I should be glad to see the Association to which I am referring with ten times its present income, for it is a nobly-conceived and wisely-administered charity, giving with tender discretion. I merely express a regret that its officers have not gone nearer to the root of the evil which their pious efforts mitigate. They are in the presence of a system that produces most of the ills against which they are doing battle. Surely, then, it would be wise to assail the system while they nurse its victims. He takes up a holy mission who travels in quest of the humblest sufferer, to heal his wounds and call a smile to his lips. The money that buys a bandage for a wounded dog is well spent. How greatly deserving, therefore, is he who, out of his experience of the woes of the few, speaks a wisdom that shall show how the privations and degradations of the many may be stayed! The experience and facts which district visitors and their clergy have accumulated should be brought to bear on the general treatment of the metropolitan poor, and, indeed, of the poor of other great cities.

The district visitor must have a deep and abiding sense of the nobility of his or her mission. The true servant of the poor must have much patience; a will to refuse, where the applicant is undeserving, and a heart at once courageous and gentle. The lady of gentle nurture, who is asked to undertake the visiting duties of a district, is required to brace her mind against shocks to her senses that she will feel at every step; to be the comforter where the miserable are coarse and degraded; in short, to taste of all the bitterness of poverty—to taste the rent and dirty vestment of Lazarus, and to feel the faint breath from his hungry lips upon her cheek. It is trying enough to pass the doorways and loiter in the neighbourhoods of the poor. To pass the thresholds daily, and spend hours where the dainty would hold it almost death to enter, is the district visitor's bounden duty. It is a severe task, yet it is done, and by an army of volunteers whose moral prowess is an honour to the country to which they belong. They are a martyr band doing their good by stealth, without fee and without applause. They are soldiers, with Conscience for captain.

These servants of the poor are to be counted by

the thousand in England; one London association alone has nearly 1200 under its wing. They are of every sect that flourishes in our midst. I have led the reader to see the Roman Catholic Little Sisters busy at their pious work, and he shall presently learn that there are bands of Protestant ladies equally mindful of the distressed. There are even guardsmen in the ranks of district visitors, who travel once a week to Bethnal Green, call on the incumbent, find out cases of distress, examine into them with their own eyes, and relieve them. But there are broad fields of poverty yet unexplored. A district visitor does not, as a rule, give more than a day per week to visiting. The Rev. John Tagg, incumbent of St. John's, Bethnal Green, who has about twenty district visitors under his direction (all females), told me that they paid fortnightly visits to the poor—twenty visitors paying fortnightly visits in a parish of 11,000 inhabitants, about 6000 of whom are of the working class, and of the lower working class. It appears that a district visitor will generally spend, or distribute among the poor she visits, between 10s. and 15s. at every visit. An East End incumbent's wife spends double this amount every morning she spends among her husband's parishioners. The Rev. J. Trevitt, incumbent of St. Philip, Bethnal Green, has the spiritual direction of a parish that includes 14,000 souls. They are on a dead level of poverty. They include hawkers, toymakers, costermongers, dock labourers, and thieves, dog-fighters,—in short, the various company poverty brings together in the low-rented neighbourhoods of London. Club Row, at the corner of which is the solid brick schoolroom, is a fair sample of the streets round about Mr. Trevitt's parsonage. The bird-fanciers are in great strength. Mounds of old rope and rusty iron encumber the pavement. Ragged children by the hundred are playing in the muddy road, with shuttlecock or old barrel hoops; and others are using costermongers' barrows as see-saws. The elder children are squatted in the doorways, nursing babies. The idle men, the peaks of their caps pushed aside, are smoking black pipes. The Bethnal Green undertaker is busy. The coal-sheds are not larger than horse-stalls. While I was passing, a cry of fire arose. The turncock appeared, and turned a fountain of water into the street. This was a signal for a rush from every court and alley. The wild children of the street danced frantically about the bubbling water and played tricks with it. I doubt whether any other city in the world could produce at a minute's notice so large an assemblage of children—all stamped with the marks of poverty; all born in poverty, and destined to live and die in poverty. Where is hope for them? Their parents live by shifts—from hand to mouth. When the winter comes severely upon them they suffer horribly; but in the summer, when there is a little work about, they are merry; they have no plans that reach beyond to-day.

Looking at the crowd of children shrieking and laughing round the water, we are looking upon the effect of that massing of the poor with the criminal, on which I dwelt in my last letter. This is the district nursery and playground.

In this street these children spend their days as thriftless, thoughtless, and cunning as their parents. Imagine the effect twenty district visitors can make by a weekly visit in this vast district where every man is as poor and distressed as his neighbour. Some time back the parish of St. Philip boasted forty visitors to the poor, but the funds at the disposal of the incumbent were not sufficient to give useful employment to so many workers. The district visitor cannot travel empty-handed, and so the list was reduced to twenty. In this parish, where all are poor, where distress is in every house, I see by their last report that the Association for Promoting the Relief of Destitution in the Metropolis granted Mr. Trevitt £140 in the course of the year. Let the reader mark how much the reverend gentleman was able to raise in his parish. In the year he raised 7s. There are the hard tradesmen of the poor in the parish who live by giving the distressed bad pennyworths. These contribute nothing to the work of relief. They make goodly sums out of the spendings of dock-labourers and hawkers, but they never help the poverty on which they prey. Middlemen, greedy for penny profits, haunt every byway. These filthy houses are speculations of men who live among their luckless tenants, and drive and screw them. Yonder coarse fellow can now produce and afford to risk his £1000, every shilling of which has been grubbed out of these tumble-down tenements—he renting them at a low figure, and letting them to the hawker, the dock-labourer, and the thief, at a high rent. St. Philip's is a commodious church that will accommodate 1500 sitters. It was well attended, morning and evening, on the Sunday of my visit. It is supported by the voluntary contributions of its ragged congregation. The pence contributed by the attendants at the two services in question amounted to 3s. 7½d. The truth is, that they had not pence to give. Mr. Trevitt's congregation is entirely composed of the poorest of the poor, as his parish is. He then requires more help than an incumbent who has well-to-do folk in his cure. His parishioners can subscribe only 7s. per annum, whereas the parishioners of St. John will furnish £20 or £30. In this parish there are flourishing industries and less suffering than in the adjoining parish, yet Mr. Tagg is crippled for money. The operation of the district visitor system, indeed, is well illustrated by the experiences of the incumbents of St. Philip's and St. John's, Bethnal Green. The machinery is good, but the steam fails. London includes no parish where district visitors should be more active and numerous; and we find that the incumbent can employ only twenty, and distribute among them £140, 7s. for the relief of his thousands of poor. Mr. Tagg has had to contend during this winter with the misery caused among his parishioners by sickness. Sickness among the poor presses severely on the funds of all charitable societies that relieve them. The help of the Association for the Relief of Destitution in the Metropolis is sent only four times a year. Let there be a sudden and severe pressure upon the fund at the incumbent's disposal, he is unable to rely upon the Association for instant help. The forms to be gone through before an extra grant can be obtained from St. Martin's Place usually fill up the time between the application and the regular period when a quarterly grant would be due, so that it may be said the Association can be relied upon only four times in the year. The many rules of the Association are, however, broken through when a sudden frost or fatal epidemic makes instant relief imperative. Fortunately for the poor of Bethnal Green, Clerkenwell, St. George's-in-the-East, Walworth, Shoreditch, and Whitechapel, the district visitors, directed by a clergyman, and the funds dispensed by the great Association in St. Martin's Place, are not all the poor have to rely upon in their distress. That many of the clergy do their utmost, with the limited means at their command, it would be most unfair to deny. But the means are in all cases wholly disproportioned to the work that should be accomplished.

Let us take as an instance of Bethnal Green incumbent's work among the poor, that of the Rev. John Tagg, of St. John's. His labours are various, and, so far as they go, useful. He directs National and Infant Schools, the Sunday Schools, the District Visiting Society, the Maternal Fund, the Provident Fund, the Weavers' Aid Association, and branches of the Church Pastoral Aid Society, the Church of England Scripture Readers' Association, the Society for the Propagation of the Gospel, the Church Missionary Society, the Society for Promoting Christianity among the Jews, and the Free Lending Library. It will be observed that, while the rev. gentleman collected last year about £65 in subscriptions for extra-parochial purposes, all that he collected for the relief of the poor within his parish was little more than £30.

In the St. John's National and Infant Schools, Peel Grove, Old Ford Road, Bethnal Green, there are 200 boys, 117 girls, and 140 infants—making a total of 457 children receiving instruction under a master, two mistresses, and five pupil-teachers.

The financial statement for the year 1862 shows that the receipts amount to £413, 8s. 3d., and the expenditure to £396, 8s. 2d., leaving a balance in hand of £17, 0s. 1d.

The number of scholars recorded in the teachers' manuals as usually in attendance on Sunday mornings or afternoons at the three school-rooms in Peel Grove, and at the Bible-room in East Street, is 150 boys, 162 girls, and 106 infants—making a total of 418 children. There are 37 teachers engaged in the instruction of these young pupils.

Prizes of books are liberally awarded to the most deserving scholars twice a year. There is a library of religious books for the use of the elder children, and contributions towards it are earnestly solicited.

The district visitors are now twenty-one in number, and during the year 1862 they paid 12,638 visits to the houses of the poor, and distributed tickets for bread, meat, coals, and clothing, to the amount of £86, 18s. 1d. During the year 1861 the amount was £116, 16s. 1d.

During a portion of the year 1862, the visitors have been precluded from giving any assistance whatever in consequence of the exhaustion of the funds, caused by the diversion of the alms of the benevolent to the relief of the distress in Lancashire.

The treasurer's account of the Poor's Relief Fund for the year 1862, shows that the receipts, including grants, amounting to £70, from the Metropolitan Relief Association, were £115, 12s., and the expenditure was £88, 18s., leaving a balance in hand on the 9th January 1863, of £26, 14s.

The Maternal Fund, an institution intended for the succour of poor married women of St. John's district parish in the time of trouble, had given relief during the past year to twenty-seven women, many of whom have had the additional benefit of professional attendance from the London Hospital.

The number of members of the institution called the Free Lending Library is at present 265, of whom 195 enjoy the use of the library gratuitously, and 35 are honorary members. The number of books now in circulation is 906, and the issues of volumes during the year 1862 amounted to 5056. The Free Lending Library is, of course, an excellent institution. It smooths the path of the deserving poor to knowledge, and it strengthens the hands of the district visitors, who are allowed to distribute quarterly tickets of free membership. The Weavers' Aid Association, established to provide outfits for deserving emigrants, is also a most useful society in the permanently distressed district which is within a stone's-throw of Mr. Tagg's residence. While we perceive that only £5, 13s. 6d. were collected in the parish to help starving weavers to a new home, £13, 11s. 5d. were collected for the Church Pastoral Aid Society, £11, 15s. 11d. for the Church of England's Scripture Readers' Association, £15, 16s. 7d. for the Society for the Propagation of the Gospel, £6, 13s. 5d. for the Church Missionary Society, and £13, 13s. for the Conversion of the Jews to Christianity. I think that it will occur to many readers that these sums, collected in the midst of the hungry and the ragged, while money was wanting to soothe the sick-bed round the corner, would have been better expended where charity begins, namely, at home.

The district visitors who visit from house to house, distributing religious tracts and calling upon parents to give their children the education within their reach, could have done many little acts of welcome relief with the £60 sent out of the parish, chiefly to rich Church societies. Mr. Tagg says in his report that his district teachers mitigate temporal destitution when possible by the relief placed at their disposal. Last year the possible temporal relief consisted of bread, meat, and grocery to the value of £57, 2s. 1d., of coals to the value of £22, 11s. 4d., and of flannel to the value of £7, 4s. 8d. The possible temporal relief in St. John's, Bethnal Green, is, it will be seen, of the smallest.

The Association for Promoting the Relief of Destitution in the Metropolis, in the report for 1853, dwell on the importance of systematic relief, and a proper selection amongst the various objects presenting themselves to the charitable mind. Everybody will agree with them on the importance of knowledge and sound judgment in the distribution of alms. I believe it is the opinion of the committee of the Association that they could not judiciously distribute a larger income than they now enjoy with the machinery for distribution at their command. They have bound themselves to certain forms, from which they are not inclined to depart. They must have certain rigid papers filled up; their money must all be filtered through the hands of incumbents and gratuitous district visitors. No money must be spent to help a man suddenly stricken with illness or deprived of work, to keep his little household gods together. Bread, coals, flannel, meat, and grocery are the comforts which, when funds will allow, the district visitor can distribute in small quantities. Show us more good district visitors, and we will give more money, say the committee of the Association. They are right in having a care of the manner in which their money is spent; but let us judge of the Society by the amount of good it does in the parishes of St. John and St. Philip, Bethnal Green.

In the parish of St. Philip, the incumbent has been compelled to reduce his staff of visitors, as I have already stated, by one-half, he being the spiritual head of a parish that is one even level of destitution. Surely, to this parish, if to any in the metropolis, the grant given should have been enough to keep at work every good district visitor the incumbent could obtain. Twenty visitors have £140, 7s. to distribute over a mass of 14,000 poor people. That is to say, each visitor has at his or her disposal the sum of £7 annually for the spread of temporary relief over a district. Taking a low average, it may be said that each district visitor comes in contact with 500 distressed objects in the course of the year. During the year she is able to distribute 140s. among them. These figures will show the reader the amount of temporal relief afforded to the metropolitan poor through the channels of the great Association in St. Martin's Place. A mite wisely given is of greater value than a pound recklessly bestowed. The Association hold that gratuitous district visitors are wise distributors of alms; yet, where alms are most needed in the metropolis, their donation is so small that the hands of half the incumbent's society of visitors are paralysed, and hundreds of the sick poor go untended. The grants of the Association to poor parishes might with propriety be quadrupled in some cases. Clergymen, earnest in the work of relief, would find trustworthy agents for the distribution of the money of the charitable in proper places; and district visitors, seeing that they could give something more than a tract or advice in every scene of real and undeserved distress, would increase in numbers and in activity.

Before starting on my rounds with the district visitors of Limehouse, Walworth, Poplar, Shoreditch, Stepney, and Whitechapel, where the poor and the criminal are massed, I am most anxious to impress on the reader's mind the vices of the system under which London is growing. This system forces the poor honest with the thriftless dishonest into the same low house. There is only a little lath and plaster between the burglar, snoring with his jemmy under his ear, and the plodding, hollow-eyed slop-woman, who is wearing heart and soul out that Jeroboam and Sons may offer a cheap counterfeit of West End gentility to the shop-boys of London. Every thing is ready to the criminal's hand. The fence and the gin-shop are next door. Thieving is a ready-money business. The "souper" stolen round the corner may be realized in good current coin of the realm in a very few minutes. The crucible is ready for the stolen plate. Don't let the careless reader imagine that where the criminals live, with the honest poor, and continually recruit from the ranks of Lazarus, that the business of robbery is carried on in a careless, hap-hazard way. The thief and the receiver of stolen goods transact business with the greatest regularity. The thief might inform against the receiver, or the receiver against the thief; but they trust each other freely; there is honour of a savage kind among these thieves. Then there are snug organizations of pickpockets, with their patrons and employers. Some of these bands live a long way from their work, but they go to it, and dress for it, regularly, returning home in the evening to rest for next day's labour. So that it will be seen the robbery trade of London, favoured by the admirable organization of vast centres of misery, is not likely to die out. The poor must consort with the criminal. A labourer who can afford only one room for his family, must be next door to a nest of vice. It is, therefore, high time we should take into our most earnest consideration the causes of this dangerous massing of the poor and the profligate, and see whether they may not be removed. I shall show the results of this massing, in sad stories of tempted poverty and hopeless vice; but let me first show the reader how it is that certain quarters have a reputation for the criminals they produce—as Spitalfields was celebrated, in bygone times, for its weavers' cunning floriculture. If I had "that force of ancient phrase which speaking paints," I should be tempted to describe in colours vivid as the rainbow, the wandering of our London poor from place to place.

Improvement of a neighbourhood means, driving the poor from it. The streets are widened; fine houses rise upon the sites of the dreary tenements of empty-purse and cut-throat, two gloomy mortals whom we chain together, and banish from every "improvement." With a ragged crew of children at their heels, the twin wanderers are driven whence the light is penetrating, to places that are not undergoing improvements. They are certain of an abiding-place only where there is not the faintest whisper of well-ventilated rooms or other sanitary nonsense. Let them seek the narrow courts that remain, and here, more confined and jammed together still than in their old quarters, they fester faster. The parish officers watch them with angry eyes, for they appear in a parish already overburdened, and they come from one where the rates are low. So reduced as to seek union relief, the law of settlement steps in, and may complete and consolidate their ruin. It may make them break up even the miserable shadow of a home, and put them in the ranks of permanent paupers.

Mr. Henry Pownall has recently issued a pamphlet on "A National Poor Tax," in which he has brought together a long series of facts, which all go to prove that, let the causes be what they may, the poor are still concentrating with the criminal in the centres which sanitary doctors have hardly touched, and where improvements have not been attempted. The creation of Regent Street drove the poor to Westminster and Lambeth. The planning of Trafalgar Square added again to Westminster and St. Giles's. The turn of St. Giles's came next. That nest of vice and poverty was cut up, but it was not destroyed; the birds migrated to other densely-populated purlieus. A broad road was cut by Field Lane; another displacement of the poor and vile, but only a displacement. Their houses were swept from the face of the earth, but no houses for the poor were raised in their stead. The poor were a parish leprosy to be cast out; they must not effect a settlement; let them tramp and fasten themselves on other ratepayers. Mr. Pownall estimates the money spent in removals of the poor from parish to parish at not less than £60,000 per annum. He cites a recent case which occurred at the Middlesex Court of Quarter Sessions, where more than £250 were spent "in contesting the settlement of an aged woman, upwards of eighty years of age, who was ultimately sent to the north of Yorkshire," where she had not probably been for forty years. But there are on record more remarkable removals than this; the law of settlement being one which has given considerable sums to lawyers. To see how this law operates in massing the poor in poor districts and parishes, the inquirer must visit country places, where the labourers live many miles from their work, because the employers or landlords will not have labourers' cottages built lest their men should obtain a settlement within their parish. The question of national or parochial poor-rates is one beyond the scope of the inquiry into the condition of the London poor which I am conducting. I deal with facts as I see them. Figures show, however, that the less able a parish is to pay the poor-rates, the more it is compelled to pay. The poor, driven from improving places, repair where the poor are already located; for here alone can they find lodgings cheap enough, because bad enough, for them. When new arteries are opened through densely-populated neighbourhoods, all the lodging-houses are swept away, and few, if any, are raised in their stead. Mr. Pownall shows that, since 1821, no less than 1170 houses have been destroyed to make way for docks, railways, and improvements in this locality (about the London docks), while scarcely 400 have been built." It appears that these improvements displaced about 14,000 poor human creatures, leaving them to find nooks and corners among their already overcrowded neighbours. While the population of the City Union has been rapidly decreasing of late years, that of Bethnal Green, Shoreditch, Poplar, etc., has been greatly increasing. Poverty has been concentrating itself, and must continue to flow to poor centres. The East of London must receive the migrations of the decayed tradesman or the poor labourer and his family. It must be in a low and vicious neighbourhood that he cannot avoid; but it will be very soon under conditions that will secure the inevitable degradation of his children. The descent from moderate comfort to absolute and irretrievable pauperism is one that, once begun, cannot be easily stayed. Stagnant trade has the effect of pauperizing permanently thousands of men, who, living where poverty is the rule, abandon themselves to the tide and to the pauper's dole of the docks. These vast London docks, which are the pride of our merchant princes, are worked by armies of almost starving men, who hang about the gates all day, hoping to get a few pence by rough labour within. Wanting this pitiful work, they are compelled to fly to the parish. The ratepayers give them almost as much as the dock authorities. These dock-labourers, the fallen of all classes, are levant and couchant near the docks, for here alone are there houses foul and bad enough to receive them. These dock-gates are crowded more and more, day by day, and the pauper army is thickening round about. How many people in London know what is to be seen along the shores of the wealth-laden Thames? The ships laden with riches from every quarter of the world are unloaded by our social outcasts. The man who has sunk to be a dock-labourer is worse off than a Paris rag-picker. He starves when the wind keeps a fleet in the Downs, and earns only the very poorest pay when the fleet comes up. The competition is so furious that he cannot demand reasonably good wages. The crowd pressing behind him compels him to take what he can get. The dock companies buy labour in the cheapest market, and their market-places are swarmed with a hungry multitude. Surely, then, the tendency of the powers that have London improvements in hand should not be to send more hungry men hither. There is a movement afoot for carrying some of the distressed Lancashire operatives to localities where work is wanted—a most rational and humane movement, but diametrically opposed to the system pursued in London. We find certain centres of poverty, and we drive more poor to them. We depopulate the City to cram Poplar and Bethnal Green! Our parochial authorities vie with each other in keeping their parishes clear of paupers, or of workpeople who may become paupers. They never trouble themselves to seek out for their poor new fields of labour. They sulkily keep the penniless whom they cannot turn from the union gates, and let them pick oakum, and drink their mess of food, taking care not to

"Make the gruel thick and slab."

The truth is, that the law of settlement keeps labour in a condition of slavery. The unemployed man cannot freely go and come. We have free trade in corn, but we have yet to obtain free trade in British labour. The valuable labour that is always shut up in the workhouse is enough to create a flourishing colony. We find that sixty girls have resided an average of ten years in the Waterford workhouse at an annual cost of £500. Here they will probably remain all their lives, since there is little or no hope of finding employment for them where they are. After having spent £5000 on them, it appears to have struck the guardians that it would not be an irrational proceeding to send them to a place where their own labour will provide them with the necessaries of life. For £500, or a year's keep, the parish can send them to America, where they will find a welcome. Why, it would be cheaper to the Waterford ratepayers to pay their passage to Australia than to maintain them in idleness throughout their lives —cheaper for the ratepayers and better for the girls. The experience of the Waterford guardians is that of many metropolitan unions. There is not a sadder sight in London than the ward of the London Union, where able-bodied men are housed. Here is labour wasting that many a colony is craving; here is a man kept in forced idleness out of the industry of people who are not many steps removed from the union gates. Some years ago certain metropolitan guardians of the poor mooted the question of emigration by the help of parochial rates, but vigorous opposition was offered, and the question fell to the ground. But the scheme was worth a trial, if only as a matter of economy. There are hundreds of families who are always more or less chargeable to the parish. Indeed, where once parish bread has been tasted, it generally becomes regular food. The cost of a settled pauper family to a parish is often treble the cost free emigration would be; as, in the course of my rounds with district visitors, I shall prove by special cases of undoubted authenticity. Out-door relief enables the poor to keep body and soul together, in the purlieus where the garotter and his family live; and the poor are indeed strong who do not get some taint from the rascals with whom poverty compels them to consort. They have been driven from "improving" neighbourhoods to the haunts of the footpad; and their children must play with his children. Now, as Mr. C. B. Adderley recently put it, "Will any man, hoping to escape damnation, deliberately propose the institution of another Norfolk Island?" Here is a question it is dangerous to answer. But can there be any doubt as to the propriety of doing all that in us lies to stay the stream of pollution, to snatch innocent children from it, so to act as to shield the poverty-stricken from contact with the criminal, and so to rob the cracksman and the sneak of their recruiting grounds? If the price of the parish allowance given to the pauper, whom misery has sent to rent a room next to the felon's, would speed him on his way rejoicing to fat "pastures new," where his labour would keep his children, and raise a godly race, is there a question, then, what should be done? How this sin and stain of our time are to be wiped out is a question more important than the relief of the poor, since it is one of the reduction of the numbers of the poor.

Lord Ebury has boldly stood forth to mark where much of the blame lies. He observes that large aggregations of poor people have been allowed to squat wholly uncared for, "having no kindly superintendence, moral or physical, to light the lamp of life as a guide to their ways, to succour them in distress, and encourage them in the warfare of existence." Then his lordship proceeds to show how the members of the National Church are to blame. "It is," he says, "our pharisaical, lofty bearing towards Nonconformists, almost refusing to come in contact with them; it is the schismatic provisions of our Act of Uniformity, and our decrepit canons, coupled with our refusal to attempt the smallest remedy; the separation between our clergy and laity, caused principally by our making a kind of sacerdotal inequality; our stately, but tautological liturgy and formularies, with their obsolete phraseology and iron-binding of rubrics, which have sown formalism broadcast through the land." This formalism has undoubtedly narrowed and weakened the action of the National Church in our dark centres of poverty and crime. A great, united effort of the Christian Church brought to bear upon the plague-spots of our towns—all formalism put aside—would go far towards a cure. It would awaken the public conscience, and give power to the practical men who see a better state of things. But it must not be said that the London clergy of the National Church have been idle. They have worked —at least many of them—most nobly; and if they have not done more good than can be shown at the present time, it is because they have not been backed as they should have been backed. The statistics of the Association for Promoting the Relief of Destitution in the Metropolis, which I published in my last letter, conclusively prove how faint and inadequate is the support they are able to obtain from the public through the agency of the Association. A note from one of these hard-working metropolitan rectors of poor parishes lies before me, and most touchingly describes how he is paralysed for lack of help. He tells me that the narrowness of his means compels him to pay attention to "the very destitute" only. He writes,—"Myself, my curate, my curate's sister, and one or two ladies, are all I can muster now for a visiting society. I know it is breaking my mind down to visit the deep distress. We were not always so bad. I have a week class who meet at my house for Scripture reading and prayer. I give them a tea, and to see many of them at tea would at once tell how it was needed. I think the Lancashire distress has increased ours, because any general stop in trade affects all, and we are not so much helped. Our Metropolitan Society have been obliged to curtail their contributions, which were our great winter stay." This is a fair sample of the complaints the metropolitan clergy have to make. Impossible to "scotch the snake" with a reed. Let us glance at the amounts raised from all sources, including the grants from the Association, which some of the rectors of poor parishes received, in aid of their labours, during the year ending July 1861. The rector of St. James's, Clerkenwell, with a population of 25,275, received £209, 12s.; the rector of St. John's, Clerkenwell, with a population of 10,000, received £102, 2s. 10d.; the rector of St. Paul's, Walworth, with a population of 12,000, received £70, 9s. 9d.; the rector of St. Peter's, Walworth, with a population of 32,000, received £133, 19s.; the rector of St. John's, Hoxton, with a population of 24,879, received £202, 10s. 3d.; the rector of St. Mary, Haggerstone, with a population of 34,000, received £85; the rector of Trinity, Hoxton, with a population of 10,000, received £40; the rector of St. Dunstan's, Stepney, with a population of 40,000, received £152, 12s. 2d.; the rector of St. Mary, Whitechapel, with a population of 16,000, received £177, 7s. 1d.; and the rector of St. Mark, Whitechapel, with a population of 15,326, received just £67! These figures will give the public a faint idea of the help that is afforded to the rectors of poor London parishes, of the reeds with which they are left to "scotch the snake."

The right to relief which the Poor-laws give do not dispose of the question. The Poor-laws never give the unfortunate the treacle-pudding the Portland convict eats in the handsome establishment which, as a punishment for his crimes, he inhabits. It is of little use to discuss these matters with mere theorists. They only who have visited poor districts, who know what the hand-to-mouth living of Spitalfields or Whitechapel really and truly is, are capable of giving an opinion worth a straw on the question. I can imagine well the conversation a penal servitude man might hold with an honest Drury Lane pauper. Why, a model lodging-house can hardly be compared for comfort with a model prison. We have a "system" for the criminal, but we have none for the poor. Oakum-picking is common to the gaol and the poor-house. The parish overseer is as repulsive an official as the prison warder. There is, by the village of Herne, in Kent, a workhouse, beautifully situate, but not a window whence the pauper inmates may look out upon the landscape. Pauperism is regarded, in short, as something very little short of a crime; hence we cannot wonder at the misery that is borne by people who have been accustomed to earn their bread honestly before they consent to apply at the poor-house. Every man, woman, and child has a right to relief; yet coroners sit to record deaths by starvation. Every minister of a poor London parish can bear witness to the horrible sufferings of the poor who are trying desperately to keep out of the pauper class. The room is stripped of every comfort; and the back is nearly bare to the wind before recourse is had to the workhouse.

If the workhouse, in short, disposed of the London poor, there would be no need for the hundred and one charitable operations I have described in these letters. Trudging among the cinder-sifters over the Border, among the weavers of Spitalfields, about the crowded thoroughfares of Seven Dials, Drury Lane, and Whitechapel—why do I pass hundreds of ragged children, starvelings of the gutter? Whence come these hundreds of sleepers in this noble Playhouse Yard Refuge, with every one of whom fate must have played very savage tricks before they came hither to beg this leather wrapper and this deal box to rest in? Whence spring these famished crowds that come to lap the gratuitous soup of the Leicester Square Soup-Kitchen? What mean these poor invalids' dinner-tables? Why should the cart of the little begging Sister of the Poor come round to my door to sweep the crumbs from my table? A Cripples' Home, and bazaar in aid thereof! Asylums for orphans, idiots, incurables! Homes for the fallen and afflicted! A house of charity, like that where I saw the boy slowly dying of consumption! The scowling ratepayer pays his money because the law compels him to support the poor of his parish. How comes it then, when he has paid his poor-rate, there remain great hordes of starving creatures, who make us ashamed to walk the streets in decent clothing, and with the healthy quantity of flesh on our bones. The London rector cries that his mind is breaking down under the misery he sees unrelieved around him. I leave our social doctors to explain this to the indignant ratepayer. Here is the want; here is the foodless babe; here is the blanketless bed; and here is the Association for Promoting the Relief of Destitution in the Metropolis. The clergymen in connexion with the Association say to all who will not believe in the heart-rending tragedies that are acting about them—Come and see. Enroll yourselves in the ranks of our district visitors; examine every case for yourselves before you relieve. Last month, Mr. H. R. Walthew held an inquiry in Whitechapel respecting the death of Charles Whitwell, a man who had died in the infirmary of the union. The evidence proved that the poor man had been for some time without employment. He had wandered about the streets in a state of "absolute starvation." In four months he had only been traced once to a lodging-house. "Dr. Champneys said that so broken down from destitution was deceased upon his admission, that he ordered him at once into the infirmary. On the Wednesday following he was found dead, in a pool of blood, between two beds. The change from habitual starvation and the cold of the streets to the comfort of the infirmary, had caused him to rupture a blood-vessel."

Lord Ebury says, let the work be taken up by a united effort of the Christian Church; and let us see what can be done to wipe away that which is a world-wide reproach to us. It is to the chronic distress of London that every Frenchmen points, when he has contemplated the abundant landmarks of our wealth. He sums us up in that rapid way of his—great wealth, and great poverty. He just plants the Marquis of Westminster beside a Charles Whitwell—shoulder to shoulder—and says, Behold mighty Albion; a millionnaire twice over, and a wretch without a crust!

We shall see whether, taken up in the liberal spirit Lord Ebury suggests, the system of district visiting might not strike at the root of London pauperism. Let us see what it has accomplished with the slender funds it has commanded. Little help can the rector of St. Dunstan's, Stepney, afford the poor of his parish of 40,000 souls out of the £152, 12s. 2d. placed at his disposal from all sources. In a parish of 10,000 what relief is to be given with £40? But if strength, and practical ideas, and sound sense were brought to bear on district visiting, if it were unswathed from the benumbing bandages of formalism, and given up freely and earnestly to the activity of all Christian Englishmen and Englishwomen; if the wrappers of sect should be unloosed, and the true man be permitted to appear "supreme and erect," something more than a crust here, and a cup of tea there, and a blanket in a third place, might be done. Patchwork charity covers a wound here and there. There are hundreds who live to bless the doers of acts of charity. They who spread a dinner-table for the poor sick; who send abandoned boys out to the colonies; who consign fallen women to a refuge, and provide a Christmas dinner for the outcast, are good Samaritans who take something from the long sum of suffering that every winter adds up in London. But these little taps will not "scotch the snake." They cannot relieve the labour market. They leave the poor in low, defiling neighbourhoods. They strike, in short, at none of the causes of pauperism and crime. It has been held by phrenologists, that your full-grown, thorough-bred London criminal is the nearest approach you can get to the supreme rascal. He is the product of want and vice. He has festered from childhood to manhood into that blurred and brutified semblance of the erect man, about which there is no mistake. If this supreme rascal could, as a race, be extinguished, or, at least, be made a rarity; if strong, earnest, united action could be brought to bear upon the hotbeds where the supreme rascal grows—surely vast and radical good might be accomplished; the spread of pauperism might be arrested; the flooding of the poor from the rural districts to town might be checked. The gentlemen-beggars who reach London every fall, for a winter season of mendicancy—who filter themselves through all the London charities, and know the colour of every soup-kitchen in the metropolis, and the regulations of every refuge—these might be more thoroughly dealt with than the Mendicity Society can deal with them. By a vigorous assault on the nurseries of crime the budding vagabond might be turned into the good workman; and men we might have been compelled to export to some of our labour-craving colonies, might turn up there in the more welcome shape of lusty and honest free labourers.

CHAPTER XIX.

CONCLUSION.

Miss Nightingale has said that "to be able to visit well is not a thing that comes by instinct, but, on the contrary, is one of the rarest accomplishments. But when attained, what a blessing to both visitors and visited!" I have dwelt on the short-comings of the district visiting system, particularly in the east of London, and on the lack of earnestness among the clergy, to which many of the London rectors bore witness before the House of Lords. I have examined the extent and description of help extended by a great association to the poorer parishes; and I have shown how weak this help is, and how little is done where there is much to do. Were space at my command at the present time I might complete these studies of the London poor, and of the charitable organizations their distresses have provoked, by a series of visits to the metropolitan workhouses, and a thorough examination of the household economy, or waste, of the London poor. How the poor "keep house" is a study that must be gone through by all men who desire to make home happy in Whitechapel. We are about to see cheap dining-places for working men spring up all over London, where, for 3d. or 4d., the labourer may (for himself) fare sumptuously. I should like to see the cook who has taken the direction of this movement preaching in the poorest districts of the metropolis this doctrine, viz., that a poor family in London throws away what would go far towards feeding a poor family in Paris.

Having dealt with district visiting as it is feebly conducted on a large scale, I am most anxious to show the healthy shoots it has thrown off, and to give educated women a notion of what good may be done in small and humble ways when there is a will in the work. Miss Louisa Twining has published a pamphlet on "Deaconesses for the Church of England;" in which she has shown how admirably the deaconesses of France and Switzerland succeed. She does not ask for women to be again "enrolled in communities, in order to gratify a selfish love of seclusion and contemplation, nor even to rest in peaceful and innocent repose, however congenial and harmless it might be. Such a demand would be so entirely contrary to the spirit and every feeling of this age in which we live, that it would have no chance of success, at least in our own Church. Only in *work* will this success be found; and we have said that there is a real demand abroad for such persons who will perform it. A voice is heard from prisons, hospitals, reformatories, and workhouses, calling for the help of women. Multiply the clergy, Scripture-readers, and missionaries as they ought to be multiplied, there must still be the want of women to do that work which God has by many indications of his Providence assigned to them as their province and their sphere." Just as the London rectors declare that the Oxford or Cambridge undergraduate finds it difficult to condescend to the low station of the London poor, it is alleged that the fashionably educated young ladies will find it almost impossible to act as district visitors. Where the humble Bible-women have succeeded they would fail. These are the poor ministering familiarly to the very poor; teaching them thrifty and orderly habits.

It is insisted by many ladies, who have the good of the poor at heart, that, whether they are called sisters or deaconesses, associations of women should be formed—to live together in establishments situated in the poorest neighbourhoods—whence they might act in common. They would take no vows, and be submitted to no regulations that were not necessary to the orderly government of a common home. They would come and go when they pleased. They would be able to live economically, in sisterhoods. No fear need be entertained of Romanist tendencies; they would be in constant relation with the clergy. Banded together, all dressed alike simply, they would have a collective force that would make them respected throughout the neighbourhood. They would be known by every person in their district. Their vocation would be acknowledged and reverenced. They would become welcome visitors in the homes of the poor. Their constant presence would enable them to exercise a permanent influence over the morals and habits of their *protégés*. In places like Bethnal Green, Shoreditch, and Haggerstone, they would supply the absence of district visitors—they would come from all parts to these head-quarters of penury and crime—self-devoted servants of the poor, ready to spend their lives in the work to which the ordinary district visitor devotes a day per week or per fortnight. The experiment has succeeded among good Protestants on the Continent, and it has been successfully tried in America. It is not easy to see why it should fail in London. If there be hundreds of now idle ladies who desire to teach and help poor women and ragged children, as there are, we are told, who seek to toil in the wards of workhouses, and protect pauper children after they have left the union (on the plan of the Workhouse Visiting Society), why should obstacles be put in their way? It cannot be denied that their object is a noble one, and that if they carry it out the community will be greatly benefited. The clergy confess that the labour is beyond their powers. They desire lay pioneers. And all the objection appears to consist in this—that whereas there are ascetic sisterhoods belonging to the Roman Catholic Church, there should not be free, self-devoted sisters of the Established Church. Because, for the sake of economy and of being near the scene of their labours, twenty ladies decide to live together, and to dress alike in grey (artificial flowers, flounces, and crinolines not being in keeping with the character of the woman who spends her days visiting the poor), they must needs turn towards Rome!

I pray the reader's company on a visit to Bloomfield Terrace, Pimlico. A row of small, quiet, unpretending houses, the lodgings to all appearance of City clerks. One of these houses, where the knocker is fastened to the door, is the St. Barnabas Orphanage. This, and St. John's School and the Invalid Home, all situated hereabouts, are under the care of a sisterhood. When a little girl opened the door of the Orphanage, I was ushered into a front parlour of somewhat sombre appearance—the table covered with a cloth like a pall. The room was hung round with prints, the character of which led me to the conclusion that I was in a Roman Catholic establishment. Presently a lady appeared—a nun, to all appearance, dressed in black, with the close bound white cap, and with a large silver cross round the neck—as like one of the Little Sisters of the Poor as she could well be. I beg the reader will bear in mind that I am exactly and truthfully recording my experiences; and that I altogether abstain from offering opinion here (as foreign to my purpose) on the Sisters of St. John the Baptist, to which sisterhood the lady I saw in the Orphanage belonged. I inquired about the Orphanage, and was at once referred to the Sister Superior, at No. 11, in the row. There is nothing in the Orphanage to call for particular remark. The children are admitted under ten years of age, and are put out to situations at the age of seventeen. With every child sent an annual payment of £10 is required. In most respects, then, the Orphanage is like the Cottage Row Home I noticed in my last letter, save that whereas one is a quiet, thoroughly homely establishment, the other is as unlike home as anything can well be. It is more like a slip out of a religious house brought direct—say from Belgium. I confess I was mystified at the St. Barnabas Orphanage, and that by the time I reached the house where the Sister Superior dwelt, as old ladies say, "putting this and that together," I had made up my mind that the charity was a Roman Catholic one. At this time I had not heard even the name of the sisterhood. The Sister Superior's house was St. John's School. As I rang at the bell I could hear the tinkling of a young scholar practising at the piano. The drawing-room was severely well furnished, and a large cross stood upon the mantelpiece, while round the room scriptural quotations were emblazoned. I mentioned the

Little Sisters of the Poor to the Sister Superior, who had received me very graciously. "I never heard of them," she replied.

Never heard of them! I then discovered that the sisterhood who govern the Orphanage, the St. John's School, and the Invalids' Home, belong to the Church of England, and have their head-quarters at Clewer, near Windsor. I had made a great but natural mistake in mentioning the Roman Catholic Little Sisters of the Poor. How could I tell, in the presence of these ladies, habited like nuns, and wearing vast silver crosses, that they were of the Church of England?

The duties which the Sisters of St. John the Baptist perform are honourable and useful duties. They educate the young, have a care for the orphan, and nurse the sick in their Invalid Home for Poor Gentlewomen. This is work that may be done without Romish costume. The opponents of sisterhoods and deaconesses point to the Sisters of St. John the Baptist, and cry, "Behold the result of befriending the poor by communities. These ladies are as near Rome as they well can be!"

I am not to inquire whether this is reasoned well, but to state that which I find to exist, viz., a very strong objection on the part of a great section of governors of London charities to communities of servants of the poor. I express only an individual opinion when I say that I cannot see the force of their argument. St. Barnabas's has long enjoyed a peculiar reputation. In search of Protestant nuns the inquirer would certainly explore that parish. The Sisters of St. John the Baptist are not habited in nuns' garments because they have been banded together to wait upon the poor. Women who hold this uniform of piety in aversion, and who still desire to help the sick and wo-begone, would not be led to adopt the manners and the forms of a nunnery, because they were Sisters of Mercy, or Charity, or Deaconesses. The example of the Sisters of St. John the Baptist has possibly frightened the weak-minded, but it would be monstrous if an argument should be drawn from it that would prevent the formation of families of earnest women who wish simply and unaffectedly to minister to the children of Lazarus. I am careful, I trust, in doing full justice to the Sisters from Clewer. They are conscientious and devoted helpers of the poor at St. Andrew's Home, Clewer, and in Pimlico. Their Invalids' Home is, for instance, an admirable little institution. In this house some twenty-five poor gentlewomen, who are invalids and cannot afford the comforts an invalid requires, are boarded and well cared for. The terms, I find, vary from 17s. 6d. to 25s. a week, according to the size and situation of the boarder's bedroom. These terms include the diet recommended by the medical attendant, and advice and medicines. Wines, spirits, and the washing of personal linen, appear to be the only extras. Some boarders are received whose means are inadequate even to the above moderate payments. The regulations are strict; no reading in bed by candle-light; no fires in the bedrooms in the day, when the patients are well enough to leave their rooms; no patient to be absent from the Home after nine P.M., "without the permission of the Sister Superior." No servants of the Home to be sent out without the permission of the Sister Superior, etc. These regulations will appear to many—especially to the sensitive mind—unhandsome bandages. I have dwelt thus on the disputed question of sisterhoods because it has been, and is, the subject of, I may say, angry dispute. I may dismiss it with the warning of a wise man that "in any controversy the instant we feel angry we have already ceased striving for truth and begun striving for ourselves."

The field for woman's labour among the poor and the unfortunate of London is indeed wide. It is a field in which, by their gentleness and by their very weakness, they can do more than men. Whether acting in communities, or separately, they may achieve incalculable good, ay, and where they have been wholly inactive up to this present time. It has long been urged as a reproach against women that they are the obdurate enemies of their fallen sisters. Hawthorne has written:—"Most men—and certainly I could not always claim to be one of the exceptions—have a natural indifference, if not an absolutely hostile feeling, towards those whom disease, or weakness, or calamity of any kind causes to falter and faint amid the rude jostle of our selfish existence. The education of Christianity, it is true, the sympathy of a like experience, and the example of women may soften, and possibly subvert, this ugly characteristic of our sex; but it is originally there, and has likewise its analogy in the practice of our brute brethren, who hunt the sick or disabled member of the herd from among them as an enemy." This hostile feeling has been cherished by women towards their erring sisters. They will watch by the sick bedside, venture into dangerous neighbourhoods—but the Traviata has their unsparing enmity. They will look at her at the opera, when Piccolomini makes her enchanting; but with the unfortunates who have been wronged and flung into the cruel streets of London they will not meddle. The thief they will reform; the outcast they will clothe; but their sister they will not approach to lift her from her shame.

The midnight mission has brought many startling facts to light. There are 50,000 outcast women in London. They are not all, nor nearly all, of London. They are fugitives from country places, in the main, who could not wear the scarlet letter along the lanes of the native village, with every neighbour pointing at it. They are outraged, deluded ladies'-maids and humbler servants. They are the cast aside prey of the rich and educated. Again they are the children of sin—sold to shame; the offspring of want and ignorance bred in the gutter, to supply the polluted markets of Shadwell and Poplar. They are of all classes, and from all classes. They drive phaetons along the ladies' mile, or loiter against sailors' lodging-houses, by the docks. They are elegant, *spirituelle,* flirting the fan with dainty wrist; or they are smeared with paint and dirt, and muddled with gin. Between the two extremes there are many classes it would answer no purpose to describe. But it is with these outcasts, at once hungry and disgraced,—these hapless, painted creatures who laugh while their heart aches, and sport hired finery, and carry about with them—weary to the inmost depths of the soul—the slavery born of their sin; with these creatures, from whom the virtuous shrink as from toads, that the work of the midnight mission lies. Not by mere midnight meetings is this, the ulcer that has shown itself of late hideously prominent, to be rooted out. These meetings are a beginning, and a mere beginning. The refuges for fallen women, to which I have conducted the reader, are admirable aids, but the radical cure has yet to be originated.

Let us glance at a few of the facts realized by the mission. From statistics recently published it appears that thirty-four meetings have been held, and upwards of 1000 women rescued.

Similar meetings have been held in Manchester, Liverpool, Nottingham, Edinburgh, Glasgow, Dundee, Dublin, Cardiff, etc., and homes opened in those places, as well as in Plymouth, Exeter, and Hull. The results are as follow:—7000 women attended the meetings; 50,000 books, tracts, and Scripture cards were circulated; 123 females were restored to friends, 250 placed in service, 8 had married, 2 were reconciled to husbands, 2 had emigrated, 1 had been sent to France, 1 to Holland, 1 to New York, 2 were placed in business; 27 were now in Homes, 30 left the Homes after a short residence, 36 were assisted and enabled to obtain a livelihood, and 600 rescued in the provinces. Total 1081, besides a large number who have turned to honest ways of living.

The last published balance-sheet shows that the receipts for the year amounted to £1607, 0s. 4d., and the expenditure to £1579, 7s. 1d., leaving a balance in hand of £27, 13s. 3d.

Some good, then, has been accomplished; but how much more might have been effected if good and conscientious women had helped in the work of reclaiming their erring sisters. This is women's work, if ever woman's work existed. Instead of 1000 fallen women reclaimed, there would have been 10,000 had Christian gentlewomen taken part in the labours of the mission. When the virtuous woman will turn an eye of pity on her fallen sister, and help her from the earth, and bid her sin no more, the radical cure will be begun.

A London workhouse is the scene of every abomination. Here are a few unfortunate broken-down parishioners, and wards are devoted to the bed-ridden and the insane, and the sick; but the vast majority of the inmates consists of hereditary paupers, tramps, prostitutes, and their unhappy offspring. The schoolmaster despairs, the inspector turns away hopeless. In the forty-five London workhouses there are generally between 25,000 and 27,000 men, women, and children; and about 70,000 persons are generally receiving out-door relief in the metropolis. The pauper army may be fairly computed as 100,000 strong. In these wards are gaol-birds, artful mendicants, idle vagabonds who have considered the workhouse their rightful home; bastards who were born in the workhouse lying-in ward—all mingling and contaminating each other. The workhouse schoolmaster throws up his hands in despair. Ill-paid, the subordinate of a master who is, socially and by education, his inferior—having to deal with the lowest class of children—he can make no stand against the influence of the men, with whom his scholars pass nearly all their time. The workhouse girls are the hourly associates of unmarried mothers. They are sometimes the offspring of shameless mothers, and have first seen the light in the workhouse lying-in ward. They are friendless in the world, and have for companions the very worst examples. They have learned to look upon the workhouse as their home, and to them it is an easy-going home, from which they are not very anxious to raise themselves. The observations I have to offer the reader on London workhouses, and which I have obtained from the evidence of Poor Law Commissioners and assistant-commissioners, City missionaries, and others, are necessary, in order to understand the *raison d'être* of an institution founded by the Hon. Mrs. Way, known as the Home at Brockham. London workhouses are prisons which the public never enter, and to which very few people give the least attention. The ratepayer surlily hands the rate to the collector, and seldom troubles himself to learn how the money is spent. Parish matters are generally left in the hands of a few ignorant busybodies. Poor-Law guardians, considered as a class, are not the intellectual aristocracy of the kingdom. How many ratepayers trouble themselves to visit the union and examine for themselves the working of the poor-laws, and the character of the inmates. How many who live within a stone's-throw of the sombre walls know that within, a population of pauperized men, women, and children is for ever shifting; that they are descendants and progenitors of paupers; and that they supply a very large proportion of the population of our gaols. The workhouse school-master may well utter cries of despair. What can he do with children who are the companions of the dissolute and criminal; born of unmarried mothers, and for ever on the move? Many that are in the workhouse should be in the bridewell; for they are lusty vagabonds. They declare that they can get no work—so, by law, they must be fed; be they deserving or undeserving, saints or gaol-birds. Let them pass into the wards, and live and sleep in company—the unfortunate herded with the criminal, as it is outside. A missionary bears witness that in the Hackney Union, in one year, of 38 births 27 were illegitimate. It is calculated that one-fifth of the inmates of London workhouses die every year. A metropolitan chaplain gives evidence to the effect that about 50 out of 500 paupers are deserving poor; and that "the residue are a mixed multitude, brought to pauperism respectively by every shade of moral obliquity, generally arising from idleness, the seed of all vice, and proceeding to the most hardened and veteran criminality." He points to generations of bastard paupers born in unions. Then there are the tramps who can claim a night's lodging; and so, provided for at night, can shuffle through their day's begging and stealing. The acute knowledge of their rights which pauperized men and boys obtain was illustrated only a few days ago at the Westminster Police Court.

George Jones, "a miserable-looking boy, 14 or 15 years of age," was charged with breaking a pane of glass at the workhouse in York Street, Westminster. The boy had applied for a night's lodging, and had been refused on the ground that the casual ward was full. Whereupon he declared that, if he could not sleep in the workhouse, he would in the police station. He broke a window, and effected his object. Before the magistrate, Mr. Selfe, the boy displayed a lively familiarity with workhouse forms. "I stood there a long time," he said, "and I only counted a dozen tickets given out, so I thought there was room." The workhouse porter confessed that applicants were turned away nearly every night. The boy had tramped from Dartford, and was on his way to Barnet; a workhouse bird, born to the life, I make no doubt. He was committed for seven days, as a punishment for breaking the window; and when released he would go on his way, from casual ward to casual ward, looking miserable enough, but keeping to this, the positive vocation to which he was born. The remedy for this lies without the workhouses; within there is no hope. The Poor-law Commissioners have expressed their fears of the results of the training of pauper children in union schools. They say, "A workhouse cannot, with the greatest attention to classification, be made a place in which young girls can be removed from the chances of corruption." A workhouse teacher reports:—"The boys in this union will never be depauperized; they have to mix with the men, most of whom are gaol-birds. I have found them talking to the boys about the gaol, and of 'bright fellows finding their way to the gaol.'" The evidence—official evidence of the failure of pauper training—is startling. Another teacher reports:—"Nothing can be done while the boys are in the union." Again: "The common topic of conversation among the children, is the arrival of the women of the town to be confined here." The children in the union school are, moreover, subject to the daily contamination of the stream of tramps' children that pours incessantly through the house. Mr. Cumin reports, that "one of the most fatal effects produced by the pauper children being brought up in close contact with adult paupers is this, that the child loses all desire to earn its own living, and is content to spend its own days in a workhouse. . . . Boys who have never been accustomed to handle a spade, and girls who have never been accustomed to scrub floors, naturally rebel when they are put to such work. They sigh for the workhouse, in which they can spend their lives in eating, sleeping, reading, and play." Let the reader take the verdict of the Commissioners themselves on the effect the workhouse has upon the young:—"The children who enter a workhouse, quit it, if they ever quit it, corrupted where they were well disposed, and hardened where they were vicious." No wonder, then, that the union schoolmasters, who are shamefully underpaid, should despair; and that men who profess to teach the young idea, shun the workhouse school-room. They receive half the pay of ordinary elementary schoolmasters; and their scholars are of the very lowest class, and continually shifting from the forms. And so, after many years' trial, after generations of paupers have held a union as an ancestral hall, the Royal Commissioners come to the conclusion that children could not be educated in workhouses "in a satisfactory manner, because the influences of workhouses are in themselves pernicious, and because proper teachers cannot be induced to take charge of the schools."

Proper teachers! The office of workhouse schoolmaster is shunned, because it is a task at once ungrateful and under-paid. The schoolmaster is under the workhouse master; one almost wonders he is not under the cook. His scholars—a ragged, ever-changing crew—are for only a few hours under his control. The precepts of the school-hours are laughed to scorn by the adult paupers, who are waiting without to mingle with their young friends. Much of this evil is wrought by the thousands of sturdy tramps and vagabonds who are for ever on their rounds from workhouse to workhouse. The law is too lenient with these idle gipsies, who bring forth children to fill our workhouses and our gaols. As a matter of duty to their innocent offspring, the case should go hard with the vagrant father. He should be compelled to work, and that lustily, not only for his own food, but for that of the creatures he brings with him. We have seen how difficult it is to obtain money from parents under the Reformatory Act, but here we have parents who continually put themselves *en evidence*. Labour should be rigorously extorted from them. It may be answered that they would desert their children. For such desertion they would be punished. The fear of this punishment would keep them from the casual ward. They might be detected in any workhouse. Their children would cost the parish in which they are left the price of their support; but in the end the parish would be the gainer, for the system would be broken up. The race would be cut off; the race of tramps would no longer breed a posterity of tramps.

The Hon. Mrs. Way has a comfortable Home for Pauper Orphans at Brockham. The girls are taken from the polluted pauper schools to taste some of the gentleness and kindness of home. The Pauper Education Act, introduced by Sir Stafford Northcote, makes such Homes possible. By this Act, parish authorities pay towards the support of their pauper children in these homes of charity. Mrs. Way's children cost about 7s. a week, of which cost the unions to which they belong pay 5s.; so that, while the parishes are lightened of a burden, and while numbers of girls are rescued from a life of pauperism and vice, voluntary charity is lightly taxed. Brockham Home is a modest little work, and it is a model work which might be copied with advantage by many rich ladies of the land who desire to do a little good to their poor fellow-creatures.

In these letters on the London Poor, which I now bring to a conclusion, I have been compelled to restrict myself to the examination of representative charitable institutions. The mere list of orphanages, retreats, refuges, reformatories, homes, missions, almshouses, infirmaries, philanthropic societies, working men's colleges and clubs, dispensaries and dormitories, and funds of all descriptions, fills columns of the *London Directory*. Many of these, that would have afforded instructive matter to the readers, have been necessarily left unvisited. I have endeavoured to deal with systems rather than to paint scenes.

One part of my subject, at which I have now an opportunity of glancing only, viz., that of the improvement of the dwellings of the working classes, deserves the close attention of the people who devote themselves to the wellbeing of the poor. The Metropolitan Association for Improving the Dwellings of the Industrious Classes was formed more than twenty years ago. Its operations have been extended year by year, and have been copied in many places. This is a most important association, possessing many clumps of model lodging-houses; but its operations are not so extensive as those of the Labourers' Friend Society, with its income of £12,000 a year. A few figures will give the reader an idea of the nature and extent of the Metropolitan Association's operations.

The eighteenth report of the directors shows that the mortality for the year, in the entire property of the Association, was 40 out of an average population of 2496, being at the rate of 16 per 1000: 23 of the deaths were of children under 10 years of age. It appears, therefore, that the average rate of mortality in the buildings of the Association has been at the rate of 16 per 1000, while that of the metropolis generally has been 23 per 1000.

The balance of the profits of last year, after providing for the dividend then declared, has been carried to the guarantee fund account, increasing that fund to £1656, 16s. 11d.

The net profits of this year exceed those of last year by £191, 15s. 6d., and amount altogether to £2625, 2s. 8d.,—sufficient to pay a dividend of 2⅞ per cent.; but the directors recommend a dividend of 2½ per cent., free of income tax, which leaves a balance of about £351, 7s. 8d. to be carried to the guarantee fund, increasing that fund to the sum of £2008, 4s. 7d.

Philanthropists may, therefore, invest their capital in the improvement of the dwellings of the poor, if they will be content to receive 2½ per cent., "free of income tax," for their money. The two Associations to which I have alluded do not represent all that is done for the metropolitan poor in this direction. There are Marylebone and other associations for improving the dwellings of the industrious classes. That which concerns us, however, is not what has been done, but what remains undone. These associations can rescue from squalor, and expensive squalor, only hundreds, where there are tens of thousands to be rescued. The great Metropolitan Association, after twenty years of activity, now lodges about 2400 individuals.

The low neighbourhoods are untouched. Here and there, at very wide distances, a model lodging-house or two; and all around, dirt, disease, and crime, in tenements not good enough for rats. Here is suffering fiercer than that which even, with the help of Mr. Adderley, we can inflict on our criminals. Very knowing satirists, indeed, have amused their readers with pictures of darling criminals conning their morning paper in gaol over their steaming coffee, aggravating the leniency of the modern penal code, in order to arouse the indignation of the public. This end has been attained. The public are indignant, and an era of severity towards the criminal has been inaugurated. Might we not, at the same time, set about a more rational treatment of the poor; endeavour to break up the ranks of pauperism, by dealing toughly with our ragged army of 50,000 tramps; by setting up strong partition-walls between the poor and the criminal; by persuading rich and virtuous women to have a care, a heart for their fallen sisters; by taking actively to the work of charity in some of the hundred and one forms in which it is rooted, to our honour, in the midst of us. Charity has taken ridiculous as well as noble forms, and it has been, and is at times, most perniciously exercised. In these failures there is no cause even for depression; for, if we have bungled, we have done great things also. If we have put too blind a faith, now and then, in the rapid perfectibility of the human creature by means of marks, or by hymn-humming, we have, at least, made ground against the brutal old judges, who hanged men up at Newgate as coolly as they suspended the contents of a day's sport in their roomy larders. Enthusiasts have done as much harm as open enemies. Consider the effect the Maine Liquor Law advocates have upon the temperance movement. Let brave men preach honestly against intemperance, and the manifold evil consequences of it, and they will be warmly supported on all sides, for the question lies at the bottom of the crime and the poverty I have had under consideration. The distillery is the artificial mother of gaol-birds. Drink goads men to beat their wives, to rob their employers, to grow lazy, and to stumble from the honourable ways of life. Therefore, war against intemperance; but effectual war. Total abstinence is a violent measure; but the prohibition advocated by the friends of the Maine Liquor Law, is a bit of tyranny that rouses the ire of men who would be the strenuous supporters of a rational temperance movement.

CPSIA information can be obtained
at www.ICGtesting.com
Printed in the USA
LVHW110811120522
718525LV00003B/64

9 783375 001896